The
Rock
of
Achill

JIM SHEEHAN

NEWMAN SPRINGS PUBLISHING
320 Broad Street
Red Bank, NJ 07701

First originally published by Newman Springs Publishing 2020

ISBN 978-1-64801-452-9 (Paperback)
ISBN 978-1-64801-453-6 (Hardcover)
ISBN 978-1-64801-454-3 (Digital)

Printed in the United States of America

To the goddess of passion from whose touch can
fire the mind then change the world.

PROLOGUE

Upon the shores of green-laden Achill Island, at the close of the age of the faerie and the dreambeast, is a man of opportunity yet unborn. His fate is coming for him in places far and near which will become a great flicker in the dying embers of ancient Ireland. And so, the story begins on Achill with its maligned refugees and rogues.

Lorcan was wandering in boredom. He meandered through a narrow treeless valley, its fall grass now fully grazed. His father was counting cattle on the other side of the low hill to the west that misty morning and was sure to miss him shortly. He squatted and reached down to pull a tuft of grass from the ground, sighing. He threw the broken blades of grass on the turf and looked up to the ridge of the southern hill. From over the top of that hill, he saw a massive red stag dashing toward him. Lorcan paused in shock for hopping quickly just behind the deer was the largest white rabbit he had ever seen which was covered in green markings. No sooner had he absorbed that fact when suddenly, it was transformed into a spinning prism, with each facet of color, then assembled into its new form—a naked woman, covered head to toe in a green ribbon that glinted and glowed. Her white hair streamed behind her as she and the stag both looked up at the sky repeatedly as they ran. Lorcan stood up slowly and placed his hand above his eyes to block the sun, not really comprehending the sight before him. He backed up defensively and apprehensively searched the sky as well, wondering what had perturbed the two of them.

As they approached closer, running nearly directly toward him, he saw panic on the face of the woman. Now no more than twenty feet away, the dark-red animal kicked in several directions and barely moved forward discernibly once it was at the bottom of the converging hills where Lorcan stood. The woman came to a halt beside the beast, staring above her in obvious fear. Lorcan was frightened for them but watched in stillness. Neither of the creatures seemed to take any notice of Lorcan. The wide eyes of the stag told of terror, and Lorcan briefly considered the distant cattle whom he didn't hear in any distress. After those few moments, the buck then rushed back toward the hill, away from Lorcan, its hooves tearing away wet mud beneath it. The woman hesitated a moment before following. Lorcan heard her scream. Twenty yards away, the deer collapsed, as if shot, but there was no report.

Lorcan saw the predator that brought down the deer, which quickly departed, but he couldn't believe his eyes. A white-tailed type of bird that ruled the skies across Achill had made a fast dive then had torn out the fallen animal's nape. The oversized bird then—just as quickly—ascended into the clouds with tremendous speed. The deer lay there, trying to breathe, coughing, with its black tongue protruding. The woman darted toward the deer, collapsing by his side and crying loudly.

Lorcan moved toward them, his eyes sweeping the sky in case the bird was insane—and returned. The woman looked up at him, her winter sea-colored eyes, with irises rimmed in coal, were red from tears.

She spoke slowly. "How could I have saved him? I could never fly." She buried her face in her hands and continued sobbing as she threw her arms over the stag's corpse as if to shelter it as it garnered its final breath.

Lorcan could think of nothing to say. He stood quietly, in full view of the deer, their eyes locked. He quietly mourned for its destroyed life. He saw the blood on the grass and felt ill from all the excitement and terror. The deer released one last breath just as the brown eagle landed beside its still prize's head. The bird heedfully looked around, like a dog first sensing if it was safe to eat, unconcerned about the presence of the woman and Lorcan himself.

Lorcan thought about how the deer behaved, as if it knew it was being hunted, and wondered how miserable an end that would be, pursued by such an imminent doom. It wasn't a year before, he had witnessed a cattle thief get sliced by the blades of two watchmen who caught the man trying to escape uphill, away from the village. That dark night, Lorcan had called out for help as he, while out playing, discovered stones that had been moved to open a passage on a pasture wall for the cattle to funnel through. He could barely see the thief, although he heard him stumble loudly as he looked back at his pursuers. The light from the torches of two villagers lit up the vagrant's face. The ill-fated thief showed the same horror in his eyes as the deer.

Lorcan looked at the monstrous bird with a fear that numbed his legs and caused his mind to consider grisly fates. Lorcan glanced over at the woman. She was oblivious to the presence of the eagle, bending over to kiss the snout of the stag, her hand on one of his black antlers. He could hear her whispering to the deer. Lorcan quickly returned his eyes to the eagle. The bird tossed its head up and looked at Lorcan, showing his height to be as tall as an adolescent child. Lorcan took in the sight of the predator's dreadful eyes, like globes filled with the blue sky. He wouldn't have proceeded to react the same way, had he not been so frightened, but rational decisions took too long to consider. Thinking back on the stories he was told around the hearth flame, Lorcan started to dance as feverishly as he could in front of that winged monster. He was desperate to please whatever supernatural power was inhabiting the bird.

The bird arched its neck, opened its wings, and screeched at Lorcan with its massive beak. Lorcan kicked his heels and turned directions as quickly as he could, trying to remember the dancing he saw the villagers do some nights when an occasion demanded it. He glanced at the green-striped woman, whose naked arms and torso still cradled the buck, and saw her studying him with a curious expression on her face. Of course, he knew he looked foolish but he had just witnessed a massive rabbit turn into a woman and a giant bird kill a great stag with ease. If there were any old gods to please here, he aimed to do it.

Lorcan struggled to remain on his feet as his dizziness only increased with the smell of blood and the sound of the bird. The thought of being in the presence of a supernatural being was not easy. He was sweating and would have shed some tears had he not been so cold with fright. The bird screeched three times and then hopped toward him, finally landing close to the deer. The woman hissed through her teeth and scrambled backward, away from the eagle; her eyes focused on the bird. Lorcan lost his footing and stumbled backward a few feet. He closed his eyes and prayed desperately for the angels, or his father, to rescue him.

The eagle looked upon the child with a deep focus. Lorcan decided pleasing this creature was futile and that seconds were going by that may be his last. There wasn't anything nearby to throw at the bird and he had no weapon. He dropped his arms to his sides and opened his eyes to find the bird appearing to prepare to dart toward him. The bird's wings began to push back while leaning its head forward as if to cry out for attack.

Lorcan felt a wind suddenly appear against his back, and as the tall grass moved, he felt his heart beat so hard that it caused his head to shake and arms to flex forward. He winced as he heard the eagle shriek. What happened next, he'd never be able to explain. He charged the bird as if he was meeting a challenge from another child. He met it halfway with the bird just coming into flight. With no thought, only instinct, his head slid under the creature's chest and he rotated violently in order to reach out for its menacing claw.

Quick sharp images of what he was doing ran past him like focusing on a single raindrop in a waterfall—but he was in control. Gripping the bird's claw brought him upright from a backward tilt. The bird attempted to turn to face him. He felt his hand slice open, but how badly he didn't have time to contemplate, for what happened next could be far worse. His blood fell to join the fallen stag's and he let go to have two free hands to protect himself from the coming attack. He put up his left forearm to brace against the terrible bird's life-ending sharp beak.

With the impact, he hit the ground on his right shoulder. He was calm, even though he felt every moment his head beat off the ground with each thrust of the enraged beast. He looked to the side and before his moving eyes was the woman, glaring at the eagle with intensity and panting like an enraged animal. And again, with one whirling transformation, she became a huge white-and-green fox which charged the eagle. The bird and the fox rolled away from Lorcan, locked in battle. Lorcan heard the cry of the fox before she bit into the upper-left wing of the eagle. The eagle screeched and jabbed its beak at the side of the fox. Exhausted, Lorcan lifted his battered head off the ground and watched the brawl for a time.

The giant bird had left deep gouges in Lorcan's pale chest but beneath the torn blood-soaked shirt and flesh pounded a strong heart. He struggled up to his hands and knees. Lorcan looked around him again for any weapon and then his eyes fell upon the crown-like rack of the stag. He noticed a part that had been broken with the animal's collapse. Without hesitation, he crawled over to the buck and reached out for the broken piece with his wounded hand dripping blood. He gripped it and twisted, breaking it completely away from the antler.

The eagle and the woman-now-fox were still struggling and rolling on the ground, neither appearing to have the upper hand. Both were muddied and bloodied. Lorcan pulled himself to his feet and approached the chaotic bout carefully. He stood next to them for a moment, uncertain, not wishing to accidentally harm the fox. The raptor was able to readjust its talons as it hovered before finally pitching the fox on its side. The eagle perched upon the submitting fox which was too exhausted to give further resistance. Then the eagle stopped and raised its wings and screamed again at the fox when Lorcan saw his opportunity. He darted in, the stag's final gift in his hand, and found a soft spot in the eagle's left side under one of the wings that hid the sky with full extension. The bird made overlapping sounds, like a rambled ancient language, while stumbling back, then finally cried out in a horrified feminine tone. Lorcan could see the sun's full reflection in the winged monster's eyes as it collapsed to the ground, breathing no more.

The fox lay on the ground, panting, it's muzzle covered in blood. In a momentary haze of green glittering embers, the woman now hung her head between her shoulders, her bare back glistening with sweat, among the streaks of mud and deep scratches, as she held herself up on her hands and knees. Her long white hair was bedraggled and filthy, hanging all around her. She lifted her head to the sky and Lorcan could see pain in her murky gray-green eyes but was disconcerted by the blood all around her mouth.

She cried out to the sky, "Why! He was my loyal last and only companion! Now what will I do? Oh…so many of us have died wretchedly through our own madness or by another." She tore at the ground with her nails. "How I tire of this existence, Lord. In the darkness, hiding from you for so long and now…so alone." She looked straight up, pleading with her hands cupped toward the sky in an open-palm prayer before her chest. She trembled as she meekly begged, "I need a reason to live. Give me a reason to live!" She placed her hands over her face and sobbed quietly. Through her fingers, she whispered softly, "Once I was the one who chose those bloodlines, the strongest who brought glory to your creation. How can I serve you again, God, to set things right between us?"

She wiped her hands from her face and looked up at Lorcan who was still bewildered from her speech as well as the battle. She cocked her head to the side and said in a musing tone, "You saved me. You have a powerful spirit in you, boy."

Lorcan retorted, "Much thanks. It's mine. You can't have it." He narrowed his eyes at her. Feeling woozy, he put his hand on his head and tried to keep his balance. He then tucked his chin a bit and took a deep breath. He offered, "I am sorry about your friend."

She grimaced slightly but ignored his comments. Raising her eyes to the sky again, she stated clearly, "I have a decision to make. I'll bestow a gift. I will raise a champion for you. In time, let me know if my sacrifice was enough to enter your kingdom and be by your side." She looked over at Lorcan again and lifted herself to her feet.

Lorcan was still amazed and somewhat confused as she began to walk toward him slowly. As she walked, her wounds disappeared and the glowing green patterns that decorated her entire body began to dissipate until they completely vanished. Then she reformed as an adolescent girl, about Lorcan's own age, still naked, now with brown hair. But the same dark ocean-colored eyes centered on Lorcan.

"What's your name?" the girl asked Lorcan with a new voice fitting her appearance.

"Umm… L-Lorcan," he stuttered. "Who…what are you? What's going on here?"

"Well, you may call me Aine. I've given up my immortality as you might see. You have saved my life and I am indebted to you. I will go with you now."

"Oh?" said Lorcan. He swallowed and suggested gently, "Perhaps you would like to borrow my tunic?" He jerked his torn shirt up over his head and carefully handed it to her. "The wind is starting to blow."

"Certainly." She beamed at the ripped clothing in her hands for a moment before putting it on. She ran a finger across her forehead to push her wild hair to the side. "Ta." She looked down at her barely covered form and he noticed her slight grin. "This is quite adequate."

There was silence for a moment then Aine reached forward to take one of his hands. "Lorcan, what happened here today will need to stay between us. Don't you agree?" She nodded her head at him and raised her eyebrows as if looking for his answer.

Lorcan didn't need to think about it long. He didn't plan on telling a soul. "Yes, you're right. Let's keep all this to ourselves." He squinted over at the hill to the west and said, "My father will be looking for me." He looked back at her. "Will you come with me?"

She smiled mysteriously, with a twist to her lip, and replied, "Certainly. We will be the best of friends. I could use a good friend."

Croaghaun

Dublin Port, August 1, 1805

Bridget gripped the railing at the edge of the obsidian pier, its smooth stone reflecting the moonlight, and looked out at the ceaseless waves. She sought shapes in the clouds as they rolled and crashed into each other in a desperate attempt to find a sign to set her compass. She knew that if her lost love should now find reception in the court of her heart, then it would be condemned by the gavel.

She imagined him riding on Croaghaun, the gray Iberian he was always so damned proud of. He was a terrifying animal in which she never once dared to touch him as though it would be dishonoring the fierce creature. She envisioned his hooves pounding in a gallop atop the waves and her man riding in his dark leather coat, retrieving her yet again from this pier. *That will not happen anymore,* she thought.

The cobblestones next to the pier were wetted down by the ocean spray and damp air. Her heavy gray dress billowed with the sea winds and her black jacket was hardly enough. She was dry but just as cold to the touch. Her lips wouldn't warm anymore and they often trembled, a trait that developed after the first month without a letter.

The ship was boarding.

*****

Croaghaun Cliffs, September 3, 1801

"Donn!" he hollered out. Lorcan frustratingly called out again and tossed a stone into the thick fog rising from the sea that invaded the valley that morning but no one responded. Often he felt he was too old for herding and the aggravation of reckless young men.

He looked around him and wondered about the grass that seemed all too abundant at this late autumn date. With the ground turning into the anvil of winter, it was his people's practice to bring the cattle into the valley. They were tied to their livestock for prosperity so he had sent Donn to search for stragglers on the cliffside.

Feeling the cold through the holes in his boots, he staggered across the slope, using whatever stone he could to better serve his failing footing. The sunlight glanced off the stones of Croaghaun, and the mountain, sacred and vibrant, was crowned with heaven's light. The glow encircled all as he climbed.

He pressed his trusty walking stick into the wet turf, always uncertain of his next step. He continued carefully up the mountainside toward the top of the cliff where he went with eagerness as a boy, and now, only begrudgingly with his advancing age. He needed to find his son Donn so they could pack up their belongings and leave the booley for the winter season. It was time to leave the cold salt air behind for the safety of the meadow village.

His mind raced with worry as he considered possible reasons why his boy hadn't called back to him. The cliff—a terrible and fabled cliff—had swept the unsuspecting into the wash to break against the waves. The view from the cliff was so grand to behold as to hypnotize the unwary then to seal their fate with a nudge from a treacherous sweep of air. Donn knew better than to venture so close to the edge, but still, uncertainty gripped his mind.

Time passed as he inched his way, denying himself rest. He could feel the silver watch his father had given him beat against his chest from the inside pocket of the ragged brown vest he wore. Its presence reminded him of the many moments he'd endured without knowing his son's condition.

His father, Tadhg Feeney, was given the watch as a gift on the sealing of a cattle deal with a trader from Galway. He had been a great man whom the island leaders always relied on for answers regarding issues of economy and trade. That small ornate timepiece was dear to him and provided lustrous evidence of a world that existed far from these hard shores.

His son, Donn, was a firebrand, just as his grandfather had been. Tadhg always pushed events to react to him like a finger piercing a puddle of water. When alive, Tadhg was resolute and one color of personality, full of integrity and strength that was a bottomless well. Lorcan often felt like the herald of his father. As if a thread through the island's history, his family helped tie the knots.

He could hear the sea now. His unkempt hair was blown back as the growing winds met his face. Rage filled his chest as he wanted to demand that the mountain reveal his boy. The sun would soon tear away the mist that choked the valley and he hoped to see all the way down the peninsula that cut into the Atlantic.

Feargal Butler, the long departed butcher from Slievemore, used to speak of hearing voices on top of the cliff. He had felt warned that he was eavesdropping on the angels' business so he never stayed long. Lorcan thought as he neared a lookout, *If I'm to be in the presence of such fine company, perhaps they'll lend a hand to find my only son.*

It wasn't many years ago—and the memory was clear as yesterday to his tired mind—that Donn was dangling his short legs in front of a stone bench at the outdoor sermon of Father O'Malley, asking him where the angels resided and if any lived on their island.

"Of course," he had answered. "Your mother was certainly one."

Lorcan took a deep slow breath as he surveyed everything his eyes could take in. Sweat dripped from his forehead, not simply from fatigue, as his sight denied him knowledge of his child's whereabouts. The waves below pressed upon the north cliff wall in a thunderous repetition.

He briefly looked over the sharp edge of the cliff. It always reminded him of the time he threw the flowers from his wife's grave over its steep sides. He couldn't let go and see them lying on her grave so he had kept them and taken them up the mountain. Over and into the surf, he had tossed the wildflowers—back when he could get up there without the aid of a stick. He sent them to a divine destination unknown, one that allowed the sky and ocean to celebrate the memory of his lost darling.

Lorcan gazed across the verdant valleys below that rolled into the ocean's cold spray. Rubbing his jaw, he looked down upon the hill he had climbed and the meadow that lit up golden with the rising sun. The walls of the ancient summer camp for herdsman, the booley that acted as an outpost could be seen in the distance on the rugged landscape.

"Donn!" Lorcan yelled again. He wiped his brow with his almost-white sleeve, mixing yesterday's dirt with today's.

Suddenly he heard a faint grunt and the sound of plodding hooves. As he spun around, he caught a glimpse of gray hair before getting slammed and then hurled into the air. Lorcan hit the ground with a thud and was nearly knocked unconscious, but as the blackness began to clear from his eyes, he pushed himself up from the ground and saw Donn chasing the black tail of a fearsome beast.

Donn was trying to calm a magnificent stallion with his bare hands. The neck and shoulder muscles of the horse reverberated with tremendous energy in a symphony of erratic movement that was only half as noticeable as his flashing dark eyes. Donn and the horse were circling each other, only feet away from the cliff's edge.

"Watch the ground, Donn!" Lorcan yelled.

The animal was snorting at Donn before assuming an aggressive posture. Enough smoke left the steed's nostrils that Donn was coated in a white cloud. The sun blazed behind the horse as it stood, still and threatening, while casting a mighty shadow over both men.

The gray horse, with a black mane, appeared to be on fire from the red glow around his silhouette and it seemed to present itself as a god of horses, demanding immediate servitude. It thundered the ground with its front hooves, refusing to let Donn come near.

Lorcan could feel the watch in his pocket and wondered if this was the final seconds he'd have with his son. Donn lunged forward while gripping part of the stallion's mane. The horse tried to jerk away before making a rear quarter-turn back off the cliff with one hoof, the ground giving way slightly. It appeared as if Donn had a good grip on its mane but the horse violently turned his neck toward the cliffside, delivering a short side buck, sending Donn's legs flying off the ground to roll off the sloped edge.

Lorcan started to dash forward the almost-twenty feet stretch to reach his son. The young man lost his grip on the handful of hair and fell, catching a rocky outcropping with his hands. The gray stallion turned his attention to Lorcan then readied itself for a charge through him to freedom.

Donn was out of Lorcan's sight, hanging off the cliff edge on the other side of the horse. Lorcan was enraged as he needed to get past the beast to save his son and he squared off with the animal as it began to charge. The horse got as close as his chest before landing its hind quarter upon him and lifting him, momentarily, off the ground. Lorcan staggered and nearly fell but it was almost as if the stallion sensed his desperate determination to reach his son as it stood to the side, pawing the ground.

Finally Lorcan could see Donn finish pulling himself over the cliff's edge. Lorcan exhaled in relief. His son didn't take long to get to his feet, although his forehead bled from a deep gash. The wind blew wet grass off his scraped hands. The gray depths of the ocean below had only claimed some of his sweat and blood.

The horse readied itself to dash to the side, between Donn and Lorcan, but Donn was able to grab its mane before it picked up speed on the wet slope. He swung his hips over the back of the deep-chested animal and held onto it as the frenzied horse flung itself everywhere. Donn yelled, "Stop now!" And it was as if a door slammed on the animal's will. Defeated and suddenly still, the stallion slowly collapsed over on its side and Donn kicked away from its back.

Donn saw his father walking toward him with hands outstretched. The horse lay motionless behind Lorcan, breathing heavily. Lorcan pulled Donn up then stopped. The father bent over as he held a knee between breaths and then dropped down and grabbed some turf with a hand. Donn limped past his father and observed the fallen beast. The horse's eyes were closed, as if asleep, and its mouth gaped as if in shock.

"What happened to him?" Donn whispered as he put his hands on the horse's torso.

"He gave in to you. Thank the Lord you're all right, boy," Lorcan continued between strained breaths. "You were just a little stronger than him and he finally had enough."

The Feeney men, although generally easygoing, were always known to have extreme ferocity when demanded like giant stone wheels crushing anything in their path once they were pushed hard enough. Lorcan tore some earth with his hand like a claw, threw it beside his black boots, and stood. The father glared at Donn with those eyes that nearly hid under his low brow and thick eyebrows. Donn's face quickly reddened as he began to realize how impetuous he'd been.

Lorcan allowed a grimace and queried, "Have you done enough today that we might start back?"

Donn looked down at the quietly breathing horse and quickly replied, "Why can't you stay back at the bay? I'm old enough to gather the cattle myself."

Lorcan squinted and took in the damage done to Donn's head. "You nearly murdered yourself just now and you'll not tell me what I should or shouldn't do. This was the reason you weren't gathering the cattle for the journey to Slievemore?" he asked, pointing at the silent and still horse. "You've taken three days longer than I had planned and the fair at Ballinasloe is next month. We can't afford the delay."

Donn looked at his father with pleading eyes behind his dark-brown hair that blew around his bloodstained forehead. Lorcan put both sets of knuckles against the top of his breeches and waited for Donn to start moving. The horse gave out a slight grunt and then let out a deep breath, shook a little, but remained mostly still.

"I like the horse," Donn feebly offered.

Lorcan loudly retorted, "That's a one-sided feelin'."

Donn convinced Lorcan to help him lead the horse down mighty Croaghaun. They made a makeshift halter using Donn's torn shirt and slipped it around the gray stallion's long neck. The horse awakened and gave no resistance as if it were suffering from a long night of drinking.

"I'm going to take this horse to see the captain at the mutineer outpost while you round up the cattle at the booley camp and head them to Slievemore," Lorcan said to Donn. The mutineer outpost was on the west end of Keem Bay.

Donn was gathering the few heads of cattle he had found in the morning as the fog lifted around them. "Why do you want to take the gray to the mutineer outpost?" he asked.

"They are the most likely ones to have lost an animal like this from their stables. If this is their horse, it must be returned to them. We don't want to be taken for thieves," Lorcan explained. Donn simply nodded his understanding.

After Donn finished rounding up the bovine stragglers, they began carefully making their way down the mountain's slope in a slow diagonal pattern, crossing over patches of grass that were tipped in gold from the sun and glistening with droplets of dew like pearls. The horse had a pompous gait, despite its apparent daze, and held its nose pointed parallel with the ground, seemingly to show contempt and superiority over the men.

Although quite hungry at the moment, Donn was distracted by imaginings of how he'd now be sure to impress the ladies of Slievemore, now that he had this fine horse. Donn had grown up, sometimes, seeing these young women, in their long colorful gowns, stroll on well-kept paths near the sandy northern shore at Dugort and Slievemore. He would see the ladies from the road while traveling past the tall orchids that covered those walkways, flowers that seemed to bloom as the result of the patronage of such fine women. He noticed their smiles—smiles he hoped would, one day, be meant for him.

The women that visited from far-off places, sometimes escorted by men that he envied, seemed to him resident angels. This magnificent horse was sure to bring him favor with those beautiful ladies. He would ride up through the wildflowers and—

"Donn!" grunted Lorcan, interrupting Donn's reverie.

Donn was startled to realize he had walked a good twenty yards in the wrong direction, away from the cattle. He bent his neck, looking down, and pulled the horse toward his father. They had arrived at their summer camp home. Donn entered and sat down on a chair to rest. Lorcan came inside and stopped in front of the hearth in their old booley lodge. Donn noticed the disrepair of their surroundings. Ever since his mother had died, his father had avoided the premises and the house had gradually looked more and more deserted. Dirt—forbidden when his mother was alive—coated the various pieces of furniture.

Lorcan was apparently lost, deep in thoughts similar to Donn's. "You know, son, I could smell her cooking in the cauldron long before I ever walked in the door. We always had some wonderful stew, followed by a dessert of honey and milk. We had a home, Donn," Lorcan continued grimly. "Every time I enter and see that cauldron empty is a reminder that she's gone. It's my firm hope that you'll never have to live without that sort of bliss once you've come to expect a warm home to return to." Lorcan briefly shook his head and bit the inside of his mouth. "I never thought anything would change."

Lorcan scratched the back of his head, turned, and went to the table to gather up a few possessions into an old sack. Donn hurried over to help him. Nothing more was said as Donn couldn't think of anything to say. Donn never questioned why his mother was not here with them. She had died, leaving him and his father alone.

Having helped his father pack, Donn grabbed a halter and went outside to put it on the gray stallion. He put on the shirt that he had used to halter the horse. His father came outside to join him with a sack slung across his back.

"Don't forget what we're doing here," Lorcan reminded Donn as he walked up to him. "Keep the cattle calm and close everything up to keep the weather out. If I'm not back by tomorrow, then start heading the cattle to the pasture at Slievemore and I'll catch up to you. My pace should be twice yours." He tousled Donn's hair, smiled at him, and continued, "I'll make sure I look out for your horse. Make sure you keep the hearth lit to please your mother. Clean up and dry your clothes." Just then, the horse snorted and looked away in apparent frustration.

Lorcan set out at a quick pace with the horse in tow. He knew he'd have to climb some hills and rugged terrain to reach the small horseshoe bay so he wasted no time.

*****

After Donn watched his father lead the horse away, he decided to build a fire in the hearth before heading out with the cattle. The six red-and-white cows and three calves Donn had found this morning had joined the herd and grazed greedily as the mountain grass they left behind was now sparse. The meadow was lit up with a brilliance by the afternoon sun, and the cattle swished their tails around their box frames in a constant rhythm. Little brownish birds, with red splotches above their eyes, were here every winter as the weather closed in and speckled the pasture among the cattle.

Donn didn't have to fear the cattle wandering off with no strong wind for them to push against and such good grazing and what wolves there were didn't have a distinct advantage when the cattle weren't in a spot favorable for ambush on uneven ground. He sat down near the cattle and began to eat the oat bread and curds stashed in the sack he filled at the booley village. He was contented to have made it back to the booley with something to show for the effort.

Donn thought about how sustenance was growing scarce as they relied on his aunt's cooking while in summer pasture. She had departed for Slievemore days ago. He missed his aunt's warm bread—not unlike the many things that were also absent with his mother gone. He would finish packing his belongings and securing the hut tomorrow since his father was impatient to get the cattle to Slievemore. He was fairly ready to move the cattle toward the pastures by the island dock tomorrow where he expected his father to then return. They would leave shortly thereafter to the mainland.

It was somewhat lonely here since the village was almost deserted. The herdsman liked to depart at nearly the same time with their herds for mutual protection. Isolation wasn't unique to the boy, but as a child, he had enjoyed the Catholic hedge school where a rotation of tutors came from villages and the mainland to educate children with language, music, and philosophy. He had spent summers in the village, helping care for the crops and going to the school down by a small inlet under some birch and ash trees. However, that special education had ended a year ago, and now, he was under his father's guidance to become a livestock herdsman and island trader.

Vibrant, and not yet a distant heritage, was the ancient land of the people of Achill. To the south lay Clew Bay, and the treacherous islands of sunken drumlins were scattered toward Clare Island; and all were far down below the demon-breaking bell of St. Patrick. Not a soul in Ireland dare place a hand on that black bell and tell a lie.

Donn would dream many an hour away, imagining the feared O'Malley banners fluttering above a choppy sea. During his boyhood, before a night's fire, storytellers retold the history of the O'Malley ships that challenged all for supremacy for the rights to Clew Bay's waters and its fishing. Southeast, over the sliver of sea that separated Achill from the rest of Ireland, was Galway and beyond that the fertile farm grounds and decay of a once great kingdom.

The nearest cow swished its tail back and forth as Donn quietly ate and daydreamed to that rhythmic sound. There was plenty of time to dream in the life of a herdsman, in particular, plenty of time to dream about a horse.

*****

The Feeney's had always been herdsmen. Lorcan thought it special to take Donn to the October fair outside Galway just as Tadgh had done with him at his maturing. That fair had grown in size every year and their family had been an active participant since nearly the founding of it. With the lifting of the English export ban on Irish cattle, it had given his father, Tadgh, a chance to thrive.

This year, he wished to bring a group of young heifers to the market fair and auction them but leave the other cattle and breeding bulls for the winter in the community pastures at Slievemore. All the two-year-old oxen went to the local market for decent prices since there was always a demand on this small island for beef. Some angst hung over this upcoming fair since the unforgiving past winter caused half the calves to perish. The cold wintery ground and wind had been too much of a shock for the newborn calves.

Lorcan had plenty of time to think on the three-hour journey to the tower. He dared himself to disbelieve that Donn had the short attentiveness of youth with their stumbled-upon passions and week-end destinies. He could hear the horse breathing and the grass give way under their feet as the wind passed through the valley like a great invisible hand. He remembered an old herdsman who had told stories by campfire to the village children when he was a boy. At the worst, it undid all the good the local father achieved through Bible study, filling their minds full of superstition and legends about Achill and Ireland. The children would huddle beside the sleepy liquored-up man and ask questions like, "Where did Gol the giant die?" They'd ask how many mysterious fairies watched over Clew Bay.

The old man—of many years and great respect—would squint before offering another of his inexhaustible answers as he seriously considered each question, then he'd move only his eyes toward the young child with great focus and speak without any uncertainty in his low voice. Lorcan would always wonder if any of the old man's tales were true but he'd make sure to never forget them. The old gods were run out by the Christian God, according to his father. However, as a boy, he wondered if they weren't just hiding and perhaps this rugged isolated island was just such a place. Lorcan remembered asking, and the answer was, "The rocks themselves echo the ringing church bells which thin out sanctuary for the faerie races. The timber harvesting of the great Irish forests has diminished the merry and solitary existence of a faerie." His memory of the red buck running by him, just like the horse he led had earlier, seemed worth recalling. Often he thought, a grand strange fate can reach him, even in the quietest places.

The Visitors

"There!" She reached out and picked up the doll from the black mud. Bridget pushed the hair from her eyes before brushing off the sticks and dirt she could from its faded dress. Her little sister was so overjoyed when Mr. O'Brian, the old sailor in Slievemore, made a doll just for her. While running around, exploring every hidden flower on Achill, little Ashling would be in agony if she misplaced her stuffed companion. Mr. O'Brian, whose own four daughters so loved the sewn dolls he'd make while home from coastal fishing, retired to his family cottage while his younger brother continued the trade. His smile was rare but infectious, with all its mischief in his old face often visible, and it most often appeared when a young girl would beg him for a doll or when he'd have one to give.

Bridget started back up the rocky hill from near the beach and inlet that led to Slievemore's small dock. Her simple dress, that was covered in dirt and which she tried to keep from dragging on the wet grass, reminded her of the doll. With the sun setting, she felt lucky that the precious object was recovered and that her family need not worry any longer about her absence from home.

Bridget and her family had arrived on Achill Island just less than a year ago at their father's inspiration. Her father, Daley Savage, was a master tailor from Ulster who left there both due to religious persecution of their Catholic faith and hope for a new and better future in the west of Ireland. They had moved into the inn near the sound when they arrived, and it was so nice not to be living there anymore, but otherwise, her sister would have never encountered the kind old sailor that made her feel less a stranger in this new country-side. Bridget recalled her mother rushing to prepare the house so that they could escape life in the village.

She continued over the dirt path as her feet grew colder. The sun was setting and the red in her dark hair dimmed with the disappearing light. The trees that flanked the road whispered as the wind and sunlight snuck through them with tiny beams of radiance that helped her find her way. She shivered against her shawl and looked out at the fog-laden hills that looked untamable.

She passed through the family gate that joined the neglected hedgestone walls. She became aware of the light emanating from only one first-floor window of the country manor she still saw as unfamiliar. There was no indication of unexpected visitors but she tried to make her hair presentable as she neared the door. Certainly they hadn't had dinner so early without her?

A flush of birds broke over the trees, giving shade to the hedgestone fence surrounding the Savage estate. The birds made a conical departure up away from the chimneyed roof above the family sitting room. The birds typically graced the lawn below with colorful discarded feathers that Ashling loved to gather. Little Ashling watched those active little creatures depart and return, and she fancied that those that made homes in their trees were delightful neighbors. Sometimes the birds would sing so she thought it fit to sing back. Bridget thought it was strange but adorable how her sister took to relationships with whatever had wings.

Her father opened the door, and before she had a chance to say anything, he pulled her into the house with a quick tug and closed the door behind her.

Her father's salt-and-pepper hair was slicked back and he was wearing his typical gray shirt and black trousers. He had trimmed mutton-chops and a sharp angle to his jaw. His wide eyes under thick eyebrows showed his seriousness. Once she was inside, he had the noticeable look of relief but still-unannounced concern filled the air. Bridget looked toward the small sitting room where a group of five men surrounded a large map on the floor. Candlelight flickered off their grave faces as they traded words while Bridget tried to absorb what was going on. Her father placed a hand on her shoulder.

"You best get up to your room and get cleaned up." He usually paused before every statement, as a man thoughtful in action, but now he seemed harried.

Bridget clumsily dropped the doll to the floor. She saw three of the men, who were standing, look over at her with a glance. One of the men, kneeling before the map, seemed out of breath. The final man was sitting in the corner, smoking a black pipe that caught the light. His eyes were half-closed and he never took his attention off the worn-out map.

Her father spoke in a hushed monotone, "These are our guests for tonight. Please don't disturb them."

Bridget picked up the doll, feeling silly. The serious conversation was further disturbed when young Ashling burst into the sitting room.

"Look at my pretty shoes!" Ashling repeated to each man in the room as she skipped.

The men acknowledged, one by one, in affirmation, however awkwardly, and with grunted short answers, that she, indeed, had pretty shoes. She turned to Bridget holding the doll and quickly exclaimed her gratitude while snatching it from Bridget's hand. Embracing it left mud on the front of her dress and face but she beamed happiness all around. Bridget briefly looked around in annoyance.

"There now, what is your dolly's name?" said the man with the black pipe as he puffed out a roll of smoke.

"Princess!" Ashling replied with gusto.

His compressed lips around the pipestem allowed words. "Emmm, Princess, well, it is an honor then."

"Yes!" She giggled back.

Bridget's mother came into the room and interjected, "Go to your room now. Thank you, that's enough."

Ashling vanished out of the room just as she had arrived—with a clamor. The man with the black pipe chuckled a bit as he resumed whispering to his associates.

Daley's wife walked over to him and took his hand. She whispered, "Are we rebels now, husband?" Mrs. Savage spoke with a disappointment that was added to the accumulated dismay that had trailed its way from Ulster.

"Come, Ella." Daley moved her toward the main room away from the travelers.

Bridget decided she should also leave to clean off the road's wear and prepare for bed. Bridget departed from the room and turned to the left, heading up the narrow staircase where she found her dark bedroom. She closed the door and opened the one window a crack to free the room of its stuffiness. She carefully lay down to hear the conversation of the men as she pressed her ear against the floor. What she could hear made no sense and she only heard clearly something about a horn they could not hear which seemed to trouble them. While still hearing the boots of the strangers below her, she succumbed to slumber.

Soon after dozing off, she heard a noise that startled her awake. It wasn't wind rustling through the trees, it was—music? She moved to the window seat, gazing out the thick glass panes. She could see a small ember like a firefly near the biggest tree behind the house. It seemed to exist alone. She decided an investigation was demanded! Anyway her still-muddy clothes were perfect for an adventure.

She quietly left the house and moved toward the tree and saw that the ember was the pipe of the stranger she had met earlier.

"What are you doing here?" she asked, upon approaching the man.

"I thought it be a fine night to delight the faeries, and besides, this is how I'd like to tell 'em farewell," replied the shadow smoking from upon a tree stump.

"No, I mean what are you doing at my parents' home?"

He tucked his fiddle underneath his chin. "Your father has been kind enough to allow us to stay the night. Would you care to join our concert?" Bridget caught a glimpse of a tattoo that seemed to wrap his neck.

"Our? You're alone." She puzzled at her surroundings.

He bit down on his pipe and his face lit up upon a strong draw from his pipe, and then he began to play. A stream of light poured from the lone tree in the valley. Little various colors flickered in waves around the landscape in harmony. The moon flooded Achill like a nobleman glorying his entertainer with attention. With every rush over his bow, her heart jumped and she danced across the green grass below her. She was moving faster than she ever had as she felt no need to breathe or think about her next movement. The fiddle commanded a celebration and all would surrender to it.

The little resident faeries added a drumming hum that complemented the dash and pleadings of his mad reel. She felt the delight of a hundred souls with the frolic and grandeur filling the air. Her heels never touched the ground and instincts came alive in her blood with a fury. The rosin on the strings never failed as the tempo quickened while the reel continued until the faeries left ribbons of vibrant rainbows across the valley.

All life was connected by his music and she reveled in the new sensation. She could see the man smiling with eyes shut as he played with natural grace. The sweat trickled down his brow and cheeks. The squinting reminded her of a man thinking of a lover that remained in his fond memory. She could feel the faeries flit through her hair as she danced. Butterfly-sized were these delightful dance partners and many took their turn to beguile her with a flight, gifted with whips and spins just for her; then she granted each a nod before they continued on. The host stomped the ground and it was like the earth was his drum that beckoned an audience to the grand gallery he had created in the valley. Her shadow cast off a stream of flying things and fell upon the hills.

A bloodcurdling scream erupted from the sky and it drove away the audience back into its old hawthorn tree, quick as a snap. A woman's scream, that seemed to replace the sound of thunder, echoed through Bridget. The man lowered his instrument, grabbed his pipe, and said with another squint, "That'll be the end of it." He carefully and solemnly put away his fiddle and bow.

A shaken Bridget had so many questions, all while wondering how her parents didn't wake. "How did you do that? What were those things? Wha…"

"Calm yourself and I'll tell you a story before bed as thanks for the company."

She bit her lip and darted her eyes before sitting on the ground.

He made himself comfortable on his tree stump and began. "Long ago, my clan was led by a young king against a very dangerous threat to Ireland. Before that time, we lived with many different races in peace here. Our home was like an Eden—like tranquility. Then a monstrous horde arrived at our shore. Black banners terrified the people and threw us into dark days of survival. They were giants that seemed to control nature itself, and we became their livestock."

The man puffed his pipe. "After that bleak time and a dead king, a strange band of warriors arrived. They claimed they were sent to aid us, and the wise ones among us joined them. They became our leaders and trained us in how to kill the invaders. The new king had many powerful weapons but used mainly a harp against them which proved more deadly to them than any sword. The surviving enemy were reduced to hiding in the dark places."

He continued at a faster pace. "However, our kingdom was torn apart by the poison that war leaves behind. The old heroes eventually died, or left for other kingdoms, and the lesser of us struggled over who should be in power. Every family that had served felt that their banner should be hoisted highest which tore apart the knot between us. Temptation to harness the music and sit on the throne caused countless battles. Men soon forgot what started the fighting and only the bloodshed remained while the rebels hid wherever they wished."

Bridget interjected, "What happened to the harp?"

"No one's seen the harp in centuries. So many of the wondrous things from those days were stolen by dark creatures while we were distracted which, in turn, they hoped to turn against us. They found them worthless since they were created to fight rebels. Those that love God rejoice at His authority while others that try to defy it can only run." He took his pipe from his mouth and put it in his deep chest pocket.

"What business brings you to Achill?"

He squinted. "Oh, we have to attend a meeting for certain."

"A meeting?" asked Bridget. "I see. Are you here to meet someone to trade wool?"

"No. We're not invited to the gathering of our prey nor do we know where or when it is."

"A little frustrating, I might imagine. Still you find yourselves here under our roof. Did you bring danger to our family for boarding your men?"

"Your father has always been a generous man as long as I've known him. What we're here for…" He paused a moment before continuing, "You're in no more danger than any other in this troubled country. We're on the hunt and we travel across all Ireland, if need be, to be successful. The riddle to their path has a mad answer, but as long as we chase, they run. Since we know there is a destination, then we know it's possible we can corner or cut them off."

Bridget considered this. "How would you know you're in their way if you aren't aware of the meeting's location?"

"As long as we chase, then the meeting cannot be convened. The criminals we're after scatter when chased, but eventually, their own arrogant nature gets the better of them and they hasten our encounter. They become furious toward those whom they believe are beneath them. To state it plainly, they want to rally to exert a wicked harm. For me to say more about what we're off to find would make me guilty of putting you in the danger I told you would not threaten you for having met us."

The man paused and picked up his fiddle and Bridget got the sense that he was not going to explain any further. She offered, "Well, then, my name is Bridget." Her wide eyes and fidgeting legs betrayed her inner excitement.

He rose, gave a deep nod in respect, and then said, "Kite Collins, have a fine evening, Bridget." He walked back toward the house and disappeared through the doorway.

The Shipwreck

Lorcan reached the last hill before the guard tower and heard a terrible crash, including little snaps in the distance. The horse stirred and Lorcan hurried his steps to the top of a bog. The grass was burning where he stood. A few hundred yards away, he could see waves crashing against the jagged rocks and the great hull of a damaged warship. The ship had been scuttled on the shore as another was anchored in the shallows. The British tower was a pyre of black smoke as a victim of the white-and-black-adorned ship in the bay. Lorcan could see men by the tower, dragging loot across the shore back to the sea. The beach was littered with debris from the ship and black soot where explosive shells had hit. A small group of men struggled to pull a deep raft onto shore. On the beach, two men were conversing—one mounted and the other on foot. The old man on foot wore a beaver hat and dark robe and looked up to speak to the rider.

"Of any place we could have landed, we find ourselves now on Achill Island," the older burly man said with his hands stuffed in his pockets as he shook his head.

The mounted man with floppy red hair commented, "We will depart, but first, we'll locate our absent brothers. Then either the *Perilous* can be made to set sail again or at least be salvaged."

He asked his leader, "Perhaps they were captured?"

"I don't think so. I do find it hard to believe there isn't a reason for this though. Seems as if when we took the time to look, a reason was there to help us move forward." He looked past the smoke on the crest of the hill. A figure was standing there with a familiar horse in tow. "And there be the good grace of destiny, standing on the hill, I wager. Do you have a match? Mine are soaked." The old man didn't smoke; he knew this but teased him with the question anyway. With a smirk, the energetic man spurred his horse forward and his mounted bodyguard followed.

Lorcan saw the small group of riders headed toward him from this shore of great turmoil. He saw that the bearded men on horseback all had large wolfskins draping their square shoulders but none of their horses were saddled. They had horseman sabres with intricate silver guards over the grips secured to their sides. The lead rider, with his black cloak floating behind him, halted his gray charger in front of Lorcan and did a salute with a mock bow. His twin beechwood pistols were tucked away inside his blue sash, wrapped around his waist, inside his thigh-length leather jacket.

The red-haired rider shouted, "You brought me my lost friend? The most hospitable shore of all Ireland! Your name, sir?" He spoke with an almost-relaxed lilt to his words which was in contrast to the carnage behind him. The apparent leader focused on Lorcan with a large smile, hiding his exhaustion. The other riders stopped all around the hilltop and waited quietly. All the mounts of the bandit crew looked like the steed he led by rope.

Lorcan, with one hand on the halter and the other on his suspender, said, "What in holy heaven has happened here?"

"We lost a ship, and when we came to reclaim it, a disagreement ensued with your jailers. We object to disagreements, especially since we're a peace-loving sort." Then the man dismounted and introduced himself with an outstretched hand, "My name is Cathal O'Ruairc. What is your name, my dear friend?"

"Lorcan Feeney." He shook the deerskin-gloved gentleman's hand. "My son found this animal on Croaghaun and it about killed him, catching it."

Cathal combed back his red hair with his fingers and then pulled out a short bent cigar, bit it, and spit to the side. He knelt quickly and tore himself some burning peat to light his cigar, puffed, and said, "So you say a boy caught my horse? That's quite a story. Only a certain kind of man can come near these stallions."

After he lit his cigar, he pointed at Lorcan's chest pocket, indicating an offer to light his pipe. When he reached out, Lorcan noticed a tattoo running down his wrist beneath his jacket sleeve. Lorcan pulled out his trusty pipe and Cathal came close and used his cigar to light it.

Lorcan clamped on the bit and explained the story with some pauses and revision. They smoked and Cathal patiently listened to the bizarre recounting. Lorcan interlaced a few unexplainable mysteries into his discourse that islanders simply used to validate a story that would otherwise be dismissed. In Ireland, a faerie tale was as much credited with honest delivery as any other oral history. Lorcan was uncoordinated in his memory, affected as much by Cathal's sharpened brown-eyed gaze as the burning destruction beyond them. When Lorcan finally served the full worth of his impressive story, Cathal gave a murmur of acceptance, then mounted his horse and said, "Please take me to your son. I'll conclude the matter of the stallion with him then."

Lorcan dropped his arms and postured defensively. "Is that necessary? If it is any retribution you seek, then I'll stand for it but I won't bring harm upon my boy."

Cathal let out a chuckle and stated, "Rest yourself, good sir. I want to meet the boy that could catch my stallion. Honor must be bestowed. Your hospitality need not extend any further."

Lorcan nodded then mounted the horse. Cathal shouted to his men to continue looking for their lost brothers before departing.

As the two trotted along together, Lorcan considered the man who flanked him. It was clear that the two horses were used to riding alongside each other since they nearly moved in natural concert. Lorcan considered that he was in the company of an outlaw and his life may be in danger associating with him. He determined to give haste to this request to place this situation behind him. It occurred to him that Cathal revealed confidence by leaving the safety of his formidable crew for a destination unknown to him.

As they rode, Cathal emanated a regal presence that Lorcan couldn't deny which commanded a respect that Cathal need not demand. However, Lorcan's mind was heavy the entire journey, for it seemed that he was caught up in events that could upend a man's fortunes. But then, as his nerves calmed, another thought came to him that was the most troubling. When you spend your entire life waiting for a dashing Irish leader to appear on your shore and now suddenly confronted with one, would you wish to remember that you didn't aid him? Although an Irishman must weather the disappointment from many grand expectations that fell short, he remains a dutiful victim. Lorcan frowned as he thought of his honor and the burden he carried keeping it.

The Meeting

It was dark when Lorcan arrived back at the booley camp with his new companion. Donn was in the house when he heard a horse approaching. He was elated at the prospect that the horse was not taken and he hopped up from the smoldering hearth. The soft glow emanating from inside exposed a second rider to his sight. Cattle crunched the grass in a sleepy grazing pattern as he squinted toward the figure. The riders appeared to be on matching horses. Donn didn't know who the other man was so he decided to keep quiet instead of giving his usual greeting.

Lorcan dismounted just outside the door and stated simply, "Donn, this is our guest tonight. He wishes to speak with you about the horse. Tie them up and join us."

Donn didn't waste any time. He brought the matching pair to the shed and ran back to the booley. He quietly walked into the remote settlement's only occupied residence. It was always eerie here where all around was blackness, defied only by the fire in the hearth.

Cathal gave the impression he was relaxed wherever he found himself to be. He sat and leaned a shoulder against the wall near the fire. He looked tired. Donn stood near where his father sat and waited.

Lorcan spoke up, once noticing Donn's strong stare out of the corner of his eye. He pulled off his damp vest and said, "Son, this is

Baron O'Ruairc, the man whose horse escaped. He'd like to have a word with you."

Cathal pulled a small red-and-yellow apple from a deep coat pocket. "That horse is very special to me. He is like a brother to me. You have in your stable a bloodline that traces itself to the greatest warhorses and companions of the ancient Irish warriors." Cathal looked at Donn. "Did you know that to even be allowed to touch him, you'd have to be a Fiann?"

Donn was pale with worry. "No, I didn't know that, sir," he replied.

Cathal looked into the fire and continued, "It has been my great honor to watch over these horses since I was a child. My father guarded them with his life—hundreds of years of care for the Irish kingdom."

Donn was worried the lord would think he stole the horse. "I found him running in fear. When I caught him, I did it only to protect him."

Cathal gritted his teeth. "It's why I'm here myself to speak to you. I've assembled a crew and I'm looking for the right kind to join us."

Lorcan sprang to his feet and went into the bedroom, shaking his head. "Please excuse me."

Cathal looked back quickly at the apple and raised it toward Donn. "Could I interest you in an apple?"

Donn was flabbergasted by the turn of conversation but continued to listen patiently. "Aye," he replied.

Cathal looked at the apple with a hangdog look. "What might you do for it?" he quizzed.

In awe of the stranger, Donn responded, "Anything."

Looking startled, Cathal said, "Anything? Well, if you'd do anything for a piece of fruit, then you're hungry enough to sail with me." Cathal stood up and moved close. "My name is Cathal. I'm a lord of a land controlled now by foreign invaders. The Villiers are fat and arrogant and will soon be rolled into the sea, back to wretched Normandy."

"Can you manage such a thing?" Donn asked in a loud distrustful way.

Cathal placed a hand on Donn's shoulder while handing him the apple. He replied, "If you join my crew for the next voyage, you'll never wonder again. I hear you like my Irish stallion you found."

"He is magnificent, aye," Donn said.

"I'm impressed you could catch him." Cathal raised his eyebrows. "Only the Fianna can handle these horses. If you want him, then you'd have to become a protector of Ireland. You think you're up to it? We won't have much time."

Donn was bewildered. "My father needs me to help him with the livestock."

"One voyage after your training, just one. If then you don't want to continue with us, you can stay here and be a guardian of Achill Island—with your great stallion to ride." Cathal sought the focus of Donn's eyes to his, and then, when he had it, he added, "Give your choice to me if you remain lost to decide a pursuit. With me, ne'er a day will pass that your time would be shamefully misspent."

"You'll let me keep the horse?" Donn looked at the door.

Cathal whispered and leaned forward with an intense gaze. "Yes, so what will it be now?"

Donn nodded and Cathal grabbed Donn's forearm and shook it strongly.

*****

The next morning, Donn woke up to the fierce gaze of his father. Perturbed, he sat up in bed slowly. "Sleep well?" Donn asked.

Lorcan stated emphatically, "I know you're thinking about heading off on some adventure. Back when I was a young man, my blood was a river of fire just as yours is now, Donn. Listen, I understand you."

Donn responded, "You never did anything to change anything. You didn't fight in the rebellion or recover our family land."

"I held on where many others didn't. You have to have patience, boy. Your time will come," Lorcan replied.

Donn rubbed his eyes wearily. "I know what I have to do to make things better."

Lorcan narrowed his eyes in fury and spat out, "Fine, you'll never make it back here alive and then we'll have nothing. I'll have nothing. Everything would have been for nothing." Lorcan waved his hands dismissively and added, "Be done with this after the horse is yours. God save you, boy." Lorcan ran his palms over his suspenders, looked to the ground, and seemed as if he had more to say, but he turned and left the room quickly.

Cathal was busy looking for the crew of the wrecked ship so that left Donn even more uncomfortable sitting around, watching his father avoid him. Donn decided he would put aside his misgivings and go off to woo a woman. It wasn't a cattle sale that had his attention at the age of seventeen. He remembered a valley where flowers grew that were unlike anything he'd seen. He wagered that ladies love flowers based on what he knew of the ladies of Slievemore.

Donn left the booley camp and headed to the valley. He soon spotted the small white petals that shot out from bright-pink petals bunched in the middle. He was relieved that the cows had missed them and quickly pulled a few. He continued east from Croaghaun to Slievemore where he would hunt for his new love. He would have enough flowers so that he could offer one to as many pretty girls as he could. How could he know which one he'd fancy until he'd met them all? It would make it simple then to pick his favorite. A thought shot past his mind, *What if he gave them to two sisters and they found out?* He shook his head and decided he would still take the risk.

*****

Bridget was walking one of the many narrow cart paths that converged on West Slievemore. She tried to pick a different route often but knew she needed only to turn the other way to head home. It allowed her to escape a stuffy home and some of the dullness. Her father was kept busy with visitors from the mainland that were being introduced for business. She found she grew dizzy from the constant pleasantries offered to those lucky enough to escape this island.

Walking away from home felt exhilarating and to see anything new was a welcome distraction. She often found herself lost in thought of a past home during the few hours she would be gone. She remembered when she would steal one of her mother's roses that she kept on the main table. She would rub the petals on her lips to change their color. Often she would witness her parents being affectionate on her father's return from work, and now, she imagined herself having a man to expect. Bridget knew that if she were ever going to meet a gentleman to fall in love with, she'd have to get away from this windswept island.

Bridget's shawl had slipped down so she pulled it back over her shoulders. The chill would be terrible without it, a gift from her father on her last birthday. Its fabric was from India and the pattern a maze of elegant burgundy flowers and green vines, and beneath, a muslin brown.

She could see the waves reaching the coast, painful reminders of her exile from the world. Bridget could hear the sounds of cattle in the distance as she walked past the vanishing trees and hedge bushes. She sensed a break in the sunlight. She looked up where the top of the hill split the sun and met the sky. On the high ground, there was activity of moving livestock and also something still. It looked like a boy, standing motionless, focused on her. He was kneeling and holding something pink. She stopped her pace and a hint of regret for wandering so far from home cropped up in her. The boy rose and cast a shadow across all the ground around her. He started toward her and she knew avoiding an introduction was impossible, but this seemed improper and concerning.

Strangers were a common sight on Achill and a high wall of caution was observed by the islanders when coming across new faces. Too often, those visitors would be desperate to escape a pursuer and all they saw before them was an expendable obstacle to freedom. People did not arrive on Achill's shores casually but with a purpose, be it benevolent or cruel.

She stood and fussed with her dress and hair as an ingrained, but regrettable, habit. The boy approaching her was wearing a long-sleeve brown tunic and dirty black trousers. He took large steps down the hill, holding in front of him some pink flowers. How ridiculously awkward!

Donn took a quick breath then smiled while asking, "Hello… what is your name?"

"My name is Bridget, and who might you be?"

"My name is Donn, I work my father's cattle. I saw you strolling." He was disarmed by her eyes, like glowing amber in a dust storm.

"And now, why did you decide to come over here with those?" She pointed gently at the flowers he carried in a tight-knuckled grip.

"I saw you from across the moor and realized these are meant for you."

"Oh?" She noticed his hair, a little long and combed every direction by the wind and cemented with dirt, testifying to his pastoral livelihood. River water without soap could not tame those locks.

"Aye, I've decided to pursue you, Bridget. Distance between us will be but a memory."

He pronounced her name like a rustic but it didn't sound too bad—she was surprised. He offered her the flowers and bowed slightly. Bridget thought he must be simple since he was overly gentlemanly in such a rough setting.

"Th-they are beautiful like you." Donn smiled with a grin she mistrusted. His eyes were so intense that she became flustered.

Bridget couldn't bear the attention. She thought that he obviously was a ruffian with that fresh cut on his forehead. She elected to shock him with hope that he would leave.

"I have nothing to offer you back, really, but let me give you this since you're being so hospitable." She quickly picked up a rock about the size of her palm and handed it to Donn. He looked at it then up at her, through his dark bangs, in complete confusion.

"It was the closest thing I could find that reminded me of you." She grinned and was quite proud of herself. Donn didn't drop the rock but instead pocketed it and threw his head up at the setting sun.

"Very gracious of you, Bridget. I'll work very hard to live up to your fine opinion of me."

"I'm sure." She giggled. "Thank you for the introduction but I must be heading my way home." She nodded and turned away.

"Farewell, Bridget." Donn waved and headed back the way he came.

On the way home, Bridget delighted over the flowers. He was the first man she'd met that treated her like a lady on this island. That was worth something. She wondered if she would ever see him again. *Probably not.*

Donn cursed himself all the way back to the herd for giving her all the flowers. He tripped in the near darkness, heart beating fast with disgrace. What came over him? He put his hand in his pocket and felt the hard rock. Donn could sense that Bridget was fearless at heart. He liked that about her.

The Crew of the *Perilous*

On the rock-laden shores near the village of Gweeselia, under the bell sounds of Christian order, there was a waiting man. He looked across the gray waters. The gentle rain added a somber beat against the waves and hills. Luke looked for sails and saw none. He had traveled the ocean and now was tied to the seas as a result of a failed rebellion. His ship, the *Perilous*, was broken up and now waiting was all the leadership he could offer his crew of Ulster men.

"Captain O'Connor!" a distant voice shouted out.

He turned around. "Yes, what have you?"

Cathal's band had found them at last. Two burly men wearing wolf pelts and riding gray horses were on the ridge near the village. The crew of the destroyed ship huddled around their rescuers.

Luke yelled out, "Where is O'Ruairc and where is the *Mistress*!"

A heavy man with twin pistols secured and a sharp-edged ax aside his mount trotted forward a little. "He waits near a southwest bay on Achill, near Keem, Captain."

That's where I lost my ship, Luke thought. "Come with me and refresh yourselves with meat and beer. Then we'll go!"

They approached an establishment in disrepair with a muddy front walk. The outpost, sitting below a large dead tree, was a bleak proposition for the band. Luke and his entourage pushed in the pub's door and startled the sleepy gathering of locals. The scuffed black boots of the intruders were dry for a rare occasion and the dirty blue sashes, tied around their waists, were intriguing to the patrons' eyes as they made way.

Luke was at ease and tossed coins on the table, which promptly were exchanged for dark pints. The poorly lit pub had a massive goblet-shaped firepit with a detached flume pipe exhausting through the thatch roof. Its hot coals warmed the guests and could offer stew from a stove in the base. A glow gave the room a rosen-drenched appearance. The brown floorboards, cracked at the nails, met a flat brass sheet that plated the base of the bar.

An old man crept up to the bar. He was gaunt and sick with age and his breath stenched of beer. His tall height had been stolen by backbreaking labor.

The stranger spoke with a near mumble, "What do you want here? We've soaked the ground with enough blood in Mayo for your kind of foolish dreams. Or are you not rebels?"

Luke calmly stated, "We tossed away our rebel green to follow Irish blue. A way forward for all our people is what we wish." Luke took a drink and looked at the old man who was stiff and fearful. "Don't worry. We only have a thirst for beer today and not loyalist blood. I'm sure you were there that day at Castlebar?" He declined to answer, pulling his short brown hat a little lower and retreated slowly back to a table. Two shipmates followed and slid chairs up to the man in retreat; acting like two bookends, they sat in place. Each nursed their drinks and leaned in toward the now-uncomfortable stranger. Never seen apart were Fig Gallagher, a young Jamaican who lost his father to yellow fever, and Jacko Dillon, a gunner who followed his elder brother to serve on the *Perilous*; and now, this stranger got the joy of their close attention. Luke knew that his crew wouldn't allow anyone to catch them off guard by informing of their presence, especially his castaway sons of the Caribbean.

Although it was unsettling to be under the patrons' study, the crew began discussing their way back to Achill. Daniel MacIntyre, a typical proud farm boy from Dungannon, said, "We kept moving to avoid any attention, and now, we expect to return to Achill without finding a British patrol? Do we expect to dress up as sheep and bae our way there?" MacIntyre was always noticeable in his stolen cocked bicorne which sported a large colorful feather from a carnival celebration.

The two scouts from Cathal's crew were not remarking but looked unimpressed by the lack of enthusiasm for the return. Luke replied, "As hungry as the folks around these parts are, I imagine a stray flock of sheep would receive attention. We'll move only at night and stay close to shore, same as before. We'll cross back over to that Achill Bay with little trouble."

Their quartermaster, Michael Devine, was visibly filled with regret as the supplies in the hull of the *Perilous* were either sunk, looted, or in complete disarray. He ate while breathing heavily as his eyes darted around, unable to commit a direction to rest. He finally paused between tearing away at some cold mutton and said, "I'll need to spend some time figuring out how to maintain the crew." He glared a little at Luke past his sharp nose, swallowed, and declared, "We shouldn't have tried to come near shore during the storm. The fog was too great and we joined a hundred ships' fate, breaking up ashore like so. How can she sail now?"

Luke felt an uncertainty, like a rock in his gut, but he sensed that morale was at its lowest since their old leader Munro was executed and it pained him deeply. He would always remember when he and his crew were taken prisoner to the Caribbean. They agreed to sail with Cathal who had liberated them from indentured service. Their usurped ships were under Cathal's command and he promised them a fate other than throwing themselves at English cannons. Cathal offered them a compromise to achieve a free Ireland. Two years of sailing to ports for their leader at least kept them busy but it was like a mutual denial of a fate that seemed always on their heels.

Luke responded, "We make it back, then we'll make it known that we intend on O'Ruairc to keep his promises now. Eat and let's rest until evening sets."

*****

When the men of the *Perilous* rejoined the *Mistress*'s shore party, it was a happy but brief reunion. Luke was anxious to inspect and refit his ship.

"Our copper sheathing was damaged and our sailing ability will be greatly reduced," stated MacIntyre.

"You cannot repair and rebolt?" Luke responded.

"Not timely nor do we have the chance with these unwelcome shores to dock and take on supplies. I'm sorry, Captain."

Luke bit on his tongue and then ordered, "Pull off the copper."

"Will do, Captain."

Devine looked up from his ledger and mentioned in a hushed tone, "The ship will last not long."

Luke looked over at Devine. "Long enough, we're on borrowed time. Besides the en'my frigates run disadvantaged before our sails, now less burdened."

Devine adjusted on the stump he sat upon and his eyes squinted. "Weight won't be an issue with empty bellies."

Training

Cathal trained Donn in swordsmanship while he waited for his crew to repair the damage done to his ship and for Luke's crew to be found. Donn was quick to follow the baron's every instruction. Not a patch of dirt around the house was undisturbed by Donn's crashing body. When Donn wasn't getting brutalized by Cathal's discipline, he was learning philosophy and Irish history. It seemed that every time he sat down, he was dripping blood from one more part of his body. He'd sometimes grow light-headed from either the beating or the voice ceaselessly shouting commands at him. The unbridled gray horse was always a quiet spectator while grazing; he'd swear its eyes followed him. He found himself locking eyes with the feral animal more than once. Cathal explained to Donn that the horse has an exalted place in Irish life and that he should be treated as a brother.

Cathal had a habit of turning a light sword exercise into a sudden violent attack that would leave Donn hitting the ground as if thrown by a trebuchet. The tutor would then yell at him to repeat what he was taught.

Cathal excused his rough treatment of the student by affirming, "You may face combat unlike anything even I can prepare you for so…accept impossible odds as your new daily wager."

Donn drank a handful of water from a bucket and asked weakly, "When may I learn to shoot? Certainly sword fighting cannot be as useful."

"Without a concentrated fire from a musket line, it acts merely as a shock to your enemy and can only hit its target not much greater than the distance from where a sword fight is imminent anyway. Just pay attention and the rest will come in time."

They continued. Donn was exhausted from the awkward foot placement and trying to keep the burdensome sword in an ever-ready defensive posture. Cathal made a move toward him with a low cutting stroke to his right side. Donn reacted by parrying with his blade so it caught under the hilt. Hardly a moment after the impact, Donn was slapped on the head.

"Did you see what you did there? You never block an attack with the edge of your sword. You use the flat…where the strength is. If you break your blade in combat, that'll be your last mistake."

Donn rubbed his head and dropped his blade down on the ground. Cathal pushed Donn over and he hit the ground and struggled to catch his breath.

"*Never* let your sword touch the ground. You have a scabbard. Use it."

Donn recognized this was considerably more difficult than Latin.

Cathal said, "Now stand and face me. Train yourself to outlast your opponent. Learn to evade an attack instead of exhausting yourself blocking the blows. Make your counterattacks and aggressiveness set the momentum of the contest."

They continued training and Cathal made the point. "Our enemy finds it impossible not to offer the first strike. That gives you an advantage."

Days went on and Cathal explained the heritage and customs of the Fianna. Even a summer holiday for his horse would be observed, as it once was, where no labor should be demanded. Donn was told that guardians, like Cathal's father, were entrusted to aid those that would protect Ireland. Cathal's father kept a royal equine bloodline alive in his stable and he told Donn that he had Cormac Cas to thank for these wonderful Iberian horses that served the house of the king of Ireland so well.

Meanwhile Lorcan remained patient and didn't converse with the pair as he tended to the cattle. Donn didn't know how his father felt but he knew his father was giving him space out of respect for him. In the morning, it was obvious to Donn that his father was upset since he kept going back to the bags hanging from the cross post on the ceiling, acting like he couldn't find what he was looking for. He knew it was his father fighting off the urge to speak to him because the idea of him being so uncertain as to what to have for breakfast seemed comical.

More tasks were set before Donn before his training would be complete. He had to reach Cathal behind a staff in a defensive position. He was made to drill with his horse and learn to maneuver on command, always wheeling to the right for cover. Saddle tricks became second nature. He was taken into a small square marked on the ground and had to learn to avoid a sword blow without any shield. He learned to wrestle with his father's bulls and topple them. He had to name and speak to his horse as a family member. Croaghaun, a name of fitting respect, was the only name his tired mind would conceive.

He was led to a raised dirt mound and told to dig. Cathal handed him a pickax and shovel. Donn worked alongside the cattle as they chewed and paced. Sweat and dirt covered him completely and he lost himself in his toils like a spirit driven mad. His lower back would grow numb so he would walk a minute and then resume the digging. His shovel broke through a layer where the heavy soil found way to stones. He lifted a few rocks out of the hole with a struggle. An opening was apparent although too narrow to allow more than his arm. He was so tired he couldn't hold his own spit so he climbed out of the mudhole and lay on the tall grass with a thud, lest he pass out. Through his half-closed eyes, he could see the sunlit blades of grass appearing bejeweled. His breath was short and he was close to drifting off into sleep.

That night, he was awakened by a shaking in his ears, like the air was erupting. The world was black, except for a beam of light shooting straight into the beyond above him. He waved his hand through the swimming colors that it carried. His hand carried the light with it, like it was painted on, before slowly dissipating. His curiosity drew him to the source, and when he braved the strange light so that it bathed his body, he could continue to dig. After creating a hole big enough to crawl through, he shimmied through the portal and dropped onto a solid floor.

He was in a small chamber, the walls of which surrounded a table. There was a narrow door that would have faced the sea, partially caved in and covered with sod. The table was flanked by bowing lions carved from a white wood. The walls were smooth and painted in biblical-like images of angelic people at battle with ghastly creatures. There were scenes of ships and sunlit meadows with gentle animals. There were men covered in green marks and waving blue banners, following a man with a staff. Directly in front of the table, he saw a large group of men rising to the heavens, being called there by trumpet.

He approached the table and all that was on it was a large plain bowl. In the bowl was what appeared to be water but it contained a light that could barely be seen. Donn questioned if he should be in this place but found himself quite thirsty. He put a hand in the bowl and drank. His mouth was stained with the light and the water filled him like bread but the effect was sudden contentment. His eyes were relaxed as he looked into the bowl. He saw his reflection as though he was a different person that he had yet to recognize. His inner doubts suddenly went to flight. A whisper ran to his ears and around his neck with a warmth. "Go forth, brother, in His name."

Donn left quickly and made his way back home. Cathal listened to him blather about what he had seen. No response was offered. He simply said he'd return and told him to hold out his hands, palms up. He placed a rock in each of Donn's hands. He had to stand with his arms raised up for hours in the sun, never being given any food or water. He didn't remember fainting.

*****

Luke looked cheerfully bespelled. "How odd you are."

Cathal quickly took bread from Luke's hand without him noticing and ate it while listening with a relaxed focus.

Luke shook his head and continued, "A stolen ship isn't meant to be sailed into the waters controlled by the very bastards you stole it from! Cathal, are you trying to kill me? Does that excite you?"

Cathal responded unabashedly, "You landed here."

"I *shipwrecked,* you stranger of sanity! You listen now, the next time you wish to rendezvous in the most treacherous bay in the whole of Ireland, consider the cost. By god, I may have been injured!"

Cathal chuckled. "The next time, I'll be sure to consider your safety, my friend. Does the *Perilous* float?"

Luke quickly spat out, "Like a corpse buried at sea." He waved Devine over. "Tell the baron about the ship we turned into firewood."

Devine rushed over with his book, protected beneath his arm. "The provisions are safe. I believe with some repair to the keel and plating, we should be able to pull her into the surf safely before long. The masts are intact as well as the hull."

"I have every faith the *Perilous* will be in parade form before the month is out. Fancy a cigar?"

Luke broke a smile and said, "You know I hate those damn things. Be off with yourself."

Cathal was relieved to see his men safe.

*****

A giant of a man picked Donn up off the ground where he had passed out for the night. Donn woke to a blinding sun and Cathal's cigar wafting into his face.

Donn asked, "Why did I have to hold up the stones?"

Cathal responded, "It had nothing to do with the stones but to prove to me you'd carry out my commands."

Cathal's men were all around. Cathal let Donn eat a breakfast of foul-smelling mystery-meat soup with biscuit. He could barely move his mouth to consume the broth.

Judge whispered, "I fear you rush this lad, Cathal. He has too much to learn."

Cathal replied, "I've got a feeling about this kid. If I can't trust my instincts, I'd be lost." Judge sighed heavily but said nothing.

Cathal, smiling, dropped down next to Donn. He quietly told the tired boy what he must do. "You're going to go mount Croaghaun. You're going to circle that campfire there, while repeating what Judge there tells you to—all night long."

An elder man with a furrowed brow, wearing a beaver cap, walked over and placed a spread hand on Donn's sweat-matted hair then muttered a prayer. He gave Donn a piercing stare and instructed him to say the prayer until told to stop.

"Lord above, below, beside me, I pray to you. Make my hands yours. Fill my spirit with your will. Bless thy blade to serve and protect your people. I sacrifice now and forever in your name, Jesus Christ, my King." Donn practiced the words a few times to a patient teacher.

After Judge was satisfied, he walked over to the small fire. He dug his hands deep into his jacket then knelt before it. The men were silent and still as Judge sat. Then the wind ceased blowing, the horses quit stirring, the crackling could no longer be heard. The flames pulled higher and straightened like they were reaching for the sky. Judge opened his jacket and unsheathed a sword. He placed the blade in the flames. He closed his eyes.

Cathal whispered, "Is he ready, Judge?"

The elder nodded and rose then solemnly stepped back.

The men continued their silence while Cathal handed Donn the bridle. Cathal slapped the dust from Donn's back, knocking his tired frame forward, and spoke plainly, "Remember, once a Fiann and horse have partnered, it is for life. You become each other's concern. If it's death you encounter, you meet it together. Now mount and you'll both submit yourself to God and His Ireland."

Donn mounted and took the reins. As he started his ride, Cathal followed him briefly. He offered advice to his weary pupil. "It's not just the bounty of horse flesh I be offering to ya but a rank of significant responsibility as well. That is, if you can earn our trust this long night." And so, Donn repeated the prayer and rode Croaghaun all night long.

The next morning, Cathal helped Donn off the sweaty mount, and the holy man prayed over him. Judge retrieved the sword from the extinguished flame and gestured Donn to kneel. The sword now had gray symbols emblazoned upon the steel. Donn wondered if he was imagining the blade's transformation but he couldn't deny what he saw. The markings meant nothing to him but he felt a charm by them. When he saw the sword, he felt a need to hold it as if he was reclaiming a part of himself.

Cathal waved his sword over Donn's shoulders and called him Fiann, knight of the Irish race. With care, Judge handed the sword from the flames to Donn. The mysterious markings, vertically designed, caught the light.

Cathal explained that they protected God's followers from the outlaw government of demon legions. "With the banishing of the mischievous, genocidal Caorthannach and her demons into the ocean by St. Patrick, the Fianna adapted to the new heavenly government's methods to protect mankind. Before that, the Fianna were in a constant state of war against the Fomorians, or organized demons, with the pendulum of freedom swinging back and forth through the generations of Ireland. Evil King Balor, on his black horse, leading his legions, was forced back into the sea by the holy Tuatha de Danann. However, as the Tuatha de Danann died or departed and were replaced by lesser men, they let wickedness corrupt their kingdom of heaven on earth. The Fianna were seen as a threat, and without leadership delivered from Heaven to command them, they were scattered to covertly operate or fight for secular whims."

"Who were the Fianna though? I mean, where did they come from?" asked Donn.

Cathal offered his hand to invite Donn to stand and said, "The Fianna trace their heritage to the bloodlines of the Nemedians, who were the lost people, that came before the golden age of the Tuatha de Danann. King Nemed's honorable and valiant kingdom was another example of wickedness entering the hearts of men and the covenant with God being torn asunder."

Cathal taught Donn all these tales and their importance so that Donn understood his place as a member of the Fianna. He now had a responsibility to his people that traced itself back thousands of years.

Late that day, Donn was sitting near the fire as some of the crew ate dinner all around. He ached all over, feeling exhausted beyond measure. The old priest was looking at him from the other side of the campfire and seemed amused. After some time passed, his near-faint composure was interrupted.

"Try this. I think you'll like it." Judge pointed to his open bottle then walked over. He seemed, to the young man, like a giant draped with a curtain.

Donn grabbed the thick glass container by its long neck. He held it over the flames and saw its dark brown contents.

The old man sat on the log Donn was on and then began fidgeting with his cross. "Rum from the western oceans. Every sip sends me back to the beginning and a tropical port and then, like revealing myself clearly again, reminds me of my purpose." Judge snickered and closed his eyes.

Donn took a draught from the bottle. He winced with friendly surprise. "This is fine!"

Donn put the bottle back down. He pretended to examine the label and decided he'd say something about his stomach not agreeing with it. He never cared for drinking, except when a festive occasion demanded it. He would always have a hangover and that reminded him in precisely the same way of an accident he once dealt with as a young boy.

As a young boy, Donn was sitting on a hedgestone wall, tossing hay over into a small enclosure with a bull. His legs were dangling along each side of the wall. He was sweating tremendously from the sun and exhaustion had gotten the better of him. He fell over into the enclosure with one of his pitches of hay. He quickly looked up and a bull was readily charging him. Donn felt himself taken up from behind by its furious impact, flipping him over and driving his head into the packed dirt of the other pen. His muddy face was stained with blood when he looked up at his father who had rushed to aid him. He vaguely remembered coming in and out of consciousness while riding home on the hay wagon. Donn ached terribly when he'd move too quickly, and soon after, fever set in. His mother nursed him for three days and nights next to a fire while she prayed and vigilantly tended the flames. She was always suspicious of authority so she scoffed at sending Donn to any healer. Not only was she rebellious by nature but she only allowed outsiders to see what she wanted them to witness and she felt safest with her independence intact. Meanwhile his father was convinced whiskey was the answer to ease the pain and help him sleep so secretly he bade him to sip when his mother wasn't looking. Unfamiliar with alcohol at the time, Donn soon found that the drink supplemented to the dizziness as well as gave himself another reason to feel ill. He recovered, of course, although hangovers will now always remind him of that injury and had thus largely soured him on drinking.

Judge muttered, "I made the mistake of having this rum one night when Cathal was near. He was just a boy then, you see. I ran my mouth about how I truly saw the world. I said that all our heroes and nobility are gone, long perished—only sheepherders being left behind. You can see, I was upset that evening. I had grown frustrated, witnessing the competition between louts that performed daily in and out of the pubs. That isn't really the truth though, our senses tell us lies. These men that you know, working the land, are soldiers, disguised to fool our enemies. They wait to be called upon by those who would be brave enough to lead them to restore an Irish kingdom. They don't know any of this but a few…lucky ones? My complaints had an effect on Cathal far longer than the rum had on me. A man is valued by his timber, his substance, that which is within that can weather disappointment and crisis, that will eventually prove his worth. Cathal is an oak."

Donn spoke with intent, "What can you tell me of what we have yet to face? Everything Cathal says to me sounds like a faerie tale he expects us to live in."

"All these things you're raised to understand are just details of a cloak that covers the truth. Beyond the distractions, the old ones, that some once called gods, are still at work. The war over humanity still rages like pieces moving across a board. I think of it like chess and sometimes wonder which pieces have been lost to us and what that represents. Perhaps instead, it's like cards, we play with dark forces but then, certainly, we always will carry the strongest hand since ours was drawn for us by the Lord. Alas, we can still play those cards poorly if we lose faith." Judge paused then added, "Do you have business before we set sail?"

Donn hesitated and looked at his boots and knew exactly where he wanted them to take him. "I wish to say goodbye to someone before we go, if there is time."

Judge responded, "Very good. Then off we'll go together to involve ourselves in heaven's battle royale."

*****

The next day, Lorcan was busy being busy which meant he was restless and not accomplishing much despite his hurry. Lorcan had witnessed the trials his young boy endured and it was painful to accept his son would soon leave. He hadn't been alone the whole of his life and it was unsettling to feel the impending emptiness. He wanted to send with Donn something he had never spoken of before. He opened his wife's storage chest. He dug under her things, careful to look as little as possible, so as not to draw out a mournful memory, then pulled out the skin of the red stag that was slain so many years ago. She had saved it and he sometimes would see her touch it and have a quiet moment. Hard to imagine, even now, that young girl accomplishing the preservation of the hide. Lorcan rubbed his hand across the dark deer hide. He had then decided to see the tailor and have a jacket made.

Lorcan went to see Daley Savage at his residence where he took on clients. Lorcan introduced himself and then instructed Daley to make a short jacket to block the wind on Donn's voyage. Savage shook hands with his new customer and promised it would be done in haste.

The Harvest Party

Bridget watched Ashling for her parents as she played in their yard.

Bridget felt little resentment for being taken from Belfast society after she was only recently introduced to the social circles. Although she had friends and familiarity with all of Belfast, she always felt afar in spirit, like being invited to a stranger's birthday party. Her sense of ease and confidence—now on this foreign shore—came from the relief of being spared temporarily from the choices that all young women in her position must make. Surprisingly contentment filled her heart. Daily she felt this contradictory understanding since she barely knew anyone on this island and there were few balls, even in nearby mainland, at which to meet suitable gentlemen. Her curiosity was increased about the type of man she would fancy. Watching her parents endure the pain through their tired expressions and attitude wore her down in Ulster, moving her to quickly accept the move as necessary. Bridget saw this as an unexpected challenge, and perhaps, what she had expected to transpire with her life in Ulster now seemed too conventional.

Ashling was sitting with her pet goose in the hedgestone-walled front yard. Mr. Buttle, the long-necked goose, was always the dapper guest, whether rain or shine, in his long blue-ribboned bow. Ashling decorated him and treated him as an always-welcome neighbor. She would walk over to tend her pretend garden of wildflowers while he would waddle along beside her in apparent secret conversation. Bridget would sometimes roll her eyes when her sister would approach with the goose and her doll in hand.

Bridget could hear feathers, honking, and a dress passing over the grass approach. "Where are you all off to then?" she inquired with a disinterested far-off gaze.

"Mr. Buttle has invited me to the harvest dance! I'm discussing what I shall wear with him now."

"Oh, has he? He shall be the sharpest-dressed gentleman there, I'll wager." A tinge of sarcasm couldn't be contained.

Bridget thought of the large gatherings, or ceilidh dances, where she danced throughout the evenings at grand estate halls in Ulster. As she understood, the front of the Slievemore Inn was a gathering spot for a country dance. It was to be an event of gratitude for whatever crops the beast herders found that survived the growing season. The harvested feed was important to complement the reserved grass over the unpredictable winters.

She did like the thought of going to the dance for the sweet red punch. The food would be heaped upon the black-lacquered tables inside while the white rock walls on the outside would be lit up with a hundred torches. The tavern keeper at the Drenched Rat held it there instead of at his establishment since the reek of months of labor wafted off the building at this time and it was impossible to keep clean. Traveling musicians would arrive in time to complement the glee already felt by the tired farmers. These socials never brought visits of the gentry but the locals came without any thought to propriety.

Her parents arrived home. Her father appeared exhausted and it added to her mother's concern for his health. Tailoring for clients that were mostly on the mainland was difficult, and he was required to travel without pause. Ella helped him pull his boots off and they spent time talking. Bridget would sometimes notice her parents holding hands in such a way that their world revolved around where their flesh found each other. She knew their quiet acts originated from a love that found expression in subtle adoration. She saw them share conversations with their glances so Bridget was ever so careful not to intrude on them during such moments. Bridget pondered on who might like sharing her hand and if that inextinguishable love could be so returned.

Bridget went to get ready for the dance. She must have taken out every dress she owned and waved it in front of her mirror at least once before selecting a flowing cerulean-blue dress adorned with a trim of white lace flowers lining the sleeves and meeting at the center bodice.

She had always thought her neck was her best feature, but now on this island, it had to be her hair—so much brighter and well-kept compared to these island girls. The elements of wind and rain, combined with a lack of accessories, made keeping it long impractical and rare. She decided she would never cut hers no matter how long her family chose to stay. Being here actually made her wish to be more attentive to its care. In a land where a ringlet was only a rumor, she would be unique on this mossy rock surrounded by a cruel ocean. Like banished nobility, she aspired to stand out among her neighbors.

Bridget, to her growing distress, was wearing out heaps of her shoes during her many walks. Something that was acceptable for outdoor wear in Belfast was quickly found to be lacking in her new surroundings. Her need for exploring could be stifled by her father's tightness with his purse. She had her favorite leather slippers for around the house, covered in dark-blue satin, that she dare not wear outside. She did have her short black lace-up riding boots, with small heels, but she didn't find them comfortable on long days. She was determined not to let Achill change how she saw herself and that included her pride in fashion. She didn't go a day without a sponge bath and she was meticulous about her hygiene. Before long, she was presentable enough to attend the party.

When Bridget arrived at the festivities, the attendees were everywhere like a flock of geese that had amassed for a meal. She was happy that although she liked her dress the best of any she saw, it was still understated so as not to appear out of place.

She wandered through the conversing crowd. The working men were relaxed and the families were together; the children dashed around the skirts and legs of their parents. She felt awkward not knowing anyone and wished her parents would have come. She wandered over to the long refreshment table.

The tavern keeper, who typically made mince pies for daily guests, had made *bolo de mel*. The sweet treat was a favorite of his Portuguese wife and the fishermen who frequented the lodging. Bridget enjoyed the cake then picked up a cup of punch. She moved into the full tavern where pints were being sipped. She wiped the sugar from her fingers and then saw him.

"Here-here I am, my Bridget," Donn stammered. He looked at Bridget, seemingly unaware of the party all around him.

"Yes, here you are." Bridget fought back a grin as she remembered the silly boy with the odd flowers. Her dress, graceful and blue, danced about the floor as she swayed slightly, as it picked up the candlelight with a scattered shimmer like calm port waters at noon.

"You'll be absent from me a short while." He let out with a sharp breath.

She had merely expressed a slight interest. However, through the music, Bridget noticed his rushed tone and serious eyes.

"You see, I can't marry you…" Bridget's eyes widened as he continued. "Until I've bought back my family land. I'm leaving tomorrow and I'll return soon."

She leaned into him in shock, showing her concern. "Marry me, you can't marr—"

He interrupted, "I know, I promise not long." He suddenly reached forward and took her left hand. She was going to pull it back but a dancer bumped her elbow back toward him. Donn kissed her hand and it warmed her entire arm. Donn placed his hands on her sides and then stated earnestly, "I would not be without you nor would I content myself with remaining a gentlemanly acquaintance. I will demonstrate with good effect my intentions toward you. Upon every challenge that is set out before me, I will vanquish any obstacle that could result in your absence from me so that our union can never be questioned or opposed. You are my desire and my just God will give me a path that leads to you." The zeal in his eyes froze her.

A quietness overtook them as words became stuck in her throat from the emotional confusion. Donn stared deeply into her eyes.

He then turned and quickly left the establishment into a pitch-black world. Bridget realized, as she watched his receding back, that she didn't even remember his name.

*****

Bridget was fidgeting with her hair, sipping a teacup of punch, while the others danced. She watched from the wall and thought about her parents and if they had discovered her missing. This hall was full of joy and laughter so that had encouraged her to sneak away. Away she needed to be from the sadness in her mother's eyes from having the family uprooted and the stress that surrounded her father. She had not planned on meeting a man swept away by a romance she had never offered.

She walked outside and looked past the crowd to see if she could spot him. She wandered away from the town center, mostly lost in thought. She found herself at a small dock that sprang from a rocky outcrop against the shore near the main pier. Many small fishing vessels were tied to one side of the pier and also tied upon the shore with stakes. The torch-like bonfire in the village was only candle-size as she wandered far. She sat at the last wooden plank and curled her knees under her chin, arms wrapped around herself. She could see dolphins in the distance, pushing against the water's surface while playing. She thought about the boy and what he must see in her. She started humming the reel that she danced earlier. She felt like she was somewhere west of the civilized familiar world.

She saw, out of the corner of her eye, the moonlight shine off of a wave headed the wrong direction. Suddenly she heard a scream, followed by a dark shape, and she fell off the dock, partly from the wind at her back and partly from panic. She threw her arms out of the water and grabbed onto the dock. The weight of her dress wouldn't allow her to pull herself out. She fought to keep water out of her mouth as she cried out for help. She tried to move, inch by inch, down the pier, but she was tiring and the screaming that she was hearing was horrifying enough that focus was hard-won.

The sky above became alive with the flight of faeries. Close to a hundred of them took her by the hands and arms and pulled her to shore. Bridget lay on the ground and stared at the sky in shock. An intermittent giggle emanated from her throat, like hiccups, as she watched the faeries crisscross away into the black hills. She held the sand with the palms of her hands for a moment then struggled to stand. She stood there, dripping wet, and heard again the other-worldly cry of the dark creature and, with her back to the sea, she knew she had nowhere to run.

She watched as a black apparition shot past like a falcon that fluttered the starlight and lifted the dust off the ground around her ankles. Eyes, menacing and bright, appeared static a few yards away, like spears touching her soul, and it caused her to panic again. The dark form slithered below on the ground, as the eyes grew larger, and then another scream of agony crashed into her, muffling her cry for help. As she was falling to her knees, she was grabbed away.

Donn stood on the shore with a sword in the air. He was as affected as a barbarian witnessing an eclipse when he saw the banshee. Donn demanded, "Bridget, stay back!" She fell back into the surf and pulled the hair from her face. The banshee flew straight up into the air, lightning appearing to spark off the creature. Then all was calm. Bridget was helped up by Donn after a few anxious moments and he beckoned her to follow him. They began to make their way back to her house so that she could have the sense of security once again.

"How were you able to scare the banshee away? I mean, it meant to kill me." Bridget shivered as she held her dress, heavy and wet.

"Why was that? What did it want with you?"

She felt so hopelessly vulnerable at the moment that she spoke as much as she could about the night the guests came to the house and the creature that scared the tree faeries. "You must think I'm right mad but that's what happened. I thought it could have been all a delusion until tonight. What are you doing with that sword?"

Donn uttered, "I'm a Fiann now." She stopped and stared at him with confusion. He continued to walk and explained as she slowly followed. "It all started with a horse, but I bargained for a chance to keep him. Now I've found myself a part of something far larger than anything I could have guessed. A group of men said I'd have to become an Irish knight and serve them for a voyage, then guard Achill from there on, if nothing more."

She started shaking her head and flipping her hands around, all the while biting her lip between questions. "What does this have to do with you throwing yourself between me and a banshee? Are you such a chancer? Never have I felt more like a square circle than I do right now. I'm so scared that blasted thing will return to take me away…tell me, what am I supposed to do!"

"I'll take care of it. I'll learn how to send it away for good. At least it knows you will not be unaided. As for why it wants you, I don't know. I'll ask my new friends about whoever stayed at your home."

Flummoxed, she exclaimed, "You sound entirely new to this!" Her eyes fixed on Donn with an icy glare. She looked away and quietly carried on. "I make the faeries happy so I suppose that horrible creature hates me for it."

Donn began asking her about her family and her story as much as a means to distract her as to learn about her. She was mumbling less and less as she became engaged by Donn's questions. She was starting to believe that she was safe with Donn, although she still felt disbelief about what she had experienced.

"Wasn't this a wool trader's house?" he asked.

"Our house is part of the Clark family assets which was once lived in by my mother's uncle. He used to summer here to watch over the sheep he contracted and he was apparently quite happy to escape the busy muddy streets of Galway."

She explained to Donn that her mother's family directly imported high-quality wool, stored it, and resold it to various customers, mostly English merchants. Her father, a Catholic, had no trouble finding customers in Belfast to tailor for, at least at first. Then new English nobles flooded in that couldn't hide their disgust of not only Catholics but also the old Norman families that had assimilated into Irish circles.

Donn listened, and when she asked him about himself, he explained his intentions to buy back his family land. He spoke of his father and grandfather. He wondered aloud about what this voyage would mean and how his father would manage at the fair without him.

"Where is your mother?" she interjected.

Donn thought of his mother and slowly started. "Her name was Aine. She's buried near Dooagh Bay. Since she passed, my father has changed a great deal." Donn exhaled sharply and looked over at Bridget. She could see the deep well in his blue eyes. "There was a cradle that best describes why. He built it for many children he would share with her. She died and he had that to remind him of those hopes dashed. I'd catch him gazing at it. There was nothing that would fill that void."

Donn relaxed a bit and spoke of happier moments. How his mother would pour him as many bowls of soup as he wanted. How she would always make sure he wasn't cold at night and never let the hearth fire go out. When his father met his mother, she was an uneducated orphan. His grandfather, Tadgh, sent her to a small mission at Keem Bay to the southwest. When she returned, it was as if only the quality of her clothes changed with much of her mystery remaining. She could eat and carry herself in a civilized manner. His father had told him that his mother's eyes carried within them the soul of Achill.

They walked by the windswept trees that guided them to her home. Donn mentioned that Cathal had told him that the seeds that became these trees they passed were brought by the Nemedians to guard against evil. Their red berries were marked with pentagrams as visible symbols of their allegiance to God's natural order. The ancient Irish would make drinks from those berries and fill themselves up as an act of inner defense against corruption.

Bridget was shivering more and more so she was elated to be nearly home. Still she dreaded leaving her defender. She was growing fond of his stories since it gave her some reason to appreciate Achill for more than her low opinion allowed.

They made it to her front door and she felt him staring at her. Suddenly she didn't know what to say or do. How she could blush, as cold as she was, was remarkable.

Donn paused and held Bridget's hand. He looked her in the eyes and said slowly, "You can always count on me, Bridget. I have to go help my father now while I still have time before my departure. I wish you a good evening."

Bridget hesitated and stammered, "Good bye, D-D…"

He smiled and responded, "Donn." He kept looking at her, still not leaving.

She looked at the ground and noticed that he wasn't letting go of her hand. She felt strangely uncomfortable to be the one to remove her hand from his grip. She could no longer deny his gaze. She was fully clothed but felt naked to him. Perhaps it was this uncertain world she lived in now or maybe a bout of recklessness but she reached her head up and kissed him with a hint of awkwardness.

She smiled and was unexpectedly happy with herself. "Goodbye, Donn."

Donn kissed her hand and released it. "Goodbye, Bridget." He turned and disappeared into the dark night.

She dragged her miserable self inside, careful not to cover the floor with her mud. Her thoughts were scandalous the rest of the night—thinking about her guardian and his strong hands.

The Departure

A fresh merchant business, built on a well-located lot next to a barber, was initiated by Sven Davoy. Sven was of Swedish descent but with nearly no custom or identity that harkened back to the land of his forefathers. He was born and raised in Galway to a family of fishermen. He had, at a young age, noticed his father haggling with a merchant over his catch who, Sven despaired, should not deserve such fine fish without catching them himself. Although he felt the buyer was ignoble, he felt a party to the fool in the trade, no matter the deal struck. Because of this, Sven decided he too would become a trader and live off the sweat of others so that he would no longer feel so humiliated.

When Sven was old enough to be called Mr. Davoy, he gathered capital and storehouse space, enough to begin his enterprise. Before Sven had gotten used to scratching a proper ledger, he was introduced to Cathal O'Ruairc. The baron spoke to Sven about finding his younger brother, Chancey. Sven, startled by the unusual armed patron, darted around answers that wouldn't endanger his brother. Cathal grew impatient and told Sven that Chancey had written him a letter, explaining that he "has the location for the Rod of Lordship and he wished to share it with me." At this jarring revelation, Sven dropped his quill and stepped back into the wall in shock.

Sven's little brother was having a pint at the tavern when both Cathal and Sven sat down with him. Chancey was grinning under his long blond whiskers when he confessed that it was Sven who Cathal should be speaking with as it was *his* map. Sven was distraught and his focus was on his fool of a brother while Cathal waited for the deal to begin.

"How did you acquire it?" asked Cathal.

Sven rubbed his fingers together on the table and said, "This is just a piece of parchment I found one day while playing as a child—he's pretending it's more than a novelty."

Cathal quietly looked at Sven as Sven grew ever more uncomfortable. The rookie trader took Chancey's drink and finished it, then offered, "The nun wanted to burn it when she saw it. It was covered in beasts and directions to a distant island that reeked of forbidding unholiness. I found it in an old barrel that was supposed to contain butter."

Cathal grit his teeth, smiled slightly, and said, "What do you want for the map? I've been passing word to every sailor across the North Atlantic of the possible whereabouts of Hy-Brasil."

Sven had to drag his right arm off the table since he was injured in a childhood fall that made it hard to lift that shoulder. He pointed his left hand at Cathal and said, "I was raised never to take advantage of fools in a trade. You say you're interested in this scratch paper and my brother thought you might pay us to acquire it. Take it and be off. I'll be pleased to be freed from it."

Chancey had a troubled look on his face and rubbed his brow.

Cathal shook Sven's hand and spoke, "I'll be the fool. However, allow me to recompense you. Take this." Cathal pulled a little brown leather bag from his coat then placed it on the table with a heavy thud. Sven took the bag and then the party rose and left to acquire the map. After Cathal took the small rolled map that Sven had kept in his lodging, he bade them farewell with a smile. Chancey stomped off, apparently disgusted with his sibling. Sven, later that evening, opened the bag slowly by the candlelight of his bedside table. He found inside solid gold coins with faces of Roman emperors upon them. They caught the light and Sven rubbed them hard, worried they might be an apparition. He could hardly imagine how much wealth was in this bag or how Cathal may have acquired such a rare treasure. He quickly hid the bag and slept little that night out of excitement for the future.

*****

Lorcan and Donn met on the small golden shore. The sun was bright and caused them both to squint, an unneeded excuse to look concerned. Lorcan was silent; Donn noticed his father's hesitation but also could see the beaten look he wore. He quickly embraced his father.

Lorcan stated, "You're all I have, boy. Come back home safe." He slapped Donn's back twice.

Donn gave a sad smile and struggled to move away, realizing that the forces of fate were driving his actions. He murmured, "You as well, Father, be well."

Lorcan looked at Donn and said with conviction, "Listen to me since I may not get another chance. Friends of mine, and your grandfather as well, made tragic mistakes supporting rebels in the past. I was warned by your grandfather not to join secret societies, and now, I'm warning you of the same. I know these words wouldn't affect your decisions but please consider that warning whenever you have a chance to just come home."

Before Donn departed on a rowboat to the main vessel, Lorcan gave him the jacket he'd had made and Tadgh's old timepiece. "Take these. Something from your mother and myself to take with you so we'll never be far from you."

Donn pulled on the jacket and put the watch in his pocket.

Lorcan added, "I cannot hold you back forever. I know I'm condemnable for that. I can't apologize for it. Just go and let me put it out of my mind, dear boy." He gave Donn a playful slap on the face and smiled once more at his young son before turning to leave the shore.

Donn boarded the ship by rope and laid eyes upon the deck. It was a long narrow vessel, meant to cut through the waves with speed. It was lined with fifty, mostly short-range, cannons and wasn't suited for a fight unless it was up close and of their choosing. The horses were in the hull on swings. The thick white sails appeared golden when the light pierced them. The outer hull wall was blackened with pitch and the only ornamentation were Celtic images of creatures carved on the small walls guarding the helm. He noticed the deck as he walked upon it with its red hue that gave good traction for its black-booted deck hands. The stern held an unpainted large wooden coat of arms. It represented County Down, a leading symbol in the action of the uprising against British Protestant oppression.

Cathal welcomed Donn aboard the ship. Donn wasted no time in explaining the threat that lie in wait for Bridget. After Cathal heard the story, he answered with calm concern.

"If the banshee wishes Bridget dead, then it's because she angered the demon somehow. It won't forget."

Donn was alarmed. "How will she be safe without me there? There was mention of a group of men that boarded at her father's home. The way she described them, they were like your men."

"She isn't any more safe with you there…now. The creature is hiding from the Fianna, and although they are simply a deterrent, they will keep it at bay. We will vanquish it together in good time." Cathal grabbed Donn's shoulders and gave a reassuring smile, then resumed inspecting the ship.

"How do we prevent being boarded by British patrols? These days, it seems it would be impossible to travel freely," Donn said.

"We raise the Union Jack and put up pennants to show we are on the king's errand. That way, we cannot be questioned or detained by other British ships without a great risk to them. Also these frigates have been transformed enough to never remind anyone of the *Adamant* and *Andromeda*. We can pass through the wooden wall that Britain has placed on the world's waves."

Just off the coast was the *Perilous*. Although the worse for wear, it was still serviceable and a match for the *Midnight Mistress* in ability. The two ships cast a long shadow and were in full magnificence to Donn's mind.

He hoped he would get to know the crew, even if slowly. They were ready for the rough autumn surf spray with their wool sweaters and caps. The men seemed to look up to Cathal but also his first mate.

Shipyard Farrelly was fit and a large man whose presence demanded respect. He commanded the men with his booming orders as well as his own example. When Donn shook his hand, he thought his knees might buckle from the pressure. There were members of the crew whose fathers were Irish and mothers were slaves of the Caribbean. Other than their darker skin, they were nearly indistinguishable from the other crew members. Donn spoke to one such man named Tymon MacNamara while coiling yard rope. During casual conversation, he learned that his father was an indentured servant and his mother worked in the cane fields. He mentioned how hard she had worked. His father stayed after his service was finished and educated Tymon with a passion for Greek history and sailing. Tymon was educated and beaming with confidence. Obvious to Donn was that these children of the islands were the experienced sailors of the *Midnight Mistress* and *Perilous*, most with naval experience, so respect was fully expected and given by all aboard. Tymon said his father gave him a compass that was a family heirloom which he most treasured. He told Donn how Cathal had told him, when they first met, that he'd need it if he sailed with them. Tymon laughed and said, "How could I refuse such an offer to use it?" He departed the exchange and was quick to climb the mast to make repairs.

Donn could tell that Cathal had built relationships with each of his men and they were infected by his hope and ambition. The crew worked hard on the ship they treated as their own home. Like animals that had been the object of many hunts, they all carried an ever-alert posture. To Donn, they seemed too anxious to leave much time idle as they were always facing the unknown with each day. An Irish rebel had a short career, and these men were experts at cheating death.

After they all set sail from Achill, they headed northwest across the gray Atlantic. Donn's jacket worked well to break the frosty winds that swept over the deck. He got his sea legs quickly enough, imagining the people of Achill's traditional seamanship to bolster his confidence.

The men had their daily maintenance routines for the ship to protect the ship's seaworthiness and also keep discipline in the ranks.

Sand was thrown out in order to smooth the deck by way of a stone and a lot of muscle behind it. Everything, in terms of the operation of the ship and her inventory, was checked every day. Anything unusual was corrected or brought to the captain's attention. The spirits locker was the most revered asset of the ship but Cathal only opened it weekly for the mess or on a declared occasion. The half-deck below was where Donn slept, and a few officers slept in a neighboring cabin. The baron's aft apartment was above his study, filled with artifacts and books. Cathal kept the musket and pistol complement inside chests within his study.

Donn quickly had to get used to the salted food and tasteless meals aboard the *Mistress*. He wasn't used to such food, preserved as it was, but getting used to the roiling sea made him grateful he never wanted to eat his fill. One evening, in the mess, Donn noticed a sailmaker at supper who wasn't eating. The fierce man, with a shaved scalp, conveyed a natural isolating posture. He had a piece of torn linen wrap that he appeared transfixed upon. Donn didn't look over long since the act felt intrusive. He heard one of the other sailors call the man Conri. He decided Conri wasn't an approachable sort so he simply kept his distance.

The fleet's closest thing to a doctor was a French free black man from the Caribbean who quartered within the *Mistress*. He was in his late years of usefulness and dressed smartly in a long black suit. His name was Cassart. Cassart was not easy to understand since he spoke very little English and didn't use his hands to express intention. "What is the bother?" and "feel better" were the only two things Donn heard him say. Apprehensive crewmen would persuade French-speaking crew members to translate their affliction to Dr. Cassart lest they receive a cure that could kill them.

Over time, Donn came to believe that the doctor enjoyed the anxiety over a possible misinterpretation. In fact, Donn tried to introduce himself and was calmly asked immediately, "What is the bother?" Donn backed away and quickly dismissed with his hands, worried what might happen to him should a misunderstanding take place. It didn't escape Donn's attention that the doctor was perhaps the only man with two African parents in the crew and was potentially also the most educated man aboard. Donn found out, in short time, from the crew that the doctor was given his education late in life. It was granted by the governor of Trinidad so that the African people in his village would have medical care they might trust, plague and labor shortages being a constant concern. Donn, much to his wonder, was told that the doctor considered this voyage a retirement. He couldn't help but see him as, perhaps, the only adult to watch over the brave children that sailed these boats forward.

In the wee hours, Donn was surrounded by the sound of snoring shipmates; however, his mind placed him in distant solitude. He would focus his eyes on a lantern's flame. Disquiet clouded his contentment. He had been swept away by the events leading up to boarding the ship, and now, he met the challenge of reflecting upon his choices. He wondered how his father was faring with the cattle. He considered that if something might happen to him, his selfish actions would cost his family everything. Then there was Bridget. That was the one and only thing he truly struggled to cope with, being away from her. He asked himself if becoming a man had an inherent selfishness by nature. His decision of what his true destiny was could have been deemed arrogant but his needs, if he was correct, could then be a forfeit of his place beside her.

Now his rashness had cast him off his home island, with a group of men he scarcely knew, upon an ocean of peril. He followed a horse to a fate he made his own. Irish stories are countless about a fool being led by a tempting creature to his doom but away he went. He couldn't stop himself when the moment to act pulled on his spirit, otherwise he would condemn his very being. So a Fiann he had become, aboard a fleet of living fable, to seize that glory that lies beyond the horizon so that lovely Bridget's hand would be his alone.

The Island Kingdom

Donn had become accustomed to the rigors of ship life and the days continued. At last, the lookout shouted, "Land!" And the ships approached the little island, unmarked on any map, which rested under a bloodred sunset. The trees were a man's height wide and the soil was a sparkling black. A low mountain rose in crescent shape around the valley with a purple cloud wrapping it like a neck scarf. They neared the coast and lowered boats down. A quick but silent departure to the beach then followed.

Donn was with Cathal in his boat. Between grunts of pulling the oar he manned, he asked a question. "How did the rod find its way to Hy-Brasil?" Cathal broke his concentration off the quiet shore and answered.

"A monk created that lovely little map—back when the church was investigating the history of our curious people. I suppose he had spoken to someone who had the oral history still intact enough to help him draw it. Based on what I could gather, refugees escaped some great chaos on ships."

Donn shook his head, thinking about where Cathal got the map. "Why did the church not care about this map?"

Cathal shifted in his seat and squinted. "Probably decided it was a fantasy since the Irish had been using a rod long after. That was simply a needed forgery in a broken kingdom. Either those escapees stole the rod or they were entrusted to protect it. There is something that bothers me though."

Donn looked up from his oar, having to breathe a little harder to keep up the conversation. "What is that?"

"The images depict them as being led by Druids. When Druids feel threatened, they are known to be downright wicked. They would have led the fanatic kind. I don't believe whoever they were running from missed their company." Donn remained silent after that statement, feeling the ominous mystery dry his mouth from further conversation. It was dark enough that Donn jumped a little when he felt the boat bump into the beach sand.

Cathal led his party, under cover of night, through the dense woods. Donn noticed that the ground, an odd mixture of sand and lava rock, seemed to sink in and leave a perfect track. The softness of the ground made their advance tiring.

No underbrush existed between the mammoth trees, and therefore, the island appeared fragile by nature. Images of snakes and triskelion symbols decorated the island on randomly found erected stone tablets or even etched on tree bark. Donn felt like they were wandering into oblivion but Cathal seemed to be guiding them by the location of those obscure markers. The party tramped through ponds of collected rainwater and carefully avoided numerous low branches that obstructed every path. A bright light hung in the distance and became stronger as they approached. It was apparent to the crew, marching through someone's nightmare, that they were nearing their destination.

They eventually came to a moss-covered limestone structure of raised platforms with bizarre and frightening carved faces. The carvings were similar to those found in some old churches Donn had seen back home. Their boots touched down on the hard surface of the stone and Donn realized they were at a pagan altar. They walked up the steps to a long length of floor that extended to the far platform which framed the rollicking flames that did honor to nothing they understood.

As they continued to walk forward, Donn saw small obsidian pillars with ogham writing facing each other in a half-moon surrounding the shrine. The etched words shone like glassware when reflecting any light they might capture. The flames, that were fed by no visible fuel, flickered blue with heat and were contained in a long recessed pit that finally ended at the altar. They neared the gray rock altar which appeared set upon a burial mound with narrow canals meant to outlet a blood offering, shown by the black stains and terrible smell. The altar was like a circular table with a lid. In the center of the front wall was a large depiction of a screaming-faced deity. The ominous female in the carving was depicted as causing a mountain to erupt from waves below. The structure's base was scorched and blackened by many past ceremonial fires.

Cathal looked anxious and spoke low, "This is a funny cromlech and, by the looks of it, one that still gets attention."

They had walked into the center of a strange hill fort. Donn wondered who lit the fire and why it was left to burn alone. Some of the men took their pistols out, tucked in their sashes as Cathal slowed his pace near the fire. Donn smelled something terrible that he thought was burning flesh. He watched as Luke grimly investigated the fire. Luke calmly walked over to Cathal to report, and even though his voice was in an undertone, Donn heard Luke tell Cathal that there were human bones in the fire. The expression on Luke's face showed great disgust with their situation. Meanwhile the men flanked the pool of fire in front of the altar where Cathal and Luke stood, their faces looking into the dark abyss around the formation, illuminated intermittently with the flickering of the flames.

Cathal, who had been stone-deep in thought, ordered four men to lift the altar cover with haste. They tried but failed to elevate the seal. Their grunting was loud and it was an unwelcome noise. Cathal snorted then grimaced before he lit a cigar in the bonfire. His eyes darted around while he puffed, then he rose again and his eyes gave a clue to a plan formed. Donn noticed Cathal's hands were alive with action and never shook or wasted a movement which acted as a testament to his unshakable confidence. Cathal commanded Luke to retrieve black powder to blow the lid. Luke slapped the shoulders of four men and they dashed away to the pile of supplies at the base of the hill, even dropping their rifles to make speed. Donn, like the other men, attempted to watch for natives in the woods but it was like looking for light in a shadow. Some of the men kneeled and acted as sentries for the captured unholy place but anxiety kept them all counting the seconds which never kept up with their heartbeats.

Donn could hear noises like the sounds of birds chirping some announcement. The Irish instinctively gripped their weapons. Not a leaf nor branch was disturbed since no more sound emanated from the forest hugging their position. Suddenly, with a maniacal rage, the crew was attacked from all around them, sending a shock through the men. The new screaming menace had red paint spilled over their naked bodies. Their teeth and their eyes were black and they were all as big as Shipyard. Their shriek was like an eagle before striking which caused their prey to hesitate in fear.

The Irish met the danger by filling the hollow in the woods full of gunfire and smoke. The men would use their spent firearms as a blocking tool while drawing their swords to cut down the waves of human monsters. Donn heard the sailmaker, Conri, cry out, "O'Ruairc Aboo!" before he set two blades into the flanks of one of the enemy. It bull-rushed him into the flames without fear. Nimbly Conri rolled him over, while engulfed in flames, and leapt back on the main floor. He was like a charred and smoking timber but his ferocity was not abated as the fight continued.

The strikes of swords and gunfire were chaotic while the returning seamen tried to rush supplies to the altar without being taken down by the raging battle. Cathal spit his cigar out and moved down the line of crewman, acting as the tipping point in combat between sailor and beast. Donn saw a couple of the men forcibly dragged down the hill in a tumble, howling in terror, followed by the victim becoming overwhelmed by the predators. Donn tore through his first attacker with tightly gripped sword in hand and then, without hesitation, moved on to the next assailant. Donn couldn't absorb the fact that he'd killed a man because of the desperation of the situation and the fact that it was like slaughtering nightmares as opposed to humans.

A fellow crewman, a boots' width away from Donn, was impaled by a spear. The man crashed down against his leg, forcing it to bend forward, but Donn recovered while fighting on. The spilt blood made the ground slick and it was a horror to look back upon his friends as much as into the darkness that was flooding devils upon him. He could tell that the young man who had been impaled was fighting to breathe due to the puncture in his chest but the brave man gave out no effort to cry for help. Donn's head was broadsided by a spear in a swinging motion and he could feel blood escape his mouth. He rolled out of the path of the follow-up fatal thrust. Donn quickly cut away the spear and then kicked the knee of the attacker so that he collapsed back off the embankment.

A loud command in another language, from behind the veil of night, sent another wave of tribesmen forward against them with renewed ferocity. Donn watched as the rest of the crew faltered before the onslaught but miraculously saw them hold their fortitude. As his nervous excitement abated, Donn began to realize there were human bodies attacking him instead of the paint and masks that they wore. The longer the fighting lasted, the more enraged Donn became and the more recklessly violent his attacks became. A heavily robed figure with a pagan stag mask stepped within the light behind the altar, sur-rounded by spearmen, and looked directly at Cathal's doings above him. The baron locked eyes on him and yelled down, "You no longer have a right to the rod so kindly go back to the devil empty-handed!"

Cathal set the charges on the altar and an explosion blew the altar's bronze slab upon the robed figure. The short man cursed as it crippled him. Donn thought he understood the Latin word for Roman in the denouncement. The men yelled out the war cry "Faliagh Aboo!" as they jerked forward together like a living wall. Cathal grabbed the rod from the rubble and his bodyguard of wolf-pelted warriors were like castle towers protecting their leader against the copper-plated spearmen below. The pack loudly barked in calls to the enemy that shook the mind for attention.

Luke called for a fallback into the woods and they commenced, waving their swords and keeping their would-be attackers in check. Their ammo spent, the men would swing the stocks against any attack-ers blocking their escape. Donn saw Conri, who appeared almost blind from the heat of the fire he endured, hit anyone that might be near him with both arms like a tripwire's surprise. The natives barked at the Irish that had the blood of their kinsmen dripping from the Fianna swords. As quickly as they were stumbling in flight through the dark forest, they were pursued, announced by bird-like rally cries that echoed off the surroundings. The crew that were too wounded shortly became fatigued in the sandy ground and were overcome by the pursuing doom, their screams testament to their fate.

After what seemed like an eternity of terror, they arrived at the beach to man the rowboats. Shipyard, upon seeing the retreating crew members, set the ship's cannons to fire repeatedly into the woods above the sailors' heads. Donn felt like the ship was a guardian angel erupting for their defense. The whistle of the lead balls flying into the hellish little island sounded wonderful to him. Trees snapped and broke against the barrage as the cloaked ships functioned like sea monsters that spit fire at the pagans.

The crew toppled over the bulwark onto the deck with wet thuds. Cathal was onboard shortly after Donn was. A white rod, about a foot long, was in his right hand and he soon thrusted it into the air. The men cheered with what breath they still had in them. Donn saw that Luke and Cathal were more reserved and wondered if they were thinking of the battle losses. Conri was lying on the deck as if paralyzed from exhaustion. Cathal ordered a departure and the mast stepping began. The waves were rushing about the ships as the sails unfurled and cracked with seized winds and they were off again.

Donn felt sick to his stomach and was bruised and bleeding nearly everywhere. His ears still rang from the explosion at the altar. He wanted to wash the blood from him with seawater but he decided that drinking water to restore his spit was most needed now. He slumped against the mast as he watched Cathal go into the main cabin. Donn wondered how many men didn't return to the ships and what the significance of that so-called victory was.

Donn decided to drink some water from a barrel with some effort. After he drank two ladles full, he couldn't help but focus on the doors to the baron's quarters. He decided he would have words with Cathal about why he risked his life. With the slow opening of the cabin door, Donn saw Cathal investigating the white rod. Surrounding the desk where he sat was a myriad of tattered books and rolled-up papers. On the left wall was his long coat, a weapons rack, and a large nautical map. On his right was a small clerk's desk with too many small drawers to count.

"Am I surrounded by pagans, Baron?" Donn lowered his head as if waiting to be scorned.

Cathal broke his attention and raised an eye to Donn. "Certainly you were this morning on that forgotten rock."

Donn reiterated with a glare, "Why do you risk our lives for that which clearly only pagans would bow to? I ask with respect, sir."

"Ahhh. Well, I see…this is Ireland you risked your neck for." He suddenly tossed the rod to Donn, totally startling the young man who barely caught it. "It's not for the pagans that may worship it or the museum that would kiss our hand for possession of that stick. It's to give our people back their pride and you can't have pride without an idea to support it."

"An idea?" Donn ran a hand down the solid and etched-white bleached wood.

"It doesn't matter what we see in this bit of almond tree but you can still build a kingdom around it. Otherwise our stories remain myths and our people's history begins like an unknown ghostship that spilled our people out upon a mysterious coast. Remember that this relic was a divine gift to our people and it will be our honor to retrieve it for them."

Donn focused on the rod and his gaze found a million details so small that a pattern could barely be discerned. "Why would anyone care about this?"

Cathal was slapping a removed boot to clear it out while loudly responding, "The Irish are counting the seconds until they have that in their sight! That is the physical manifestation of the Word of God that you hold there. Boy, we are the heroes that have been missing, except in song to your neighbors." A few moments of silence passed. Cathal took a drink, looking at Donn misty eyed. "Do you think yourself chivalrous, Donn?"

"What?" replied Donn.

"Are you a heroic man?" Cathal raised an eyebrow and smirked.

Donn paused then responded, "Of course, I'm in your service, and I don't think of myself as anything."

Cathal pointed, underhanded, at Donn and said, "You're one of us in the thirty-three. If you're one of my thirty-three or I am of yours is yet to be seen, my brother." Cathal had nearly tipped his drink so he leaned back and stared at the young man.

Donn knew the significance of thirty-three men in making a king but he wondered why Cathal was suggesting their company related to such a statement. "What are you chasing after, truly? Isn't this whole expedition personal vanity? It *is* beautiful, isn't it?" Donn placed the rod back on Cathal's desk.

Ignoring Donn's obvious skepticism, Cathal continued, "I'm after what can again make us impossible to overcome, ever again. The tribes will unite, elect a king, and never bend a shameful knee again." Cathal jerked his arm up and pointed at the ceiling. "You see, the Irish have been roaming around with wandering souls because they're really led by what's been stolen from them long ago." Cathal walked forward and placed a hand on Donn's shoulder and quietly added, "Our families, our people, will be united again to free our island."

Donn asked who the tribes mentioned were and Cathal spent considerable time explaining. As the result of so much of the Irish history being burned and storytellers being slaughtered, little remained in memory of the original guardians of their island. The high kings of Ireland were paid allegiance by many tribal leaders whose bloodlines tied them to a time that now exists only in dismissed legend. Those tribes still owed obedience to the one who carried the white rod and the accepted tribe that heralded its path forward.

Cathal added color to the explanation. "Luke himself was brought forth from the late Airgíalla Kingdom which ruled many tribes. His were the now-scattered people of the Li and they are forgotten, even by their own descendants." Cathal rubbed his face and snorted, then added, "We are headed back to Achill now. As long as you honor your oath to protect Ireland when called, then you, your sword, and your Croaghaun may leave our company. It was a pleasure to have your service… Fiann." They shook hands before retiring for the night while the ship creaked and slipped over the waves ahead.

The Fair

Since Lorcan was going to be late for the three-day fair, the usual man that he used for tending the cattle, Seamus O'Healy, was certainly already hired out. That was a pity since he could send out Seamus with his cattle and never have to worry about what care they were receiving. Seamus had known him since Lorcan was a boy. Seamus worked for Lorcan's father, beginning their relationship when he arrived as a roving laborer. Seamus was a quiet and stern man who chased objectives vigorously. Tadhg had appreciated these traits and made sure to use him whenever possible. It was enough work to keep him on an island that otherwise wouldn't fulfill such a man's need for daily toil.

Because Seamus wasn't available, Lorcan hired two local men he knew that normally fished in currisks off the coast. They were strong and sober which should be enough for them to make the journey and return. There was nothing like a fair to entice a helping hand. Lorcan made one final check on his livestock in the village pastures and then prepared to set off.

Lorcan had spent the morning loading his best heifers aboard lighters. These were always available, for half a shilling per head, to cross the short distance between Achill Sound and the mainland. The two floating pens held the thirty-eight cattle he hoped to profit from at auction. The dock charged him a fee of four pence per head for the handling and tax. As the flat boats were untied and pushed away from the dock, the skittish cows busied themselves by chewing on the hay thrown down for them. The planks were aged, letting out a loud creak against every wave. That made the cows jerk their heads to check their predicament. The cold salty air gave rise to favored memories. As he departed the island with the livestock, he remembered being a young boy about to go on an adventure with his father.

A youth no older than Donn was in charge of the vessel. After a short conversation, Lorcan could sense that the boy was very mature for his age as a result of harsh labor. Avoiding drumlins and other obstacles was not an issue on this short transport so it wasn't necessary to have anyone more experienced to manage the boat.

Lorcan admired his stock with pride. Tadhg had invested in bulls at every fair and culled what disappointed him so that now they had a reputable bloodline. Lorcan had even sold some cows that were later sent to farms in Western England by way of the dock in Liverpool. Lately Lorcan hoped the new developing port at Milford, on the Welsh coast, would bring new customers. In the meantime, however, he would have to focus on the ten or more days that it would take to arrive at the fair.

Le Poer Trench were the local landowners that kept the fair a yearly success. The head of the family, William Power Keating Trench, was of noble Norman descent. William, the recently promoted Baron of Kilconnel, was his father's friend and Lorcan's as well. The tireless and industrious, albeit elderly, man came from a no-nonsense family of traders. Lorcan's father, Tadhg, envisioned the expansion project after buying cattle through private treaty with William. Tadhg and William decided that it would be a valuable resource to strengthen the agricultural economy, adding cattle to William's October horse fair, after many herds had been rounded up for the winter. Invitations were sent out to large livestock dealers to come and bid on the finest bloodlines in western Ireland.

The Trench family had always been staunch supporters of the English crown due to its stability. Loyalist sentiment was useful to the landed class like pants to the horseman, demanding Tadhg's apolitical nature. During the uprising of 1798, William's brother-in-law was murdered which led him to become withdrawn from the native people. Nevertheless, William enjoyed the fair and looked forward to seeing everyone in good health and at peace.

Lorcan and his shoremen set out with the cattle and camped every night. They passed near the village of Newport and followed the roads south of Castlebar. They had camped near the gentle waters of Lough Carra under Toormakeady Mountain to the west. Green and flat was the landscape and the dirt paths only rarely encountered a patch of forest. They passed bogs before they arrived at Ballinasloe. The bogs were near Sir Thomas Ffrench's castle, son of Sir Charles Ffrench, another business associate of Tadhg's. The local turf cutters had already collected and dispersed the dried sod to warm homes in the winter; the area was relatively quiet in the autumn season.

Already a great crowd had descended upon the festivities near the buildings and woodlands outside of town. Wagons were set up with goods to sell, taking advantage of the crowd as a makeshift market. Hay wagons were filled to the brim all about the grounds. Most numerous were the scores of sheep and many herds of cattle. Well-bred horses were also spread out as far as the eye could see. The livestock industry in Ireland was here for this fair as cattle and sheep production were on an upswing market. The sound from so much commotion was great and nearly everyone hollered for attention.

Lorcan's hired men kept the cattle near the main road while he announced his arrival. He took his registration papers in a leather folder and looked to retrieve a pen number for his cattle. Lorcan patted down and tugged at his vest to smarten up his outfit before walking onto the grounds. With a palm to stick his oily hair into a better part, he moved his way in.

Lorcan was no stranger to many of the usual attendees there and he was immediately shaking hands and laughing with many in a steady procession. Some of the faces he recognized looked worse for wear but they all put their best foot forward. He found William near the lead sale grounds. The old man kept his hands warm in his vest and smoked a pipe. Lorcan was warmly received and they promised to have dinner before he would depart. Lorcan inquired of William where he could find the foreman, Mr. Coyle, to locate a place to pen his livestock. William told him, with a disgruntled look, that the new foreman, Mr. Hanlon, was in charge of the pen order and he could find him near the main auction house.

Confused, Lorcan asked, "What came of 'Fit' Coyle?"

William chirped quickly while looking away, "He no longer is under my employ. Fit couldn't move past his son dying in the uprising so his work suffered."

Lorcan remembered the old foreman looked unwell but he passed it off as stress and perhaps a little too much stout. "Pity, that. Please let me know if I can be at your service." William nodded in appreciation and they chatted about events at the fair, the weather, and a couple of old stories about Tadhg.

Lorcan shook William's hand and proceeded to find Hanlon. There wasn't much time to waste since it was nearly evening and he wanted his cattle resting as long as possible.

Lorcan passed by the bustling crowd. Many dignitaries could be spotted mingling. Colonel Peter Daley, mayor of Galway and once-commander of the loyalist Clanricarde Cavalry, was at the fair. Bankers from Galway readily exchanged notes to ease transaction difficulties. The merchant class and families that ran Galway rubbed shoulders with the patrons and, thereby, giving them a platform to exchange stallions. They also enjoyed the opportunity to see how the producers performed at the market. Typically they'd disperse before the evening since alcohol and potential misfortune mixed poorly with visible creditors.

Lorcan was bemused that the horses were so popular. Many firm hands were shaken as deals were struck each moment. Not a tree could be seen that did not have at least three animals tied to it. Exhausted men were working their ponies by lead rope for interested parties. The bidders, with paperwork in hand, might sit upon stone fences and call out requests to the horsemen. The teeth and body of each horse were carefully checked by intrigued horse traders. Carriages carried wealthy families who looked on for something they might fancy. Little boys, with halters on tame horses, followed their fathers' directions in front of prospective bidders. Crowd-pleasing events abounded as tug-of-war teams competed and traveling merchants showcased inventions from mock podiums.

The piles of hay filled the air with a sweetness. Failed barley crops were used as a good livestock feed and always made enjoying a beer at the fair that much more tempting to the senses.

Torches were being lit all around the grounds as Lorcan arrived at the small Sale Cottage, equipped for the fair with all the paperwork to record sales. The floorboards he walked on had seen an endless procession of boots bringing in livestock transactions and creaked from the wear. Lorcan saw Mr. Hanlon, a dour-looking young man with a snub nose and well-kept chin beard. He was sitting, eating his dinner without looking, and keeping his records book close to his face. There was also a bald and heavyset man sitting by a front-facing window. He had a blanket over his shoulders and didn't look healthy but he appeared to be watching the crowd intently. Lorcan paused in front of Mr. Hanlon.

"How can I be of assistance?" said Hanlon in a nasal voice.

Lorcan introduced himself and then spoke, "I'd like a pen to keep my cattle while I take on potential bidders."

Mr. Hanlon raised his eyes while wiping his hands. "Space is limited now! I'm afraid a great many more attended this year and you're late. How many cattle are we speaking about?"

Lorcan narrowed his eyes as he detected trouble. "Thirty-eight head. Do you have room for that?"

"Well…" Mr. Hanlon shook his head. "I'll have to check if we have availability. Where are they currently located and do you have any men to tend them?"

"To the northwest, near where the woods end. I have two men that are watching them now."

"Do you have their papers?" asked Hanlon.

Lorcan handed the papers over to Mr. Hanlon who raised them to the light of the dirty window. Hanlon then looked engrossed as he glanced at the registration documents and moved his mouth as if talking to himself. He closed his eyes and said, "I've heard of this stock from Achill. Known to be impressive foragers in all seasons, are they not?"

"Yes, people seem to think they're all right. Look, is there going to be a problem finding a place for my cattle?"

Hanlon looked at Lorcan and responded, "You're quite late and I find it impossible to accommodate you adequately. I may have a solution, however. Allow me the opportunity to purchase these cattle—at an excellent price—and your business will be done here. You'll be able to forgo the uncertainty of an auction, especially since as such a late arrival, you'll be at the bottom of a long list of pens ahead of you."

"That's not my plan here." Lorcan dismissed it with a solid tone to his voice.

Hanlon put a hand up in a pleading motion and added, "Please consider. I'm only trying to alleviate your troubles. Certainly you see that the enthusiasm and capital will be long spent before your cattle are up."

"I thank you, no. I know the owner of these grounds personally and, if I must, I'll take it up with him about your 'accommodation,' as you put it."

Hanlon leaned back in his chair long enough to whisper in the other man's ear who affirmed with a slow nod. Hanlon then continued, "Very well, if you insist. It is not space that will be a problem, it's available hay. There is a cut of barley from a late delivery that arrived today." Hanlon quickly marked a journal then handed Lorcan back his papers. "Move to the empty lot past the covered market to the south. The enclosure will be next to the sheep there. I will include you in tomorrow's program."

"Water, clean water, present on dry ground?" Lorcan asked. Lack of water was always a concern and a thief of body condition when long apart from adequate supply.

"It is—troughs have been placed. I'll mark it down that you'll need attention before the last round tonight. Is that all then?"

Lorcan nodded and left.

Soon after, he spoke to his men about the destination so they proceeded to move the cattle. Lorcan was exhausted, age a constant depriver, so he went quickly to the tents for supper. People he hoped might have a hand raised to bid tomorrow strolled past him. He could smell the pies as he neared the stalls. Apple and pear pastries, fresh from pie rings, were laid out before a tired-looking woman.

He pointed at the pastries he wished for on a back table past the sale window. He gathered his sweets, a stick of mutton, and a mug of ale, then sat on the grass near a stone fence. He consumed his delicious meal and listened to the stirrings of thousands of livestock fill the air.

The sun was now gone and the lanterns were illuminating the pathways nicely. Carriages were taking gentry back to their estates for the night and it allowed for some breathing room on the grounds. Men had filled tents to sit and tell stories or to trade before bidding began again. Serving girls carried endless rounds of drinks to the tables and the surrounding ground was perpetually soggy from the spilled contents. The shadows that threw themselves on the walls fluttered like flames on that gentle night. The night was serenaded by a flute player. He was the same man that played every year. Lorcan didn't know him personally but had been told the man learned his music while attached to the British military and was originally a local. His striking notes gave a background to every conversation and, after so many nights, his music became an integral part of the delightful fair.

Lorcan was nearly finished and ready to go procure the night's feed when he saw the fair organizer fast approaching. To bed down by his cattle that evening seemed more unlikely upon witnessing the demeanor of Mr. Hanlon's face as he approached.

"Mr. Feeney, I've been requested to retrieve you to meet with Sir Trench this moment."

Lorcan briefly hesitated while focusing on the man stuffed in the black chimney-like hat and motioned. "Lead on then."

Lorcan arrived at a manned coach at the edge of the fair. A grave voice emanated from inside. "Please join me, Mr. Feeney. We have business together I'm sure you'll find worth your time."

Into the coach Lorcan climbed to find a sleepy Sir Trench with his arms crossed. William punched the roof and bade the coachman an immediate departure. He opened an eye toward Lorcan and said, "Allow me to head for home and he'll return you shortly thereafter." The driver beckoned the team forward with a crack of the reins and they were off.

"Very well. How can I be of service?" Lorcan asked.

"Tierney Hamilton died last week. He had 400 cattle and 1,200 sheep. Fifteen hundred acres and the dispersal of his livestock will be sold here on the morrow."

"I've heard the name but not of his passing."

"Seamus O'Healy worked for your family a great many years. I'm sure you'll be troubled to know that Seamus has been arrested as an accomplice in the theft of the late Hamilton's cattle."

"How could that be? I… I don't understand." Lorcan was raising his voice a bit in bewilderment.

"When Hamilton died, his foreman took the opportunity to draw from the estate's wealth himself. Tierney kept detailed records, and although the criminal altered them before absconding with the livestock, his banker had a duplicate copy. However, he was not captured before involving poor Seamus in his actions. When Tierney's foreman and Seamus arrived at the fair to auction the livestock, they were both detained and sent to jail."

"How could he sell the cattle without papers granting permission?" Lorcan asked.

"They were forged. Certainly a dirty plot. The Hamilton's are crying bloody murder."

"Seamus could not have known the cattle were stolen," Lorcan said in disbelief.

"I assume you may be correct. However, I decided to give you the opportunity to ascertain his innocence." William rubbed his hands to relax their arthritic condition.

"I can give a character testimony and pay a fine if that pleases the court. Do you believe I can help him? You must have some pull."

"It won't be an issue. Give me your signed document that he is an upstanding man and that you'll take him back to Achill at first opportunity. There really is no worry. I'll have the driver drop the correspondence and Seamus will arrive at your pens in the morning."

"Many thanks, William."

"You're quite welcome. Come inside while you complete the letter…and please share some brandy with me, old friend."

Lorcan and Lord Trench had conversed until midnight when Lord Trench offered a bed to the exhausted cattleman. Lorcan accepted and retired. He washed his face and the arduous road he had traveled suddenly bore down on his joints. He slept deeply, despite having reservations about being away from his herd, especially in the care of two men he didn't know well.

The next morning, Lorcan and Lord Trench returned to the fairground by coach. Lorcan waved goodbye to his friend and walked to his pen. On returning, he saw something that tore his heart open. His cattle had been butchered and the remaining carcasses were being loaded into carts. He spotted Mr. Hanlon taking notes and directing his employees. He saw his two men sitting in silence with heads low.

Lorcan immediately got Hanlon's attention. "What has happened to my herd! Who is responsible for this!"

Mr. Hanlon calmly turned to Lorcan and stated, "The livestock clearly had rinderpest and had to be immediately killed to prevent an outbreak. I secured willing buyers for the meat of the few that hadn't exhibited symptoms and can hand over the proceeds."

Lorcan was instantly infuriated by this fool's actions. He felt he could drive in his teeth if he heard Hanlon utter another word justifying himself. "There has never been an outbreak of rinderpest in Ireland and it certainly didn't start on Achill. You're mad. You had no damn right to destroy my livestock!" Lorcan charged over and lifted Mr. Hanlon by his jacket collar.

Hanlon was nearly drowning inside his clothes when he squeaked, "You…you'll leave my person or be arrested!"

His assistant struck Lorcan with a rock over the head. Lorcan's head gushed blood and the stained grass joined his fallen livestock on the green. He grabbed onto a fence crossmember with a forceful hand and attempted to pull himself up. His eyes lost focus. His great hand slowly lost its grip and a desperate thought rushed through him that he must return to his son. As his shoulder slid to the ground, he imagined Aine coming to heal him. The shocked onlookers could sense his soul escaping him. There was silence as Lorcan's last breath left his body.

*****

Having heard of his rescuer's fate as he left the jail, Seamus arrived at the pen, looking as though he hadn't washed in weeks. The mustached man had sweaty black hair that was swept to the side above his dark skin. His blue eyes, unfamiliar to tears, felt irritated as he took in the scene with difficulty. Suddenly the scars that littered him gave fresh pain and his exhausted body felt too heavy to stand. Seamus knelt about the blood-drenched grass, shadowed by the trees in the midday sun. The lanky man looked over at the hay inside the pen near the few dead cows still remaining. He climbed over to see it more closely when its color caught his attention.

Seamus held some hay near his nose and then tossed it away. He felt the belly of a fallen cow and then slowly stood in contemplation. He took a look at the sticky slobber pasting the gaping mouths of the fallen livestock. He was grim and an intense fury filled him. It was plain to Seamus that the hay was what made Mr. Feeney's cattle sick.

Seamus barged into the fair office. He abruptly confronted the fair manager with the evidence by throwing a bit of the hay on his desk. "This hay was cut too low and died of drought. That made Feeney's cattle fall ill. Who dared give permission to feed this poison?"

Mr. Hanlon locked eyes with Seamus and coldly responded, "I would have thought a freed criminal would be anxious to leave this area in case his good luck might run out." Seamus waited a moment, slowly realizing the threat that was cast at him. Mr. Hanlon waved his associate over who menacingly approached, then added, "You shouldn't have to pay the price as well for your foolish friend's mistake of not inspecting the feed he purchases. Are we going to have trouble?" Hanlon brushed the hay off his desk with a finger as he didn't break eye contact with Seamus, not even to blink. "Shall we call over the constable about what you're doing here now?"

Seamus didn't utter a word though reluctantly proceeded to escape this impossible situation. He solemnly loaded his old boss's body, wrapped and prepared, into a wooden cart and made the long trip back to Achill, heavy with guilt.

Land

The ships were soon to arrive at Achill Sound. Donn was on the foredeck, leaning against the railing, when Cathal approached him.

"What will you do now?" asked Cathal to Donn.

"I'll go see my father. He will have returned from the Ballinasloe Fair."

"Pray you be prosperous?" Cathal puzzled.

"I would say we are nearly always neither prosperous nor misfortunate. However, it has long been my dream to own the land we work," mused Donn

"Our goals are not so different. Do you usually go to the fair?"

"Yes, my grandfather helped start the fair with Trench. It has given us a better market."

"Trench? I know that name well. Does he have a son?" Cathal took on a tense look.

"Yes. I believe he does."

Cathal rested a palm on his sword pommel. "I knew an admiral with that family name. He wasn't pleased to see us leave the Caribbean, especially with two of His Majesty's ships."

Donn raised an eyebrow. "You say I'm standing on a British ship? I didn't realize it was so easy to help yourself to their transportation."

"Hardly. Broken backs and empty hearts were all the Irish had at Montserrat. We, the crew, made a pact as brothers and escaped by moonlight. We slew the night watchman and set sail. I found out later that the admiral, a young ambitious man, didn't want the scandal so he quietly called them shipwrecks and his deceit carried forward."

"You sailed back to English waters instead of escaping? Why?"

Cathal's face took on a considering expression. "I made an agreement with Luke that if the rebellion could be saved, we would first attempt it. When we were too late, he agreed that we could serve Ireland other ways. I retrieved my family horses and we never looked back, as if our lives began when we set foot on these ships. I'm surprised you haven't asked me sooner."

"I didn't know if the questions would be received with welcome. I have wondered but everything has swept me away enough, I put off asking."

Cathal raised his eyebrows and took a step forward toward Donn.

Donn continued, "When did you become a Fiann then if you went to Montserrat as a boy?"

Cathal smiled. "I met a wily priest who took me under his wing. He taught me all I wanted to know about Ireland. He taught me about the greatness of our people when all I knew before was the destruction. I began to see us as a refugee kingdom instead of a broken one." Cathal turned with his hands behind his back. Rubbing a thumb in a palm, he tucked his chin and then said with a little concern, "Its leaders forced to flee—with one tie that bound us all, we should return and one day bring her people their kingdom again… Do you think old man Trench will realize you're associating with me? That may go rather poorly."

"I doubt my father would bring up the subject. He isn't the gossiping sort. However, my absence may be noticed. The priest, was he a Fiann?"

Cathal nodded toward Donn but kept his gaze averted as if deep in memory's trance. "Yes, Judge *is* a warrior and a father who is even responsible for the sword you carry… This vessel is a king's chariot for exiled, for free Irish. It is not English." Cathal pointed at Donn. "It is Irish and you are an Irish knight now." With a jerk of his hand to point a finger above his head, Cathal continued, "I say to you that is not wind that fills the sails! It's the spirit of your ancestors pushing us along. Now you understand."

"Lord Fitzgerald of the United Irish would have been dismayed at the thought of a restoration, as opposed to a republic. And who might be king?" Donn shot a knowing smirk.

Cathal raised his palms up and comically spoke aloud, "Let the ancient tribes know their king when I arrive on our shore." Then he followed with a light chuckle before slightly bowing his head and becoming misty eyed. "I don't care who is king, only that the Irish are ruled by Irish and our fate is our own to choose. As for the *United* Irish, show me some that truly are and I can sympathize with Republican ambitions."

Donn crossed his arms and said, "It appears I sail within the lyrics sung by the forlorn dreamer. It is proud I am to have been a part of your quest, Baron."

*****

After a few days and nights, the ships arrived at Donn's well-remembered towering cliffsides.

Donn had gotten to know Tymon better as he apprenticed on the vessel. He learned that the men who operated the masts and ship were originally in the service of the crown under General Abercromby. They invaded island after island, defeating the Spanish; but at Puerto Rico, they were defeated after a bloody struggle. Donn had heard the name Abercromby since that man later commanded the British forces in Ireland for a short time. It occurred to Donn that Tymon was a highly skilled marine. When Donn asked why Tymon was not a part of the landing party on the island they had left, Tymon laughed and said, "I don't like to leave the *Mistress* in another's hands."

When Donn's departure was imminent, he gathered his things. He shook hands with those brave souls he had come to know. Cathal offered an invitation before Donn departed. "Go with us. Take another voyage. Be a part of an Irish adventure, one that won't be written about just as all our old stories worth remembering."

Donn kindly replied, "I've business to attend to but your offer is generous and appreciated. I wish you all safe travels."

A rowboat was lowered to bring Donn to shore. Croaghaun was lowered into the water with sheep bladders to float him and tied to the long narrow boat. Cathal called out and caught Donn's attention. "We'll be at Slievemore until we finish resupplying, if you require us. *Slán abhaile!*"

Donn rode up the bank toward the village. He thought he might go see Bridget first. He felt so proud to show off Croaghaun and his longing to see her was growing by the moment. As he passed the pub, he saw Seamus sitting. Seamus looked up at Donn and quickly alerted him to halt. Seamus bade him to accompany him to the cart as he stammered out the story of his father's fate. Donn dismounted and touched his father's wrapped corpse. Donn shed no tears but a great while passed before he spoke. Seamus was sitting against the wall in silence, giving Donn peace to mourn. A couple of hours had passed when Donn told Seamus, "We cannot tell anyone of his death yet. I need time to make financial arrangements. We'll bury him next to my mother, and by that time, I'll have a plan."

Donn and Seamus quietly buried Lorcan under Croaghaun's anxious gaze. The ground was hard from the cold but they managed after some ordeal. Donn quietly paid his respects and then asked Seamus if he'd watch the remaining cattle while he was away on business. Seamus quickly accepted and said, "For as long as you require it, my service is yours, Donn."

Donn didn't hesitate. Sleep was no longer something easy to come by so he learned it was merely an option for the world he found he now lived in. Although it was dark, he traveled directly back to Slievemore. Each moment that passed felt like it was counting down against him; for so young a man, the irony didn't escape him. He needed to work out a deal with the landowner to purchase the land and the best way to do that is to get a letter of introduction from a gentleman. He only knew one, however, unorthodox the choice.

Donn found Cathal at the inn in Slievemore in a rented room. Cathal motioned to his sentry to allow him to pass.

Donn spat out a greeting, "With respect, sir, I need a favor before you depart. Also I have a proposition."

Cathal was taken aback briefly by Donn's rough appearance and directness. "My service is yours," replied Cathal as he blew at the steam coming off his mug.

"I need to meet with Sir Neal O'Donel and I want to know if you could help. An introduction so he might give me a moment of his time."

"That bastard?" Cathal ripped laughter from his throat and looked up. "I can give you a letter. I don't know what you hope to gain from it. Ever since it was no longer fashionable to plunder Spanish vessels, the nobles in Mayo have become a rather boring lot. Long ago, the amount of saltwater you sailed over dictated the greatness of a noble on the western shore. Now it takes nothing more than ring kissing." Cathal coughed and pulled his blanket over his shoulder. "Why waste your time with him?"

"I need to meet with O'Donel to understand what it will take to own the pastures in west Achill… Are you unwell?"

"If I have a curse, it's a recurring flu I picked up as a boy." Cathal slid over some paper and began to create the letter. "Now I only met him briefly and it wasn't a time of mutual admiration. Anyway unless you play cards, I doubt you'll entertain his attention." Cathal stared, less amused than before.

"I've heard rumors that he loses a lot at cards. Is that right?"

"Yes, it's known that he lives despite a pile of markers with his name yet unpaid. He is vexed by endless rounds of basset." Cathal gave a roguish grin. "He once mentioned the game was probably created to torment him personally."

Donn nodded. "Perhaps I could use his vice as an opportunity to buy back my family land. I need leverage."

"With what funds will you put up?" Cathal raised an eyebrow and dropped his smile. "Not the horse, by god!" Cathal quickly dropped his quill and resumed his hot toddy with exerted tranquility.

"No, I'll let him name any price and hold him to it. But a gambler is always short on funds… I need to do this now but without cattle revenue. That brings me to my proposition."

Cathal raised his face, wide-eyed in anticipation.

"You must have opportunities for fortune that I couldn't ever have here. I'll sail with you and earn enough to secure a future for me and my bride. In return, you'll have my service for as long as you require it."

"Bride?" Cathal swallowed his drink carelessly and grunted, then winced. "When did you have time to get married?"

Donn broke a smile. "She hasn't had a chance to say no yet but I'd make a poor choice until I have my own land. Before it was a desire, but since I met Bridget, I know I can no longer wait. Can you help me?"

"You're a man of worthy ambition, Donn. All those that came before you, that claimed Achill as their home, belong to the island and it to them. An Irishman is born knowing the promise of land unto him. I'll help you gain yours. It shouldn't be difficult to work with O'Donel since he is known to despise the crown and acts contrary to its interests on a regular basis… You know, he even voted against the Act of Union, even though he knew it was dangerous to his livelihood."

"After I make an offer, I'll need to secure those funds to make that payment. Stay long enough that I could join you on another voyage. My father is dead and I desperately need this."

Cathal looked shocked. "Oh dear god, man, I'm sorry to hear of your father's passing." He sighed and slowly rubbed the first finger of his right hand above his eyebrow. Donn wasn't sure if Cathal was considering the request or if he had a headache. "Naval squadrons sweep this area often but I'll give you a week and then, if you join us, I'll give you every opportunity to see your dream through." Cathal cocked a brow and, with a whiff of amusement, added, "I beg you consider firstly, where we go, I cannot offer guarantee when, or if, you'll ever return home to the warmth of your bride's bosom. Where your terrors reside, where your nightmares breathe, you can bet we'll soon be setting sail toward them."

Donn didn't respond but simply took Cathal's hand in his and they shook on it. Cathal nodded and said, "I'll have your letter of recommendation ready for you in the morning. Then hurry yourself and may God travel beside you on your journey."

Donn went to his family's cottage in Slievemore and slept. Tomorrow, after receipt of the letter from Cathal, he would tell Seamus of his plans. Before departing Achill, he would visit, finally, with his beloved Bridget.

Romance of the Rock
and the Flower

The early winter light entered through the frost-kissed windowpane as Bridget enjoyed breakfast with her family. Bridget wore a dress she loved. The high-waisted dress had a solid burnt-orange skirt covered with a generous translucent white silk skirt and was topped off with a reddish-brown bodice with white lace trimming and embroidery that ran up from the cuff to near the elbow. Flower patterns with branches covered the collar of the bodice, meeting silk-puffed shoulders. She wore a quilted wool petticoat beneath to keep warm. Ashling was sitting beside Bridget, swinging her legs with her typical routine of pretending to eat while waiting to be allowed to go play. Bridget's mother and father sat next to each other with her father at the head of the table.

Daley was always focused in the morning and never very social. He wore his usual black vest and white shirt, always a contrast to whatever he was creating. Her mother, Ella, always carried a gentle smile, practiced through the years, as she endlessly assessed the condition of their home. She dressed without excessive embellishment although very smart in cut. She had the well-groomed appearance of someone who held herself in high regard, projecting a regality which was powerful for the unprepared.

The breakfast had been fully served and Mrs. Murphy had just poured Daley his tea. Ella noticed he didn't thank the housekeeper as did the rest of the family. As Mrs. Murphy left the room, Ella whispered, "Daley, darling, you should thank Mrs. Murphy for her services in the morning. She frets that her cooking is not up to the standard to retain her employment. Remember her sensitive nature."

Daley abruptly said, "Sensitive? One might consider carrying a rain jacket in case she ever becomes saddened."

Ella pursed her lips and then tactfully changed the subject. "I need to broach the matter of our circumstances here, husband. Our fortunes are limited here. At best, you provide wedding finery for the local brides or a tailor for the desperate gentry to call upon. Also although we have moved here because my uncle offered his lodgings, the girls have no proper school to attend."

Daley leaned over with his elbow on the table "My ability will become established as an asset to the area and then business will call on me from afar. Our choice of residence is of little consequence."

Ella shook her head disapprovingly while sipping her tea. "When my family made the offer of a loan to purchase lodging in Westport, we should have considered it longer. The Bank of the Four Johns was willing to provide you with letters of credit to set up a working shop. Mr. Ewing thought it was a splendid venture."

Daley shook off the remark. "Mr. Ewing was not taking a personal risk that the export market would continue to be prosperous around Clew Bay. Imagine if the British economy collapses with a French victory. Also he knows full well that your family will bail out the debt if necessary. The man is a nincompoop."

Ella was clearly appalled. "He said very nice things about you, Daley! I'm taken aback that you'd say such a thing."

Daley nodded, then coolly offered, "Well, he can shock us with honest words, although truth remains the best disguise self-interest can don."

Bridget said, "I hate it so when you both bicker in front of me."

Ella comforted Bridget. "The bread of our marriage is in our passion for each other. We adore each other, and through that, we overcome any challenge."

While everyone was talking, Ashling had begun humming a song to express her boredom. Ella said, "Ashling, please eat something."

Ashling reached for honey butter and greedily spread it as Ella spoke on with Bridget. It wasn't until the third helping that plopped on the drowned toast that Ella couldn't ignore it any longer. Her head snapped back to her young daughter.

Ella said, "I think that's quite enough butter, Ashling!"

Daley added, "If you were to drop that on yourself, you'd slip clean out of the room."

Ashling opened her eyes wide then took a large bite. The cream splashed itself about her face and her lips smacked. Ella's fierce look did little to hide her frustration as she observed Ashling follow up by wiping her face with her sleeve.

Bridget began to consider the people of Achill. "Father, why do the people stay here? There doesn't seem to be much of a future here."

"Well, I understand your confusion." Daley wiped his mouth and mustache with a napkin. "Everyone has their own idea of where their place is, Bridget. We're here though, aren't we!" Daley chuckled. "It's as Cavendish is proving and Newton wrote about that the gravity of one mass exerts a force on another mass. I believe there is a type of gravity that exists which pulls us toward the familiar. This island exerts such a great pull on the people who live here that they have trouble escaping. Of course, there is the fear of the unknown, however, I—"

Ella rolled her eyes and interrupted, "Please, husband. I think you made your point well enough for breakfast."

Daley grimaced and covered his mouth as a mock gesture to catch muffled laughter. He rose and kissed his wife before retiring to the sitting room. As he exited the dining room, he added, "Do not mistake the love for home as anything other than that."

Bridget smiled and nodded at her father. After Ella excused Ashling from the table, who sprang up like a trout from a river, she went to take inventory for a trip to the market for Christmas provisions. Bridget planned to join her; although the weather was so dreary, she dreaded the trip in a frigid hackney. She moved into the sitting room to see her father reading a Galway newspaper, *The*

Freeman's Journal, always at least a week old but a pure enjoyment for him. It wasn't a well-rounded paper like *The Belfast News-Letter* and was of a focused interest in Irish rights and the politics involved. Before asking if he may need her help sewing, she thought twice about disturbing him since she could lose the morning getting swept up into one of his stories. She peered out the window to see if the sun had made any progress through the fog.

She saw Donn riding a fine steed over the land that slumbered beneath a blanket of sparkling snow. Snow was kicked up around the horse quickly and slowly floated away and dispersed in a glittering cloud behind them. The trees appeared as ice sculptures covered in winter's jewelry. She quickly wiped the glass to make sure of her sight as joy overtook her.

She hurried out the door and nearly walked into him as she was so happy he was there. Her short breaths and uncontrollable giddy laughter made it useless to hide her excitement.

Donn's eyes swept over her and greeted, "How are you on this fine soft morning, darling Bridget?" His open hands cupped hers by their sides.

"Oh, Donn, you're like ice!" She warmed his hands in that white-knuckled season.

"With my time sailing, I don't really notice anymore. Have you been safe?" His questions to her spoke with a truth-seeking concern, accompanied by an investigator's gaze.

"There has been nothing to concern you, really." She shook her head and looked away. "All excitement has appeared to have stopped since you left. Perhaps I should worry about what tomorrow brings, now that you've returned?" She playfully smiled and tilted her head back to him.

Donn was relieved and joyfully responded, "Well, *leannán,* I carry with me restful tidings for you."

"Please, won't you come in and meet my family? Christmas is nearly upon us."

Donn nodded and brushed off his jacket that was worn over a gray wool sweater. His hair was casually combed back and darkened by the morning snow. He carried himself with a very present confidence and she suddenly didn't see the boy she knew but rather a man at her door.

Bridget led Donn to the sitting room. Donn felt a little hesitation since he wondered about the impression he might make with her parents.

"Father, I'd like to introduce to you Mr. Donn Feeney. He has come to visit us today. He is a friend of mine from the harvest dance in Slievemore."

Daley dropped his paper to his lap and stood quickly. "Christmas greetings! Very nice to meet you." He strode over and shook Donn's hand. "I'm Daley Savage. What brings us your company on this fine holiday?"

Ashling had her piano lessons after lunch and could be heard practicing scales in the living room. Small amounts of "Greensleeves" repeated as Donn gave Daley his background and how he first met Bridget. Daley's eyes couldn't hide his surprise by his daughter's secret friend but he remained polite and welcoming. Mrs. Murphy served black tea in splendid queensware while biscuits and jam were placed which was certainly unique for Donn.

Daley explained that he was a tailor and asked Donn if he knew about fashion.

Bridget rolled her eyes and said, "Of course not. Pardon my father, he is rotting for conversation about design." Daley took no offense and chuckled with Donn. Bridget continued, "Donn has offered me a ride before Mother returns so I'll put on my cloak and we'll be off."

Both men looked surprised but Donn quickly added, "Yes, if that's all right with you, Mr. Savage, if I escort Bridget around a bit? I thought we might take some air before I'm off again today." Bridget quickly began pulling Donn from the room.

Not wanting to lose track of the young man before learning more about him, Daley called after them, "You will join us for dinner tonight! You can meet the lady of the house then."

Donn and Bridget took a morning ride on Croaghaun. The horse snorted up the snow-blanketed hills and trotted across the slopes that glistened under the bright sun. They headed west to the little valley where Donn told Bridget he had picked the flowers he had given to her.

They finally had ridden down a hill into a meadow which appeared like a porcelain sugar bowl. They dismounted in the splendor like visitors to a wintry Eden. She moved about the icy field, seemingly ever untouched by a human presence. Her cloak bonnet, edged in black fur, barely hid her eyes from his gaze. They shared a daydream that this could be their valley as that is the only way they could ever remember it now. The act of doing something together pleased her—to play as a couple. Although surrounded by such beauty, Bridget was aware that Donn's attention was solely on her. Donn slowly moved over to her, the snow crunching beneath him. She pretended not to notice immediately. She felt her presence in his hidden kingdom had rendered her vulnerable.

Bridget's cheeks and lips became flushed from the winter air or was it Donn's approach, she wondered. She could hear the horse pawing for vegetation behind her. The cold air was sweet with the meadow's scent. She could see the trees had been cleared in the center of the valley which drew her attention to the possibility that some structure used to exist here. The snow had divots in areas and she wondered if a bird could see a pattern, but the brush obscured her curious search. All the ground around her glowed brilliantly. The trees were like white-coated paintbrushes and stood tall below the clouds that moved along above. The clouds appeared to be created by a sky that scraped against these trees.

As she was darting her vision around the area, she suddenly noticed Donn standing very close to her, very quietly, which startled her. She stammered and looked back at Croaghaun. "I'm sorry, do you wish to depart?" She motioned to move away.

Donn grabbed Bridget by the front of her cloak and pulled her back to him abruptly. He exhaled deeply and his breath billowed below his chin. She placed some fingers upon the arm that had grabbed her. He moved in like he was diving into a river and pressed his lips to hers. The kiss felt like her heartbeat was in lips, throbbing with ecstasy. He raised his head back to look into her eyes and they stood, quietly.

She considered what had happened and if she should be upset. Bridget put a finger over Donn's lips and said, "You know, darling of mine, I've never met anyone like you. I feel flattered every time you look at me." Bridget let out a laugh. "You think I'm really something grand but you should be warned, I'm not very unique, and where I come from, you wouldn't even notice me." After she spoke, she perceived a wondrous taste on her tongue from his kiss.

Donn winked and said, "You know, I can tell, when I'm looking at the stars, the one that is special to me. I can find it every night. Just like you, my gentle Bridget."

"Oh! And now I must compete with a star?" she asked playfully.

"Only the stars could compare to you." Donn leaned forward and kissed Bridget gently.

"Did you pass over others before you came to be with me, Donn?"

"There was never another and you are so set apart that there would never have been. The dawn of my day comes with your smile."

"Oh, Donn…" She struggled to make her face show the frustration she thought she felt. If she didn't find a voice soon, he'd receive her words as an endearment! She continued with an analytical tone, "The curious avenues of my heart have no direct path and you seek like a man with a hidden compass." She bit her lip and blushed.

Donn cocked his head to the side a bit and spoke, never losing his focus on her. "Tell me about Belfast. Where do you find yourself when you think back on it?"

"For visitors to Belfast, it is considered quite the frontier town. I saw the radiance and excitement there—a city just born, filled with magic—where I hope to find myself again. In Belfast, there was a lovely walk along the Lagan River. If the Nile was responsible for the rise of Egyptian greatness, then the people of Belfast had the Lagan. Ceaseless lighters upon the quiet waters, filled with cargo, floated down the canals and made it radiate with their lanterns' reflection. Couples who were happily courting strolled along and I so looked forward to having my turn to share a walk beneath the oak trees. I had hoped to expect the same. I should embarrass myself, now telling you such things."

"It must be a wonderful place, if you come from there," Donn responded. He stared at Bridget intently.

Bridget blushed again. It was in the way he looked at her. She cherished every time she could feel his strong hands in hers. He could unburden her mind with just a little sweet attention. She declared with a teasing tone, "You should return me home now as I am growing far too fond of you."

*****

Returning to the Savage home, they joined the family in the living room. Decorations adorned the warm fireplace and tree. Laurels were tied to the table edges and walls with bright ribbons. Ashling was rolling around on a rug in a green wool dress with her hair brushed and tied back with a satin bow. Ella had on a crimson velvet gown and beamed with smiles. Daley, wearing a green silk waistcoat decorated with embroidered fall leaves, was dozing off over his book on his chair. Bridget's family warmly greeted Donn, approaching with proper Christmas greetings.

Candles were lit about the house for the holiday, and Ashling lit the one by the window as it was the custom for the youngest to do so. The plates were removed by Ella and Bridget. They savored in chocolate puddings while Ashling gleefully gave a vocal performance of "Hark the Angels Sing." Daley always delighted in hearing his children sing and it showed in his misty eyes. Bridget felt very at home at that moment and the occasion soothed her heart.

Evening shadows grew and Daley offered Donn a port. Donn finished his glass and thanked Daley for his hospitality. Daley bade him goodbye with tired eyes and then dropped on his wing chair.

Bridget drew near to Donn and asked softly, "Can you stay a little longer?"

"I must not. I have a long ride, first to Carrickkildavnet Castle, then across Corraun, and over to Westport. Anyway…" Donn took Bridget's hand with both of his and looked upon it longingly. "You have a Christmas to celebrate with your family and you've given me the only gift I could have wished for—your affections. I promise to return to you shortly. I have another Christmas miracle to seek out."

Bridget couldn't withhold her dismay and abruptly said, "What could possibly be so important in Westport that I must share you? And so late in the evening!"

"I know where I'm at, even in the dark, and I can wake up ready for the transport if I leave tonight. I must meet Sir Neal O'Donel to make an offer for a part of his Achill title."

"How can that be so important as to rush away?"

"I've lost my father…" Bridget placed her hand on Donn's arm in sympathy. "And I feel compelled to do everything in my power to turn my family's fortunes around. It's hard to close my eyes at night. Besides…with land of my own, I can court you knowing I can offer you the future you deserve."

Bridget thought about the things she overheard her father say, even when he thought she wasn't there to hear. "My father is a tailor for Sir O'Donel. The rumor is he has lost possession to his holdings on Achill to the Marquess of Sligo from a bad wager."

Donn considered carefully. "If this is true, it's Sir Browne that I should find. I will have to ask Cathal for another letter of introduction. Where does your father go to meet him?"

"He goes to Westport, all the same, since that is where all the well-to-do and nobility convene to pursue the industry they are rapidly building. Even my mother's family are selling their interests in their mills in nearby Newport because there is such a demand for manufacturing floor."

Ella walked over and carefully interjected, "Thank you for the visit, Mr. Feeney. You brought us rare company on this festive occasion." Donn reciprocated, nodded, and walked out of the door to his horse.

Ella closed the door behind Donn. Bridget peered through the window, savoring these last moments. Ashling was standing inquisitively with her little hands in her mother's hand muff which forced her to lift her chin to peer over the fur.

Ella was becoming noticeably frustrated with her daughter. "You need to learn quickly that you do not have a choice in who you can associate with and how you behave. Our family must survive and that means you will not disgrace us. Do you hear me, Bridget? We expect you to confine your attention to your schooling and your household chores."

Bridget knew only of men who were refined. Growing up, the cadence of stilted conversation saturated her. At rare times, flamboyance would overtake someone's behavior and it would be infectious to her. She wanted to be around those whose emotions were bravely uncaged. Words became curtains that she sought to open by elevating honest meaning through the speaker's actions. Kind considerations that gentlemen offered deepened a hunger within her. The taming of her spirit was a daily torture as she approached adulthood. She spoke admirably to her mother of the courageous people in her beloved books but she could never impress upon her the restlessness she felt. Recently she found the coarseness of life on Achill aroused a longing within her.

Noble Bets

Donn went straight to Cathal for yet another letter of introduction. He then immediately set out in the direction of Westport to visit the Marquess of Sligo. Donn slept on the beach by Achill Sound that night. In the morning, he took a lighter to the mainland. He passed Rosturk Castle on his right in the early afternoon. Later, as he approached Newport, he could still see the majestic white-blanketed Nephin Mountain, home to the now-vanished rulers of ancient Connacht. He arrived in Newport after dark and took a room at the inn. He continued his travels the next morning, arriving in Westport around noon. He kept to the shore. The Quay, the port of Westport, was bustling with ships being loaded and unloaded by merchants transporting goods. Donn made his way past the numerous crates and transports at the dock. Warehouses and taverns overlooked the bay and men of property conversed freely with smugglers and shore-men alike.

In the far distance, the towering mountain, Croagh Patrick, overlooked the town. It was not like Olympus, a home to the gods, but a center of Irish identity and a place of divine importance, none-theless. Croagh Patrick reminded Donn of St. Patrick's love for the Irish people and his sacrifice to protect them from hell's creatures of mischief. The mountain was omnipresent and everyone felt its shadow while all good men paused before disgracing its witness.

Donn hoped that under that mountain's jurisdiction, his fate was well-destined.

Tattered drifters and vagrants seemed to be littered along these sad roads. Although industry was rumored to be a welcome guest on the horizon for these folks, he simmered with despair over the poverty. Donn witnessed these wretches that he should call his own but, as if entering a different kingdom, he didn't recognize this foul and upside-down land that surrounded his senses. No pride prevailed and the memory of such was generationally forgotten. The home he knew seemed as a distant dreamworld, unknown to these downtrodden Irish people.

He left the town and arrived, by the afternoon, at the Browne estate. Donn was shown into the office of the marquess who was standing by his fireplace with a palm hand to his brow as if he was fatigued. He was of slender build and his wig was unpowdered. He glanced over to Donn.

"For what do I owe this meeting, young man?"

Donn nodded. "Thank you for the kindness of the introduction. My name is Donn Feeney."

His lordship inclined his head, otherwise motionless, and his eyes nearly closed.

Donn continued, "My father, Lorcan Feeney, had been running livestock on Western Achill under a lease with Sir Neal O'Donel. The land once was Feeney land and I wish to proposition your lordship in regard to it."

The marquess subtly reacted with a flick of his eyes "I've never visited this land that has recently dropped in my lap. I am aware of your father and his account. What is your proposition?"

"It's my fervent wish to establish my family again. Could his lordship be persuaded to offer the land for a bounty that would transfer deed?"

The marquess walked over to his desk. A massive wolfhound stood up from near the fireplace and followed. When the marquess sat, he simply stared at Donn and remained silent.

Donn felt uncomfortable and spat out, "The parliament allows Catholics to own land, your Lordship."

He raised his eyebrows. "You have funds for such a purchase?"

Donn nodded. "I will in short time. I'm to take a voyage, and on my return, I'll present it to you."

The marquess seemed disinterested as he browsed some correspondence on his desk. "Ah, yes. A voyage? How interesting indeed. It must not be on a whaling vessel, and you certainly would never make that sort of coin on the king's wage. How will you come by it, may I inquire?"

"I've been employed to assist in the delivery of goods for an eager merchant."

The marquess grimaced. "There is some fortune in war, is there not… Do you not value your life, sir?"

Donn resolutely responded, "I do, enough that I'll live it on my own terms. While I'm still young and my body still works as it should, I have a chance to change my fate for the better."

"Whose ship do you sail upon?"

"Baron O'Ruairc's vessel."

The marquess noticeably became still and then withdrew his hands from his paperwork. He straightened his posture and solidly gazed at Donn. "Youth, with all its advantage, accompanies an untested mind which can act tyrannically upon sound judgement. Could you consider myself your friend, sir?" The marquess never exhibited public noblesse oblige but allowed exception for acts of private paternalism toward his provincial neighbors.

Donn dipped his head and raised his voice, "I would be honored to entertain such, your Lordship."

The marquess struggled to rise from his chair, not because of any physical deformity or infirmity but as the result of the burden of timeless responsibility that had debilitated his soul. "Your wish to own land may come at an ongoing cost that years of burden will uncover." The marquess suddenly changed the topic. "What is your association with O'Ruairc? I've considered him a Caribbean myth a time or two. His story is not widely known due to the politically sensitive nature of the topic. Imagine my surprise on receiving his letter for you."

Donn answered, "I know only a bit of the baron's story. He offered me work in exchange for a bounty on his voyage. He and his crew have thrown off the yoke and are seeking fortune. I feel my immediate opportunity lies with them."

"My son, Howe, is sympathetic to reform in the Caribbean, at least as far as the indentured and slaves are concerned. I myself do not personally invest much thought into those politics since, again, the responsibilities to my family's holdings are quite enough to manage."

A brief pause overtook them and Donn added, "I wish to grow my holdings for a prosperous future for my family as I'm sure you do."

The marquess responded, "Only after my third dram of scotch do I even amuse such whims, the discouraging result of hard experiences, I'm afraid."

Donn queried, "Is there an amount of money that would entice his Lordship to allow me to make such a mistake myself?"

"There is no fine estate house on Achill. A pauper-landowner would be your future. You'd never attract a worthwhile bride with no decent home to offer. The arrangement would also carry no title. What you'll learn, in short time, is that no one loves a landowner and your friends will dwindle. You still wish this fate?"

"I do, sir. The risk is mine."

The marquess put his hand on the scarlet lacquered desk and pushed himself back. He shook his head. "No. The answer is no. It wouldn't be responsible of me nor to the tenants of that property to leave their lives in the hands of someone that may be imprisoned for his actions." The marquess sped his words, "Anyway I only carry it on a marker, Sir O'Donel may purchase it back one day and the right isn't mine to sell it without that attached obligation. That concludes our business, I believe, so good day to you, sir."

The footman immediately walked in front of Donn to show him to the door. Nothing more was said so Donn left. He mounted Croaghaun and rode away.

He trotted toward Westport in no real hurry. He was shaken by the abrupt failure of his proposal. Donn heard a carriage and team rumbling toward him on the narrow uneven road he was traveling.

He sidled out of the way to let it pass. A hand appeared from out of the carriage as it passed by. As Donn turned Croaghaun around, he heard the driver reign in the two-horse team and halt the carriage.

The passenger introduced herself, "Good day, sir! Good day!" He heard a thump like she tumbled forward before reaching the window. She waved her hand again, simply peeking in a childlike manner out of the window. "Were you leaving my husband's estate? Are you the new groundskeeper?"

"My name is Donn Feeney, my lady. I'm afraid I'll have to disappoint you that I'm not your new hire. I'm a farming tenant on your husband's land on Achill."

"Oh, please, ride up if you would." Donn moved Croaghaun forward to the window. She breathed heavily and sat back and waved her fan to cool herself. "My, you're a farmer? What a fine horse and you sit him so well." That was followed by an examining purr-like hmmm. She was certainly playful like she was filled with scandal and was having great fun at his expense with rounds of bombarding jests. The endless curls upon her head were as magnificent as her joyous nature. "I'm the Lady Louisa Browne. Pleased to make your acquaintance. Then what does a gentleman, or rogue is it, such as you desire from my husband?"

Donn quickly told of his offer to the marchioness. She explained that with all the fraudulent deals that had plagued the area, all the gentry were soured on new business. "You see, my darling, there was this private bank near here that would perfectly explain my husband's mistrust." She spoke of a private bank that was started by a blacksmith under the name Westport Bank. This bank issued notes on deposits at preposterously small amounts. "The blacksmith was found to be short of the guaranteed funds on several occasions and often traded goods or services to settle debts. Finally the uproar against that institution and many others caused legal action in the highest courts in Dublin to settle and close down those petty operations. Now all the gentry will only trade paper with their very trusted associates or non-Irish banking groups."

Donn replied matter-of-factly, "It so happens I was going to present the gold upon the transaction so there could be no suspicion."

Her eyes flashed open large. "Well, if I were you, I'd go see Sir O'Donel in Westport. He could help you since he's quite the dealmaker and still the titleholder of that property." She paused and smiled sweetly. "Otherwise… If such a handsome man such as yourself ever decides he could leave the life of animal husbandry, then look me up again and I'd be delighted to employ you as a gardener. I could keep you all to myself at the Seamount House." She smacked the roof with her umbrella and the carriage began to move. She waved her goodbye and added, "Go to where drinks are being poured and you're sure to find Neal!"

Donn raised his hand in farewell and started his horse back down the path. After the chance encounter with the marchioness, he considered their conversation and wondered if he should find Neal O'Donel and offer to assist him in paying off his marker in trade for the deed he sought. He didn't have long to weigh his options before the ships would leave without him. The light cut through the woods in streams of grace as the shadows flickered past his gaze. He rode toward Westport and Sir O'Donel.

*****

Donn stabled Croaghaun for a well-deserved feed and rest. He found himself hastening down unfamiliar streets, asking any passersby where he might find Sir Neal O'Donel. He stopped into a pub called Clare's Bog. Donn entered and looked at the faces of the patrons while a barmaid quickly offered a seat and took his order for an ale. The active tobacco smuggling into Clew Bay made it easy to fill a pipe every day so the establishment was smoky. However, that also made hushed trading proposals commonplace, and Donn's ability to seek out Neal was not a simple matter. Donn saw a small boy in an apron carrying empty mugs so he asked the boy where he might find Neal O'Donel. The child took a coin and silently peered around the room then slapped Donn's shoulder and pointed to two men he had passed near the main entrance.

Donn stood and casually walked within earshot. The barmaid brought him his beer and he tried to pay her without raising any awareness of his presence at the table.

The clean-shaven dandy of a man said, "I already am heavily invested up north in the Argina mine. I won't be able to convince the bank of another risky endeavor for that would be my undoing, if unsuccessful."

Neal, visibly frustrated, responded, "You know the demand is there and I'm ideally located to exploit linen production in Newport. How do you ever do better if you don't take a risk—£30,000 and I'll have a monopoly there with those empty buildings we can put to use. Galway and Sligo will be an afterthought when it comes to linen weaving and its export."

The banker took on a dismissive tone. "Adding a potential financial disaster here in Mayo to match mine in Roscommon isn't so tempting as you might suspect. Besides I'm exhausted from local bereaved widows of men that have died burning culm approaching me for reciprocity…as if I was responsible! Let me speak bluntly about what turns the wine sour in the cup you're offering me… How is your gambling?"

Neal persisted with a tightness to his throat. "Peter, I have the answer to creating a fortune that will change this area. My past frivolous actions do not define my character and I will prove that to you."

Donn had heard of the man Neal was conversing with, Peter La Touche, partner in La Touche Bank of Dublin who owned the ironworks. *This is like witnessing an event before it makes the newspaper!*

Peter shook his head and slapped his knee before standing. "With much regret, I cannot supply you with the funds you require. If I have a change of mind, I'll contact you straightaway." He straightened his cloth waistcoat and grabbed his straight cane. "Now if you'll excuse my leave, I'm needed back at Harristown to be with my family. This unscheduled detour cannot prevent me from returning home on Christmas. I won't add an O'Donel to my shareholders' misery like an O'Rielly has done through mining failures."

Neal looked glum but shook Peter's hand and bade him farewell.

Neal grabbed the unfinished bottle and briskly pushed through the door of the tavern to the road. Donn quickly matched Neal's stride and said, "Excuse me, sir, if I may take a moment of your time."

"I'm quite busy right now." Neal seemed completely absorbed by some inner rage that he struggled to contain.

"I have an urgent proposition to offer your Lordship. We can solve each other's challenges and mutually gain prosperity. Please, sir."

Neal took a slug off his bottle and lengthened his stride to break away from Donn. "I have no patience or interest in rebel strategies that will put me in a court for high treason against the crown."

Donn countered, "They who harbor Frankish supporters find little peace in Ireland as do men that settle a family on leased ground."

Neal turned toward Donn while wiping the whiskey from his chin. The gentleman's jet-black hair was uncombed and his cheeks were shadowed by a razor that perhaps was purposely misplaced. His fierce brown eyes were intimidating and his posture looked prepared to throw a punch. "Why do you interrupt me? What family are you referring to that could possibly improve my day?"

Donn replied, "My name is Donn Feeney. I'm aware of a marker you gave Lord Browne. That marker carries the land in West Achill which I call home. I can give you funds to pay off that marker and for your investment in Newport mills."

Neal gave a toothy smile and lapsed into brogue. "I don't see a large bag of gold you would need be dragging behind you for such a bargain."

Donn asked, "When do you need these funds and how much money would allow you to sign over West Achill to me?"

Neal was losing his smile. He poked at the boy's chest and spoke quickly, "Fine Mr. Feeney—find me thirty times the annual land rent for the acres west of Slievemore to the coast, then add £1,000 to that. If you deliver that treasure to me, I'll survey and then sign over said property." Donn didn't immediately respond so Neal continued, "Decide now. I need to finish my business so I can return to Newport this evening."

Donn put his tongue in his cheek and looked around quickly then spoke. "I'm going to sea but I'll return to provide you those funds."

Neal whimsically responded, "I can't promise I'll still need the funds by then. If I do, then you have a bargain. Good enough, lad?"

Donn grabbed Neal's hand and they shook on it. Neal offered Donn the bottle and they both took a pull off of it. Neal shook his head in a sign of disbelief and then Donn watched him enter a bawdy house with playful sirens hanging out of the windows. Donn went to his horse knowing he finally had all the pieces in place.

Lust and Promises

There wasn't time left to hesitate with Bridget. Donn dreaded the possible fates—if, like the hare that bolts at suddenness, she might falter before his conviction. His imminent words and action would be heavy with destiny so he focused on his intent. He determined that he would have her in his arms before dusk, then by dawn, she would be in love with him. And so, he rode. Croaghaun blasted down the dirt trail and across the marshland with an understood urgency. His shadow painted the whitewashed stone walls and landscape for an instant only as his arrival was as certain as the sun would soon be buried by the sea. Donn approached the Savage residence and saw the bright halos of candles lit behind linen curtains. He sensed his father's timepiece counting down in his vest pocket which reminded Donn of every passing moment not spent with Bridget.

He boldly walked up to the door and used the knocker to announce himself, straightened his jacket, and waited.

*****

Bridget opened the door and the snow on the step feathered around their feet. She squeaked, trying to form words as she locked eyes with Donn.

Donn offered, "Bridget, might I please have a walk with you?" She hesitated and he added, "Please."

"All right, if that's what you'd like." She pulled a shawl over her shoulders and looked back, sure her parents were upstairs sleeping. They strolled out to the main path, past the gate, and then stopped. He untied a small lantern from his saddle and lit it.

She raised his hand, with the lantern, up, and slowly formed a smile as his face was illuminated. She placed her other hand on his wet cheek, then it shook a bit like touching in anticipation.

Donn grabbed her wrist, so near his face, and buried her in his embrace. She let out a gasp. He stole a kiss that put the color back in his bloodless lips. The lantern hung by her side and was swung under his cloak. She quickly matched his desire by offering her mouth to his. Their clothing was aglow from the light below them and Bridget thought they must appear from afar as the fiery manifestation of a passionate kiss.

"Bridget."

"Yes?"

"I'm in love with you. Would that be all right by you?"

"You jest, sir. How can you understand love?"

Donn glanced down and sighed. He grabbed her hands and held them in front of him. He locked eyes with hers and spoke with determination, "Years I've spent looking up at the stars. Many nights, I would shuffle them in my hands…like diamonds on a black cloth. I used to imagine I could put them in my pocket so I might have them during the day. When we first kissed, I felt as if I finally had them in my pockets."

He settled her on his horse and led them awhile so the animal might rest. Donn climbed up and began a trot. Bridget pressed herself tightly against Donn. Her hands reached past his thick warm coat and she felt his heart beat. Croaghaun moved swiftly where he may in the dark hills. She closed her eyes against the piercing night air. She felt her tears run across her cheekbones straight back like icy daggers. Bridget was frightened the horse would rear back or act in a way that would loosen her tired grip. She could feel every heavy step the horse made. They came upon the destroyed British outpost tower. He carried her inside and placed her on a blanket. She saw the fireplace was filled with peat and burning hot. Cannon-shot had left a view to the coast. She could see the light sea wind move the waves while the moon and stars multiplied on the water's surface. Donn looked upon her and slowly undressed them. He explored her with a careful hand. He traced her with his fingers as if he was claiming her for his own.

It didn't matter that she wouldn't move her hand from his chest. It didn't matter that she violently shook away against the wall like an animal pinned down by a predator. It didn't matter that her hair, soaked with sweat, nearly cut off his impassioned labored breathing as it fell upon her face. It didn't matter that her thighs burned to the touch as he lifted her again and again off the ground. Although gently he began, she was then being conquered. He stayed still when she needed him to, after he first entered her; the feeling so powerful for her that it did relieve some of the initial pain. Now she knew the ravishing of her body wouldn't cease until he had all that his lust demanded. He kept readjusting his left hand upon her sweat-slicked upper back while his right hand gripped her left thigh like a vice without mercy. She put the back of her shaking left hand against her mouth and struggled to bite her index finger in order to focus her pounding heart or pocket some of her racing blood in one place, if only for a moment.

Her mind couldn't complete thoughts, but when she closed her eyes, she saw bright colors through the tears that welled, trapped in her black eyelashes. She placed her right hand above her which allowed his chest to more fully crush her full breasts. She pressed against the wall in a vain attempt to save the skin on her back since she half-expected the wall to be red and her back to be swollen. He grunted and thrust his hips against her as she gasped and tilted her head to rest limply on his shoulder as his manhood impaled her too deeply for her consciousness to handle. Her left hand dropped to his hand on her leg. He thrust again and she threw her head up and leaned her body back enough that it allowed Donn to turn and kiss her top lip forcefully. He let her lip go and looked into her eyes. She had her eyes locked onto his and she moved her left hand to lightly touch his lips with her fingertips. Suddenly he was completely still for a moment and thrust again, releasing into her.

A fog wafting from the shore crawled into the tower. Their intertwined bodies existed within a cloud that couldn't overtake the warmth of their coupling. The sound of the landing waves against the beach had muffled the sounds of her pleasure and his labors.

"On that day, when you kissed me in your meadow, were you in love with me then?"

"Oh, yes," Donn replied.

"Why?"

"I realized soon after I met you that I would only ever be in search of you. I had never known the extent of beauty in anything until I witnessed yours." He rolled onto his back and looked up and away from her twitching lips, apparently avoiding her burgeoning need to laugh at him. He let out with distinction in his words, "There has never been a moment since the first that I did not bear the pain knowing you are meant for me, although not in my arms."

"You are so dramatic, dear! Certainly you know I'm not your uninformed torturer!" She playfully pushed away his head.

He smiled. "Ahh, the sweetest torture." His eyes gazed far away. "Made me see my life as one of purpose which I cannot unsee."

"God in heaven is kind to us, love." She bit her bottom lip and teared slightly before kissing his neck. They soon fell asleep in complete comfort.

They awoke each other under the stars' last twinkling encore before sunrise. He brushed her hair aside and placed his palm on her cheek. "The divine holds the stars in His palm. He gazes down on us and I believe it pleases Him that we're together. My heart beats with yours now." She rested her head on his chest. He whispered, "Bridget, I'll never be far from you because this is *our* world now."

Late that night, Bridget was awake when Donn opened his eyes. She was nestled close enough she could feel the warmth of his entire body.

"Hello." She looked toward him and said carefully, "While you slumbered, I resisted shutting my lids since I considered I may disappear and find myself at home in Ulster like this was all a dream. I'd find so much without value where once I called a good life. Once this island was the world to me, and now, it seems so small." She pulled his coat up and over her shoulder and looked away, whispering thoughts, "Why should I feel so happy here, regardless of all that lies ahead. Like a mare returning to her stable, I'm safe under my master's roof. Fate has favored me, and now, I'm done away with all other known homes." She felt closer to the island, to its people, to its land. Making love to Donn made her a part of him. He was Achill's finest so she would be his fairest.

She saw him looking at his timepiece. Sudden anxiousness came upon her. "If you love Achill so much, then why do you not stay?" Bridget forced out.

"You mean…if I profess that I love you so much, then why will I not stay?"

She tepidly nodded as a jury awaiting testimony.

Donn stood and poured a bowl of water, saved for the fire, over his face and hair. She was startled that he rose after the question. She was nearly convinced he wouldn't offer a response until he started pulling on his trousers and boots.

"I'm going to make a home for us. That's my purpose. To do that, I must travel. If I stayed, then what we have here now wouldn't last long since my future is in question without the land."

"What makes you think you can keep such promises? Do the clouds make the shapes you desire as well? You don't need any of that. You have me now. We can be happy here, my love." Her tone changed to convey an order. "I'm telling you not to leave." She got up and moved toward him. He pulled her to him. He touched her face carefully and caressed her top lip with his bottom lip. He let out a deep breath, eyes shut, and gripped her hair.

"I would be a forgery if I didn't try, Bridget. I must be true to you as well as myself."

Bridget pressed her index finger against Donn's chest and gave a sly smile. "Make sweet sounds quickly now to sway my continued desire of you before you take your leave of me." She shook her head disappointedly at him.

He acted. When she felt his hands grab her body, she felt the sensation of being captured. As if a disguise had been lifted, now she was revealed as his prey. She felt no fear when that revelation swept her being which made her his—to never need chase again. A constant stream of fire shot from his eyes as he dragged his hand up her arm. One finger at a time, he wrapped his hand around her upper arm. He pulsed his grip when his heart sped up and he exhaled. She was frozen, looking up at him, inescapably drawn to him.

"Say it to me, Bridget. Tell me you're mine." Donn didn't wait for the response as he slammed into her lips as the words were forming.

She rubbed his resting hand with a finger that turned to a palm pressing against his bicep. Her fingers spread out and her palm slid up toward his shoulder as she tilted her body toward him. As her head turned and placed itself against his solid shoulder, she then joined both hands upon his warm cheeks and rolled her grip back into his hair. She looked up past his chin as he wrapped his arms that bore certainty around her. She spent a little moment breathing him in, safe in his strong embrace. She felt his upper body tense as he further drew her near. She dropped her arms and caressed his jawline which caused him to look down into her eyes. She bit her bottom lip, then pulled on his head to beckon. Donn spoke not a word but drove his kiss hard upon her mouth. He swallowed her startled exhale as he lavished wild kisses against her flesh. His touches and tongue delivered a passion that branded her senses. When her tears came, the awakening within her levitated her soul beyond the confines of her physical being.

Farewell to Eden

Donn saw two guards posted outside the Slievemore Inn, the chilly drizzle leaving the quiet men soaked. It did not take Donn long to locate the baron. He found Cathal inside, entertaining some willing ears over a stout. Pipes were lit and Cathal had the locals enthralled, not a whisper allowed while he recited his tale. Donn didn't interrupt, just took a stool at the bar. He realized Cathal was taking liberties with the recounting of the island expedition. Donn tried not to listen as he found it impossible not to groan. He ordered another draft and he drowned his objections in its milky froth, hoping to escape the agony of hearing every request by the audience to expand on each detail, already suffocating from its own nauseating drama. After enduring the bloviation of each moment of the expedition, victim to excruciating lengths of exaggerated detail, Donn finally had an opportunity when Cathal picked up a fresh drink so he interjected, "The only whistling I recall hearing was from cannonballs hitting the forest, not faeries chasing us."

Cathal tightened his lips and gave Donn an annoyed look before relaxing and stating as fact, "Trim the magic and murder the legend. Anyway you've been on one voyage, and now, you're a trusted chronicler?"

Donn flippantly suggested, "You must think of yourself as King Gillomanius, charged to protect Ireland's heritage?"

Cathal responded, "Not at all but I'm not a folktale either. Gillomanius is useful in a very English parable to suggest the subservience of Ireland. I tell another sort of story. One just for us." Cathal smirked and then rejoined his gathering to continue his saga that had yet to find a boundary to contain its epic nature.

Donn thought, *He'll embellish that story like a brass doorknob.*

The empty mugs multiplied in front of Donn as he waited—and waited. He considered how his path had diverged from everyone else patronizing the bar. His drifting memories carried him into the past. Danny Shea was Donn's good friend growing up. They ran the same paths together. Danny's father, Gearoid, was a keen carpenter that busied himself with fishing vessel repairs and odd jobs around the island. His mother, Orla, was very kind to Donn and she did the wash for the inn and others. Donn enjoyed Danny's company because he could make a game out of anything. Once Danny ran down and caught a young fox. He tried to feed the frightened animal, but after two days of trying with no success, he finally set it free. Donn always remembered that fox and how it would rather die than be tamed. He silently debated with himself whether or not people were so principled. Was it not simply overwhelming fear in the fox's eyes or something else there like a conviction? Finally he felt a hand on his shoulder which startled him.

"I should take this time to lay my plans before you. Is your cup full?" Cathal asked. He continued without waiting for a response. "We'll search for our right to rule, and then we'll recover our promised arms to defend our people—the rod, the spear, and the sword. Only then will we return home." Cathal paused then his lip curled on one end. "I know not what our future holds but I know a heavy cost awaits us, Donn." Cathal seemed pleased with himself when he winked at him as if that grim statement was a dare to be met with laughter. They finished their drinks and walked out together. Cathal told him to make ready for departure on the morrow.

*****

Donn traveled a muddy road, went to bid farewell to Bridget, knowing this visit may be his last for a great while. He had arrived near the Savage residence when he saw Bridget reading a book, sitting against the flat side of a tree trunk. She didn't notice his approach until his boots were on the grass next to her. She only glanced at him with a disdainful look before she threw a shawl over her shoulder, averting her eyes back into her book.

"Why do you cover yourself and wrap your arms on my arrival? Are you cold? It isn't cold out tonight. Perhaps it's your way of telling me to keep a distance… Your eyes tell another story." He moved forward, close to her, and his shadow covered her. "How goes your mind, lovely Bridget? Do I not vex your thoughts longer?"

Bridget slammed her book shut and stood. "You suggest that I cannot shutter my feelings, safe and unconfessed, and now they must lie in wretched nakedness for you to mock? You labor to cancel my affection but only after my willingness to love has grown will you now leave my life." Bridget became hysterical in tears. "I tell you to stay and you leave me! How is *that* love?" Bridget walked toward her home with Donn trying to follow.

Donn said with conviction and haste, "Bridget, hear me clearly." He pulled at her arm to stop her. "If there was a river between us, I'd become a bridge builder. If there was an ocean, I'd sail over those waves." He pitched his overcoat upon the dirt before them. "I start my way toward you when I depart." He grabbed her cheek and chin with a hand. "Nothing can keep me from you."

As he leaned in to touch her lips, Bridget rolled her eyes and pushed him away. "What makes you think you can just have me as if I was your precious horse?" She tossed her hands up at him and gripped them tightly in an act of rage. "I'm a lady and you, as a *would-be* gentleman, must show propriety in engaging in courtship!" She then threw herself into his embrace and pressed her breasts against his soaked shirt. She kissed him like she was devouring a feast after a fasting. His eyes shut tight and his muscles tensed in a physical act to merge their souls. She ran a hand down his lower back. He quickly grabbed her hair and pressed her into him, willing her to accept his powerful kisses. He felt like a wild animal that would leave spare nothing of her.

"Disarm yourself, lovely Bridget. Do your lips not seek to curl at my arrival? Gentlest lady, you must fear not as I am the same man you met before. I do not deserve such reproach so speak to me not as a stranger."

"Stay with me." Hastily she added, "Don't you dare let go of me." She rose up by standing on her tiptoes and desperately pecked kisses upon his neck and face before wrapping her arms around him tightly.

As they held each other, Donn whispered, "I must save the madness for tomorrow, tonight I have you within reach. This love controls my thoughts and needs as I lose the gentleman and put on the rogue. Save the lust for me, darling. Save nothing of the day but that which I share with you. Find the breadth of my love for you which exists in my eyes, if you dare to gaze into their depths. Render your heart unto my strong hand so I can shield against this world's oppressive nature. Demand your knight and I'll kneel again before you…my love."

✱✱✱✱✱

The moonlight flittered through the ocean clouds that visited the island. While the boulders, like melted ebony upon the shore, cradled their bodies. They existed within a cloud that cycled in waves of mist that crashed in from the shore as they joined together. A sparkling curtain of stars seemed unending against the black hills with their lit towers in the far distance like tiny embers hanging in infinity.

She felt an insatiable need to be in his arms. Passion tore out of her with his every exhale down her neck. With every thrust against her, she felt like they were two souls separated by a window and he was trying to join her. She wanted him to find her, to become one. Only after crashing intimacy could he make it through to be with her. She shed away all that she knew and yielded to him.

The hours of the night passed by. She rested her cheek against his chest while he slumbered. Her naked body was chilled by the night but warmed by his touch. She lightly placed her fingertips upon his resting open palm. She felt the rough skin of a childhood spent herding animals. Donn stirred and instinctively wrapped a solid grip on her slim fingers. He took a sharp breath and opened his eyes while pulling her arm back beyond his head to pull her closer to his gaze. A peck upon her forehead was followed by a kiss upon her upper lip. Bridget smiled.

"Bridget, we can be happy. In a land that knows so little about happiness, we can claim a generous share for any lifetime."

"I'll have to pretend to have fallen asleep on the beach again when I come into the house looking like a castaway." She gave voice suddenly to the impending peril that she felt. "We've found our paradise and now you wish to abandon it? Consider this kiss before haste takes you away from me." Bridget reached forward and pressed her lips to his so forcefully she nearly brought tears to her eyes. She could feel the heat waft from their lips as they parted. As the moisture was drying from that kiss, they silently looked into each other's eyes. Donn was distant and seemed taken from her in his inscrutable state.

They both went about with nothing else said with the sun not far from rising. They washed their faces in the sea and put on their clothes. Donn had offered some cut and dried meat and cheese he had been carrying in a bag on his horse. After a long inquietude between them, Bridget finally attempted a conversation. "What troubles you? You've not touched your food and I pray you should at least breathe," Bridget said what should have been delivered as humorous but it carried a reluctant tone.

The air was thick with apprehension when a stoic Donn broke the silence. "Ah, I'm without the ability to see myself accepting less than my dream. I will own my family's land." Bridget placed a hand on his shoulder. He nodded and looked into her worried eyes. "There isn't a moment that goes by where everything couldn't be taken. How can we start a life together on dirt someone else claims as their own?"

Bridget placed her hands on his cheeks. "Donn, there is nothing left that I can imagine which could make me happier than what I have now. Can't you see? It isn't right to ask for more. You want to throw the winning dice back again and you don't know the wager."

Donn said carefully, "Bridget…your father would never accept less than a gentleman of means for you." He squeezed her arms and smiled. "Ours is destiny, darling. Just give me a brief departure to make a home for us of our own. I will not fail… Besides I had no idea you snored so much. I need a little time to come to terms with it."

Bridget placed her head on his chest to hide her grin, shielding her outrage. She then jabbed his stomach and turned to gather her senses. Donn let escape a surprised grunt and pretended to guard himself. A moment later, he swept forward and grabbed the crook of Bridget's arm and then swung her back around to him.

In his gruffest voice, he said, "Say now, I wasn't done with you." Donn invaded her with a deep kiss.

Bridget gently spoke, "Fail not to return to me. The seals will have one more guest on their shore until you do."

Donn took out his father's watch and said, "Look at this from time to time and remember that it's just counting down to the second I return to you." Bridget took it and held it close to her.

*****

Donn left with the ships, and as he looked back on the hills of Achill, he silently despaired. He sighed and felt tears nearly overtake him. He let out the biggest wave in farewell he could in hopes she might see it.

Send down a harbor, dear Lord, to safeguard my heart through these coming trials, Donn thought.

*****

Bridget knelt down on the grass and watched the ships pull out in the distance. She hardly spared a blink for fear to miss a moment of their separation.

Return and marry me, boy. Hurry home… She bit her bottom lip. *Damn you for leaving me.*

*****

With the departure of this masted herald for Irish glory, an overture that may have pleased even the divine spectator, that sailing was missed. A fledgling kingdom, without great hall, toiled aboard wooden plank to ford many a mythical menace.

Maids and Linens

A month had passed by. Without Donn, everything on the island felt meaningless. All the daily tasks were once just a prelude to being with him, and now, she was like a planet without a sun. Everything was a trivial interlude before spending time with Donn again, but now, she had to relearn purpose. She slowly learned how to quit anticipating him. Bridget became thought of as wistful and reserved by those around her. She lost interest in reading her novels. She couldn't concentrate on the pages. As Bridget looked inwardly for balance, she saw life's routine more clearly. She took a greater interest in quietly observing the world around her. She was always looking up at the sound of every footstep, in case Donn had returned, and it made her ever flustered. She had little to fill her days and neglected to plan.

Daley would fall asleep on his chair in the early evening. When he dared to lie down, he often coughed a great while before resting. The damp climate of an island seemed to make that frailty all the more noticeable. Bridget tipped her head forward, stared, and held her breath when she watched her father take his shaving blade from its wallet in the morning. He would fight back coughs with that sharp instrument next to his neck! She resolved she would assist him more to fill her time. Daley was pleased at her interest and gave her cloth to cut to measurement and errands.

Bridget slowly began to reassert herself again, but all too often, she would lose focus. She went to breakfast and idly studied the housekeeper. Mrs. Murphy's hair was pinned up and, with an industrious nature, she took care of the entire meal and all the needs of the household. Mrs. Murphy, always courteous, carried a smile and a tolerant nature that could tame any ill wind that filled the home. Bridget admired her and tried to key off of her abundant energy to motivate herself.

Bridget noticed the housekeeper's coarse brown linen dress that had been mended numerous times. The repaired sleeves, where there had been rips, and the thread, which had been pulled at the seams and resewn, were obvious to the eye. The irony was apparent since she worked for the once-finest tailor in Belfast. Mrs. Murphy worked without any visible signs of tiring throughout the day as if filled with the same energy as a team of oxen. Her hands were rough and aged past her years and Bridget felt pity for her that she was sure Mrs. Murphy wouldn't understand. She was a woman who one could hardly hold conversation with since her station made every exchange awkward. The first time they spoke, Bridget was unable to admire, flatter, or show interest in anything of their new housekeeper and that upset Bridget to deviate from her reliable conversational patterns.

Bridget's little sister cavorted about all day around Mrs. Murphy, unaware of the discomfort Bridget felt about her. Father had agreed with Mother that Mrs. Murphy's son would go to school as part of her wages. The despondency that came to Mrs. Murphy after her husband died at sea was lifted and perhaps that ability to secure her son a future fueled her days. Bridget spent time thinking of Mrs. Murphy and came to decide that she didn't have the right to act so forlorn.

For distractions on Achill, the choices were slim. Bridget didn't relate well with the girls her age on Achill whenever she happened to run into one on an errand. She did notice their curious habits though. Bridget watched them use leftover milk to treat their hair. Even an island woman can find ways to keep her appearance which reassured Bridget that her vanity wasn't wholly unforgivable. Certainly the winds were the hardest on people and aged them the most. As an irony, it was difficult to show off one's beauty when continually covered up to protect against this climate. A conversation about fashion or the world seemed somewhat rude which left her silent in their company which, in turn, came off as disinterest so was probably equally upsetting for those to whom she happened to speak. She thought, *How ridiculously awkward I've become.*

Since her father was ever more ill, she would act to relieve the burden of his duties. Bridget set herself to help her father prosper in this home he had chosen for them. When she traveled to town, it was on simple errands of delivering correspondence or her father's completed clothing. She heard many things that broadened her understanding of island politics and gossip. The last time she went to town, she overheard two men outside the tax collector's building speaking loudly about the land that had been chosen for one to farm. The village board, which was beholden to the landowner, had the right to adjust which areas a family may work and pay rent on which caused a great many arguments. It was the rundale system of tenant lease that left opportunity stifled and allowed corruption to flourish. She hated to imagine a life where her father did not have a trade skill. Those thoughts invigorated her to act with gusto upon her self-imposed chores.

One day, Bridget had arrived home, as the sun was setting, and found her father dozing off in his chair. He spoke to Bridget with lids closed. "How was your day, daughter?"

"Mostly the same. I have your receipts and cloth that you asked for. Is Mother home yet?"

"Yes, she is asleep since she was up early with Ashling's fever." Daley stood up carefully and approached his daughter. "You should know something, I think."

Bridget placed her gloves on the table and put up her jacket, then responded, "Yes, Father?"

"Your mother has had correspondence with her sister in Dublin. She made an inquiry for you."

Her eyebrows shot up and she lifted off her heels a little. Daley continued, "Your mother wants to see you get on with your life. She can see there is no future for you here and I agree with her."

"You want to send me away! How could you do that, Father?"

"We care about your well-being, Bridget. We don't wish for you to waste the flower of your life in this land that offers young ladies so little opportunity."

"I feel so alone here but at least I have my family. And now I'm expected to live on without a family as well! How many times can I be exiled from home?"

"Bridget, you've become enamored with that farm boy."

"Donn!" Bridget shouted back, frustrated.

Daley remained resolved by the important message he had to convey. "Yes… Donn. Your mother and I cannot accept…your mother and I expect more for you. You see, this life is hard, Bridget, but I'll be damned if I see you make it harder just because you can't see past your own nose!"

"I love him, Father. He's good to me. He looks at me like I've always wanted to be seen. He's kind and dear to me. Can't you understand that?"

Daley hesitated and then nodded quickly. "This is my fault. I brought you from Belfast and I knew I could lead you into peril. This is it, Bridget. I've taken you from proper society and set you up for terrible consequence. You're not to see that boy again. I forbid it. I forbid it and you can blame me all you want for your broken heart."

"Well, that's just grand! He's left! He won't be a bother to you because he's gone and I don't know if he'll ever be back!" Bridget began to tear up so she quickly retired up the stairs and into her bedroom.

*****

Daley remained silent. A pain swelled in him for the harsh words they had shared. Daley went back into the sitting room and slumped into his chair. He circled his index finger with his thumb and closed his eyes.

Daley heard little feet walk into the room and opened his eyes. Ashling looked at her father with concern on her face. The fire in the fireplace had been reduced to embers. She asked Daley in a soft voice, "Father…what is wrong with Bridget?"

Daley sighed and replied, "She's not feeling herself of late. Why are you out of bed?"

"I had a bad dream."

Daley felt her forehead and sat back onto his chair. "You need rest. You shouldn't be up so late."

"Why will you not sleep, Father? Are you upset about sister?" Ashling pinned the doll against her chest and rested her head above it.

"Ashling, when you get to be her age, things can become confusing. She'll be just fine. She…had a dream and she didn't want to wake up from it. Now go to bed."

Ashling began to move away then stopped. "It must have been a good dream then…since she was so upset about it ending."

Daley opened his eyes wide and scanned the room in exhaustion. "Yes, I suppose it was."

Ashling added, "You can make her dreams come true, Daddy. Don't worry…good night!" Ashling scampered away.

*****

Bridget awoke and made her way downstairs to find her father, visibly tired, sitting next to her mother in the dining room.

Daley cleared his throat. "Bridget, your mother and I have decided that we'd like you to learn more about my business. Also you will accept invitations to the balls that are hosted by the nobility and gentry. That season is before us now and will keep you busy until the summer. You will stay here with us but we'll make the effort so that you're not deprived of a future you deserve." Bridget saw her mother's hand placed on Daley's shoulder. Bridget smiled and felt a burden lifted from her since she knew her father had embraced her need to remain home.

Bridget worked by her father's side over the days. She knew the sewing methods but was guided in the evolution of how the cuts and patterns flattered the frame of the wearer. Daley loved sharing his trade as was so obvious by his never-ending explanations about every detail they encountered. Bridget finally found a worthy distraction from thoughts of Donn's absence and allowed herself to be engrossed by this apprenticeship.

Bridget began to understand her father's significance. Daley was a progressive in tailoring men's clothing as the English appreciated the separation from mainland European dress. He moved away from the loud fanciful clothing of the past upper class and created more subdued and masculine cuts. When Daley would see a man influenced by French fashion, he had a difficult time not showing the distress in his face as he repressed his disapproval. Fit and function was what his clients looked for. Once frustrated after a disagreement with a patron, he told Bridget, "Our nobility is in our paternalism and the ties to the land. Our clothing is to be a reflection of the pride in stewardship. The French dress only to catch the elites' eye like animals that flourish bright colors to attract a mate."

Bridget mused about how her upbringing might develop. She fantasized a fictional declaration, "I've arrived at a place where linen is seldom even bleached, where beauty must go unaided through garments." Although she might have found some confidence at her father's side, she was increasingly distressed about the social engagements that were imminent.

*****

My darling Bridget,

How far a distance a ship can carry a man but the heart ebbs not. This heart is a hearth and it contains a brilliant fire. I tend to it every day because I need its warmth and comfort. The hearth is the center of a home and that is where I find myself when I think of you. The time we're together fills a rack of new timber to throw into that fire where my soul exists to thrive beside.

I can feel your hand in mine and your kiss now so I am not far from you. I can hope, above this cold sea, that my embrace has not been forgotten by you. I'm your man and I will take my place beside you, sweet leannan. May angels spare you no happiness and be pleased to speed our reunion.

The Spear Faeries

Donn collapsed back upon some yard rope that was pooled on the upper deck, a welcome break from the endless list of chores he had to do. He rubbed beads of sweat from his soiled face as he caught his breath. As he rested his gaze upon the emblazoned horizon, the familiar view of the stirring ocean prompted him to contemplate its infinite nature. This was something he did often. Sometimes he'd imagine the depth and what might lie within its watery kingdom. It was enough to make a man cringe to wonder how a boat could stay afloat and, at the same time, keep them all safe from the dangers beneath them. Nature didn't grant the ocean to man, however, here they were, defying the territory of the creatures that call it home.

At times, Donn silently braced himself with prayers—well, conversations with God, really—whenever that fear of the infinite came over him. His faith was a vessel he traveled upon as he sailed aboard the *Mistress*. The day's labors found him flush with divinity's blessing that would keep him brave and keen. Truth was, Donn felt small in front of such vastness and he felt challenged by it. He wanted the sea to fear *him*. He couldn't explain it but there it was. He could hear Shipyard give a shout to announce the baron's pending address. He stood quickly to stand ready with the other men gathered.

Cathal reached into his jacket pocket, swiped back his hair and postured, chest full forward. He unrolled a tattered parchment with a jerk of his elbow. The men looked enthralled and were silent. After all these days waiting, nearly forgetting the sound of his voice and towering presence, he shocked them to attention with his typical gusto.

"Lads of the *Midnight Mistress*, hear me now!" He pointed to the paper raised before them. "Did your fathers speak of a land where your dreams dance across your eyes?" He stared at the closest ship swab and continued. "There is a place of flying devils, of those that court with gold cups and plates. I wish us to go and seek out these creatures and liberate them of an ancient possession, the Spear of Lugh, which they'll come to realize they have been protecting just for us. It's a secret of their tree and why they guard it. This map shows us the way. We go to Lanzarote. Now set the sails! Play the pipes." His command was a catalyst of enthusiasm and action aboard as he observed their progress.

The men yelled "O'Ruairc Aboo!" as they flew into action across the long deck. The *Perilous* was signaled to set sail. Uilleann pipes were played and the men readied the masts. Donn saw the navigator, Gideon O'Hogan, giving instructions to Kennedy at the wheel. Cathal ordered that the crow's nest lookout be rotated twice as frequently because "tired eyes will surely sink us in the waters we'll be sailing."

*****

Luke, who was watching the *Mistress* from aboard the *Perilous*, could hear the faint cheers in the distance. He put down his scratched telescope, wiped his eye, and let free a wide grin as he felt the wave of excitement collide into the ranks of his own crew. "Do you understand, lads? We sail for Ireland's honor today! Don't dally." He drew his hat and waved it. "Do not disappoint me." Like a spring, the men dashed to work. Meanwhile Devine was closely observing the actions of the crew and ordering replacement or repair where necessary.

The ships unfurled their sails with a rumble, followed by a loud slap, and were then pivoted for their new course. Energy could be felt rolling along the deck as the vessels were brought to life in a manner not unlike restarting a heart.

*****

Donn wasn't the most skilled sailor but he attempted to stay busy by helping where he could. He'd find himself having imaginary conversations with Bridget to pass the time laboring. He had to tell her about every idea that sprang to mind and what she might remark drove his curiosity. As he endured the voyage, his lips remained still and his eyes dry but his mind was captive. He approached Cathal, always in visible command, to query if he was fulfilling his obligations aboard.

Cathal responded, "If you keep a sharp eye and stay on your feet, you'll be a landman for not long at all. The most experienced seamen aboard the ships are our darker cousins who crewed vessels about the Caribbean. My advice is to learn their methods. We need to become more than we know ourselves to be if we wish to survive in waters where we're not welcome."

After seven days' sailing, they arrived at a rolling cliffside that towered into the clouds above. The blue waters of the Mediterranean met red dirt walls and rocky outlays. Cathal ordered to drop anchor. The anchors dropped with a loud splash. Cathal signaled for the *Perilous* to send officers over for further orders. The *Perilous* loaded a boat and arrived with Luke and MacIntyre in the small group.

A crowded deck of heavy breathers surrounded Cathal when he pointed at an unsuspicious cliff wall. "We've arrived. Can you see the port?"

The men collectively focused on the details. The waters were milk-like against the rocky seawall, except for one odd place. The vegetation overtook the damp rock and reached the crest of the cliff which flowed freely without obstruction. The red wall had stones that appeared worn but some predesigned placement looked peculiar.

Cathal paced by the men and explained, "The Phoenicians sailed the world and they loved Irish gold. They brought stockpiles of what they acquired here to that cothon port. Beneath us is a submerged wrecked sea tower to guide vessels into that collapsed entrance to a grand cothon."

"What ruined it?" Kennedy asked, wide-eyed.

"Volcanos! Eruptions that erased their legacy. Now its inhabitants think they've a quiet place to disappear. We will infiltrate and return to the ships before night falls."

Cathal ordered crates full of fragile glass bottles brought up to the main deck. He explained that they were packed with magnetic shavings, tar, and gunpowder. "I want you to light and throw these party favors at the faeries when we reach their home."

MacIntyre tipped his hat back then rubbed his chin, sporting a clever smile. He rolled a bottle in his palms. "I wager these gifts we be offering to the pagan guardians are likely to spoil kind introduction… I'll take two." He gingerly dropped them into his deep jacket pockets.

Cathal ordered the fifteen able crewmen from each ship with two of his bodyguards—thirty-two men in all—to ready for a swim while the rest were to stand ready for battle from the ships. Officers MacIntyre, Conri, and Donn would all go with Cathal. The crew quickly went about preparing for battle. Many of the crewmen leaving the ships removed their sweaters. The Irish stuck their hair up with chalk, like the old heroes, so that the enemy would see the white hair and be filled with dread. They prepared for battle and rubbed wet blue powder across their faces and bodies to intimidate through the dark markings of the true Tuatha de Danann. The men quietly equipped their rifles and daggers. Luke wasn't asked to personally make the assault so he returned to his ship as the commander in Cathal's absence. Shipyard would man the guns of the *Mistress* while Tymon would see to the ship's operation.

Judge was standing to the side of Cathal. "Remember, Cathal, when you had those whip-like red scars on your forearm for a time?" Judge, smirking, looked into the water and placed a hand on Cathal's shoulder. "A jellyfish you encountered. Terrified of the water for months but you overcame that."

Cathal pursed his lips like he tasted something bad. "I am still terrified of open water. I just got tired of you laughing about it."

The men were at the ready and watching Cathal for orders.

Cathal announced, "We cannot raise the ancient gate, and even if we could, we'd find ourselves hunted before we neared the tree. We are going to break in and take whoever's in there by surprise. In the confusion, we'll be away with the spear."

Cathal ordered the firing of a solid shot at the gate to unhinge it, making it accessible.

Shipyard remarked, "Won't the cannon fire tell the Sidhe we're coming?"

Cathal shouted over, "No, the volcano rumbles the ground regularly." He flashed a grin. "At least, I hope they'll pay it no mind."

Cathal was moving around the deck as the guns opened fire and Donn saw Cathal notice Shipyard grinning. "And what might you be havin' a chuckle about, master gunner?"

"I've fired guns at many things but never have I been ordered to throw lead at rocks."

The three longboats were lowered down by the davits into the choppy waves that swept to the cliffs. The boats made their way from the ships slowly, having to deal with the errant currents that cut by the cliffs. Donn turned to Cathal. "What did the Phoenicians use this place for?"

Cathal had to yell to be heard over the water crashing against the boat as he focused upon their course. "Gold! The early traders came to Ireland to trade for the precious metal that our island was filled with. They hid it in this port to protect it from pirates. The last time they came to Ireland, they left loaded with treasure but found their ships slithering with hiding Fomorians retreating from the Tuatha de Danann. They returned here to find assistance but the creatures used the opportunity to slaughter all the merchants and take over the port."

Donn was astonished. "They've been here for over two thousand years! How could they survive?"

"Who knows these things? I wouldn't be surprised if they knew how to make the volcano erupt to secure their new home." Cathal leaned in and wagged a finger at Donn. "Make sure you keep your powder dry. I didn't say this would be pleasant. However, the enemy will appreciate it when you take the gold. They absolutely despise the shiny stuff."

Donn spoke at a quicker pace, partly because the boat bobbed over the crest of the coastal waves and his balance was ever challenged. "I thought little faeries were all we were to encounter. How will we defend against them?"

"They use faeries and other creatures fearful of this new world as slaves. The Sidhe have a history of dragging innocent races of beings with them in their descent into hell. They won't be ready for us. Trust me." Cathal winked.

Donn asked, "Why are the faeries guarding the Spear at Lanzarote?"

"These kinds of faeries prefer mines and embraced that lava tube. Those faeries that ally themselves with the devils of the old world face our blade all the same. Damn them. Damn them…to whatever hell we can send them." Cathal squeezed the hilt of his sword as he finished that sentiment.

By the time Donn reached the first jagged boulders from which to tie off, he was exhausted from fighting the tide. They tossed grappling hooks, then one man from each vessel used the rope to pull himself to the treacherous rocky outcrop.

*****

The crew of the bobbing *Midnight Mistress* and *Perilous* were silent as they watched the landing proceed. The ships gently creaked as the anchors held them stationary. Shipyard was eating a wedge of Cheshire cheese while he squinted and strolled by the guns. Aboard the *Perilous*, Luke was lying back on a short bench catching a quick nap in the luxurious sun, completely at peace.

*****

The boats were pulled tight to the inhospitable sheer cliffside. Cathal was the first to climb upon a rock and he spotted and pointed out where the cliff was incomplete against the now-rusted gate. The weight and age caused the gate to tilt back, no longer flush with the far seawall. They, one by one, grabbed onto the gate crossmembers and shimmied through. Sacks of supplies were tied to their backs.

Donn found a stone landing which he stepped down upon. Only a faint light shot through the long moat below a massive corridor that led into the depths of the mountain. After the last man made it through, Cathal whispered to light torches.

As the first torch was lit, Donn could see images on the tunnel walls. Large cats were depicted in faint carvings and worn paint, some with wings in a regal pose and others where the animal seemed to aggressively force a walled fortress to submit. The colors were bright where they existed and were swirl-designed. Long flat boats, trading vessels, were painted floating on waters with strange creatures peering from the seas. The air was stale in the chamber as the light flickered across the eerie surroundings.

Cathal spoke to Donn as they walked. "Light and dark can be seen by mankind but the armed Tuatha de Danann couldn't pursue the Fomorians into the dark of the earth."

Donn responded, "Baron, I think I have a guess why the Fomorians hate gold. My teachers once told me a lesson of Plotinus. He once likened God's power to the sun. The One's power is not diminished by being a reflection. The light banks off the gold and terrifies them."

"Pardon my trouble understanding you. Our ancestors did believe the sun was a symbol of God, but since it is not and Plotinus was using an analogy, then why pray is the sunlight so important?"

"We make the mistake of attempting to understand that which is beyond us. I'm surprised that you'd question the strange." Donn smirked.

"It helps to better do battle, if nothing else. Humor me, schoolboy!"

"Gold is an element rare and treasured for ages. Perhaps it, along with the sun, are holy poison—at least since their rebellion. Where there is the sun, there is life and His promise."

Cathal responded, "Fair enough. The Tuatha de Danann loved wearing gold which seems strange since as armor, it's fairly worthless. As for myself, I left my suit of gold armor somewhere else so I'll be making do with sword and shot!"

The wolf guard started sniffing the air and scouting further ahead of the party. They made no sound as they pounced, using their arms to lessen the sound of their movements. Sunlight passed through the shallow canal water, producing a lantern effect on the walls with a gentle wavy blue glow. The tunnel had been designed with tall, masted vessels in mind, and the men passed supporting arches every twenty-five feet.

The crew continued walking for five minutes until Donn could see, in the distance, the canal give way to a larger pool of water and a central island with structures upon it. An ominous white glow emanated from the far reaches of the chamber, and a few white crabs could be seen scampering beneath their feet. The men began creeping carefully to the first stone wall embankment that marked the beginning of the circular shipyard.

The mountain seemed hollow now to Donn, looking at the sight of this open chamber. The grand shipyard was like a massive cathedral with drilled vertical channels on the ceiling that expelled the smoke from the flames of the docks' open torches. Each slip had flanking statues of panther-like creatures in various fierce poses, acting as silent guardians. The stench of foul and filth was everywhere—from discarded fish remains to assorted garbage. Each slip on the outer ring, facing inward toward the central island, had a set of overhead hoists that allowed for the dry docking of vessels of over one hundred feet in length. A structure of scaffolding and platforms allowed personalized storage and repair tools for each vessel. There were several slips without vessels and some had fallen away from their hosts with only bits of lumber remaining tied up. Each slip was a lock that allowed a vessel to be pulled into the flooded dock and then tied up before that dock was sealed and drained.

A channel guide for a ship's keel was on the central platform then that platform was mechanically rotated toward its designated slip. Donn was in wonderment at the thought that thousands of people may have been present here at one time when the port was operational. Now that they were in the central chamber, he saw behind them a strange feature. The likeness of a fierce goddess was carved above the tunnel entrance. Her entire image was coated in cracked red paint, except for inlaid obsidian eyes. She was holding a black iron gate above her that appeared as a bulbous disc with chasing lines surrounding it.

Donn heard ripples in the canal and he watched a school of merrows slap the water with their tails and emerge near the stone island. The hair on their heads was long as their bodies but had the appearance of bundles of whiskers that merely played at being long hair. They threw sacks of fish upon the stone landings. Then Donn saw the Sidhe.

Two pale creatures with long bodies came to retrieve the net sacks. They were adorned in plated leather armor and moved like half-asleep drones. Faeries, with flashes of random lighted discharge throughout their wings, darted around the middle chamber, different colors bouncing off the waters like a private celebration between them. The crew could see the branches of a massive tree growing right into the ceiling.

Donn whispered, watching the activity, "Will the faeries fly over us, Baron?"

Cathal responded, "Not over moving water, they certainly won't. Trapped, they are."

The barkless tree was breathtaking. Its glassy branches possessed traveling sparkles that encircled and pulsed. The broad transparent trunk was laced with thin ribbons of silver traveling within as if life-giving veins. The branches of the tree periodically erupted with tiny lights like a startled flock of birds. The inner chamber was awash in the tree's glow. The structures surrounding the center tower that directed the ship traffic in and out of the shipyard had crumbled. Their flickering torches illuminated the watchtower once tasked to direct the docking boats. The crew extinguished their flames in the canal, then moved further down the stone path.

As they neared the tower, Donn spotted a table fastened together with leather ties where a little person sat, busy with quill and vellum. The creature was no taller than a man's knee and difficult to bring into focus for its diminutive size and quick movements. A smoke cloud hovered over its head from a pipe and seemed to abate only when the creature paged through a document. Donn and the other men knelt since the two Sidhe had walked up to the table where the creature sat. The Sidhe had black eyes and their bodies that, although upright, looked just as much amphibious as human. The Sidhe dropped a sack upon the table which further revealed golden coins that tumbled out onto the floor.

The men were like statues and only the water dripping from their trousers made any sound. They waited for Cathal's orders. Cathal looked over each shoulder, seeing his men waiting, and whispered, "Apparently it's not just dinner the merrows are useful for. Sunken treasures."

Donn was kneeling beside Cathal and added, "It's one of the little folk, Baron."

The little woman leaned in to argue over something pertaining to the contents. She palmed her pipe and let two fingers curl over above which split the smoke. Her small frame was stiff with anger as she spat out both insults and smoke. She would rock back and forth in her chair as her following quill strokes were quick beyond measure. The rocking gave Donn an awareness of the rattling of a leg chain on the woman. The eyes of the bookkeeper shot around as if assessing wealth in order to serve her masters through thievery.

Donn whispered, "Why do the Sidhe still have gold here if they despise it?"

Cathal pulled out his sword and responded, "Other creatures lust for it, and the Sidhe use it to get what they desire. Now let's move forward."

Powder bags, shots, and pistols were dropped into two sheep bladders. The men slipped quietly into the water and swam to the circular platform of the port. They pulled themselves up carefully and crouched in the ready within the shadow of the tower. The Sidhe sentry had already begun walking away on patrol, and although the little woman seemed to notice the intruders, she chose to do nothing and continued to work. The wolf guard pointed at the slips filled with sleeping Sidhe for the commander to take notice. They were on the opposite end of the oblong stone platform that seemed to be floating in the canal with the far end being where the tree stood.

A sickly Sidhe, with an oversized helmet, appeared from the darkness next to a massive bell in the central tower. He hopped violently upon seeing the intruders and reacted by shrieking and striking the bell which gave off a deep sound, sending ripples through the canal water. Cathal started walking boldly forward past his guards. He shot the tower sentry in his bony ribs, sending him forward off the ledge into the water. As the sentry fell down the steep stone wall, the sleeping army began to wake. Donn saw the first head turn toward Cathal from off the floor, and as the Sidhe rose, Cathal squared up and broke his jaw, forcing him to tumble into the canal to accompany the splash of the sentry. The crew continued to move deeper into the canal behind their baron as the cave came to life with shrieks of terror. The wolf guard sprung forward, in flanking position of Cathal, to smash heads into the ground. Donn unsheathed his sword and followed close behind Cathal.

*****

Conri always felt the same when a fight began. His breath quickened, his hands sweat, and his blood ran hot. Seeing the enemy, so numerous, was granting him an unspoken wish. He felt the least amount of pain when he could inflict it on those that did evil. He entered into a frenzy that seized up all external feeling and gave way to rage that demanded tribute, as if rage was a god he embraced. No longer able to hold his discipline, he ran forward into the unknown, away from the rest of the crewmen like one who might carry the colors in full assault.

He saw a Sidhe near the edge of the platform on patrol. It screamed at him with a hollow pitch with its ghastly mouth wide. Conri vibrated from his hate, which cracked many of his bones at once, and kicked at the ground. "*Abhastaird!*" He bellowed in a bass voice that echoed as if it was inside of a large cellar. He tackled the sentry, who was slow to swing his ax, which led Conri off a slip's pier and onto the deck of a docked ship. The two of them crashed through the galley's fragile deck and into the hold below. Conri crashed through dusty sealed jars, and as they shattered, he rolled to the front of the tilted ship. Tin ingots were piled at that end of the storage so that it imbalanced the ship to the point of tilting forward.

The surrounding Sidhe rushed forward toward Conri, past skeletons of ancient rowers slaughtered on their benches. Conri grabbed a metal block and slammed it into the side of the Sidhe's head so that its helmet caved into its skull. The ropes on the hoist broke loose from the ship and it crashed upon the floor. Conri rose from the pile of wood above him. His lower body still stuck in the ship's debris, he saw other Sidhe surround him on the edge of the pier above him. He felt like death as one who had arrived to claim hiding souls. Nothing had time to fear him if he wished them dead. No darkness could hide them from him. Conri took hold of a broken plank and awaited their foolish assault.

*****

Cathal shouted a rallying cry, "They will release that bright beautiful spear to us and it'll shine a light to our promised kingdom! To the tree, men!"

They moved forward into the remainder of the sentries whose true numbers were in the shadows. The squad around Cathal was rushed and overwhelmed, so much so that Cathal was pinned down by one spitting Sidhe. Cathal pulled a small pistol from his inside jacket pocket. He pressed the brass barrel against the chest of the assailant and fired. The ferocity of the ball that passed through the Sidhe was lethal and shocking. Cathal tossed the blood-drenched pistol out of the way and threw the now-lifeless corpse off him.

Donn noticed that the Sidhe hesitated around him and didn't commit to an attack with him as quickly as they had opportunity. They snorted the closer they got to him and had to rebalance themselves. Donn saw the Sidhe staring at his stag jacket and wondered why the creatures seemed to be repelled by it.

The crew were startled enough to turn and look when a waterfall of lava poured from a raised steel door behind them. This action effectively cut off the retreat for the Irish but Cathal, again, disregarded the danger and advanced. The Irish were now also attacked by the faeries which glided toward them in multitudes—as many as raindrops falling from a cloud. The Irish soon found themselves being sliced about their bodies in little cuts. Cathal grunted a command, "Cover the room in shrapnel, throw the bottles now!" After the bottles crashed against the walls all around, the faeries appeared to lose sense and their velocity was their enemy. The faeries pounded the walls to die or break wings. Some ran into the rushing lava and burst, screaming into the flames. Lava fell through a merrow attempting to escape. The steam wafted across the chaos and made fighting clumsy and increasingly dangerous.

The tree now dimmed with the full evacuation of the faerie residents and they filled the room with flickering rainbow colors that continually repainted the surroundings.

More of the Sidhe began to stir and wake from their slumber. A couple of the sailors were bitten as they ran past them but were quickly cut away from them. The awakening Sidhe struggled to use their muscles as they staggered up.

Cathal ordered, "Guard, tear through them before they attack!" The wolf guard sprang into action with heavy blows upon the heads and bodies of the Sidhe. Necks were crushed and heads were pounded in until the floor was covered like the unkempt floor of a butcher's shop. After a minute, the Sidhe joined the guard in hand-to-hand combat. The guard proved ferocious enough to hold the attention on themselves and not the tree.

The sailors lunged at the tree but were tossed away time and again. Their bodies were hammered and that taxing effort was slowing them. Cathal was kneeling near the step before the tree, defended by three crouching armed sailors. As the men rushed to reach the tree, their bodies began to float, and although they kicked forward, they failed to move forward. Only feet away initially, they were repulsed ten yards or more then recklessly dropped onto the ground. Some men fell on the little screaming faeries, crushing them into glowing bits. As Cathal was tossed to the ground, trying to lead the assault through the waves of faeries, he was deeply wounded on the right leg.

A Sidhe hissed and his large black eyes set upon Donn. Donn had to use his knee to brace against the creature as it lunged its weight forward, trying to wrap its arms around him, apparently, to tumble Donn into the canal. Donn put his hand against the Sidhe's cheek and turned its head to shift its center of gravity, making it harder for it to succeed. The Sidhe planted its feet so it could relieve the pressure from Donn's hand but Donn used that opportunity to sweep its legs out from under it. Donn quickly kicked the creature into the canal as a fellow sailor walked by and fired his musket into the Sidhe's chest. Bleeding profusely, it sunk into the canal, aided by the weight of its armor.

Donn rose to his feet, finding the battle in full chaos and the tree still unclaimed up ahead. He was flanked by three men who had shakily regrouped with him. Donn pulled his sword from his waist and yelled, "O'Ruairc Aboo!" That sound rolled down the canal and reverberated into the enemy soldiers. Whatever Donn did was effective since the enemy appeared to cower as if their spirit itself had been suppressed. Donn waved the men forward in a fast walk then a jog. They hopped over and away from the Sidhe that they couldn't engage while keeping pace. Donn's sword was swung like fine music to cut his way forward. Donn's group acted like a bowling ball through the battlefield. His men were in a raged frenzy, overapplying viciousness when encountering the Sidhe. When they arrived at Cathal's side near the tree, they were covered in blood. Cathal was leaning an arm on a large piece of pillar that was broken off its base to support his injured leg.

"Where's the little clurichaun?" asked Cathal.

Donn looked around and saw the wee woman hiding behind her tipped desk. Donn commanded, "Here now, you, quickly!"

The faerie peeked its head above the table and shouted back, "Nay!"

Cathal, frustrated, shouted, "We need your assistance!"

She quickly growled, "I won't be trading monsters for lunatics!"

Cathal stumbled, as he tried to stand, then erupted and threw a rock at the table. "Trade with me, bookkeeper!"

Donn added, "The options are better with us than here with them. You have my word, we're honorable!"

"Fine! You free me from here and swear not to enslave me and I'll lend you aid!"

Both Cathal and Donn shouted in unison, "Done!"

"Break this chain from me then and I'll get you what you came here for."

She stomped on an iron-gated door on the floor near her. Donn moved over to her and looked in. He saw unimaginable treasure in piles sparkling within.

Cathal yelled over, "What is it?!"

"It's a fortune in gold." Donn looked over at the clurichaun and said quickly, "It's the spear we want in that tree."

The little woman stared with obvious concern at Donn and then declared, "I've been here all this time and my opportunity to be rescued is by the only human not interested in gold!" She threw her hat upon the ground in a fit. Then she, despite the battle around her, lay down and looked up at the ceiling as if suddenly exhausted. She lamented to herself, "The foolishness I must deal with is surely served from Dagda's cauldron!"

Donn stood over her and repeated, "Can you help us? It's what we seek and we can help each other."

She wearily placed a hand on her face. "Only those with a kinship to the tree may come near it which may prove difficult to negotiate since you're roasting its brethren." The miniature woman got up and pulled on her red hat. She squinted at the battle around her.

Cathal was using the table as a shield as the enemy was rushing in from varied directions. Cathal cried out, "MacIntyre, bring up the gunpowder!"

Donn saw all the crew fighting throughout the center island, some facing gruesome deaths by being bludgeoned to death or getting tossed into the water to be torn to pieces by the merrows. He looked over at the little clurichaun and noticed her staring at him intently. She spoke, "Do you notice how the Sidhe are barely attacking you? They seem to be avoiding you! It's that strange hide you wear—it repels them! Quick, have you tried to reach the tree?"

"No, but the others—"

She interrupted him with a hard punch to his knee. "Listen to me. You must go. You try now!" Donn winced at the pain she dealt him which nearly made him reconsider the hasty partnership.

Donn wiped some of the dirt from his face into his hair, nearly solid with sweat and saltwater. He sheathed his sword and looked upon the ground in the area. He picked up a mallet dropped by a warden, then swung down with a grunt, breaking the chain that held the diminutive woman in rags. She immediately snuck over to Cathal beneath the raging chaos of faeries in out-of-control flight.

A second line of defense had formed behind a stack of ancient cedar logs that had never been delivered for trade. Out from behind that pile of logs moved a crewman with a barrel he was rolling forward. MacIntyre moved that barrel with haste past a litany of skirmishes that proved a constant interruption to his progress. MacIntyre was at the lip of the platform, which was situated before where the tree was rooted, while Cathal stood near the base of the tree. Then an inflamed faerie ran into MacIntyre's lowered head, like a boulder from a catapult, which threw him on to his side. A black fanged Sidhe hobbled over and attempted to stab his spear into him. MacIntyre, with black smoke rolling off his burning hair, rolled to his side, avoiding the strike. The hissing bald Sidhe's feet appeared like alligator claws and were planted like posts into the ground, ready to deal the killing blow. When MacIntyre rolled back, he forcefully grabbed the chest belt of the attacker and lifted himself up a little. He stuffed his pistol gunpowder pouch into its open mouth then shoved the burning carcass of the faerie in to follow. Its head lit yellow and its eyes exploded, followed by its skull cracking and the body collapsing without its brain to control it.

MacIntyre was covered in its black blood and was pinned under the body. The barrel rested under the legs of the dead Sidhe. Donn watched as his comrade would be killed soon if aid didn't reach him. A sailor, whose tattooed body was splashed with red and black blood-like paint, approached from the tower. He wore a bent helmet and walked with the confidence of a war god enjoying the spectacle. He grabbed MacIntyre and threw him over his shoulder before making his way toward Cathal. Donn saw it was Conri and was relieved that MacIntyre was still breathing.

Donn took in the horrors around him and heard the chamber echo with the screams of his friends. None of the Sidhe were guarding the tree, and the faeries were in disarray. The ships in the port sleeves were burning and collapsing. He made his way to the tree and no one opposed him. He arrived at the blinding trunk and placed his hand upon it. The spot Donn touched lit up, just like when the faeries landed upon it. The light in the tree gathered itself into a ghostly image of a many-horned creature whose body reached through a void. The otherworldly beast seemed angered at its awakening by Donn. It snarled, causing the branches of the tree to shake from the sound. It looked at Donn and swiped a paw near where the hand was placed, leaving large claw marks. Donn felt the impact and it was like something breaking a mirror from the inside out.

"You will release the spear to me now!" Donn commanded. The mighty trunk of the tree fiercely vibrated. A black energy spilled out from his hand into the tree and the creature screamed in terror as it tried to shrink away. The black energy, like venom, invaded the breadth of its timber. As if split by a giant ax, the tree tore apart from itself. The force of the tree breaking in two threw Donn back onto the ground, showered in a million shards of crystal, filling the chamber with the snow-like powder.

Donn heard the volcano rumble and the entire chamber rattle from the strain. A massive branch, as wide as a hay wagon and long as a sloop, snapped off the tree and landed in the canal. It floated until it came near the falling lava which seemed to be repelled by the magic still remaining in the branch. The lava pooled in midair, yards above the branch, as if it found an invisible ceiling, then flowed outward until it sprayed the nearby area. The unaware enemy, who had blocked any retreat, now found themselves melting in agony across the entrance to the chamber. The ceasing of the flow of lava into the canal caused the hot steam to abate to a degree sufficient for the crew to see the walls of the room again as well as the tunnel exit. The exhaust chambers began dripping with lava which soon became a flow that landed like pillars of doom. The once-great tree would not melt but instead guided the landing lava down its broken branches in terrifying streams back onto the platform.

Donn saw, in a solid carbon ash, a spear that rested at the bottom of the split of the trunk. He reached in and grabbed the smoking spear, feeling none of the searing heat he expected. Donn then pitched himself in an awkward run back to Cathal. He had to place a hand on the ground twice to keep from helplessly falling. He made it to Cathal and handed him the spear. Cathal shouted an order, "Regroup to your baron now, lads!"

The little woman adjusted her hat, pinned up in front, and waved Donn over. He sensed no danger, although perhaps he should have been more cautious. She pulled Donn back to the gated floor portal and pulled a key off her neck.

"You bring me along and wealthy I'm proud to make you all."

Meanwhile Cathal was struggling to avoid a slow bull-sized Sidhe that was attempting to grab him. He looked at Donn and mentioned to him, "The gold you need for your land is there. Grab it quick since we have to retire. MacIntyre has grown tired and I believe he'd like to rest in his bunk."

Donn, exasperated, yelled back, "Wouldn't that anger the faeries!"

Cathal grunted and raised a brow. "Not any more than I already have!"

Conri yanked the Sidhe back away from Cathal. Cathal pulled a pistol and shot the Sidhe in the head before rallying his remaining men for the escape. Bare-chested men lay dead around the huddle as Cathal quickly told the exhausted men the plan. Donn took his sword and quickly made bags of the now-empty bladders. The chamber ceiling filled with rippling ash clouds. Volcanic lightning rolled above the Irish and its sound trembled off the waters.

Donn used the key and grunted to lift the heavy gate up and away and then jumped down into the pit filled with gold. He tossed filled bags up as quickly as he could. One of the men helped Donn carry the bladders. They then joined the rest of the crew as they fled. The clurichaun hurried with a large golden goblet over one shoulder, kicking her boots up as she ran.

They halted at the edge of the platform. Cathal said, "We'll swim in the canal, under that branch, and back to the boats!" Donn came up beside Cathal, dragging two bags of loot. Cathal pointed at the bags and said, "Two men to a bag, let's go! Get in the water!" Conri stood with the barely conscious MacIntyre leaning on his shoulder.

Donn remembered the merrows and asked, "Is it safe to swim with the monsters in the water?"

"I believe them to have perished. Besides I grew up near a volcano at Port Plymouth and these gasses will cause you to fall asleep and never awaken. We must go!"

Donn leapt in the water, holding a bladder with another man, and swam under the branch. He then climbed up onto the tunnel's walkway, dragging a bag of gold up beside him. He looked around and saw that four bags of loot had made it to the other side of the canal. He ran with the other men and saw the lights of faeries following, now able to escape over the water between the tree branch below and the lava above. Donn arrived at the boats with the crew and they attempted to cast off into the sunset. A swarm of faeries hovered above the longboats, darting down to attack as the crew was trying to cut the ropes loose. The powder for his pistol was too wet but Donn used the butt of his weapon to crush the faeries onto the floorboards who were disoriented from the smoke that was pouring out from the canal. The planks were littered with the tiny bodies of the faeries. Donn sighed in relief as the ropes upon the boulders were finally dropped. They pushed away from the shore, leaving the mad swarm of faeries behind.

After the boats were reattached to the hoists, Donn and the other survivors were pulled up into the ships. Donn watched as Judge collected the little broken faerie bodies and packed them in a crate without explanation. As Judge went about the gruesome task, Donn noticed that the tiny corpses would vibrate and move slightly toward the island. Before he could ponder the possible implications of that mystery, Donn heard a shout that cast itself higher than the top mast which caused all the crew to make instant economy of action toward departure. Their careful skill, from long-traded sweat, granted ease in escape to the sailors still above the sea. Donn worked side by side with the men, suddenly feeling himself to be a mortal. The majestic flourish of the sails was then filled with the powerful trade winds, pushing the ships into the Canary Current.

The anchor broke loose from the mud of the seafloor and was aweigh. The ship caught the wind as soon as the sails were unfurled. The vessel let out a loud creak as it broke away from the glittering violent coastal surf. Donn saw the *Perilous* bombard the shore to cover the landing party's escape.

Donn was resting on the deck near Cathal when O'Hogan walked up to the railing nearby. O'Hogan's eyes lit up with the dancing lights on the black horizon. He gripped a yard rope and tried to focus. "Are you looking at this?"

The baron nodded and said nothing. He had bandaged his leg and was inspecting his surviving crew. MacIntyre, his head lying on his pillowed sweater, was awakened by the baron before he continued on.

O'Hogan stated to no one in particular, "They have the entire shore lit with torches and they're running like madness."

Judge answered, "Those aren't torches. Those are the faeries and they cannot depart far from their tree."

"Why?" O'Hogan was visibly disturbed by that statement.

"Because they are tied to it like a magnet. If they resist its pull long, it'll kill them."

Shipyard trudged by Judge, carefully carrying a wounded sailor, and commented, "Perhaps they exaggerated a bit when the storytellers spoke of the beauty of the Sidhe. The survivors act like they've seen monsters." With his heart finally settling, Donn grew sick at the sight of the blue mixed with blood dripping off the injured sailor upon the deck.

Judge responded, "Their shame stretches millennia. That's what the absence of love can perform upon you." He clasped his hands together.

MacIntyre, holding his head with some focus, closed his eyes and happily said, "That makes fine sense. Considering my ravishing nature and the time spent with accommodating cailins."

Judge peeked over at MacIntyre and unwillingly let out a short chuckle. He picked up MacIntyre's hat and tossed it at the sailor whose wit was never injured.

Meanwhile Donn could barely hear the clurichaun on the top mast platform laughing hysterically and cursing its foiled captors, using ancient and English words both. Since the odd creature was Cathal's guest, no one questioned it as all the crew were so distracted by the day's events.

The black clouds, which had covered the horizon, appeared to fold in upon themselves and piled higher as if attempting to reach the heavens. The ship glided forward on waters pulled toward a building storm. The moon was hidden but Donn thought he saw terrifying creatures sitting on the water as the distant lightning flickered. He imagined their black eyes watching him as the ship passed. The childhood tales he had heard as a boy, he now found himself sailing through it seemed. Those heroes from long ago braved a sea that frothed and bit at the sailors that dared her frightful domain. The merrow and monster were ever prepared for those that fell in her embrace. As he retired to the cabin, he thought he heard a moaning, which echoed against the hull. *Perhaps a whale*, he thought but his instincts warned him of a dangerous presence in the sea.

Tied Destiny

Bridget was out strolling near Keem Bay on a family outing. She noticed a small entrance to what appeared to be a small cave, nearly hidden, facing the surf. Its moss camouflage had been disturbed, making the entrance visible. She climbed down the bleached rocks that stretched into the shallow waters. She moved toward the cave, careful not to slip on the slick boulders. She peered through the opening but it was too dark so she tore away at some of the overgrowth of moss. She pulled it away and climbed down through the rubble of the wall to see what mysteries awaited. It was a structure built into the hill, looking as if it had been kicked by a giant. The wind ran through and piled bits of grass and dust against the walls and dark ground.

She lightly touched the ground with her feet and lowered herself inside. A blanket of soft glowing light poured about the room from behind her. She saw that the room seemed empty so she headed to a great old door that faced the sea. She pulled on its iron ring. The light streamed through and she let out a yelp of surprise. An old man, thin and frail, was eating a raw fish while sitting against a wall. He looked over at Bridget and he slopped the fish down onto a ragged woven net and picked up a tall splintered walking stick to rise.

"Who enters my home?" He narrowed his eyes and gripped his dark shillelagh with both hands. "Who disturbs me!"

Bridget was so startled she didn't know how to react so she grabbed her dress, half-ready to attempt a dash to safety. "I apologize. I didn't realize anyone was here. I'll go!"

The old man looked around and his eyes grew wider and softer. He tripped slightly but kept his balance. "It's I who must apologize. Don't be frightened! I'm afraid that since I'm used to avoiding people, I no longer know how to greet them."

Bridget momentarily felt calmed and curiosity claimed her again. "Why are you here?"

"I'm a *seanchai* which is what you'd know as a storyteller, though I haven't told any in ages. I've always taken joy in watching people in the quiet to learn new stories." He waved at his cave. "However, you can't be a part of the story if you wish to tell it and know you'll live to tell it so…here I am."

His appearance was revolting to Bridget with blood stuck to his beard from the fish.

"Would you care to hear a story?" he asked.

"No, I'd better get home to my family, they'll be worried. I'm so sorry."

"Oh, I beseech you! I've had no one to prove my trade in so long. I live here because my tales upset people and they no longer wanted to hear them. Just a short story and I'll make sure it brings you joy."

Bridget looked into his eyes. There was great pain there. He didn't look menacing, just disturbing.

"All right… I didn't mean to ruin your lunch."

"Sit and I'll begin my story then." He wiped his face and brushed his ragged yellow gown as best he could. He stood with both hands on his stick, trying to appear appropriate for a performance.

"Once the great Cu Conor protected the property of the high king Fiacha. The Cu, for his many years of service, was offered a young and beautiful bride, Rowena. She sang for the court and her beautiful voice shamed the instruments of the land. He was glad and fell in love with the girl. Before they could wed, the king sent him on an errand to recover stolen cattle. Samhain was the night he had seen a pyre above Rathcroghan and the cattle that had been slaughtered along the way led him to its flames."

*****

The Midnight Mistress

Donn awoke to shouting and then a sharp scream so he fell out of his hammock, pulled his boots on, and climbed the two ladders from the berthing deck out onto the top deck to see about the turmoil.

The ships were encircled by a massive wall of upright waves that blocked much of the horizon. The walls of water lit up randomly with arching green flickers. A giant reached out from the sea. He was angry and his voice was like firewood cracking apart. His eyes were like massive ivory pearls reflecting the sea. His body was wrapped in swirling patterns that appeared like ocean water, still and sparkling. He looked as if the ocean was his washtub, his arms as large as a mast. The *Mistress* and *Perilous* were slowly drifting away from one another.

*****

The Perilous

On the *Perilous*, a crewman fought to hold his balance. "Look at its size! Do ya see it, Cap'n! Look at it."

Calmly Luke responded while gripping a rail, "Yes, yes, I do. It is impressive." Luke looked up to see the monster's head. "Perhaps you should load the forward guns now?"

Visibly embarrassed, he responded, "Aye, Cap'n, right away."

*****

The Midnight Mistress

Men were violently being thrown into the surf. Donn saw Cathal holding onto the rail above the main cabin, shouting orders with little effect. The men were hurrying and couldn't complete their tasks without fumbling. The chaos was beyond what Donn could have imagined. The clurichaun was near the bow, trying to pull her hat over her entire head. The pale giant waved at the water and moved closer to the *Perilous*. Cathal interrupted his barking at the crew as the enemy moved toward the sister ship. Donn noticed Cathal was silent which was as frightening as the battle they were in for their lives. He could see Luke aboard the *Perilous,* swinging amidships on a yard rope and then shouting orders into the hull.

Donn saw the *Perilous* shoot its forward cannons at the giant's stomach with a belch of smoke and fire. The cannonballs were as mere bee stings against it and seemed to enrage it all the more on its approach. Donn watched in horror as the attack on the *Perilous* was imminent and seemingly unstoppable.

Kennedy angrily yelled out while gripping the wheel, "Why doesn't he just drop these waves upon us and destroy us?"

Tymon shouted, "Do we have no recourse against this bastard, Baron?"

Donn heard Cathal call out to Shipyard to bring him Judge. The priest quickly arrived on the deck and looked at the monster. Judge grew still a moment and then spit to the side, "Manannán Mac Lir has come. I promise you, those Druids back in Hy-Brasil will be disappointed!" Judge motioned for Donn to follow him. Donn followed Judge and Shipyard below deck. Through the portholes, Donn saw the sea god plucking men up from the *Perilous* and hurling them into the air where they plunged into a watery doom. The giant then beat down upon the ship and began to most certainly flood it. The heavy shrouds gave way to Manannán's fury and the mast timbers splintered under the stress. The mast fell onto the enemy. Its sails, crashing against the demigod, gave a momentary pause to the blows. Turning to Judge on the gun deck, Donn watched as the priest unwrapped holy linens from the faerie remains while gunmates cracked open exploding canister rounds. Judge quickly stuffed faerie corpses inside the canisters as makeshift ammunition.

Judge looked over at Donn. "Over here, grab them like so and assemble. We have no time to waste."

Donn worked feverishly. He kept his head down and worked on a single action since, if he tried to handle what he'd even do the next moment, he'd get lost in fear. Once they were done, Shipyard ordered the disbursement of the canisters among the firing squads.

"These cannon only! Don't bother with the top deck as they don't have the range. If any of you miss, I'll throw you to the beast myself!" hollered Shipyard.

The warrior priest prayed against Manannán while he used his strong arms to pass out the cartridges to the crew quickly lining up. He looked to Donn. "Go and report to the baron that we're ready to fire on his order. Quickly."

Donn returned to the top deck. He saw two men approach and speak to Cathal. They were abruptly slapped and shoved back. Cathal wasted no time resuming his focus on the divine enemy, never over three hundred yards away. Donn moved over to Cathal. Donn passed the disgruntled men as he took the steps up to the quarterdeck. They staggered away to their posts, visibly frustrated.

"Baron, Judge loaded special canisters. The guns are ready to fire on your command," Donn said hastily.

Cathal barely acknowledged Donn with a slight nod and spoke indifferently to himself while limping to the gunwale, "We must do this if we wish to live. We must do this if we wish to live…"

The sea god was howling, the sound reverberating off the imprisoning waves. Donn saw a man dry puke from stress near the aft while tightly gripping his musket. Then he watched the sea god lift his nightmarish volcanic black sword from the water. The weapon, long as a ship, had a jagged edge like shark's teeth. With the enemy putting its broad back to the *Mistress*'s guns, Cathal screamed with tremendous force, "Open fire!" The *Mistress* was shoved to her side twenty yards and shaken savagely from the magical energy leaving the cannons. The heavy shot cut over the glassy water like glowing missiles. Explosions riddled Manannán and he dropped his sword into the water, causing a large geyser where it pushed through the water. The wounds were like large gashes that pulled at his matter. Donn noticed that the streams of light that were emitted from the wounds were all pointing in the same direction—toward the shore of Hy-Brasil. The demigod wrenched back in obvious pain from the peppering he took. Donn saw that some of the shells had errantly struck the *Perilous* and it was taking on water.

*****

The old man continued, "And released the sid from the dog bone collar, his bargain now complete. A trap had been set and the Cu Conor was the target they had baited. He was set upon for blood sacrifice so that Samhain may last an eternity. He fought until he couldn't lift his arms to throw off or stab again at the evil spirits. Whenever he was allowed a breath, he was quickly sliced open by the claws of the corrupted. His torch faded dimly to mark the ending of the hero."

Bridget's eyes narrowed and her mouth drew tense. She spoke up quickly, "The hero must live. Otherwise what kind of hero could he be? He's not a hero to the woman he loves!"

The old man, with his eyes shut, said in retort, "It's as I witnessed it, now please don't interrupt."

She withheld further questions.

*****

The Perilous

"Show him your teeth, lads! Pour hell into him! He will never forget that day he faced the *Perilous*!" Luke cried out.

The gun crews, in rhythm for destruction, kept a continuous fusillade portside, firing—alas—to insignificant effect. Luke slid around on the soaked deck as the tilting ship warped beneath him. Just looking up to see the massive fist above caused him to fall on his shoulder. The clenched fingers rose above the ship as water cascaded

161

down like rain to warn the victim. Luke saw a man crushed and not even the blood, or scream, could escape the impact. The exhausted men were popped up off the deck from the reverberation with each blow of the monster. He couldn't see past the monster's torso but he could hear the firing cannons of the *Mistress* echo across the waves. Even now, he believed they were not lost. Manannán began to pick up the keel of the ship and raise it above the water. Luke found it difficult to do anything with a measure of dexterity as the ship would elevate ten feet at a time from the wake of the aggressor's leg movements. Another of Manannán's blow's landed. Luke was suddenly on his back and saw the torn mast and missing topsail. His ship was certainly foundering but he felt it pointless to send men below deck to work the bilge pump.

Fig fiercely hung from the damaged rigging above the deck. His bravery was still intact, despite this dire situation. He had closed his eyes when the fist came down upon middeck. When he opened them again, he knew his friend Jacko must have been tossed up by the reverberation and come off the edge of the deck. He pointed and yelled for the captain.

Luke was able to hear Fig despite the ship wrenching against the sea. He saw a struggling sailor unable to pull himself back aboard. He slid down the tilted deck to where he could still see a dark hand grip the rail. Grabbing an arm, he was able to slowly rise him to safety. He recognized Jacko Dillon, as he knew him; for now, he watched as the rescue was all in vain since his head wound would soon be fatal. Jacko was aboard to serve with his older brother, also a lost Montserrat child looking to find a future in a world that had no room for him. That's when Luke became angry. His men were suffering and the responsibility for it offended his core. He forced himself on his feet and looked to bring order to the chaos, to prove they're a fair threat to the enemy.

Luke shouted, "Bring up the highly explosive shells!" With only moments to spare, the crew scrambled and brought what they could from the top deck. Luke ordered the loading of a boat full of gunpowder bags, buckets of tar, and shrapnel. Then the crew of the

Perilous lit the longboat on fire and cut the ropes that held it to the upper side of the hull facing the beast.

"Touch fuse!" ordered Luke and the longboat was struck with short-fused shells from the cannon fire. A loud explosion erupted, causing Manannán to stumble, dragged away by the energy from the faerie remains embedded deep within him. The tar, in flames, clung to Manannán as it did the outer hull of the *Perilous*. The sail that had fallen against the god was lit ablaze and his blond beard caught fire like kindling. The enveloping black smoke rolled up in billows that affected the aggressor's vision. Luke was pleased as he stood on his ship, doomed as it was.

*****

The Midnight Mistress

Cathal ordered aloud, "That's it. Banish him and fire at will now that we have him considering his mortality!"

"We cannot, Baron, we used all the faeries!" Donn called out.

Cathal grunted then looked Donn dead in the eyes. "Donn. Go tell Shipyard to arm the crew and bring them up to ready the carronades." Cathal hobbled over quickly and grabbed Donn's arm. "Bring the spear! It may be our last hope."

Donn quickly tore away from the events and slid down the ladder. He had trouble steadying himself on the careening ship as he yelled to Shipyard, "To the top deck. Your baron has called you to ready for close-quarters battle!"

Shipyard threw a cannonball back into its rack and then commanded, "He's coming, boys! Open the weapons locker and see to the business on the upper deck!" The sailors quickly departed from their cannon posts and hustled for swords, grenades, and muskets. Shipyard pulled his shirt over his head and tossed it away. His massive frame, marked like long-used battle armor, had gray chest hair and intimidated any rational would-be opponent. He wiped some tar from a bucket onto his hand and grabbed his sword. Donn watched as he went up the steps to what might become his final battle.

Donn sped to Cathal's main cabin. When he entered, he saw the spear lying on the desk. The bronze head was glowing, causing there to be no dark corner in the room. Donn gripped the wooden shaft, taken from a faerie tree, picked it up, then dashed back to the baron. He watched as Manannán saw the bright spear and began his sluggish movement toward the *Mistress*.

Cathal calmly retrieved a leather pouch from his jacket pocket and pulled a cigar out. He gripped it in his teeth and told Donn, "Take the spear, get to the top of the mast. I want some space between you and the crew."

Donn was glancing above and back to his leader. "Baron, what am I supposed to do with it?"

His eyes were ablaze. "Damn't, wait for my orders. Go quickly if you wish to see your girl again!"

Donn took to the ropes and passed Conri who was trying to keep the sails pointed so they didn't drift away into a seawall. Donn climbed the tall mast, holding the spear in his sash. Donn saw that the demigod's eyes were now filled with the same green lightning as the waves and water streamed from between his lips. As Donn climbed, he could see the sky filling with black storm clouds that rumbled so that the sea shook. Day quickly dissolved into almost night. As Donn climbed, he was engulfed in the powerful glow of the spear.

*****

The old man, eyes still shut, tilted his head back and swung his cane to point out of the cave. "As the warrior bled and crawled through the stone maze, he heard a faint howl echoing like a whisper on the wind. His wolfhound was calling him and he followed, he crawled. On the ninth day, Cu Connor had found the breach out of the depths of Rathcroghan. As he set foot past the cave opening, it collapsed, and with it, the imprisoned Sidhe let out a terrified cry."

*****

The Midnight Mistress

Donn heard Cathal shout up as Manannán grew near, "Hurry with yourself, Donn!"

Donn noticed the clurichaun was shadowing his movements up the mast with far greater ease than himself. A pounding rain began and beat on them. The wind whipped and unsettled his grip with every reach. Although he didn't look to see Manannán in the darkness, he knew he was close by the splashing water of his movement.

Donn pulled himself onto the mast's foretop and held yard ropes tightly to steady himself. The storm's roar and ship's creaking and groaning were deafening. He could see a black shadow, with thick embers like gunshots dotting it, towering before the burning *Perilous*. Donn looked for Cathal and saw him through lightning flashes. He couldn't hear what Cathal was shouting. Donn turned to the clurichaun and said, "Go to the baron and find out his commands!" The clurichaun nodded and quickly made her way to the baron.

The clurichaun raced back to Donn and shouted over the din, "Point the spear at Manannán and declare him thy enemy. Declare him thy enemy…then *strike…him…down!*"

Donn pointed the spear toward the towering shadow and screamed out against the unrelenting wall of rain, "With this spear, I strike you down, my enemy, my people's enemy!" The spear gave off a fluid light that streamed every color. That light filled the immense enclosed bowl in which the battle was taking place. Manannán tried to shield his eyes as if it burned them. His expression radiated terror as his arms seemed pinned back by an invisible force within the light. Donn suddenly felt no fear with the spear positioned above his shoulder. He cast the heavenly weapon toward the sky. It traveled through the black clouds to where it joined the stars as a sparkling sister in the sky. Then it pitched down, seeming to grow in length and speed. It was over Manannán's head, as long as a lightning bolt. The demigod's mouth was open in surprise as he looked above himself. The spear passed down through Manannán's mouth and white blood spit out over his lips. Donn heard a sound, like a tomb closing, emanate from deep beneath the sea. The faerie essence from the earlier cannonade began to pull away parts of the deity until he had totally disappeared. The clouds drifted away. The waves slowly pushed away and vanished, clearing the air and once again revealing the distant horizon. White embers floated about like snow upon the sea. The men were silent as if rescued and secured by divine intervention. The clurichaun ordered, "Summon the spear."

Then Donn spoke loudly, "Return to me." The seafloor shook as the spear broke loose and returned through the water to Donn's outstretched hand, once again tranquil.

The crew chanted, "Feeney Aboo!" Applause was offered up all around the smiling baron. Donn climbed down the mast to see Judge grab Cathal and redirect his attention to the *Perilous*.

"Bring the ship about and head for the *Perilous*!" ordered Cathal.

*****

Luke and his crew had brought the horses to the now-warped main deck, using the miraculously yet intact boom. They were standing upon the ship as best they could as it tipped and threatened to sink. The *Perilous* began to break up and cave in on her port through a tear left by Manannán. The keel had been broken, allowing her to tilt irretrievably to her side. The long boards splintered underfoot which ruthlessly took crewmen down irretrievably into the rumbling sea. Horses and men leapt into the water to escape the vacuum caused by the failing ship. The *Mistress* was swift to aid the distressed crew and load what supplies they could save. Luke knew it was only the ability to swim and stubbornness that granted many of the crew another day of breathing sea air. The horses were saved but a few faces were absent. Luke fought to keep his composure, not because of the loss of his comrades but from the exhilaration and adrenaline fading from clashing with, and vanquishing, a god.

*****

Cathal approached Donn on the busy deck. Many hands found Donn's back in support of his heroism. Cathal took the blade from Donn's trembling hand and spoke, "Tell me more about this girl of yours back in Ireland. I wager a great sum that as long as you're a part of our crew, we'll share whatever charmed persistence you surely possess." Cathal laughed and grabbed the back of Donn's head and briefly pressed it into his shoulder. Cathal then jerked the spear into the air for the crew to see. They shouted in a delight, close to delirium, at the sight of their deliverance from certain doom.

*****

The old man, now interacting more that his story was complete, pressed his hands together and said, "I must offer a warning since you've chosen to live on Achill Island. Once the world was calm and the wind did not exist. When the first creature died, its breath escaped which drifted thereon like a fugitive. Any creature that hasn't accepted God remains a wanderer. When you stand on Croaghaun and a chill runs up you, you have been touched by one of these spirits. The Sluagh, as they are known, will corrupt those that are spiritually weakened so you must always be vigilant. This is not a tame land as you may have already suspected."

Bridget cocked her head and eyed the ground when she offered, "I have seen something. It screams. I hope to never encounter it again."

The old man's eyes widened as his grip tightened upon his staff.

Bridget could see the light changing to a red hue that hit the floor of the cave; she realized the sun was setting. She stood and moved toward the opening. "I must be going now. My parents will be worried." She paused and looked at him. "Will you be all right?"

He gave a raspy laugh and shook his head. "Being all right may be my curse, cailin. A very long time I've been alive. Thank you for accommodating me today, a rare day indeed." He nodded and held up an open hand. "Stay near those that love you. They will protect you when the night is darkest. *Dia duit* and until we meet again."

The Depth of a Soul

Donn felt his mortality more dearly aboard the now-cramped ship and, based on the men's desire to celebrate, thought the rest of the crew must feel the same need to embrace the joy of living. To Donn, the brotherhood among the men seemed like it was only sewn more tightly by the near ruin.

Down in the berth deck, at the mess tables, Donn and the Irish sailors were overindulging. A strange rapid flicker caught Donn's eye. As he turned to focus on the disturbance, he missed what was occurring but the sound of a small animal scurrying along the floor kept him alert. One of the men, as sleepy as he was drunk, loudly noted to the other men that his drinking cup was no longer on the table in front of him. Barrels were quickly moved and the men began to stumble about the room, looking for anything that might explain the mischief. Suddenly a little belch echoed in the chamber. Another sound of a sharp giggle and the men began to converge on an empty fruit sack hanging on a hook. They saw the faerie woman, resting in her makeshift hammock, finishing a cup of rum as big as her chest. One of the sailors tried to grab the cup, and as fast as his hand moved forward, she ran up his arm and finished her drink sitting upon his shoulder. The sailor jerked back and the clurichaun dropped her cup and kept repositioning herself on the hapless sailor until the drunken clurichaun fell off his back but not before she tore the back off his shirt. The rest of the crewmen laughed at the sailor's plight but, regardless, tried to dive after the clurichaun. As quickly as they could move, they couldn't corner the faerie and the pursuit ended when two of the men headbutted each other into an unconscious stupor.

Donn grabbed a mether pot and filled it with mead. "Now come, clurichaun. Share our beer and tell us of yourself as a friend."

Donn watched as the little woman walked over and climbed up on a bench. Her head barely peaked over the table so Donn put a folded blanket over the bench next to her. She adjusted herself upon it before the staring crewmen, then slapped her hat down. Donn took a drink, using both handles, then handed it to her. The crewmen quickly sat down by them. She took the mether and had to reach her arms out wide in order to grab two handles. She carefully took a slurp and nearly tipped back. She reset it on the table, already showing some wear from the previous drinks. The mether was then taken by another crewman.

The little one winced at some smoke next to her. Judge was puffing a pipe and she slurred, "Now what sort of weed might that be? Pass that here." She took the pipe without asking, pulling it from his startled mouth. A couple of the men snickered, and after a long draw, she commented on it with words not intelligible but obviously complimentary. She spoke up, "So ye be friends. All right then." She sped up and bobbed her head side to side. "Clurichaun, leprechaun are names you stupid humans gave us." She pulled out her long pipe from her jacket and then hammered Judge's pipe into hers, dumping the smoldering tobacco. She sipped the stem quickly then added some of her own tobacco before relighting again with a borrowed twisted spill.

Judge looked at his empty pipe with apparent dismay as he retrieved it then asked, "And what might we address you as, little one?"

"Clurichaun is a particularly nasty aspersion upon a faerie, don't y'know? We are a proud ancient race and have been subjugated by many a terrible overlord. You giants can call me Jana."

All the crew quickly agreed with one another that Jana was a good name. Jana watched them, her eyes and face showing bemusement and disgust at the same time. She smiled big at the two sitting next to her and announced, "Fine to hear you like it. I chose it just for all of you."

Donn, surprised, said, "Really?"

She dropped her put-on grin and replied, "Nay."

Donn wiped his face then shot back. "Why are you so angry? You're free from that cave of holy miscreants."

Jana looked perturbed by his words and used an iron nail, large in her hand, to tamp the tobacco. They learned from her that one Ri Corbett, king of the faeries, banished her from court beneath the mounds. "I was traveling the world, a refugee from my own people, no longer allowed to live among my own. I eventually came upon a well of no particular interest. There was a slimy korrigan there and he tricked me down that deep well and so I fell." She pulled a draw and she spoke with the smoke escaping with each word. "That's when the old ones, that korrigan's masters, took me as their slave. I only survived because…" She took a quick round with the mether which streamed down her chin. "I convinced them I was a noble leprechaun capable of accounting for their vast riches."

The evening wore on and the mether spilt upon everyone in the bonding group of merry sailors. Questions continued about Jana's past experiences. She was wobbling on the table with an arm on a sailor's shoulder to hold herself up. She looked into his eyes with a pleading look then said, "Really, a forest to build a home in and be left alone is the common wish of a faerie." She tapped her pipe on her bootheel and then slapped the cheek of the listener, as he was dozing off, so she could continue her point. As the obligatory nodding toward the soulful, and painfully unnecessary, statements filled the cabin, all the men were struggling to keep the mead off their shirts. The men began to go to their hammocks one by one. When Donn finally retired, a welcoming ease subdued his bewilderment of conversing with the mythical companion.

As Donn was climbing into his hammock, Luke strolled by. Jana suddenly ripped a belch, then a series of miserable hiccups, following from a pile of nearby rope. It was certainly a change from the chorus of snores emanating from under the blankets covering exhausted sailors.

Luke looked up and spoke, "Dear Lord in heaven, she found the champagne."

The following day, Donn was glad to see Jana moving freely among them. Although her decision to remain consistently visible was apparent, she was often twitchy in movement. He saw that her confidence was tempered by her past disappointments. Her actions, when committed to a task, were faster than the eye was capable of following. She leapt where she chose, as if height was more a choice than a limit. The intent of destination was claimed upon the instance of her pleasure. When her voice was heard, the tone was always excited and at a tight pitch. However, when Donn spoke to Jana, a sincere respect was shown through the careful attention she granted.

As time went on, the crew seemed to grow comfortable with the unique passenger. Jana carried a black humor and pulled it out, even when an unwelcome moment had come to pass. However, there was something about her need to find levity in the abhorrent that gave her a magnetic appeal. Her villainous giggle was like a flag waving defiantly despite the peril. Her charm seemed to disarm the crew which, Donn knew, was once suspicious of sailing with the little passenger.

Eventually Donn decided he needed to ask a favor of his loyal friend. He met her near her hammock. "Jana, I have some letters I wish Bridget to have. Can you deliver these to her? My burden with them grows since I write to her, yet cruelly, they remain with me."

Jana stood tall with duty but quickly surveyed the room with displeasure. "You humans are ever so afflicted by what the gods have cursed you with and so well you mistake them for blessings."

Donn added, "Then your answer is no? The spit disappears from my mouth when I speak of such a request so I'll say no more."

"I'll take leave to accomplish this for you. Give me the letters."

"Bring her this post that communicates my sentiment. Place in her hands the love that my hands can't press into them tonight."

He dropped the packet of love letters in front of Jana. "Banshee's breath, really," she said as she took in the stack that reached her waist. Jana took out a little pouch and stretched its string, then as she did, the sack grew in size by some magic. She shoved the bound letters into the bag then quickly pulled to tighten the string. The pouch was small enough to again place in her trouser pocket.

Donn, astonished, said, "I've never seen such a bag!"

"It was passed down to me. It was created by the old gods that led the tribes of iron warriors. I think humans called the court Hyperborea. Your ancestors served at their pleasure."

Donn snorted. "Why would my people follow demons?"

"They didn't look at it that way long ago. Besides they gave you all the glory and bounty you ever dreamed of."

Jana walked up onto the deck with Donn following. Donn added, "If she may be in any trouble, you'll—"

"I'll extend my obligation to her as well since it appears your very health depends on it. Your heart, without her near, is poisoning your soul… So then, I'll be off."

Donn offhandedly suggested, "Just a stray thought, but if you're in a trading mood, you can have my ration of whiskey for a month for that bag you have."

Jana laughed. "I'll need to consider that fair offer. Farewell!" Jana turned and hunched over. She looked like a cat looking for a mouse. Then she hopped into the darkness like entering a slit in reality.

Patience and Ghosts

Bridget's patience existed for and by the love she discovered through Donn. Frequently she made her walk down the winding hill paths, past where the hedge stones cease, to the little dock that was there where her love departed. And just as frequently, she left it, still alone.

She was often frustrated and sought out memories of her time with Donn, rifling through past moments and trying to detect why she was so swept away by a herder from Achill. He was unremarkable in an offered description yet he continued to be like that one stone you chose not to throw into the water. She had many occurrences where she might tell him that it would never work out but his magnetism pulled her from those plans. He'd look at her and she felt seen. When he spoke to her, she listened like his elected conscience. Whatever she found, she could tell him it was like confessing to a man unlike any she'd known before. There was a reliability she saw in his eyes, and if she was on a cliff's edge, she could hang from him with no fear of falling. It was a sweet trap she had fallen into, now that the story of her life was as well the story of their life together.

On another one of her many trips to the dock, Bridget spoke to the postboy unloading the currisk. "Pardon me, sir, do you have any correspondence for a Bridget Savage?"

The harried young man was a little frustrated by the interruption but flipped through his mail. "No, I'm very sorry but I do not appear to have a letter intended for that name." He then brushed off his trousers and moved up the dock.

*****

Bridget arrived home and Ella saw her daughter's concern veiled with distance in her eyes. Women were getting married younger than when Ella was a girl and the competition to attain a prime match was ever pressing. Although Ella felt ill of the pressure she had put on her daughter, she also had seen, all too well, the risk of a woman poorly married. A woman had to depend on her husband to protect her assets as well as her family's reputation and future. The responsibility of Bridget's courtship was not taken lightly by Ella.

Ella approached Bridget in the sitting room and flatly said, "Bridget, we need to discuss what your father and I have planned for you. I've lost my patience with melancholy over that boy who has left you here." Her hands rested upon her dress in the most nonthreatening posture possible, although she was fully aware she needed to divert Bridget's distant mind. "Our family cannot afford a scandal. I cannot allow you to destroy yourself. That means you'll conduct yourself and make us proud. You will go to the socials this season and entertain like a proper lady. This must happen because you have a tomorrow you must face and handle, *without* your parents, one day."

Bridget responded, choking on her words, "I don't know why I feel as I do, Mother. I only know that I do. How do I forget my love for him? Could you so easily forget Father if he vanished from you?"

Ella explained, "It is not our allowance as women to choose such defiant wishes. You don't have to forget him. When memory becomes faint, when only the romance remains and the pain of letting go subsides, it can produce precious pearls from those memories that you'll carry with you always."

"I want to wait. I promised him I would! Why would you have me break my promise?" Bridget covered her face with her hands.

"When you met Donn, did you expect to feel as you did? No. Consider that when you doubt you could ever be so happy again. Anyway it isn't your decision." Ella walked away.

Ella had been at a disadvantage when being introduced in the social circles around this new home. She was now determined to enter Bridget into society before her reputation was tarnished. The excuse of her pupilship was wearing thin in conversation.

*****

Bridget had often gone down the hill to the faerie tree to sit. The tree showed no more evidence as a home for faeries than any other tree. It stood as a reminder of those days where she was a part of a magical world she knew only briefly and then vanished. This time, she put a hand on the tree and tucked her face into her elbow then wept into her sleeve. Frigid and passive was her spirit and her conscience was silent. Her skin felt numb, merely a wrap to something now empty. Her days she considered nothing and spent time lost in an inescapable maze of memories. The faerie tree brought her some peace because she could appreciate its ancient indifference to life's comedy and how it remained standing with noble strength.

Bridget was gripping the wet grass in her palms and opened her eyes to the gray clouds above her. She breathed out some cold air slowly to focus and regain her dignity in the face of such disaster. Her hand bumped something, and when she peered over, she spotted a letter she must have nearly sat on. She saw her name in fair hand—the sender was Donn!

She tore open the yellowing envelope with reckless fingers. Her wet hair fell around the paper. She could hardly read only a word at a time as her breath quickened, causing her to cover her mouth. She tucked her hair behind her ear and began. She could feel his hands as she read his prose. She finally could feel his presence again.

She kept the letter a secret, and by some miracle, she found a letter every Sunday she visited the tree. Every day, she nearly tripped over her feet to reach the tree. She thought about spending the night to see if she could catch whoever was leaving the precious correspondence but to risk angering the deliverer, be it faerie or human, was out of the question. She sometimes read them aloud but slowly. She wanted to think of him and where he was when he wrote them. She daydreamed that he spoke them to her in person. Her secret letters were stored in a shoebox in her room like a treasure. With a heart full, she met her daily tasks like she was born anew.

However, before long, Bridget received a proposal to court her from one of her father's business associates, Mr. MacHugh. He was a much older man, a loveless match. They met at the Newport House, of the O'Donel's, which held a country dance. He was like a gray-haired tower beside her. He was an ever-upright structure that loomed over other guests, his face just another cold unmoving stone upon it. Since this tower had eyes, then one could imagine how strange it must feel to be looked upon by one. He stood as a living embodiment of undeclared resolve. As a redeeming grace, he governed himself as a gentleman. That withstanding, he didn't smile or dance so she awkwardly spoke to the older man as she hoped to be pulled away. Thankfully, as a Scotch reel began, she was introduced to a young man that granted her rescue.

Bridget endured many introductions in those evening dance affairs. She was never less interested in dressing up to impress others. Despite her burdening reservations, the music was quite a charming escape from island melancholy. As she danced with each man, she made a study of the look in his eyes and the feel of his hands. Some of the men were gentle and others quite determined for their affection-ate gestures to not go unrequited. Bridget swiftly became a wizard in withdrawing gracefully from would-be suitors. She mastered the act of seeming preoccupied, even when alone, to the extent that she was often not approached for conversation.

That letter of intent had arrived, to her dread. She was sitting in the study and bit her tongue as her parents discussed its worthiness. Ella wasn't satisfied, at least in regard to how early in the season it was to formally court. Bridget at least knew full well that it was her indus-trious talents with fabric that Mr. MacHugh was solely interested in harnessing for his own economy. Her parents amicably declined the proposal much to Bridget's relief.

Meanwhile her father told Bridget that Lady Catherine O'Donel, who had been a fine supporter of his trade, was determined to find suitors for her. Daley mentioned that she had brought up the issue when he was on a visit to see Neal about his clothing orders. When her father told Ella of the offer, she gladly accepted. From then on, the family went along with Daley whenever he visited the O'Donel's.

Bridget enjoyed the spirited Lady Catherine, although her kind words meant to give her confidence in pursuing romance were met with merely a feign of true participation. Catherine had a collection of umbrellas and she'd make gifts of them to her if a certain dress gave her an excuse to do so to "finish the look." How would Lady Catherine feel if she knew of the letters from Donn she read underneath those umbrellas?

*****

My heart beats with purpose. A monster lives inside my chest that wraps its claws around my heart and puts it under stress. My need to fulfill my desires anger the monster, which squeezes evermore; and at night, I may sweat until dawn.

Beneath light from stars in heaven's vault, your night is ever ours. Tell those false suitors that attempt vain advances upon you that you are won. Safe from love of mine you are not and barriers set before foolish heart will fall by my will. Down in the valley of my soul, I add by day the kindling of love's promise and that fire doth consume thee.

The forecasted dance of two spirits, written for mutual destiny, entertains the angels on high.

And so, I've come to know the faerie and travel across the territory of our dreams but rest I not since you are far away.

I think of you so very often. I stagger in silent solitude with a screaming in my head. I consider the fate of never seeing you again within every danger put before me. It's because of you that I'm brave when I'm called on to be. Days go by despite your absence and my need to grab on to you and carry you away, as mine, rages within me.

Our love is filled with what forms the stars above us. As eternal as those stars above, we'll always cast that light which is our own.

The years have passed and raving mad messages are all I can yet offer you. My promises to you—still unfulfilled—are enough to condemn me to banishment.

You're yet so far away from me. I've had to lock my heart that's yours away. The suffering love within that prison waits for prayerful release. Over those high walls, its words can be heard and I commit them to paper as a prisoner's honest confession. Should mercy arrive to liberate, it will be delivered by your dear touch.

The Bruxas

Three years passed. They traded weapons at every port named on the maps and some not on the maps. Cathal obsessively sought information about an ancient sword from Gorias, a mythical kingdom. They had to fool the leadership of a British Indiaman and, later, a full French squadron during forced inspections, convincing them they had no contraband.

With hell's false horizons and sun-spared sky, hope seemed like a distant memory. Donn sought inwardly for strength. Within him was only the stubborn will to which he clung now. He couldn't find a trace of inner guidance at the places in which they found themselves, but still, he boldly moved forward. Void of grace about him, he prayed to keep it within. He often fought to calm his mind and rely on instinct alone. He thought of Achill, the cradle of his soul, and there he focused. It wasn't long before, those sweet strolls on grassy hills of yesterday led him to the girl who brought him his now lost tranquility. He chose a moment in time with her to cling to. Bridget would smile and turn a phrase to fluster his confidence as she always had an ability to disarm him. His eyes were unwelcome messengers in lands empty of her. With so little, he continued on.

They docked at Faro, in the Ria Formosa, on the arid southern coast of Portugal. The Portuguese armada had blockaded the straits of Gibraltar and hunted African pirates for their maritime atrocities. Cathal, Donn, and a small group of his officers went to that shore to alert the authorities that they were merchants and wished safe passage past. Cathal brought an obligatory crate of weapons as a bribe for the garrison of Faro.

Western Europe had flushed its bandits to the far ports of the world but also to Portugal where smuggling was flourishing. The Algarves was now a vibrant benefactor of a new lawless Caribbean that had replaced the Mediterranean by a continent at war, filled with people desperate for all the black market could deliver.

Bandoleros were a constant danger on every road and no merchant dared to travel without funds to bribe for his safe passage. The government turned a blind eye to much of the criminal activities, since those in power relied on the illicit behavior to provide access to essential goods.

The authorities, in their blue uniforms, welcomed the tribute and consistently granted passage. The Portuguese were especially careful since a major naval battle had taken place only months previous to break the blockade. News from afar, never expected, was welcomed by an eager port authority. Cathal and his band were directed to visit a restaurant near the church of Sao Lourenco. Cathal ordered their horses lowered onto the dock, then they mounted. They traveled from Faro, from the safety of their vessel, toward Almancil. They passed colorful Genistas tied to the posts, trees, and fences along the way. They eventually approached a stone walkway under a canopy lining a wall, bracing a hillside. Tables were set under and outside it in the square. The sun was setting behind the hill. A steep dirt slope wove its way above the bay. A sword dance was being performed by a matching group of professional entertainers in the square beside a carved flowing fountain. To Donn, Portugal was like a garden party inviting the world to attend with scattered guests sharing no similar traits. The tavern keeper, noticing the strangers, waved the Irish over. He directed Cathal to Bernardo who, upon first sight, set apprehension into the officers as they strolled over. He was a drunk who somehow still passed as a *sabio* or wise man. Donn overheard Devine whisper to Cathal that the old man seemed down on his luck so he might send them into peril.

Piripiri hung from the frame of the open rafters above them. The wise man was consuming a river fish with potatoes. A man sitting in the far corner was belting out a melancholy song. A dark-haired woman, a sleeve of her floral dress hanging off her shoulder, rested her head on his chest. Donn watched as another woman, with arms extended, danced impassioned, slowly, barefoot. The loud dresses contrasted against the barren landscape and buildings around them.

Bernardo rubbed his potbelly as he nearly stood from his chair, then jerked a finger toward Cathal and declared, "You are O'Ruairc, the Irishman that searches. I have something you search for." He plopped back behind the table then shoved some food in his mouth. The aging wise man grinned with a mouthful, the grease running down his chin. His head nodded in approval, like a mischievous child that knows a secret, his eyes keeping a calculating gaze on the Irish at the table.

Cathal didn't say a word. His concern was evident. He dropped a bag of gold coins on the table. Bernardo reached out to it but Cathal dropped his hand on it quickly. Bernardo ran his glistening fingers through his graying hair while chewing and swallowing. Then leaning back, he coughed a bit.

Bernardo spoke up. "Much more useful than treasury notes, that is, in this madhouse my home has become." His fingers tapped the table before continuing before his impatient guests. "Have some port from Douro. You are in the Algarves which means the center of the world." He sucked his fingers, then wiped them on his tunic. He waved for a bottle to be brought, then continued, "I know of some who can give you the guidance you seek."

Devine, with sweat beaded around his high cheekbones, quickly looked disturbed by Bernardo. "And we pay you for the opportunity to pay another that you assure us knows what we seek?"

Bernardo explained that there was a woman, known as the blue one, who was a seer. As the thick port was consumed and the tallow candle melted upon the table, they listened to the man tell them, and repeat to them, about a lady named Justina. They all agreed to travel that night to visit her who, they were assured, was traveling between cromlechs in a touring ceremony. Their next stop was only just north, near Loule.

Donn noticed that one of the cossiers, who had performed earlier, was agitated by a woman who was dancing and flirting with the men as she passed. Donn quit paying attention to the old man's rambling stories that were in pursuit of a reward.

MacIntyre moved his head around like an owl surveying its surroundings. "What do you see there?"

The cossier sprang up, jerking the woman onto a chair, then venomously shouted at her. None of the patrons appeared willing to subdue the young man's violent jealousy. He slapped her as she gripped the arms of the chair and wailed while trying to cry out excuses for herself. MacIntyre nudged Devine's arm then said, "So the locals have some salt and need to relearn proper behavior."

MacIntyre, Devine, and Donn stood up from their chairs, creaking loudly on the tile, which alerted the establishment. The previously drinking cossiers, who surrounded the dining area, focused altogether on the Irish.

Donn spoke plainly, "We might find ourselves a bit unwelcome to the argument but let's offer an opinion."

MacIntyre pushed his hat back and beamed in amusement. "Devine, have you ever seen the likes? This place is fine full with damn fools ready for a bludgeoning."

"Aye, it's grand beyond words. After we're done with it all, I might spot a souvenir. Everything was bloody broken at our last party…"

The largest cossier approached them, now armed, as were his brethren, with a wooden stick the length of a standing man. He stood inches from Devine and breathed foully upon him. His icy stare demanded Devine back away and ignore the weeping female. Meanwhile the barkeep was moving bottles and glasses away as quickly as he could.

Michael Devine, always the stiff calculator, wasn't amused or intimidated by drunken fools. Michael, without looking, put his small journal back into his leather pouch. He breathed out sharply, and then appeared relaxed, before suddenly headbutting the lout.

The herculean cossier quickly collapsed to the ground, unconscious, his staff loudly bouncing off the tile next to him. Devine's black hair was uncommonly disheveled by his efficient attack. "Oh…shame. I thought that would be more substantial."

A brawl ensued. The Irish were thrown around, using each location as a point to pivot weight and throw a blow against a cossier. Heads crashed against the ground, along with shards of wood from broken furniture. Donn had to let the cossier attack with his staff before countering, otherwise the cossiers were too skilled to approach. MacIntyre was tackled up and over the bar with a staff against his chest but managed to pry the weapon away with him as he flipped over. When he hopped back up, he gave a great swing which landed against three of the pursuers. Devine caught a staff that had landed next to him with his boot, then lunged his weight into a punch that landed against the shocked attacker. The fight continued but then Cathal had a chair thrown at him, a leg slamming against his jaw. Cathal was spun around and away from Bernardo from the impact. He grunted loudly which made the entire crowd falter. Cathal rose—with a rage—and began pulling cossiers toward him for brutal hooks and jabs. Donn saw the baron move toward the fountain. As his shoulders shot blows at men that put them to sleep, he acted as a vacuum, drawing all local challengers. The pressure was now off the rest of the Irish so they plucked Bernardo by the arms and ran to the horses. They then brought Cathal his horse who sidestepped a man whose unbalanced momentum sent him into the water, and with Bernardo behind him, he climbed up. They rode through an archway and away from the valley outcrop around the hill at Bernardo's screeching directions. They slowed as their distance grew from Almancil so they fashioned torches before continuing on.

After what was not even an hour, mounted men were arriving to block them. On a narrow path beside a tall cliff wall, and rocky drop-off, was where they met the strangers. "It's the Seven Children! They are a black cloud from Andalusia. I must go." Bernardo threw himself off Cathal's stallion and disappeared into the darkness like a creature that was looking for a rock under which to hide. The Irish, besides Cathal, tossed their torches to the ground and pulled their rifles from scabbard then held them ready. Cathal hung a pistol down beside his horse's shoulder.

The dozen highwaymen formed a barrier on the path; their drawn pistols were aimed. They seemed rather casual with their threatening actions. A lone rider presented forward from the rest. His long-maned horse pranced in place as he looked upon the Irish in a brash manner. His black vest, worn over a loose white shirt matted down with sweat, had large silver butterflies embroidered upon it. He tilted his head and pulled his wide-brimmed black hat, tied back with a leather strap. The fading light illuminated his bright-red ban-dana, tied to a stubbled bronze neck, and dark brown eyes, burning beneath long eyebrows that sharpened his heavy brow.

With a running Andalusian accent, "*Saludos a todas*! My name is Tragabuches. Thank you so very much for visiting my beautiful kingdom. If you would please grace your host with tribute before you continue on your journey."

Cathal wiped some blood from his lip and spoke up defiantly, "I think not. I don't care for your kingdom's hospitality so I'll bid you farewell and leave all the same."

The bandelero sat, thumbing his hat back, before swinging a black-booted leg over his saddle in a relaxed manner that showed his arrogance. "I'm afraid my Gypsy mother would never allow me to see you off into this wicked night without our protection which requires but a small toll."

The timbre that his throat offered, carrying the last trail's dust, went low when he started, then sped up to the last word as though uncertain of his English. Every wry judgement Tragabuches made past his dandy mustache seemed to be just as much for his own chuckling compatriots as for those he addressed.

Tragabuches gestured a hand to the Irish, emerging from gen-erous sleeve cuffs, and said, "You'll learn that the death of one's heart can occur *long* before the body perishes." He clapped his hands quickly then returned his elbows to rest on his knee. "For you, maybe you die tonight…very far from those you love. That is nothing! Free from the debt of love you owe the other, like my late Reina. May she rest in hell where I sent her and her fool, Amante. Think of those you'll leave behind like true gentlemen." The Gypsy leader stiffened a bit then swung his leg back into its stirrup. "Now even the moon tires of this so delay no more."

Cathal paused a moment. Donn saw that the situation couldn't be more dire and his grip tightened on his weapon, wondering how he might evade the fire while fighting them.

"Very well." Cathal laid his reins down with his free hand and then untied a saddlebag. He tossed it far in front of him and it slapped heavily upon the path.

Tragabuches smiled and signaled, with a small jerk of his chin, for one of the men to retrieve the bag. A bandit dismounted and stiffly moved, saddle-sore by his awkward motion, over to the prize.

Just as he reached the bag, Cathal raised his pistol and sparked the flint. The bag exploded and tore through the man, creating a cloud of smoke, blinding the bandits. The Irish spurred their horses and pushed past the confused bandits up the path. Two of the bandits accidentally fired on each other then let out screams that echoed off the canyon.

They continued traveling into the light of a new day until their fatigue was devastating.

Donn carried a heart as heavy as a desert is dry. His dehydration was corroding his determination. The eventual end of him, and the memories of Bridget, tore at his present. She was not in his world in which he was left to die alone. With all that she was to him left behind, he could never again feel whole. He allowed his reins to drop down to barely commanding Croaghaun who stomped the dirt path forward, away from their past and toward—he feared—his future.

They took a short break. Donn knelt and drank the water from an oasis. It was warm. He smelled something. It was like perfume but it reminded him of Bridget. Like kissing her warm skin. He could remember so clearly the wondrous taste that he wished, when he opened his eyes, that before him would be her face to follow.

Donn was almost too exhausted to get back up. MacIntyre saw him and asked, "How goes your fine morning, boyo?"

"My wandering rose remains distant…and my peace takes residence in a haunted abyss where memories of her gnaw at me."

MacIntyre shook his head and drank a little water from his hat before remounting. "I offer you advice. Stay clear-minded. My father was a steelboy, fighting over land rent, and when I could shoulder a musket, he tried to stop me from joining the United Irishmen. I asked him how he thought it was fair to ask that of me. He told me it was where his passions called him that destroyed his body and spirit. Naturally I ignored him and still defy his predictions."

Calmly Donn responded as he stood, "What's your point, Daniel?"

"You need to stay sharp to survive until you're finally where you wish to be. I forgot to ask myself what I wanted in life so my arse was soon farming in the Caribbean." MacIntyre spurred his horse on.

Donn continued in the treacherous heat with the others. He imagined the lanterns across the shores of Achill, in Slievemore, Dooagh, and atop the cliffside outposts. Each one acted as a light-house, guiding him home. He had known only one path in life—protecting the cattle and one day taking over his father's business, days filled with livestock on lonely green hills and rocky shores to meet his every day. Now a second door had opened to him. He needed to rush into a future with her where she was his, resting his head on her bosom when he tired, enjoying her company and her warm smiling face at every meal—a companion in bed to conquer the cold nights. Now that he knew such paradise, he wanted it, needed it. His original path now had need of Bridget and he carried her with him wherever he was now led.

The Irish were covered in a sheet of white dirt from the heat bonding the sweaty filth on them. They finally made camp in a patch of forest which they believed to be just south of Loule. They had tied up their horses on some high ground with fair forage while they ate what they had in their saddlebags. It was still day but all fell asleep soon after laying their heads upon their saddles.

The men were startled awake by the cracking of sticks. They saw three women at their camp, now under a full moon. One was adding wood to the fire, another was rubbing something wet on a smoothed-bark tree, making strange markings. The third was silently meditating, kneeling in front of the fire. Donn saw they had several wool blankets that doubled as makeshift bags, on the ground, with glasses and clay bowls set about.

Cathal spoke pointedly as he stood, "Who shall I welcome to our camp?" The companions stood, awaiting Cathal to tell them how to react to the intruders. Donn's hands shook a bit, anticipating a struggle.

The kneeling woman opened her eyes. Her billowy red blouse piled over a black corset. She raised her hands up, her silver arm jewelry sliding down her narrow pale arms, and warmed them by the campfire. She smiled and calmly replied, "I believe Bernardo introduced me to you already." Her tongue rolled a part of Bernardo's name, giving a wicked cadence to the declaration.

Cathal squinted, brushing leaves off his trousers. "Justina? How did you come to find us?"

The intense woman peered up at Cathal with a drawn gaze. "I can sense when another is looking for me. How might I assist you in your journey?"

She stood and went to her blanket, covered with vials and a book. Another woman moved over to her and placed a bowl in front of her with a prepared paste within it. Justina added, "This is Aphra, and over there is Arria. We worship at the stones of all Lusitania, and last was Valverde, which was *very* empowering. Perhaps we can find the answers you seek." The two that assisted Justina wore red knit head scarves over their hair; Donn thought them perhaps sisters. Both her followers nodded and smiled at the Irish when they were addressed. Donn thought it odd—three women traveling alone in a land that was decidedly dangerous, even for them.

MacIntyre strolled around while keeping one eye on the women. He kept a sly smile as he looked at the ground and circled their resting spot. He came back to Cathal and said, "They left no tracks coming here, Baron."

Cathal pulled a cigar out from his jacket, hung his head, and responded secretly, "So? It's dark."

MacIntyre began to move away and repeated, "No tracks at all." Cathal raised a brow a moment then breathed through his teeth which Donn thought indicated an interest in the mystery.

Cathal walked over to the fire and picked up a burning stick to light his cigar. "How did you lovely ladies come to have such talents?" Cathal puffed and stared at Justina.

"We are known as *bruxas* but it's a crude name for what we are." She waved a hand around. "We simply look to nature for answers that guide us." Her eyes were disarming, and Cathal seemed distant in mind, so Donn was, at once, wondering if he should have one hand on his sword. Devine was standing beside and behind Cathal as a cautious sentinel.

Devine impertinently asked, "What might the cost be for the information we seek?"

Justina began using a pestle to stir some paste. "That will be decided after the act is done. However, it's never more than you have to give. Now if you please, sit in a circle around the fire and we'll begin after I've finished my preparations."

Cathal looked at the men, revealing his astonishment but did nod to have them sit. Donn obeyed and, although out of his depth, relied on his superiors to keep them safe.

Justina spoke up. "Drink with us in ceremony. The ritual will begin and then I'll ask your questions of the spirits that hear us." She began to rub the paste on the end of the handle of a short broom with a woven brush of weeds tied to the other end. The men each passed the golden cup and sipped from it. Donn thought it tasted bitter and it burned his tongue.

"Do you Irishmen recognize it?" said Justina, letting out a little laugh.

They locked eyes on the goblet and saw a charioteer engraved upon it. None of them spoke up about it though and were patient to listen on. Donn's will was becoming detached from his authority and he felt that he acted on impulses not his own.

Justina announced, "That is the cup of Cormac Cas. That great chieftain from the mountainous north who invaded your homeland… It pours truth from within it. Philip the fourth gave it to my line so his son would be spared."

Donn thought, *Spared from what?*

The sisters began to whisper prayers while Justina tossed her dress over the broom. "Now I require your silence."

Justina mounted the broom, the brush acting as a base which she could lean against. She began to gyrate and moan. The men looked at Cathal with obvious concern. Cathal was simply staring into Justina's eyes. She rubbed her body and spoke in hushed words the Irish couldn't make out. The broom nearly hopped from the shaking body impaled upon it. After a minute, the woman appeared flush with ecstasy so she removed the broom and knelt down again by the fire. Trembling, she poured out what was left in the cup and placed it back down.

Justina, whose eyes were closed, breathed in the smoke from the fire deeply, then asked, "What is it you seek?"

Donn heard her voice but the sound seemed to be racing around in the air.

Cathal asked, "Where can we find the Sword of Nuada?"

"Who asks?" Her words were like vapors escaping from a cave.

"Cathal O'Ruairc."

The three women continued to exult and genuflect as they manipulated the heat from the flames.

A breeze gently blew the leaves in a circle around them. Cathal's cigar went out in his grip, but like the rest of the Irish, he was spellbound by the event.

"O'Ruairc. The wandering knight. You can call me Diabo." Justina beamed with a joyous expression upon her face, her voice sounding like it emanated from a deep cellar. She disturbingly licked her lips as her toothy smile expanded further than should be humanly possible. "Go to Derne and find Mustafa Bey. He has the information you seek. I will tell Mustafa you will come."

Cathal asked quickly, "Why can you not tell us where the sword is?"

Diabo hissed. "Where it is, I cannot see. A cost in blood will continue to be extracted. Demanded now." She shook hard and her eyes opened but her eyes were pitch-black. "By me!"

The light of the unholy fire lit the faces of the *bruxes* in their trance. In the flickering light from the flames, the officers could see the women suddenly turn into creatures of demonic horror then quickly back again to their human forms. Justina moved past the bonfire toward the Irish. Donn could see the inferno reflecting off her eyes and, mesmerized, he remained, never really realizing those flames were now behind her. Her dark hair, free on her shoulders, gently lifted at its ends with the breeze. She moved toward Cathal. Donn couldn't react to protect him, try as he might to move a finger. His mind filled with terror as his vision distorted. Aphra and Arria continued their praying to the bonfire, undulating their bodies and raising their hands up to the sky. Justina put her face inches from Cathal's face. Donn could see the fire slither across the ground. Justina leaned in and then put her hands on both his cheeks and breathed in quickly. Cathal collapsed forward, unconscious. She erected herself and moved toward each of the men as the ground continued to flood with fire, and then the *bruxes* themselves appeared to be bathing in the inferno. Donn was the last that Justina approached and she looked deep in his eyes. She smiled and then Donn collapsed, his vision going dark.

*****

Meanwhile the stallions were stirring, the only witnesses to the nightmare befalling their sworn. Croaghaun looked at the three kings, also showing that their blood was up. Croaghaun saw the glint of Justina's curved dagger pulled and so he snapped the reins from the tree with a sharp jerk of his head. Red Crow, Mug, and Rudraige followed suit and chased Croaghaun down into the valley. The *bruxas* didn't hear the thundering hooves that were approaching. Justina, offering the dagger up to be cursed, was facing the bonfire, now the shape of a spinning oval frame. All three *bruxas* began making animal sounds that escaped their parted lips like resident familiars in rapture. The spinning frame sped to a solid shape whereupon a one-eyed specter, draped in a toga, appeared within, as a sitting audience, on a throne built with the rotting bodies of the living dead. The tree leaves and branches bent up, stuck in an updraft from the intense heat.

As Justina turned toward Cathal, her eyes rolled back. She put her hands above her head, gripping the blade with both hands. Then suddenly, she was slammed into by a galloping white comet of fury and she sailed into the air until her bones cracked as she rolled awkwardly into the brush. The dagger dropped to the ground, and as it landed, the fearsome spectator bellowed in anger before disappearing into the now-dissipating fire. Aphra and Arria wailed and held their heads like children that had been abandoned. Moments later, the horses trampled the wretched women who were nearly oblivious to their devastation under the hooves. Mug flung Arria into the fire and Red Crow crushed Aphra's skull, the contents of her cranium splattering in all directions. Croaghaun and Rudraige took turns dancing on Justina until her bloody dress appeared flattened and empty. Breathing deeply, the horses went to their sleeping knights. The horses stood watch until daybreak when the officers began to awaken.

*****

Cathal had a lit cigar resting near his leg. The smoke swirled around his naked arm, caressing his wrapped tattoos. He appeared aged, missing his wry smile. As much skin was smudged in red dirt as was visible. The eviscerated bodies sent ash into the air that settled about the area. Donn saw Cathal watching the evil burn to nothing as he sweated from the scalding heat. Donn could sense Cathal's anger that recentered at the moment to his presence and not the dead witches. Donn didn't speak to Cathal but he considered it. He felt a need to calm him in case he felt responsible for their near demise. However, the sun was overhead and they were all aware of the treacherous journey they had ahead of them so there was no time for conversation. He watched Cathal pick up the scuffed goblet from the turf that claimed so much mischief within villainous fingers. Cathal poured some wine into it. Donn finally acted on his impulses with, "Baron, whose truth should we seek to gain here now?"

Cathal glanced over, with a solid expression of resignation, then drank the cup's contents. "I have questions for myself." He turned and walked toward his belongings, past some exploring black pigs.

Perhaps it was the night they endured but Donn felt quite traumatized. He had spent hours at a time writing letters to tell Bridget of the depths of his love for her. The energy she gave him in his pursuit of her should have invigorated him. Now he kept seeing Justina's face and could not banish that nightmare painted on his mind's canvas. When he struggled to think of Bridget, his feelings were corrupted with a dark passion, without tenderness. Bridget was his destiny, and without her, he would be cast off into the deep oblivion. There, with that bright ember of her within him, he quit despairing; although she became more a specter of faith than a physical presence.

His banished thoughts that considered a Bridget who could reside within another's arms, although he felt like malevolent spirits attacked his soul. He fell into an abyss whenever left alone to consider his darling. Doubt and mystery invaded his mind with an ever-greater degree between the last moment and the next. His burden was realized every morning he woke up without her and carried forward until nightfall's sweet release. Into such a void his mind ventured now such that he disoriented himself in fever. His burden of metanoia was a curse brought by Eros. He envisioned an unfavoring spiritual prytany, sitting now, where all past judgement on love's first kiss had been deemed madness. They might ridicule him since they would know full well an untempered notion of love easily fatigues, then breaks the romance when sustenance is denied.

*****

In my mind, I survive troubles like a man running down a hallway of doors—a door leading to distractions of random wild thoughts. I kick open doors trying to find peace. Thoughts that should fill a clown's mind drown mine in defense of my terrified heart.

Megaera, the fury, visits me every night. Tirelessly she casts the torment of jealous rage within me. She does it with a whisper, like an invasion, to my ear. However, this is not the truth. I relentlessly haunt myself whenever peace might have otherwise been found.

The Voyage to North Africa

Cathal announced to the crew that they would sail to Derne to meet with the governor, Mustafa Bey. Donn was called into the captain's quarters to set out appropriate maps to chart the voyage. Donn looked up as Luke and Devine entered the room. Their boots rapped on the wood boards as they walked toward the desk.

Cathal proclaimed, "Gentleman! After a long time, this day has finally arrived. The path is clear."

The daylight, dim in the cabin, was adequate only enough to barely see the maps on the desk. Cathal had his back to the light and his fists firmly fixed on the table as he leaned above the map.

Luke waved his hand over the table and queried, "So then we fetch this sword, then that is that?"

Cathal nodded and grinned. "That may be quite the errand but yes."

Luke slap-brushed his hat twice quickly while Devine kept still. "Then to Derne we go." Luke grimaced and added, "Let's not stay long, my skull isn't suited for a pirate's paperweight."

Cathal acknowledged. "Just see that those rascals, with their toy boats, don't take our *Mistress* while I'm ashore."

Luke nodded, slapped Devine's shoulder, and quipped, "Come, Michael, let's see if we can convince Kennedy that Derne is in county Cork."

Donn waited for a quiet moment after the men left then asked Cathal, "How do you know to trust these things, these statements you decide are clues?"

"Over the many years we've crisscrossed these waters, I've found that in every port, there exists nomads and secret societies always willing to sell information, that being all they have at times to survive. It is slow to come by once announced to various parties but that which one seeks, if man has ever been graced by its knowledge, will find itself sold as any other commodity. As for the information's reliability, you can tell the truth in it by where it may lead you. For them to construct an effective lie would mean they could guess the design of a building having only seen the door, the knowledge is so specialized. Anyway I've always had a luck about where to go, like standing in a valley filled with a distant music, I have always been able to source it."

Later that night, Donn wrote to Bridget. He felt closer to her that way, although he worried she'd begin to transform into the abstract after too much time away.

> *I crave your scent. I swear I catch it in the breeze at times and it drives my senses wild. At night, left again in darkness to think of you, without you, I feel every beat of my heart and it weeps over your absence. Sometimes I'll say your name in whimsical hope to hear you respond, even if only I hear an illusion my mind has created. It's like living as a creature that discovers it must have a new sustenance to survive or, at least, something that was born and is in agony.*

Luke wandered over and noticed Donn writing in his journal at that late hour.

"Oh! Stricken down with love and so young. What a pity." Luke took a sip of some champagne.

Donn was perturbed by the intrusion. He saw Luke less sober these days since losing the *Perilous* nor could he remember him sleeping.

"How so? Wait, I'm not sure if—"

Donn was abruptly cut off by Luke. "Leaping into a burn pit with all eager haste! Full banners flying. Huzzah! Huzzah!"

Donn leaned forward and pointed at Luke. "You may mock me, sir, but understand me you do not."

Luke's eyes narrowed and he spoke with false surprise in his voice. "Dost thine love's price come so cheaply? Dare and show me your secrets, Donn, for I am but your pupil at this table." Luke changed to a more serious tone and continued, "When you break from your fervent romance, perhaps you'll consider the consequences as much as the delight. You've staked yourself with purpose that unravels at the whims of young love. You say you need to reclaim the family land yet you need someone else to make you reach for it. The fire in you could lose its fuel the moment the girl wakes up too many times in a house without you in it then moves on from you." Luke smiled at the lack of response. "So her heart is meant only for you? Well, how *lucky* you must feel… Did her poor heart break when you waved goodbye?"

"She understood the need for my absence." Donn tensed his jaw and gritted his teeth, reminding himself of who spoke to him.

Luke snapped to life and leaned his neck in toward Donn. "Oh, of course, all girls understand the needs of men to go to sea! She hasn't a better thing to do but wait on you, I'm sure… Right then."

Donn was growing tired of wading through the unwelcome ridicule so he responded, "Spoken like someone who made the same promises to another?"

Luke rounded his head back around to his drink and widened his eyes. "I know no such hypocrisy. I only admire your certainty that your love waits on your word of return alone. A word from a man whose first action was to leave her to her own devices on a dreary island. Yes, I'm sure she's quite content…" Luke's grin took a stretch and he looked again at Donn.

Donn stared at Luke grimly and put his cup down.

Luke burst out a laugh and slapped Donn's back. "Calm, my brave friend! You'll return to your destined bedfellow soon enough, on a chariot of gold, I'm certain." Luke rose from his chair carefully and dropped weight on each step.

Donn was rubbing the side of his brow and proclaimed, "I trust you have a glorious return of your own planned out?"

Luke stopped and turned his head a bit and solemnly said, "We all do, boy. Experience has taught me the glory doesn't pay the debt you'll find you owe."

The lamp above the table swayed back and forth and the playful shadows would alternately mask and show a broken set of images. Donn gripped his cup and contemplated quietly in anger. He felt attacked and choked on words that ranged from "How do they get by without you in hell?" and "What business is it of yours?"

Luke explained quickly during that awkward silence from Donn. "Lord Castlereagh would have had our necks stretched if it weren't for the Marquess of Downshire being sympathetic. He claimed we were simply caught up in the passions of the times and it would be better to bake our disloyal nature out of us in the West Indies. It was long enough, I suppose. It did put a change in us." Luke looked at Donn with sympathy. "She's yours today. I'm sure she is." Luke turned away, grumbling, then jestingly added, "Anyway I'm tired so I'll leave you now. Please stop bothering me for advice, I'm very busy, you understand." As Luke began to step away, Donn spoke up which stopped him.

"I've spent my life looking after a home that I've always known to be owned by a stranger… No, not always. There was a time when I knew *I* belonged there like the animals that run across it in constant bemusement. That grass, under that sky, was my family's. Then one day, I was out wrestling with my dog in the mud by our well. I saw two riders come to the house, and when they left, I entered to find my father sitting holding a paper. He was motionless and his eyes were cast away. He explained we would have to sell more of our livestock in order to stay on the land. Apparently rents had gone up, and the world seemed fragile to me then." Donn squinted and paused while Luke listened patiently. Donn looked around and over at Luke. "So much mystery throughout what the candlelight barely exposes while the darkness that ruled before left no question."

"You wish your family never to have to endure the hardship of having their fate so terribly dictated by another. You're on the right ship, Donn. I understand you better now." Luke breathed out and shook his head. "You ask if I regret…not going back and flaming the countryside with the torch of rebellion again. I burn with guilt so that my nostrils are filled with sulfur these many years. However, I can't pretend longer that victory over the occupiers is a matter of patriotism and determination. Fuck it is. I've met so many. All the pride the Irish race can offer has presented itself to my witness. We all failed and bitter excuses took the place of unity and perseverance. You see, our home has become a place where dreams are created merely to torment."

"I beg your pardon, Captain. You sound like a man that has lost hope yet you are here."

Luke was consuming his fifth cup since the forgotten four other drinks. Donn was not far behind in his intoxication. Donn tried to focus on the conversation, to not let Luke have the upper hand.

Luke spat out with squinted eyes, "The life pursuit of Eros is the trumpeting of wastrels as an attempt to excuse the abandonment of their responsibilities. 'Love conquers all' is a notion that mollifies the hopeless fool. All love is tragic and poison to a sound mind. This I know!"

Donn spoke through his teeth. "You speak of love from the same rostrum of the cowards that mock injured volunteer soldiers returning from war, especially where glory was pursued. How would one spend his life? The dead are safe since they have nothing left to chance."

The conversation was abruptly interrupted as Cathal arrived and ordered Donn to help him clear a space in the hull for the recent supplies they had brought on.

The storeroom was empty, except for one. Conri sharpened the edge of his hatchet with a smooth stone. Quiet, he stroked the steel. He sat in the darkest corner of the room where his weapon caught just enough light to be seen.

Cathal was tightly securing the tie to a net rope that covered some light boxes of supplies to the wall. He looked over as Donn was listening to Conri's captivating blade maintenance. Cathal spoke in a hushed form between breaths. "She was taken from him. His daughter."

Donn glanced over at Conri in amazement. "Is the fabric he carries from his daughter? Who took her? Especially from him?" Donn helped heave bags filled with flour to the other wall.

"While she was still a babe, rocking in a cradle, she suddenly grew ill. Apparently his wife couldn't handle the loss so she disappeared one day. Shortly after that, we met him drunkenly brawling himself into jail on a regular occurrence. One of the Fiann happened to be his cellmate, and upon hearing his mad tale of chasing a faerie through the woods that kidnapped his child, he was invited to join us. It was the same fool who chose to fight him that day."

"What crewman brought him to you?"

Suddenly the sharpening stopped and Conri spoke, "He keeps his lousy ideas inside his bicorne." Donn saw blood dripping beneath the fingers after he stood. With a parting glance, Conri left the room.

Donn asked Cathal, "He may have nowhere else to go but what does a man with his story still hope to find?"

Cathal shook his head a bit and said declaratively, "Probably that damn faerie."

"Do you think I offended him? Those can't be memories he wants traded around."

"No. Sail long enough with us and you'll know *everyone's* particular stink. It's a brotherhood by force, if no longer by choice. Besides it's all he thinks about when not spilling blood to smother the heartache."

The Pirates of Derne

April 27, 1805

Donn recalled a story of the ice breaking at Achill Bay when the English bombarded the stronghold of O'Malley's husband. The ships were torn apart as hopeless captives of the dock. Men rushed onto the ice on horseback in vain hope to reach the enemy ships that sailed alongside the ice, firing cannons while the Irish were anchored. The bloated bodies of kinsman that froze in the water were found along the shore all the next spring—cruel constant reminders of a black day. The new ships that were built were named in honor of those who attempted a defense of the docks. Donn looked over at the good fortune of these African pirates having an ice-free port. As they arrived close to dock, he saw a few American ships anchored but that was the only peculiar display in the busy trading hub, out among the Egyptian merchant ships filling their hulls with honey and other goods. It was a relief to spot American flags since nearly all of Europe was at war.

With his head high, Cathal donned his best dress uniform on of green and gold, wrapped at the waist with a blue sash that draped over a leg. He looked out next to Donn and said, "Poor Yusuf must be still having trouble with his brother Hemet and the American Navy." Cathal grinned. "I wonder if he has tired of these blockades during this wonderful time to be a pirate." Donn knew that during a European war, it was worth a fine coin to be a smuggler of goods.

The ancient port was lined with small fast-attack vessels in slotted docks. Slave-powered oars and a large mast made them highly effective at attacking prey. The lightly armed ships transported overwhelming mobs of dangerous pirates to board prey vessels. The sails were still but appeared to bend and wave in the heat that hung like a treacherous cloud above the water.

Donn thought the long walls of the city were impressive. Derne reflected the color of the vast desert surrounding it against the seas. Also, a high gun tower looked over the harbor that cast a guardian's shadow across the city. These were dangerous waters for some but a welcome site for those that would otherwise only see more of the Barca Desert to the east.

After they docked and carefully secured the ship, Cathal spoke to the crew. "I'll speak to the harbormaster." Donn watched as Cathal conversed with a short fat man with a crooked smile who looked harried. When Cathal returned to the ship, he shouted out for Shipyard, knights, and his personal bodyguard to join him and for the rest to stay on the ship helmed by Luke. As the men were departing the vessel, Judge shouted out to them, "A day's walk from the devil is still under his shadow. Best keep sober and your wits about you!"

Donn stood next to Cathal and shielded his eyes while looking at the foreign city. He looked over at Cathal and directly asked, "So how well do you know the bey?"

"I know him through his followers on the Balearic Islands. We'd provide safe transport past the watchtowers on Dragonera to Port d'Andratx so their illicit business could be held with corrupt Spanish officials." Cathal smiled and continued to gesture to his men on the busy dock. Cathal had the horses lowered down so that they could ride into the town impressively. After an hour, the group was assembled. Cathal slapped Donn's shoulder, then mounted his horse and said, "Welcome to the lands of the Karamanli! Now let's announce our presence."

Donn noticed, outside the walls, nomads on camels bringing in goods of all sorts. As they rode, Cathal told Donn that the tribal people received money from the merchants for the products from distant trade sites. Along with their families, from wadi to outpost, they traveled across North Africa as a means to survive. Donn saw that some had frightful haircuts grown to resemble a small bush. They passed many recessed images—mihrabs—that were inlaid with beautiful religious depictions. It seemed as though every time he looked to the right, he'd see another one. Donn was in wonder of how a people could live in such an arid land. He never felt so far from home than when he set foot on this place where land and water were so divorced.

They arrived at a stable, just inside the entrance and put in their mounts for fresh feed and rest on dry land. The steady breathing and stomping from Barb stallions filled their ears. Their horses, large by North African standards, were excited and difficult for the help to pull into stalls. Cathal decided to keep his horse.

Cathal looked over as Donn left the stable and offered an explanation for his mount. "A true Irish visit isn't complete without the spectacle. The same looks best on a storybook page framed by a wolfhound." More of his crew came about so he leaned down from his horse as if to share a secret. "To leave out the exhibitionism is to dishonor the legend we're creating." With a fast wink, Cathal then clicked his mouth to ride forward.

The shipmen formed in a V around Cathal as they pushed through the tightly fit crowd. Escorting Cathal safely proved to be stressful since a clear path was impossible. Donn spotted a young boy who was like a metal spring that resisted the ground. The bronze boy, who reached barely waist-height, was excited and looked as if he had seen a conquering hero in that narrow and dirty ancient alley. The shoeless boy imitated marching alongside the crew with gusto. Donn was flattered by the boy's wide-eyed admiration so he gave him the blue sash that was around his waist. The child jumped with glee and his friends ran over to celebrate his encounter. Donn winked at them as he continued on. He also noticed the blacks that were in heavy shackles behind Moorish captors on tall camels. Wherever they went, he painfully thought, they were to always find men oppressing other men. Cathal kept a steady pace on his horse and they had to run, at times, to keep flank with him. They immediately entered a maze of stone buildings where the wind was trapped inside and ceased to move. They pushed past mobs of people in furious activity pursuing local industry. Donn saw Cathal looking down on him. He realized, as he was soaking up the surroundings, the anxiety he felt must have been noticeable. He remarked up to Cathal, "Such a strange place this is. Is the world upside down if we sail any further?"

Cathal smiled. "If you look a little closer, you'll find things are much familiar just so."

At a building of no particular design to set itself apart, squeezed into all the rest against the edge of town, was an undistinguished almost-hidden café. Bare-chested warriors with tremendous blades, wrapped with cord at the pommel, were posted at every doorway. Where the foreign merchants and diplomats escaped from the natives and hustle of this town, they drank and smoked in shaded seclusion while watching the ocean traffic on the north open wall. Donn was relieved to have left the busy street, the breeze and quiet allowing him to collect his wits. The tiled blue floor was ugly and cracked but the service was nearly overwhelming with respect shown for the coins. He imagined that people could forget they were surrounded by the busy marketplace outside. The ruler's flags were draped over the establishment. It was a horizontally striped flag with a cool green center, flanked first by red, then flanked again by blue.

Cathal was beckoned by a small trio of lavishly dressed men with long groomed beards. The baron moved near the front of the café where the governor and his entourage were seated; the others stayed by the entrance. Cathal sat beneath a hanging basket of red flowers and took a cup from a servant. The humble servant poured black steaming coffee from a long copper spout. Donn never felt more like he was a ship in unknown waters. Then another servant came over at a fast walk toward Donn and the crew. He said he was the bey's servant and claimed that all the honored guest's men were welcome for entertainment at the foreign tavern down the street. He quickly explained to head west toward the governor's palace and they would find it. The polished servant offered to lead them. Cathal waved an affirmation so Donn and the rest left Cathal behind with the bey's men, following the servant.

Surprisingly for Donn, he discovered that even though drinking was taboo in Muslim territories, the drinking establishments here never closed so off they went. With the men heading slowly to the bar, Donn wandered underneath a red-draped awning to explore a small mercantile, a most pathetic workshop overseen by a bald man with a dead leg. He carved in the back and didn't seem to particularly like to stand. Grim was he and he kept his true focus distant. Even his eyes were devoted only to his craft. He was noticeably pale, a standout among the population. His hands were his only truly animated and life-filled implements. Donn looked about the shop and saw what appeared to be Hebrew ornamentation. The man had a barrel of soap of different colors and scents. He came over and started speaking which was completely lost on Donn. He pointed at a woman in a portrait, then the soap, and shook his head up and down. Donn nodded in agreement, wondering if the old man knew he was thinking of Bridget. The doddering man handed him a bright-white bar with a shaky hand and brought him to his desk. Donn made the purchase and dropped the odd soap into his pocket.

Donn arrived to find that every sailor's cup had been well-filled and not a lip was dry. A fastidious server, whose head only reached their shoulders, was challenged to keep hold of a glass-serving vessel while being jerked around to meet requests for more wine. The entire room, grand as a cathedral, was plated in blue-gray marble which caught the lamp lighting. Copper covered the seams of the tile. There were four rectangular pools of still water surrounding the center floor. The tranquil pools, with floating plants topped with crimson flowers, were beneath hammered copper bowls hanging from the ceiling with burning elements within. The inner roof was recessed and paneless, grid-pattern windows let in fresh air and moonlight. A mural of blue tile above them depicted a migration across the sea from a land of centaurs. There were no tables but tasseled pillows strewn about over silken rugs. In the center of the rugs were terracotta oil lamps giving circular light beams below and around them. Musicians, some with long stringed instruments and others with drums, took places between the guests. Rough-looking men with rifles and curved swords were in the corners of the room, standing in complete silence.

A man called the Battus had been brought over to meet with the bey's man, and soon after, he announced to the crew, "Come, sit." The curly haired and flat-faced manager waved in different directions like a composer. Servants rushed at each wave of the Battus's hand. The crew noticed barefoot women pour through the back of the building inside, lining the front of the recessed square. They started forward in their translucent silks that clung to their intimates, little bells hanging from their ankles and wrists.

The crew dispersed among the floor seating and Donn walked to the seating closest to the entrance. He sat and looked again at the mural that reminded him of the Greek stories he learned back at the hedge schools. Three women waited on his group of six, seated upon a decorative rug. Each of the women shared little similarity besides costume. Their features portrayed exotic bloodlines and were certainly handpicked as performers and servants to excite the guest's imagination. The ladies that weren't close to a patron danced seductively to the sound of a tambourine. Donn noticed the copper bowls, some containing seasoned rice, others with broths of fish or mutton, being set out in front of the men. Then long covered trays were set out and the lids were swiftly lifted to reveal delicacies of glazed fruits and desserts. Clay goblets were served full of dark-red wine. Desserts were greedily consumed and wine poured into the men like a ceaseless waterfall. Donn was certain that this was the greatest breakfast the men had ever encountered; their usual ration at sea was no match.

Donn noticed that the eyes of the men rarely left the seductresses that commanded the center of the room. The hypnotic flames leapt in time with their quick hand gestures. A line of women covered a wall and turned toward it. They wore brightly colored costumes. They bent over while flipping their skirts up over their backs to reveal their naked painted bottoms. The petticoats were colored to look like bright petals. The drums in the back beat a rhythm to the girls' hip motions, suggesting flowers eager to be pollinated. The men's focus was transfixed as the entertainers split up into the crowd, now singling out crew members. Shipyard had a small girl enamored with him and it was as if the rest of the room didn't exist to them.

They stared into each other's eyes as if madly in love. She affectionately rubbed his salt-and-pepper cheeks.

Donn saw that Devine was busy eating gluttonously, rarely looked up. He seemed the least interested in acquiring a bouquet of flowers for himself.

Conri was speaking intimately with a woman in a long gold dress who couldn't possibly have understood him. How she evoked sudden confidence and comfort in him left Donn breathless to witness. Conri held her ebony hand and later placed it on his cheek. She would not go away from him and none would dare try to remove her. Donn could see them as Conri looked as though he was confessing passion to a true love and she was accommodating him. She drew so close that her long curly hair curtained most of their conversation from view.

Donn saw that mischievous MacIntyre was drinking his fill and wandering the room to laugh with his brother crewmates. The Ulsterman couldn't help himself and the inevitable occurred as he plucked a violin abruptly away from a shocked musician's hand. Some of the crew laughed in anticipation. Donn noticed that Shipyard was feeding his newfound darling which made him concerned if he wouldn't try and keep her. MacIntyre put the unresined bow to the violin and let moments pass as the crowd fell into silence by the drunken man's absurd actions. The bar management seemed willing to allow the display to occur as all eyes fell on the dramatic Irishman. He began to play a quick reel and sang loud, enough for the street to hear him, with an echo that slammed off the walls:

> There was an old widow from Donaghadee
> And in her back garden, a row of plumb
> trees.
> But the widow's big dog was tied to its roots
> And the town ladies, they wore a nip of its
> tooth.
> Too-ra-loo, too-ra-lee.
> Oh, it's six miles from Bangor to
> Donaghadee.

The men began to sing along. Wine was spilt and laughter exchanged.

> So she bought a wee horse and she went thru' the town
> Selling apples and oranges all the way round.
> And she'd crack her old whip and sit twisting her thumbs
> 'Till the town folk were shy of her garden and plums
> Too-ra-loo, too-ra-lee.
> Oh it's six miles from Bangor to Donaghadee.

Now all the bar was raising cups and helping with the next verses.

> But one day, a ship sailed in close to the quay.
> It had run from a voyage far away on the sea.
> The poor half-starved sailors, they made for the shore
> And dropped like the devil on the old widow's door.
> Too-ra-loo, too-ra-lee.
> Oh it's six miles from Bangor to Donaghadee.

All the women began to sway to his exciting song and the men enthusiastically clapped in unison.

> She gave them some soup and she gave them some tea.
> She dry baked the oaten as quick as could be.
> A quart of fine whiskey as they picked up the crumbs.
> Then from her back garden, she brought in her plums.
> Too-ra-loo, too-ra-lee.
> Oh, it's six miles from Bangor to Donaghadee.

MacIntyre began moving around the room while performing. Donn began to realize that the Battus left and there seemed to be more guards in the back than he remembered.

> They ate all those plums till their tummies were sore.
> In anger the skipper made for the back door.
> He cursed and he raved and he tore up the root,
> And a hundred bright sovereigns, he picked up as loot.
> Too-ra-loo, too-ra-lee.
> Oh, it's six miles from Bangor to Donaghadee.

MacIntyre was even joined by the other musicians for the final chorus.

> And now all you listeners, take warning from me.
> I sailed round the world and on many a sea.
> Many plums I have sampled as ripe as could be,
> But the best plums of all came from Donaghadee
> Too-ra-loo, too-ra-lee
> Oh, it's six miles from Bangor to Donaghadee.

The men let out a great hurrah and clapped as Ulster had again been redeemed by the wiry man's great gift. All the ex-rebels felt more at home and they conversed freely with one another.

As Donn's wine was refilled before his last mouthful was swallowed, he noticed his little server's eyes, rimmed in coal, before they looked away quickly. He could tell her face was swollen and bruised under heavy makeup. Somebody had gotten rough with her. He didn't take another sip. The rug beneath him now seemed dirty; he was immediately suspicious of his hosts and he wanted to leave. He watched the bruised servant head to the back room and, moments later, return with a new serving tray. She was keeping her head down, causing her to miss the crewman backing into her. She crashed down with the tray's contents spread across the tile. He observed that no one really noticed through the festivities, but while she was attempting to gather the mess, an armed guard approached her. The guard was a stern-looking bald man with a build that suggested he could handle a fight. He pressed food into the girl's face and pointed at the loss while berating her. She began to cry and push away like a kicked dog. He picked her up and shook her. Donn waved over a serving girl and asked if she understood him. She said yes with an accent.

"Can you tell me why the guard is treating that girl in such a way?"

"She is new. She is not happy. She will be taught." Her unconcerned face told Donn more then he wished.

Donn furrowed his brow a bit and continued to watch. The girl squirmed against the foul brute; leaning forward, she bit and spit at him. She managed to squeak something he couldn't understand so he asked the servant if *she* knew.

"My prince is away but he returns. He will run you through." The translator glanced at Donn and added, "She is crazy. She has no family. All these girls are captured from noble families slaughtered in raids."

Donn saw her get her hair pulled up above her as she was led away. He couldn't contain his anger anymore. The absurdity of an intervention was not of any concern to him. He acted as quickly as the wind that rushes through a valley. He didn't pull his blade because his right-hand knuckles had already collided against the bastard's jaw. He pulled away the scared girl and tossed her behind him and the men that were once rollicking with laughter were now stunned in silence. The enforcer had slid across the sandy tile; Donn stood like a pillar against the room in defense of the small girl. She wept and curled on the ground while Donn kept his defensive posture above her. Sunlight poured through the windows and illuminated the enraged look in the eyes of the men guarding the dervish's property. MacIntyre, for whatever impulse, took the fiddle and smashed it over the offending guard as he attempted to rise again. As the men started to stand, the bar owner screamed something that sent the room into a terrible melee. Out from the back room rushed forward a mob of armed men that had apparently been waiting in ambush. They had swords raised as they spread out to attack the Irish. Some cups were tossed at the dervish's men before they clumsily drew their own weapons.

All Donn could do was land fists on the first pair of eyes that showed up before him. When the brawl started, Shipyard's love interest threw her body against the big man's chest, like a tackle, and shielded him with her little body. She was stabbed multiple times and the blood that sprang from her created a pool underneath her man. Like a berserker, from the floor, Shipyard pulled a stiletto blade from his boot and stabbed legs which dropped a few guards. He erupted to his feet and overpowered everyone like an unbottled cyclone. Shipyard then grabbed a short angry-looking man holding a tray and slammed his face against the steel as he moved about the room, getting swift revenge. Grunting and crashes were abounding as the room swam with incredible violence. The establishment guards attempted to clumsily slash at the crew after they were unable to drop any of those swarming adversaries with panicked pistol shots.

Flames whipped around in the lanterns by the force of the fight. Conri, still injured since Manannán's defeat, assaulted with viciousness but his distance was often too great to make contact. Donn saw Conri brought down to the ground by three men, out of sight within the mob. The enraged curly haired young woman leapt up and stabbed one of the men in the neck from behind that had stolen her Conri. When she was pursued by another guard, intending to kill her, she screamed in anger at him while backing into the wall. Devine leapt onto the guard's back and dragged him to the ground. His skull was crushed into the floor through repeated pounding until Devine had to act on the next danger. With emotionless discipline, he stood in defense of the woman.

Donn was rushed by another but turned the attacker's body weight against him. He threw the would-be assassin through an open window and, just then, a gray horse leapt sideways, avoiding the tumbling guard in a wild gallop. Donn was filled with fear when he recognized the mount. *That was Cathal's horse! He must be in danger!*

The hot blood of the Irish and the Moors splashed on the floor and wall of the establishment. "The horse! Men, your baron needs you!" cried Donn. The Irish redoubled their efforts and jumped over fallen bodies to grapple with their adversaries. The women that entertained now ducked in wailing terror by clinging to walls. MacIntyre grabbed at a large tapestry and tore it away from its hooks. He ran with it then swung it over the fire display in the center of the room. Tall flames soon reached the ceiling and smoke engulfed the room. The confusion guaranteed their departure from the trap. Adding to the chaos, the hanging lamps swung wildly as men bumped into them, making wild shadows of the men clashing on the blood-drenched walls.

The Irish began spilling out into the street. They were collapsing onto the stone path, coughing uncontrollably. Their white shirts were blackened with soot and glossed with fresh blood. They poured through the open door until the flames themselves attempted to follow. The onlookers outside pushed away from the horrific sight. Donn stood among them and, with sharp eyes, assessed the situation. He was angry and he was going to make right this ambush. He saw eighteen crewmen —which means four were certainly dead. These survivors were burned and wounded but they were alive and armed. Brave Conri was dead but Devine still had that liberated woman clinging to him. Her bloodstained feet and sobbing was hard to listen to without feeling it deeply.

Donn closed his fists. The choices were simple. Return to the ship and retrieve the entire crew for an aggressive incursion or go to Cathal now. His thoughts were broken by only the screams of those still in the building. By the time he could get support, it would be too late as the city guard would be formed up and become a virtual wall between them and their leader. Now was the time, now that they were supposed to be dead. Shipyard was resting his head against a wall near a window pouring smoke. Donn tapped his shoulder and alerted him. He wiped his eyes and understood with a quick nod. They quickly started helping the men up. The wolf guard let out hollers at the crowd to shock them and stay back. With the enemy undoubtedly regrouping somewhere, past this swarm of eyes monitoring them, they stood little chance and mere moments to await a miracle.

*****

American Flagship: USS Argus

A striped flag with fifteen stars hung above a black naval command flag. The brig was a young vessel with nearly 150 American sailors aboard her. A whistle had been blown and seamen rushed to their placements. Master Commandant Isaac Hull, in charge of the three-ship-strong American contingent sent to Derne, was using his spyglass to assess Derne's defenses from the quarterdeck. He watched the marines on shore lead the Greek and Moorish force toward the city, pulling a lone carronade the USS *Nautilus* disembarked earlier. He was bemused that his vessel was named after a mythological Greek beast while he commanded a group that would swear it to be true history. Sweat trickled down below his black curly locks, pressed down by his bicorn, from the hot sun blazing above. He kept a hand resting on the ivory grip of his long sword in its black sheath. He could hear the crackling of distant muskets and then the whistles of cannonballs finding an eventual splash ahead of his ship. Hull had earlier told the marines to split their forces and flank the city while he would give covering siege fire with his squadron's cannons.

Hull shouted the question, "Do you have the twelve pounders sighted in, Lieutenant?"

"Aye, Captain!" was answered from near the capstan.

Hull then gave the command to open fire. The signaling flags were raised and the USS *Hornet* and USS *Nautilus* commenced firing along with the USS *Argus*.

*****

Derne

Donn shouted, "We go to rescue the baron. Follow me!"

They started moving forward down the alley at a quick pace. After a few minutes of pushing people out of the way, loud explosions could be heard. The panicked chattering mob became a powerful tide against which they had to swim. The crew did not know why the city was being attacked nor did they care. They knew it wasn't the *Mistress* and must be the Americans. The thought delighted Donn.

*****

The USS Nautilus

Three sailors aboard the American sloop, manning a cannon, were conversing. They could see the smoke rise from the city and the walls crumbling. They made adjustments based on active targets that could engage their land assault. The fleet had switched from long-range guns that could keep their squadron a safe distance from any land batteries that may try a counterattack, and now, as they closed near the shore, they laid and fired brutal nine-pounders to silence the enemy batteries.

A tall sandy haired gentleman, holding a fuse, was speaking with a lilt of joy. "These damn pirates sure are getting Tom's attention today. Load again, Samuel, so they get enough American tribute." The other man smiled as he placed another round shot in the gun.

The tall man paused. He rubbed an eye to clear some black smoke. "Do you see that ship there? Do you see the black one?" He pointed over toward the vessel. "There!"

Samuel responded, "Aye, I see it, Healy. What difference does it make? You want to lay the gun for it?"

Healy excitedly responded, "I recognize, I think, the insignia on her stern. It's Ulster. See…dammit, do you see it!" He slapped a shoulder of the man that held the plunger. "Where did those pirates steal her? You know…" He chuckled. "I've some family from Ulster."

*****

Derne

Janissaries on horseback appeared above the chaotic mob coming toward them. Donn led the crew into a back alley and they ran to the end. The Janissaries' horses followed single file at a lope.

They came out the other side of the narrow path into a small plaza. The cannonballs were raining and some destruction was evident. Shipyard stopped and picked up a fallen tree. He turned and, with great strength, barricaded the corridor as the horsemen arrived at the opening. His face trembled as his jaw clenched and filled with red. His eyes pulsated with rage as he stood ready for the impact. The lead horse hit the tree and the massive man staggered slightly but then planted his feet into the sand again. The horse collapsed as if his chest had been crumpled and the rider flew over. Many pursuing horses behind crashed into the fallen horse and, through the muffled screams, bones loudly cracked.

Donn knew that danger was around every corner. They were nearing the dock but they were cut off from the gate. Donn made a snap decision and knew they could make it to the stable with a little luck. As they doggedly pushed on, unseen enemies leapt from the crowd with long knives in desperate acts to strike at them. Donn took a rapier cut to his arm, but before the assassin could swing again, Donn stabbed him deeply in the chest. MacIntyre's mouth was smeared with blood. When an arm reached forward to jab at him, he responded with blows, backed with his full body weight, knocking them out. Those violent harassments continued until they reached the stable.

The men overwhelmed the terrified stable keepers and threw saddles on their horses. The gray chargers seemed to feel the energy in the atmosphere and acted angered and agitated. Croaghaun was stomping and beating his head against his stall. Donn led him outside and leapt on. Donn told Shipyard to take all those without mounts and make sure the gate was open. The Irish only formed up for a moment outside before Donn pointed his sword and shouted, "To the palace!" And the knights were off. With the streets cluttered with broken debris and bodies, the horses squeezed together to move quickly down the main road. The mob melted away from the glorious horses. The salvos continued to whistle overhead; the townspeople were cowering at every corner, unsure where to seek safety.

Devine yelled out, the girl holding on behind him, for any answer offered, "Are we going the right way?"

MacIntyre, riding next to him, responded, "I don't know. I'm still full as a goat!"

A small group of militia on foot, bare-chested with their heads wrapped in white cloth, stood in front of the cavalry. They lifted their swords and screamed, "Allah!"

Donn squeezed Croaghaun's flanks to make him move faster and the rest of the men turned their trot to a gallop upon seeing it. The would-be obstacles to the Irish advance screamed in agony as they were run over and mangled by the hooves passing over them, unable to avoid the fate in the filled space. The knights arrived at a tower with an Islamic crescent adorning its peak before the palace steps. A bodyguard of pirate mercenaries poured out into the space between them and the steps. The Irishmen fired their pistols with random aim and then locked in sword combat. The pirates proved only initially courageous since they undoubtedly saw their profit potential dwindle with every instant. The carnage was brutal but short as the pirates fled the field away from the blue-sashed Irishmen. The men rode their horses up the stairs and through the open front gate. They were in a magnificent hall where the bey was sitting on his throne, flanked by four Ottoman Janissaries. Donn moved toward the throne and swung off his mount, his sword dripping blood onto the tiled floor. "Where is the Baron O'Ruairc?!"

"Death to the infidels!" the fat leader shouted.

The knights also dismounted their horses and ran forward to meet the blades of the bodyguards. With the bodyguard forced to defend themselves, Donn saw a direct path to the petrified Mustafa.

The bey stood; Donn walked forward and put his sword against his throat as he grabbed his beard and pulled him forward. Donn looked at the servants, past the submitting palace guard, that were covering their faces on the ground and barked, "Bring the baron to me now!" A young boy ran down a dark corridor to the left and, a tense minute later, returned with Cathal. Cathal walked in confidently, seemingly unharmed. He had an angered expression on his face when he came over to the Ottoman leader.

Cathal pulled Comac Cas's cup from out of his leather satchel and filled it with wine from a nearby table. He dropped the decanter onto the floor and it smashed into pieces. He then forced the bey to drink from the Cup of Truth by grabbing his jaw and shoving it into his cursing mouth. The wine spilled everywhere—over the baron's hand and onto the floor. Cathal decided the bey had swallowed enough as he flung the cup to Devine. He backhanded the tax collector's face and growled, "*Firinne!*" Cathal demanded of him. "Where is the Sword of Nuada?"

The bey responded in a booming voice, "Where Allah's army camped in the days of the Fomorian oppression of Eire, in the permanent north. Where the officers of Tuatha de Danann learned how to destroy the demon horde."

The palace shook and screams were heard outside from the continuing siege. The crew paced around the hall, their posture on high alert.

Cathal shook Mustafa and asked with waning patience, "Where exactly is the sword?"

"It resides in the kingdom of Gorias where it was returned—"

"How do we reach Gorias!"

Mustafa began to choke on his own throat and his hands spasmed. "Go to Inis Mór, to the chapel of Benan, over the staging area of Allah's army. There, raise the Rod of Divine Right to show rule over the Tuatha de Danann."

Shipyard walked over to Cathal and grabbed his arm. "We must depart if we are to survive the day."

Mustafa had fallen to the floor when Cathal released his grip and remained there, paralyzed. The men were standing on the now-muddy tiled hall, waiting for direction. Cathal tore the dynastic banner off the wall behind the throne and pitched it over Mustafa's body and then walked toward the door with the men in escort.

"We must return to the ship now, Baron!" shouted a crewman as he was wiping his dripping blade.

"That will be a reasonable challenge," Cathal responded grimly. The crew promptly mounted their horses. Donn could see that with all the commotion of the siege, the alleys were nearly blocked with people scrambling to escape the carnage.

Cathal and the crew moved forward and the horses soon slowed to a walk as they were surrounded by the maddened local horde. They couldn't stay cohesive in formation and their mounts spooked at the chaos. While residents were pushing away from the fighting at the walls, the horses attempted to muscle through. It seemed that no further resistance was mounted against them since the defense of the city was now the priority.

Donn knew that every moment that passed brought the potential closer for the destruction of the ship and more death for the crew. Every pace they moved forward was exhausting for the wounded and weakened. Many ways to travel through the town had been obstructed by caved in walls. He spotted the boy wearing his blue sash, up ahead on a low building, waving to get his attention. He beckoned Donn to head down a side alley. Donn yelled out to the baron and got his limited attention.

"I know where to go. Follow me!" Donn pleaded.

Cathal gave hand signals and turned his horse around. The crew followed Donn as he pierced through the crowd and headed down the alley as the boy, still with other street urchins, ran across the roof. They came out of the alley and found evacuated pathways to take toward the dock. The child appeared to leap off a roof out of view from the Irish and then suddenly appeared upon Cathal's horse, riding up alongside of them. The little boy seemed fearless and, without any hesitation, joined the crew and their impending fate. The other children waved goodbye from the rooftops as a few of the men waved back in gratitude.

Cathal rode by the boy and yelled, "Much thanks!"

He quickly responded, "You share your blue. The color of my family. I go with you!"

The party made it to the gate to find Shipyard and the other men there. The gate was already breached. City guards were occupied firing from the walls into an enemy that proved a lucky distraction for the Irish to escape. With little hesitation, the Irish poured through the opening to find Moorish soldiers fleeing defensive positions in a bewildered retreat to the east.

The ship was harbored only a few hundred yards away and the horses were struggling to keep up the fast pace. The Irish found themselves becoming entangled into intermittent single engagements with soldiers that attempted to slow them. Two of the men were slashed off their mounts and covered the sand with their blood. Donn was targeted by an assault by a massive bearded and robed horseman. Donn was able to parry with the flat of his sword and pitched the arm of his assailant high up. That gave Donn a quick opportunity to force the Janissary off his horse by jabbing him off balance. As the dust from the ground whipped up, it caused all the combatants to go wild as they struggled to focus on where next to attack.

*****

The Midnight Mistress

Luke could see his comrades in the carnage. He turned away from the spectacle and grabbed Gideon. "Have the men arm themselves and prepare to defend the ship!" He shouted to Tymon, "Ready the masts, we depart as soon as we have them aboard!" Kennedy was awaiting orders by the wheel. Luke saw him and impatiently cursed at him to bring him a rifle and look lively.

*****

Lieutenant William Eaton was slogging across the sand, inspiring over fifty skittish men to push the advance into Derne. The men were struggling to pull a carronade through the beach sand to be used like a giant mobile pistol. Palm trees were broken and burning around him which wafted black smoke into his spent lungs. Eaton led a group comprised of several marines, Greek mercenaries, and many of Hamet's Moorish forces. He had been named general in chief of Hamet's forces and it was an unusual appointment for an American marine. Ahead of Eaton was Lieutenant Presley O'Bannon and Lieutenant George Mann, both who was under his command, trying to coordinate an advance of many squads facing an entrenched fire.

Eaton had his hat shot off near the start of the battle which caused him to be blinded by the sun. His white shirt was imprinted with the blood of a wounded man's head that had pressed against it while he dragged him behind a storage building earlier. His dark-blue jacket wouldn't close anymore and he had fewer gold buttons than had originally been attached. The red trim on his jacket and cuffs were brown from gun smoke and dirt. The men he led were of a shaky temperament since ten times their number sought to defend the city. They often paused too long behind walls when it came to facing another volley from enemy muskets. They knew all too well that the rooftops of the houses that spotted the outskirts of the city hid fresh opposition, ready to rain hell down upon them. Every wall had a hole carved out to allow a weapon barrel to peek through which made safety a mirage for all of his men until they drove the enemy from their positions.

They moved rapidly, from cover to cover, and chose their targets with precision. Eaton could tell that they were close to their objective which was to storm the shore guns so they could no longer fire against the American vessels. Once they had captured the guns, they were to turn them on the city. He noticed a pause in musket balls as he took a breath between dashes. The smoke was singeing his nostrils as, just then, a loud explosion caused Eaton to collapse onto the sand. When Eaton stood, he saw that their carronade had been destroyed. He gave a hand gesture of delay to his men. Eaton peered around and saw that a skirmish had broken out in front of the main gate between a group of horsemen and the defenders. He wagered they had a chance at taking the enemy battery with the fighting taking place in front of them.

Eaton, although winded, spat loudly, "Fix bayonets and prepare to advance!" Eaton drew his sword and led the soldiers into a rapid march. They moved toward walls that sent waves of lead toward them. A musket ball hit Eaton's left wrist and caused him to fall onto his back. Two men, O'Brien and O'Bannon, rushed to pull him to safety and wrapped his wrist. The advance faltered to the shaken troops— so small was their number compared to the defenders. Eaton yelled, "O'Bannon, take that tower now! Get off of me and move forward!"

*****

Presley pulled himself up and drew his sword. The sword caught the light and he felt a rush of adrenaline surge in him. The men shouted out a battle cry and began a quick pace to the last fifty yards to the battery. As he ran forward in long strides, he thought about his grandfather with stories of green Ireland and his choice to make a home in the new world. But Presley was now across the ocean doing terrible battle upon a desert. With blood-soaked sand surrounding him, he thought, *Perhaps Grandfather had best stay'd in Tipperary.*

*****

USS Nautilus

The American squadron near the port had continued its firing operation, trying to avoid a crossfire with their allies on the shore. Captain Oliver Hazard Perry, a courageous young man recently put in charge of the ship, was patiently awaiting the capture of the shore defenses. As per his understanding of previous orders, the Moorish soldiers, under the command of Lieutenant Eaton, were attacking the west side of the city. Unable for moments to take a breath to relieve his tension, he simply waited for success on the shore to carry the day. He saw the American forces victoriously scattering the west garrison. He was also quick to notice that a group of unknown horsemen had started an engagement near the dock. This engagement he was witnessing was an anomaly and he decided he would see if an opportunity was unfolding.

*****

The Midnight Mistress

Luke and the sailors were firing into a war party that had secured the dock, effectively cutting the shipmates off from their commander. Ladders were tossed against the hull to board. The Irish musket fire proved insufficient to hold back the garrison's unrelenting approach. Luke ordered the ladders pulled and tossed. The weight of the climbers and random fire made it a difficult task. Luke hopped on the ladder and kicked off an aggressor and attacked the next, dropping rung from rung. Luke's men attempted a cover fire to protect the captain. Enemy fire pelted and splintered the wooden hull everywhere and a cloud of smoke was building, adding to the confusion. Blasts erupted from grenades thrown onto the main deck which tore at and disoriented the sailors. An enemy, a gaunt wretch with a hate-filled face, reached out to strike Luke with his blade from a nearby ladder. Luke countered the attack and slew the man who fell to the sea. Then he placed a leg upon the second ladder. Once on the second ladder, he kicked the man below in the face and pulled the man above him down and off the ladder. The first ladder was pushed back into the waters. Luke began to climb back into the ship when he felt a bullet penetrate his back. Tymon grabbed him with his great strength and pulled him over the rail to safety while a gunport opened to put pistol shot into the would-be pursuers. Luke was laid upon the deck. He told Gideon to raise the colors.

*****

Cathal and his men were in the thick of the fighting upon the narrow bloody shore. Not a man was spared from the blood and labor of battle that began to ferment a shock in the ranks. Donn was swinging off an attack with parries while wiping the burning black powder from his eyes. He looked around himself and saw his fellow countrymen drown in a sea of black-sleeved arms waving blades at them. Horses screamed. His heart pounded and his teeth clenched. Their ship, green flag flying on the quarterdeck, was nearly overrun and captured, if not by the assault from the dock then by the small pirate ships that were attempting to free their moorings.

Donn's focus came when he saw a sultanate flag above an onlooker down the shore before the long dock. Donn recognized the man as an officer, on his dark horse, since he had a bodyguard of three men, giants to the common man. His anger leapt out of him as he knew what needed to be done. He must slay their leader and break their spirit. Donn grabbed an arm that swung at him and forced it forward so the rider fell forward. He spurred his mount and Croaghaun leapt forward. Donn dashed toward the enemy officer as Croaghaun rammed through the battle. The officer had been slow to see Donn among the chaos of battle but directed his bodyguards to protect him.

Donn heard a cannon fire from the tower. He looked over at the structure and could see an American flag waving above it. The Americans had turned the city guns on the sultan's forces! Donn engaged the first brute with his sword and got bashed in the face by the dropping pommel of the menacing weapon. Donn flung his head back as the horse continued so that the first attacker was behind them. The second horseman stopped in front of Donn in a defensive posture. Croaghaun smashed into the smaller gray horse, causing the defender to fall to the ground. Donn recovered and shook the blood from his nose then acted as a warrior in frenzy. He chopped the returning first rider into submission. Croaghaun was sliced by the second man on foot and let out a bellow. The attacker stumbled on the sand before Croaghaun grabbed the skin on his face with his teeth and tore it away. The man, less a nose and most of his face, crumpled to his death upon the sand. The third rider, only feet away, trained a musket on Donn and fired. Black smoke erupted around the long-barreled musket and the projectile met Donn in the shoulder. Donn dropped his sword and spit out a grunt.

A cannonball landed on the swarm of howling Moorish warriors and an opening through the chaos broke toward the dock. The bey's commanding officer was startled and grabbed his reins with both hands, then steadied his red-nostriled steed. Suddenly more cannon fire rang out. One of the American ships had thundered a volley that struck the city gate, crumbling it into a heap of rock and debris. The sharpshooters above the old wall fell to their deaths.

The volley created an opening to the Irish ship. Donn heard Cathal scream, "To the *Mistress*, lads! To the *Mistress*, now!" He saw the men begin to pile through the gap in the fighting.

Donn dismounted and picked up his sword. He briefly saw Bridget in his memories, then committed to his risky action, leaving good sense forsaken. He ran up furiously to the third bodyguard before he could drop his musket and draw his sword. Donn pulled him off his horse and pinned him to the sand but his weakened arm caused him to lose his sword again. The officer, knowing the end was near, turned his mount and began his escape down the beach. The men on the dock fighting Luke's men took flight with him. Donn and the third bodyguard rolled twice before he found Donn's neck and began to squeeze. Croaghaun circled Donn on the beach. He crow-hopped, twisting his neck in apparent excitement, warding off further attacks upon Donn. Donn reached up and took hold of his would-be murderer's ear and ripped it off. The Moor screamed and released his grip. Donn shoved him off and found his blade. The bodyguard gasped his last when Donn ran the etched Irish sword through his ribcage.

Donn stood and pulled the blood-soaked sword out and looked about. The Irish were dashing by him toward the dock. He saw no officer but noticed a presence over his shoulder. Cathal was on his horse, pulling Croaghaun in tow by his reins.

Cathal barked, "Would you like to board our ship now or perhaps we should stay and receive a full cultural experience?"

Donn grabbed the reins and mounted. He dared not close his eyes as he might have fainted. Where men were wounded, they were aided quickly by others to remount and reach the ship.

Devine rode up alongside Cathal and said, "The Americans have made prisoners of the bey's garrison. We need to move, Baron."

The Irish boarded the ship by lowered plank while the horses were hoisted in. The rickety bridge was covered in bodies after the remaining Irish boarded. The anchor was raised and Kennedy swung the wheel.

*****

USS Nautilus

A midshipman became aware of the departing frigate pulling out into the deep water. He quickly pointed. "Sergeant, if you please, train the guns on that black vessel!"

A voice quickly followed. "Belay that order, Sergeant."

The midshipman followed with worry in his voice. "Captain, we can put her out of service before she can threaten our line."

Perry proclaimed, "Would you have my mother never speak to me again, sir? Those sailors are from the county of her birth, and if you so much as wave threateningly in their direction, you can swim back to Boston!" The midshipman staggered back and quickly acknowledged the order.

*****

Donn was stumbling past the storage cabins after he turned in his weapons to the armory. He was going to see the doctor, and hopefully, his injuries warranted attention in the near term; although competition was apparent. He heard a gunshot that startled him, half-expecting a mamluk assassin to be stowed away. He went toward the sound of the shot and entered the medical cabin. Cathal quietly walked past as the doctor carefully wrapped a man with a sheet. The man had dropped a pistol next to him and his chair that he lay dead in was facing a porthole. "What became of him?" Donn queried.

The doctor responded, "Wood splinters entered him in a hundred places. He ended his life to defeat the pain."

Donn looked away. It appeared that the young suicide used one of Cathal's pistols. Donn looked through the porthole and saw the American flag being raised on the crumbled walls of Derne.

Sorrow

Donn had his shoulder bandaged, lucky that the wound didn't carry the musket ball. He wandered the ship, attempting to bring peace and attention to traumatized and injured sailors. He was soon in the orlop, the bottom deck, when he saw Luke, gravely injured.

Luke's fair hair was filled with wood fiber, matted down with blood and tar. His clothes were tattered over his body which convulsed against his caregivers. Although his face was unconcerned, his hushed tone and brief moments of focus suggested a near collapse of fortitude. The priest followed Cathal down the ladder, into the hull, on the sad errand of being available to bid their comrades goodbye if need be. A lantern swayed slowly, from the passing sea below them, and illuminated the look of the sailors' broken morale.

Luke's fevered eyes unleashed some tears. He looked up at Donn and said, "Why are you here… Aifric is in Erin. Go… Damn, you fool."

Two men rushing to bandage Luke caught Donn's attention. Donn stumbled through his thoughts. In Luke's fever, did he think Donn was himself at a younger state or had he gone mad? Luke's blue eyes, struggling to look upon Donn, projected a grave concern, even though his words were faint. The men knew it was hopeless, and Judge shook his head at Cathal. Cathal kneeled and tightly grabbed Luke's trembling hand in his, then whispered to him his goodbye. Luke, sweating through his uniform, gripped Cathal's hand tightly.

He shook hard as he lifted himself up to speak slowly, "Who shall separate us?"

Cathal spoke up and placed a hand behind Luke's head. "Find the path ahead of us, volunteer. We'll be on our way!" He carefully laid Luke's head back down as he placed his hand back to his chest. Luke then grabbed a small gold locket in his coat pocket and held it tightly near his neck. He closed his eyes, enduring tremendous pain.

As the sea rocked the boat, Donn watched Luke drift into eternity. Cathal backed away while the busy priest prayed, honoring the body of their brave fallen captain.

Donn sat, exhausted, against a hull-support beam when Cathal walked over. Donn was shocked as Cathal was clearly grief-stricken, the way he anxiously moved his head and tried to rub his arms. Donn asked delicately, "Who is Aifric?"

Cathal spit into his hands and rubbed them together, paced a little forward and said, "Back in Ulster, she was his lady, or so he told me, and she was the true price he paid for joining the rebels. He loved her quite deeply."

Donn grimly mused, "He seemed not to care about his fate, as if his mind was fighting to retain a memory, like it was his source of life."

Cathal nodded with anger. "He was a damn romantic, I believe, late to understand its burden. Like all romantics that live too long, he carried invisible wounds within him that never closed. You see, it was that certain lady, which any of us might meet, that separation from sentenced him to melancholy, wishing for a companion." Cathal looked right at Donn and said, "Luke lost Aifric partly by being away too long and partly by choosing assumed duty over family. Perhaps you might find his last words a warning." His eyes taunted Donn.

Donn stood up and faced Cathal. "Am I to believe I'll share Luke's fate for having joined this crew? I know why I'm here and I will return to her. Now you cheapen the loyalty of my oath to our people?"

"I travel the world searching for treasures and you had yours before ever leaving with us. It's my fault for making you choose so my promise is that you'll return to her or surely I've failed you." Cathal then walked away.

Donn went to his bunk and pulled out his notebook. He wrote in order to try and free himself of the guilt that camped nightly in his mind.

I feel your lips caress mine, even here on the outskirts of a desert nightmare. Those lips warm my heart, even in memory. My days crawl by without you. Your body vanishes around every corner before my head turns. I don't have you now. Your hand isn't in mine. My heart panics and I subdue its screaming by working. I nearly tore my arms off trying pull up an anchor that was in five feet of African mud but it compares little to the hell my soul is feeling. With every day away, my torment follows me with a greater intensity, with a heartbeat that threatens to seize me at any moment.

Donn closed his eyes to imagine him with her. He wanted to write what he might say to her now.

I'll find you under a rowan tree on that long-sought day. I'll carry you away and we'll make love. Our hands will be wrapped together under an Irish sky, then a family we'll be with the children to come. Never apart again, my darling Bridget.

He needed some air. The breath that left him didn't seem to return. Donn walked the ship's entirety and watched the quiet and beaten crew drift around the ship. It was as if the light of hope had been stolen from them and it aged their bodies. The bloodied crew mourned their losses and remained as quiet as ever aboard the ship. Donn had faced loss and it remained like a foul taste in his mouth during all that followed. His enthusiasm and courage were no longer dauntless. As time passed, the baron would not exit his cabin. Donn felt that strong leadership was necessary now or morale would plummet to mutiny, he feared. Donn decided to go to the baron and beseech him to rally the men.

Donn entered the main cabin and found it dark. Cathal rested his head against a bare wall and spoke in a tortured and hasty whisper. Donn couldn't understand his private monologue. Cathal's body trembled and his fingers plucked at the wood grain. Donn witnessed Cathal remain like that for a few minutes, then stay silent and motionless a great while longer. Donn left without disturbing him.

After the escape from Derne, they drifted for many long days and nights. Provisions had become inadequate; the men ate moldy bread without complaint. Donn's dwindling morale drowned him to the point of speechless stupor. Losing comrades, friends, so suddenly, caused his faith to falter. He would wander the decks in hopes to find faces now forever missed.

Spirit and Work

The years had passed yet there were so few places Bridget could go that didn't remind her of him. He showed her the island and the once-totally-mysterious island and he became one and the same to her. For Bridget, Achill was a forgery in Donn's absence. In the late evening, she would peer out of her bedroom window and openly dare the stars to light her love's way home.

She laughed out loud at herself when there wasn't anything humorous spoken. Once, as waves were breaking onto the shore, she let out a cry against the roar of the foaming ocean. She would stand so close to the fireplace that she could feel it burn, anything to escape the thoughts of misery that wound around her spirit and suffocated it. What once was a rebirth, injected with boundless hope, now crippled her mind like an addiction.

Bridget would despair and consider, *I could take a walk and what thrived would be withered by my sadness.*

"You build upon what you know," Mother had said. Bridget considered the notion as unhelpful, but still, she appreciated the naive optimism. She only knew the social graces and European fashion. Certainly her few talents were even more comical to utilize on this green rock.

Her duty, as was ever clear to ladies of her position and age, was to wed a respectable man and bear his children. Now she prepared herself to accept her fate and venture out among potential suitors.

How odd it would seem to feel shame to not attract a match to make her parents proud. She met the task to ready herself for the ball with dignity as her heart would not allow her to further disappoint her family. She resigned herself that Donn, absent as he was, was not a suitable reason to destroy her parents' hopes for her. Up to this day of the first ball at Browne's estate to open the season, she forced herself to be civil, a little at a time, and then a normalcy in attitude finally settled in with her family again.

Bridget hated curling her hair but managed a few hairpins each morning. She sat at her vanity, with its rickety seat, and endured the trial. Lady Catherine had given her suggestions on how to present herself and only out of respect for her feelings did Bridget put up with the burden.

Bridget wore a sheer embroidered cream-colored muslin ball gown. It was tied with an ivory sash under the bust. Her hair was pinned above and allowed to fall by design in soft ringlets that framed her cheeks. Her delicate shoulders were mostly at show with the straps of the gown being tied off in bows that hung down against the upper arms. She held a wrap of matching silk behind her back then wrapped about her arms. Her hands were encased in loose ivory knit silk gloves that reached past her elbows. A black velvet reticule completed her outfit.

She slowly traveled to Westport with her mother. The carriage moving and the sound of the wheels turning, while the horses sounded a rhythmic clopping, impressed upon her mind that it was a criminal sentence that was commencing. She dared to look at the door with panicked thoughts that she should jump out and see how far she might escape. Ella noticed her tense fidgeting and offered random conversation to distract her, all the while with a calming voice.

A ferry took their carriage across the sound and then again toward Westport. It seemed like she had departed a rustic dreamland and then reappeared in the real world once the carriage was on the mainland. She should have felt lucky to again partake in the company of proper Irish gentry, however, she had spent enough time with the islanders to not condemn their way of life. Bridget still felt like an intruder, an unsettling feeling now facing a new circle to enter, surprisingly still as foreign to her as Achill was.

Bridget would preoccupy herself by glancing at portraits that lined the walls, giving her a sense of being watched by a hundred eyes. Mantles were laden with sprawling bouquets that brought the garden inside. *Why did women insist flowers are to be held no matter the commonality of it all?* Some women rested on reclined chairs as they conversed openly. Ancient Greece had inspired much of the furniture scattered about the rooms. Bridget sat upon a low back seat with carved harnessed swans for armrests. The charming atmosphere arrested her inhibitions enough to allow repose.

She had developed a roving eye for fashion through her upbringing and it was in full use that evening. Bridget winced at the thought of more fabric with gold brocade drowning it. Her favorite cotton dress that she had outgrown was the same color of the first horse she rode. The bay color met shimmering chocolate cuffs, neckline, and edging. It meant something to her as should all dresses one chooses to wear.

Bridget saw her mother being introduced in a shuffle across the room. Ella looked lovely in her white empire-waist dress and seafoam Spencer short jacket. The gown had a lower hem border of raised ivory stitching. She positively made those dresses—troubled with petticoats, bows, and heavy fabric—look outdated. The dress celebrated her body as opposed to being carried by the woman like a parade of gaudiness. Her hair was lightly curled and pinned back while, specially today, sporting a transparent green ribbon.

A curly blond-haired gentleman, mingling with an air of pomp, soon approached Bridget. He wore a well-fitted midnight-purple velvet suit, with black-corded edging, like a true dandy in the soft light.

He peered at Bridget with a phony investigative gaze. "Please pardon me, madam, but are you one of the ragged refugees from Ulster I've been told about? Yes, you must be. Condemned to living in the wilds no less than a common wretch, poor girl."

Bridget was shocked by his rudeness and all while smiling in a vain arrogance. Her brow furled, confused by the unwarranted assault. She merely was able to speak, "What? Yes, I mean. What do—" Then she was sharply interrupted.

He shamed her with a mocking pity. "Still adjusting from your tumble from grace, I'm certain. Enjoy your evening in our paradise. Such a pleasure." He bowed slightly and then moved away again.

She made a mental note to add him to the list of things that unsettle her, along with spiders, well-meaning ladies, and cold hands.

Bridget was further appalled by the next man who made her acquaintance. His breath smelled of fish and he wore a full wig. Apparently he was a grocer in Newport whose wife had died. He kept speaking about his imported spices as if that could lure her into a romantic relationship. Her skin crawled when he commented on how much she looked like his daughter. She stood up and claimed to be nearly faint to excuse herself to the night air.

She peered back into the window and waited. Only a few minutes later, she saw the grocer become agitated by her absence and begin to harass some other young woman. Bridget let out a sigh of relief. As she did, she made the mistake of turning too quickly so her head bounced off the chest of a man standing in the doorway. He caught her before she fell back on the ground. "Easy now. Are you all right?"

"Yes…yes, I must apologize, I believe I became startled and lost my footing." Bridget gathered her senses quickly and looked at his chest, which must have been solid as a tree, before peering back into his eyes. She turned red with embarrassment when she saw his amusement. He was nearly as wide-shouldered as the door and wore a dark-blue frock coat over a silver vest. Since her escape was momentarily blocked, she added, "I think you can release me now." He dropped his large arms that otherwise could imprison her. Bridget straightened her dress and cleared her throat. "I was just heading back in, perhaps you'd make my acquaintance over some punch?" She couldn't help but be curious about him since he was the first surprise of the evening.

"I'd be delighted. Shall I carry you?" His lighthearted turn of phrase tickled Bridget's mind. He had wide cheekbones that seemed to stretch his skin over his impressive chin when he wasn't smiling.

She nodded with some determination. "No, I believe I can stumble over close enough to manage." She pressed past him into the vestibule.

She strolled over to the serving table with him in tow. After they were given their glasses, he asked, "To whom do I have the pleasure this evening of sharing a dance before our first punch?"

"Bridget Savage, formally of Belfast. My family is involved in tailoring on Achill now. And with whom do I have the pleasure of introduction?"

His slicked-back black hair shone under the candlelight chandeliers. She wagered he was in his early twenties by the look of his maturity in the face but still with a staggeringly well-filled-out frame. She flinched a bit, examining him, and awkwardly looked around the room awaiting his response. The other guests roamed around them, seemingly oblivious to their conversation.

"I'm Walter. Flannery. My business is corn trading for distribution and my shop is in Dover. I learned my trade on a street called Snow Hill in London, although I am from Dover."

Flannery spoke of society and cities he'd seen at the eager encouragement of Bridget. She could imagine each scene he described and it lightened her heart. She did consider that he might see this as flirting but her interest was selfish. As the night waned, guests were departing and her mother was growing restless, obviously noting her daughter's withdrawal from the social.

Bridget admitted, "I find so little to enjoy at these functions that you've given me a lovely respite. I thank you, kind sir." She tipped back her head and chuckled. When Walter asked if they might meet again, she responded, "I can think of no reason why we shouldn't. If you're here on business, won't it only be temporary?"

"I can stay where I feel my time is well-spent." His gaze beamed into her. She had grown so comfortable with him that it was as if they had been friends for years. She was disarmed. She wished he wasn't so keen on smiling at her. She could hardly resist his wry charm but she would accept his flirting to help forget her burdens. Did Bridget believe Walter wanted more from Bridget? Of course, and the poor man must be sick from drinking so much punch in fear he might momentarily look away and find her vanished.

Walter shared stories of his family as they spent time together. "My older brother is in the Royal Navy guarding the channel. When he had leave, we would meet him in Torquay on occasion on the coast. It was quite enjoyable there. The village has found prosperity, as Newport will, in this new world we're creating."

"I admit, you've opened my eyes about Newport. I wasn't aware the future was so exciting for Clew Bay," Bridget responded.

The evening had finally taken its course with everyone departing for their carriages. Ella looked miffed but relaxed as she questioned Bridget all the way back to Achill late that evening. Bridget would not dispel her mother's fantasy that Bridget was smitten with the man; the travel was much more pleasant that way.

*****

My language becomes plain the longer I remain a sailor. When I could compose my feelings toward you like the wind can carry autumn leaves, now I fear my tongue has lost its music to sing for your pleasure. Doubt not the capture of my heart but grace me with forgiveness for my roughness. I question how I may perform around you as the gentleman I hope you once saw me as. I know, with your patience, I can again be the man that you need.

You teased me when I told you I felt energy in your skin like a lightning storm surrounding us. When I only graze my lips against you, I tremble. It fills my body and I need not rest, air, or food to sustain me. My soul becomes harnessed by yours so much that I suspect this is what it's like to make love to an angel.

Where does your heart go when it wanders from me? Has it ever been so far? I miss the sound of it when it's next to mine.

Where I wish to be is outside your window and throwing pebbles so as to capture your attentions. Please don't make me ache in that cold night for long.

The Second Charge

Luke was buried into the depths of the Mediterranean, along with many other comrades. Their sashes were wound around their swords and given to Judge before the wrapped bodies were dropped overboard.

With the loss of Luke, Cathal's radiant charm seemed forced at best. Like an animal relearning his survival without a limb, the baron was shaken up and his crew knew it. The baron left his cabin on few occasions and never to give fresh orders.

Donn thought the men acted as if they felt isolated and vulnerable. What could be seen as the lone capital of the free Irish was merely an oak fortress that carried the entirety of its fragile promise, led by O'Ruairc. And O'Ruairc was absent from the men following the debacle at Derne. Without their leader's orders, a sense of doom, like a windless sea, ate at Donn's spirit. Through days of startling macabre, the relationships of the men curdled. Their confluence was Cathal and the dream he dispensed to them was as sunlight is to cave dwellers.

Donn almost tripped over Tymon. Tymon tried to hide his face. He had been drinking and had an emotional look about him, mouth hanging open and covered in sweat. He wasn't crying but he looked trapped by something as he rested there.

"Tymon? Are you poor in health or spirit?" Donn couldn't elicit a reaction so he slapped his shoulder. Tymon shot his eyes up to him like he was awakened from a terrible dream. He grabbed Donn's shirt in self-defense, his body trembling.

Donn hurriedly said, "Tymon, look, it's me!" Tymon relaxed finally and dropped his arms. Donn slowly sat next to him and waited a bit in the dark before asking, "What the hell is eating at you?"

Tymon's eyes searched the range of his vision, then he blurted out, "I'm still stuck on that bridge. Every day, I carry the same nightmare with me. It was after the victory of Trinidad. We came to San Juan like the landlords of the Caribbean, ready to throw out all the Spanish. We landed in small boats and stormed the beaches. Our landing was afforded by lighters carrying cannons that moved with us and kept up a suppressive fire. We took cover on a sandy terreplein as the bridge fort of Martin Pena fell to our colors." His breath was slowing finally.

Donn tried to venture a question. He didn't know where San Juan even was so he wanted to ask but it seemed Tymon didn't notice him trying to raise a hand. Before Donn got a word out, Tymon cut him off.

"There we held off as they concentrated artillery fire down upon us. We were not able to sweep the enemy in the myriad of land and sea fighting necessary as the Spanish militia and French soldiers were dogged in the city's defense. Every building, hill, and marsh became a source of barrage against us. As the ships of the line fired at each other and the gunboats clashed, the carnage was indescribable." Tymon brushed the top his head forward a couple of times and breathed in sharply then said, "I saw my shipmates eviscerated with grapeshot trying to storm a frigate in the cove. A close friend, a young boy named Fig Hanlon, was killed by cavalry charging across our bridge. The attack against us eventually failed but I think that day robbed me of something that I've never found again. We held the bridge for as long as we were ordered—no matter the loss. After a couple weeks of waiting for either a desperate assault to be ordered or becoming surrounded ourselves, we were ordered to withdraw silently. We left for sea and I believe it broke the confidence of our commander. Those Spanish and their flying units were capable of blunting our engagements long enough for the port to organize its defense. The whole war was over for us then. With the facade of our invincibility broken, it wasn't long until the Spanish had entirely submitted to the French. All a damn waste anyway."

Donn tempted fate with a question. "Was there any glory at all?"

"If there was, I can't remember. If you've seen your dead shipmates rotting in the sun, it's hard to get past. Lord, it was so hot… and that smell." Donn thought he saw a reflection off Tymon's cheek.

Donn tried to focus his friend's mind. "I imagine so. Despite that, you continue to serve aboard ships. This isn't the safest voyage. Was there anything at all you gained by serving in that war?"

"None of my expectations were met, although I can't say I had much of an idea what I was signing up for. You know, had we kept going, we'd have all been killed. It was good what happened for the sake of the rest of us. Heaven help me, it was good. Every now and again, you'd see something as beautiful as it was terrible at the same time. I never knew gallantry until I saw the last soldier of a routed army still fighting on. As mad as it sounds, I saw a lone woman playing a piano despite the cannon fire bombarding around her destroyed house."

Donn spent some time drinking with Tymon. They spoke of small things and it helped Donn ignore the void in which he existed. A couple of laughs passed and they both passed out.

When Donn woke up, he woke up angry. This couldn't continue, he decided. Donn took the initiative and knocked on Cathal's cabin door. "It's Donn, Baron. I should like to speak with you." He knocked again for good measure.

A low growl of a voice was heard. "Come in."

Cathal, looking like a well-used rag, was sitting at his desk with stacks of books. One was open that he had been reading. Empty bottles were in a basket next to his desk.

"The men need you, sir. We have no direction. Does something ail you?"

Cathal sounded foggy. "I'm contemplating thoughts. In my hell, there exists a maelstrom of decisions I cannot repair or replace."

"We bury our dead, Baron. Everyone knew the dangers. I've witnessed the strength of your crew dwindle yet the challenge still ahead is great. We are not invincible, even though at times we certainly have felt as such. The creatures that undoubtedly live in Gorias will be a new threat to us. We fear we might enter a kingdom full of monsters."

Cathal tapped his bottom lip with his fingers and then swiped his hair back, leaning forward slightly to say, "Many throw what they don't easily understand down into hell with Satan. You never know when you're with a benevolent creature. However, I think that's true of any stranger. You know, when I was a boy, I would sometimes hear a woman's voice. I knew it wasn't an angel's voice. However, I felt her love. She drove my curiosity and pushed me to be better."

Donn wasn't impressed with Cathal's dodge of his concerns. "Can you, if little is lost, spend just a few damn minutes explaining to me why we're here and not on our way back to Ireland?"

Cathal fumed and jerked his head as he spoke, "Do you think we're not meant to be out here? Think of our people in perpetual servitude. Where before there was shame and burden, now there can be pride and dignity. Don't give up on me, Donn, not just yet." Cathal slammed his book shut, sat back, and rested a finger under his nose.

Donn said forcefully, "Why should so many good men die for this fantastic quest? How could anyone know how this will end? These men deserve a time beyond sailing the ocean on this boat."

Cathal responded in an even tone, "God whispered a warning in my ear. By when you find peace, you'll tell me about all luster, the bombastic, the rapturous and captivating, that the time of your life can delight me. If that's not too much to ask of my child?"

"Baron, back at Lanzarote, I saw something troubling."

"Just one thing?" Cathal queried.

Donn grimaced then responded, "I saw the remains of a man in the room with the treasure. I was in too great of a hurry to take it in that there was a crown on his head." He looked over at Cathal for his reaction.

Cathal paused then said, "He was locked in with it. Perhaps left to die with what he thought made him a king."

Donn dismissed with a shrug. "Matters little, I suppose."

Cathal nodded affirmatively.

Donn declared, "This all must have an end. Lead us now for a final voyage. To Gorias. None of us have time to wait longer. Be who we know you to be."

Cathal stood and nodded. "To the end. Very well." Cathal put a fresh cigar in his mouth. "Now go so I can make a plan."

The ship duties continued without purpose until Cathal appeared that evening and Donn heard him tell Shipyard to assemble the crew the next day at noon. Meanwhile Dr. Cassart started shaving the crew without any request. Like a remedy for depression, the doctor went about pulling each crewmember to a chair on the top deck. His leather bag was open and it was like he was performing surgery on the ill soul. Donn saw the Berber woman, Takama, assisting him, as he seemed to have taken her under his wing. Alaster, who translated, had explained how they were both from the Nafusa Mountains. She was quiet but very kind. After Donn had sat through his turn, he did feel more himself. He nodded to the serene little French doctor.

Finally the time had arrived and the deck had every hand waiting with anticipation. Cathal came out of his cabin and held some maps under his arm. It was evident that Dr. Cassart had also found time to receive the baron for a shave.

Alaster saw Cathal limping and ran up to him. "May I carry anything for you Kusaila, sir?"

Cathal shot a questioning gaze at him. "Why do you call me Kusaila?"

"Kusaila is greatest hero. You are Kusaila who won't bend a knee. I serve you."

After a moment, Cathal breathed out his nose sharply then said, "You can carry black powder for me when the cannons are firing and everyone else is busily engaged pissing themselves." Cathal winked at him and then moved on.

The baron walked up the steps to the wheel and handed the maps to Kennedy. He carried a blue sash in his hand, apparently from one of the fallen sailors. Donn wondered if it was Luke's. Cathal stood under the great sails, on the sterncastle deck, and broke the malaise with a trumpeting message.

"Fewer boots now walk this ship yet this ship is so heavily burdened we might prepare ourselves to sink. We've faced a time of great sacrifice. Together we mourn. *I* mourn. The treacherous have cost us. Death follows us. Death is the uncovered stowaway upon the *Mistress* this cruel day. We have escaped to commit our heroic brothers to the lips of storytellers and continue our tale…to its end."

He grabbed both ends of the sash, its stained ragged nature held to their sight, and then tied it to the wheel. "Know now, to them that render tyranny, find your forfeit filling the blood grooves of our holy Irish blades!" He waved a finger at the men. "When death, his damn self, drags you by the beard into the gates of hell, yes, you will not submit to defeat. You'll know that by the end of that disagreement, you'll have a sickle with which to cut your next wheat harvest."

The men's eyes belied their exhaustion, filled with an unbending rage. They stood taller and Donn's spirit rose.

Cathal beseeched his crew's sense of purpose. "An Irish Parliament, without laws to protect and promote its people, is an unbearable tyranny upon us. It is a forgery of true intention—to confuse, torment, and diminish the man that would serve his neighbor. That parliament, filled with England's most deceived subjects, convened—no, performed—in a theater, scripted by foreign overlords. And now, with the abolition of said legislature, no pretense is left available to shroud our eyes longer. As an ardri, I'll act as a guardian for our land and all welfare that should be tended to shall then be made so. Our liberty will never be sold again. If the stone should give me the honor, my edict would declare peace for as long as we may enjoy it. It might enter our hearts, that long-forgotten dream, so we no longer bite at each other like the mistreated animals we have become. We have been the harbingers of the true Irish kingdom and we will provide that promise together. Never a knee shall be bent in Ireland again—for invader or nobleman." Cathal gripped the railing and raised the white rod high to a blazing sun. "Now to Ireland we go. We will bring the music back to the Irish again and free our shores from the invaders."

The men gloriously cried out in unison with outreached fists. Donn heard Cathal tell O'Hogan to plot a route for home and the wheel spun for destiny.

*****

Shipyard had duties that kept his mind off his paradise lost. As he was walking the deck on inspection, he hesitated upon seeing the boy, Alaster, sitting with his head down. Shipyard walked over and shouted. "What do you think you're doing!"

The young boy shook himself as if from a trance and squinted up past the large trousers and into the silhouette before the sun. "Nothing."

"Nothing! That won't do… I expect every member of this crew to do his duty. Do you see that?" Shipyard pointed to what Alaster was wearing. The boy looked upon the long blue sash that hung around his narrow waist.

"That there means you are a brother to everyone that calls this ship home. We rely on those that wear her colors. Do not dishonor our family. See to yourself and make useful your days of service to the baron."

The boy leapt to his feet and nodded quickly. Shipyard grabbed his head with a massive club for a hand. "Go now. To the quartermaster and help the poor man count his precious inventory." Shipyard gave a slight smile and winked. The boy seemed uplifted as he ran to go below deck. Shipyard let out a laugh as he himself felt the warmth of the sun again but also found amusing the shock Devine would have with such a sudden assistant. Shipyard added, "Tell him I'll know now if he's out of spirits!"

*****

Donn was working with Tymon when he noticed Shipyard's friendly treatment of Alaster. "He acts like the child's father. Alaster has his work cut out for him if he'll fill those boots."

Tymon stated as a matter-of-factly, "My father was a drunk. When I was a boy, the children would laugh and humiliate him when he'd sleep on the streets. I tried to protect him many times. He was my hero and I did not care if he was a drunk."

"Fathers are important," Donn said, thinking back on Lorcan.

Tymon smiled. "You know, I still think well of him. I do not blame him. In his eyes, I knew I was not a slave but his son. To be someone's son is very special for a boy on Montserrat."

Donn nodded and continued his work. The heat skinned his cheeks and scorched his eyes but it was familiar and, therefore, welcome, away from the dangerous shores.

Another quiet meal in the ship was passing. Donn was sitting next to MacIntyre on a wooden bench. Suddenly MacIntyre laid his hat on the table and spoke. "Here and another year goes by and I haven't seen the lights of Paris. What a wonder it could be though. A common man can become a king there." He took a bite of bread and spread his gaze around the cabin. MacIntyre looked exhausted but bemused by his place in the world.

"I never thought about such things. What gave you the interest?" Donn replied.

"I grew up always hearing about the splendor of France, so alive, and the beauty of ladies without rival. I wanted to make a life there. Of course, when it got hot there politically, I turned my attention to my friends and their struggles…basically I made too many promises while drinking and got swept up into more than I could have imagined. Now I know Napoleon's built a nation of merit where my service may be well-awarded."

"Certainly you've had opportunities to depart and start that life you've hoped for."

"Aye, but that's the problem with having friends. You see, I'm not going to enjoy the debt of wine and song owed me knowing these fools are out here without my greatness to protect them." MacIntyre chuckled. "Someday, one day, it'll come."

"I pray I'll be your first visitor to greet you on such happy occasion."

MacIntyre winced. "Now you see…now I'll have to make sure you're all right before I depart. These obligations are drowning me to be sure!"

Donn smiled and replied, "I'll do my best to not be a bother, my friend."

Later that evening, Donn wrote in his journal. His thoughts were random and swept around him. He centered himself when he thought of Bridget's smile the first day he met her.

My darling Bridget,

Frequent my dreams if you dare, Bridget. I shan't suffer if you're with me this evening, but if you venture into the darkness that fills my nights, then prepare for battle. I've been invaded by horrors and fears that ambush my peaceful bedtime wishes where we rest in each other's arms. Do you lay your head and breathe out the ash of another dream of us together that burned away as you slumbered? Have you shed a tear, stolen by a memory of us? Or have you forgotten about me and my love is now only my madness to beat upon me like a wretched creature that flies in endless storms? An idle day passes not for my thoughts to toil over what I must now confess. You once stroked the rough of my beard then pulled away. When you looked back into my eyes, I now remember a smile wearing hesitation's heavy chains. I've thought about that moment. Does your disappointment yet reign that I wasn't the boy you remembered? It's been a long absence since we parted that now such fear companions my days and dreams.

Jana's Mischief

As Bridget went to the dances, unbeknownst to her, she always had a little companion along with her during the journeys. Jana was her shadow so as to keep her pledge to Donn. She had to witness Bridget's obvious discomfort but hoped that would be the extent of this season's concerns.

A man approached Bridget at the very next dance. Jana heard his name given as Walter Flannery. She saw the two getting along quite well from her vantage, being upon the rafters where the party lighting didn't reach. She watched them dance together; in a monopoly of each other's time, they continued closely tied. Jana naturally decided she wouldn't stand for this behavior. After all, she had read Donn's letters as well!

As the night wore on, the guests began to retire and Jana nearly fell off her hiding spot in rage when Walter bowed and kissed Bridget's gloved hand. Jana decided she would squelch this young suitor's chances with no delay.

Instead of hanging on to the Feeney carriage back to the dock, she followed Walter. Walter was alone as he mounted his horse. On the path to Newport, he trotted forward. A lantern tied to his saddle emitted a crescent of light below him. Jana darted along, remaining hidden, and not even the sound of her breath was available for detection. Walter arrived in the nearly empty streets of Newport then retired to his lodging. Jana was there to watch him through his window. A letter was hastily written then sealed with wax. Then much to the surprise of Jana, he left the inn again and rode northwest on the path across the bridge over Black Oak River and up toward the civil parish building. He pulled a brick from the porch of the entrance and then slid the letter inside then replaced the brick. Walter then departed. Jana retrieved the letter and what she found pleased her.

*****

Bridget attended another social, this time, a daytime garden party. She was anxious without Walter there to consume the time of her attendance. As she tired of mingling, hoping to find him, finally she involved herself in a scavenger hunt. After it was over and the day's heat wore upon her, she longed for Walter to distract her from her loneliness. She eagerly went for the punch and its pink liquid cooled her chest and recomposed her. That's when she overheard an unbelievable conversation between a man and a woman.

The man nearly spit his dessert out over his plate through his efforts to chew and spoke in excited spurts. "Run out of town, was he. That Flannery boy was spying for the bloody backs."

The woman put down her tea in disgust. "Imagine an informer here! We can say good riddance to him then. Do you suppose he already has caused harm to any residents?"

"He wasn't long here. I suppose we can only be thankful the devil's correspondence was found."

Bridget grew pale, then carried her punch and left to, she hoped, better news. She thought about her friendship with Walter but his boyish looks would not parole him from his error. The scandal would have left nothing for Walter to remain for. That evening, Ella was noticeably agitated by the revelation that she found out about on her own.

"There will be others, Bridget, as I'm sure you know. Imagine, a king's informant so clumsy as to drop his secret message out onto the floor of the inn he was staying at. He won't survive long at his chosen profession. I'm so sorry." She tried to look empathetic to the plight she supposed Bridget felt.

Bridget felt honestly relieved and said little to her mother since her sympathy was a welcome respite from the unrelenting pressure to meet a suitor.

With Walter gone, Bridget had to force herself to make new friends. Bridget found some solace in conversation with other debutantes. They had such a bright outlook on attending the dances that she could nearly forget her own dreadful attitude. However, those women weren't there to entertain her. She saw the dreams in their eyes playing out before them and she dare not dampen their evening. Then she met Deirdre Cunningham, a girl whose melancholy could darken any corner. She was quite lovely with her pinned-up raven hair. Her peculiar nature was added to by a light scar that crossed over perpendicular on the side of her mouth. They started making conversation and each event was another opportunity to continue it.

Bridget adored learning about her new friend and felt she related quite well to her. Deirdre was a rare kind. At seventeen years of age, her dignity was fiercely protected and her hands anxious for the next task set before her. Her boundless energy seemed imprisoned in a dress met to put her on display rather than for labor. She once told Bridget a story to amuse her. Before her family left Cavan for Westport, she had raced, by horse, a young soldier from a neighboring family. She loved running a chestnut stallion past the fields of blue-flowered flax into the rough country and snuck off to do so again the day of the story. Shortly after crossing a stone-laden stream, she fell off that horse. Her collarbone was cracked and her breath was stolen from her. The soldier picked her up and inquired as to her health. Deirdre shook off any need to worry and hid the pain until her return home.

After leaving the soldier's attention, she fainted on the entrance floor. Her mother, a chatelaine named Suzanne, quickly tended to her and had the doctor visit. As soon as her fever broke, she was eager to ride again. Suzanne would hear none of it until her shoulder healed. Deirdre said she grew restless the longer she waited to mend, only willing to eat soup. She was quick to point out she despised a life trapped within walls.

Since Deirdre's family lived not far from the docks, there were many times when Bridget could meet up with her at her parents' house for company before continuing on to an event. Once when Bridget came, Deirdre was simply wearing a bleached muslin dress in her room. Although Bridget knew that her friend had very little appetite for fashion, before an imminent engagement, the poor choice of clothing had to be intentional. Deirdre was gazing out her window and wouldn't look at Bridget, even after her repeated inquiries. She offered up merely, "Nothing matters. The hours go by with no end."

Deirdre resisted any advances of affection from her family that afternoon. Bridget was frustrated by her rebukes to share any activity but Suzanne guided her away to allow some space for Deirdre. Deirdre's personality was changing over time; she would be quick to argue over frivolous points and seemed determined to isolate herself. Although Deirdre carried the freckles of a child, Bridget knew she was battling with the loss of the security of her grownup dreams now on the rough west shore. Bridget watched her have occasional outbursts and wished she could console her. When she'd approach her with comforting words, the slow foggy responses defeated any possible success to rescue her from those binds of melancholy. Bridget fought back tears since her only friend was so distant from her but she brushed her friend's hair in an attempt to connect with Deirdre as she stared out a window. Deirdre did not always attend the dances as Bridget did and it seemed her mood was always unpredictable.

*****

The days continued, and before long, Bridget was riding alongside a potential suitor. He was the regal type who never rested his chin. With the near-invisible speed of a clurichaun, Jana ran over and waved her hat in front of his mount while they crossed a low bridge and it spooked violently. He lost his stirrups and was thrown into the stream below. His fine riding clothes were soaked and he was badly beaten by the stones he had landed against. To Jana's frustration, Bridget went to his aid but he was too taken by his temper to let her aid him. He slapped his dripping hat on, caught his horse, and left her, taking with him what dignity he had left.

That evening, Jana was rolling around in laughter in the faerie tree while recounting the day's events to the little glowing winged residents and their animal friends. Her laughter sounded like the strangest bird with its silly song under moonlight. The smoke wafted out of Jana's pipe and out a knothole in the tree. She would grip the neck of a red squirrel with an arm while getting to the "good part" to the audience that somehow understood her. The squirrel spit out a green acorn that rolled onto Jana's lap, belly laughing in squeaks. The faeries would flash brightly when excited and so they did as the night wore on.

Another determined suitor Bridget had met was the owner of some prized hounds. Jana was kind enough to keep them howling all night and finding ways to unlatch their kennels during the day. That lasted until the gentleman became too foul to court Bridget.

As Jana was kicking her boots off in the tree that night, she felt quite pleased with herself. Relaxed, she was nodding off when a shadow fell over her. Her eyes sprang open and she looked out the opening in the tree. She could sense a conversation whispered. Then the last thing she saw was a dark bag overcoming her.

*****

Most distressingly for Bridget, her letters from Donn no longer appeared below the faerie tree. She searched and then prayed but no letters arrived. Her depression must have looked sudden and unexplainable; however, she could become hysterical with the slightest provocation. Her parents were losing their patience. Lady Catherine seemed to perspire when trying to keep her confidence about another possible suitor. Her upbeat attitude was consoling as ever but her words seemed ever more counterfeit.

At the next ball in Westport, her disgust kept her from allowing herself to dance or converse. She felt silly that if Deirdre was there, they'd be quite the pair. A young infantryman, Ensign Adam

O'Leary, who had tried several times in the past to court Bridget's affection, did approach her.

Adam inquired, "You wear your chosen misery tightly. Your beautiful eyes are cast down to my disappointment. Dare I ask, which dragons chase you in your dreams? I could chase them away for you."

Bridget looked up at the uniformed man. "Your predilection for me is flattering. It's true you're wasting your time with me."

Adam knelt in front of her. He gently placed his hand over hers upon her lap. "Search me for worthiness. Open your heart to me and I'll make you happy."

"My heart was already won by another some time ago. I'm so very sorry, Adam." She stood and his hand fell to his side. She walked away quickly from the ballroom.

Bridget's parents demonstrated their dismay toward their daughter at the next breakfast. They said she had become a social pariah. Terrible rumors, as a result of the failed courtships, prevented any further introductions. Her mother was not receiving proposals for Bridget's courtship anymore and demanded that Bridget had to recognize what that entailed.

Daley approached Bridget in the sitting room after she had gotten ready for bed. "Only every affront conceivable has been thrown at me as an obstacle to see you in a successful engagement. I've been so greatly humiliated by the outcomes of introductions that I'm having to avoid speaking of you in proper company to keep steady business. You've left me nothing for a choice, Bridget. You must depart to your aunt in Dublin where she can take charge of you."

Bridget's eyes were thrown at her father like daggers and spat, "I've lost my value as your daughter since I have no husband? Now you send me away!"

"Your future cannot be here, Bridget. You must take control of your life by committing yourself. You are setting no good example for Ashling as well!"

Bridget looked over at Ella, standing quietly in the doorway. "How would Father make his deliveries? You need me here!" Bridget sobbed.

After a still moment, Daley reached out and embraced Bridget but he was rebuked abruptly. She clumsily ran out of the house and past the gate where her mind was fleeing quicker than her feet could follow. Daley called out to her to no response.

She ripped her stockings as she moved down the dirt path in the black night. She was crying uncontrollably from overwhelming distress. She ran toward nowhere but her desire was to get as far as it took to leave her fate behind. She didn't care about falling in mud or skinning her knees on the hedge stones as she threw herself over them. She could hear that familiar scream in the distance that normally would terrify even in her dreams, but now, she ignored it. Exhausted as she was, she also became aware of another creature flanking her movements. Glimpses of it behind her told her that a wolf was following her. She ceased to cry because she couldn't find the breath to spare. Her slippers became caked in mud and weighed her down; she threw them off and ran barefoot. In her tattered night-dress, she moved through a maze of hedge flowers that she had never seen before. She scraped her hands on the sharp branches, feeling her way in the dark.

Her panting could hardly hide the noise of the predator's move-ments behind her. The soles of her feet were wet and she kept slip-ping on the grass. She ran into a running stream filled with smooth stones. She was waist-deep in the water when it began to change from a moonlight reflection to an indigo glow. The wolf followed and her heart leapt as she saw the massive creature near enough to leap upon her. As its paws hit the water, it began to be absorbed into the water; and as the body submerged, its yellow eyes were all that she could still see. The silver scales of a fish, where she would have thought she'd see fur, swam to her underwater. It was up against her and she could still see the same eyes. It didn't seem menacing since it was merely waiting beside her.

She threw herself on its back and hugged tightly as the fish carried her upstream. She looked up at the moon straight ahead and felt as if they were heading toward it. The stars began to migrate down from the night sky and play in the fog that had formed on the waters. She felt her damp hair slapping her back from the large creature's quick speed, and the spray made it difficult to see, when she saw the banshee moving alongside the shore. When she saw that the blue moon had nearly expanded to the entire horizon, the banshee shot in front of them and then hovered, awaiting her. The fish pivoted abruptly and Bridget was thrown into the stream. When she got to her knees at the edge of the stream, she looked up and behind her and saw that the fish had become a tall flat-faced brown bear. The banshee screamed at the bear and the bear returned the battle cry. The bear jumped over Bridget and into the banshee which tumbled back from the impact. As the two met, a bright light burst into Bridget's vision and there was no more.

Dublin

Bridget awoke in her own bed, quite weak. Her mother spoke softly. "Your father found you passed out along the shore. You've had a fever." She wiped Bridget's forehead with a cloth.

She was quick to remember her father's demands that she find work with family and possibly a new social circle in Dublin since her chances of marriage were ruined in their region. She couldn't go back to Belfast because the escalated hostility toward Catholics lowered her prospects considerably. The Savages were also Protestant but Daley's sympathies eventually led him to convert. Ella's family, the Clarks, were Protestant and cool toward Ella but still loved their children despite that and agreed to take Bridget in, even as a Papist.

As preparations for Bridget's departure continued, Ella began doubting her decision to send her lovely daughter away and it taxed her. Daley, realizing his wife's inner turmoil, put his hand in Ella's and said, "We may be a fixture in Bridget's life but we won't be the ropes that pull her away from what she needs."

The day arrived and Bridget was readying to leave the house for the waiting coach. Mrs. Murphy sobbed, nearing an egregious spectacle. "Casting you off into the pale. My dear colleen. Please take care of yourself." Bridget hugged her a long moment and they exchanged smiles despite Mrs. Murphy's tears. The blubbering nearly made Bridget lose her composure.

Daley approached Bridget before she boarded the carriage, very well knowing he was the source of her unhappiness.

Bridget spoke first. "Once I was in love with a man that could lift me so high, I needn't think of the ground again. Now I feel robbed of a dream. How foolish I am, Father."

Daley hugged his daughter. "He has beguiled you too long. You must let go for your own sake."

The family waved at Bridget as the carriage left. Bridget reached out and waved, seeing her mother holding back tears behind a hankie. Ashling ran to follow the carriage a short while to keep her sister in sight as long as possible. "Please come back soon, Bridget!"

"Oh, I will, sweet Ashling. Goodbye!"

*****

The horses stopped and Bridget saw the curious shop, jammed between the colorful buildings. Her aunt, Nora Clark, joyfully greeted Bridget at the mud-covered carriage. The hugs were generous as her belongings were untied from the rear rack. Between the canopies that cross-sectioned the towering windows was a black lacquered double door with brass handles. Bridget saw an ornate sign which was painted white, with a recessed black border, which centered above the shop entrance. In black cursive, the name "Clark" was boldly marked and below it, "Textile & Tailoring Expertise." Above the sign was a carved ram's head, its wood sanded in life-size detail, exhibiting an alert expression.

The bustling activity was immediately felt by Bridget. Wheelbarrows full of diverse supplies were hustled along by wiry men while slower-moving ox-driven carts also joined the commotion.

As they entered the shop, she shook the hands of the staff within what seemed a splendor of cloth inventory, crowding the messy workstations. Bridget noticed that, besides Nora, the greetings were hurried and she could feel the tension of the tight schedule they must have to keep. Nora gleefully spoke without pause about how the family was faring. Bridget nodded and smiled throughout the courteous review. Bridget was then led to a narrow stairwell adjoining the back wall which led to a dim hallway of doors. Nora carefully opened one and led Bridget in. It was a small but complete apartment that looked to have been recently tidied.

She adored her view of the busy street below, such a departure from sleepy Achill. She felt she had returned from the wilds and her once-demure poise now more a trained performance to please socially than of any true authenticity. How Bridget could wonder at the newness of it all, having been acclimated to where nature was in firm command of all life, as compared to this existence in an industrial harness. To be a subject to nature's whim was absent in proud Dublin.

Nora showed her a basin of water so she might freshen herself from the travel and invited her to tea that evening. As Nora closed the door, Bridget slumped in a pillowed resting chair beside the window. Her muscles were painfully tight from bracing herself for every sudden bump on the ride. The novelty of seeing an inexhaustible variety of new faces pass on the street wasn't lost to her and it aided in her relaxation. The excitement of the journey did drain her and exhaustion was quickly overtaking her for a welcome nap. As her eyes did close, she considered how odd it would be to wake up in such a strange new place. Would she wake up back near Slievemore or perhaps Belfast? If it might be Belfast, then she could then finally explain her experience with her darling Donn. *You see, it was all just a long dream.*

Bridget received letters from her family, especially her sister. It wasn't enough to cure boredom which motivated her to take walks. Bridget saw where the hens roosted in Dublin but she didn't hear the usual prattle that typically accompanied them. Sly incendiaries inserted within gossip pinned themselves invisibly upon the unaware victims. She was pleased the subjects here were industrious in nature, a product of an anonymity that prevails in a city.

During the shop's open hours, many fabrics lined the outside wall to impress the shoppers. Deciding what might catch someone's eye, and then hanging them carefully, was one of Bridget's duties. As an assistant, she always kept a notepad and took measurements for the shop tailor. She would keep inventory for the head draper whenever he brought in new product and whenever some length of cloth was used. The cloth-cutter was meticulous in his precision with necessary markings and cuts taking little time, thanks to long experience. The shop acted in concert continually to keep the customers satisfied.

Bridget slowly began to enjoy her time at the shop. She grew at ease when she became used to the faces and routines. She even enjoyed how, at any moment, someone might stroll in, ready to order the clothing suitable for a king or queen. The young errand boys seemed to flirt with her with their eyes which she felt was harmlessly adorable. The management of the shop was patient with her, perhaps a fortunate benefit of being family.

One morning, Bridget couldn't help but sneeze incessantly. Once she let out a noise that she swore made her dress move like a wind swept through it. Trying to stay on her heels during those sharp interruptions was tiring and her workload daunting. Her eyes were red and tearing up and having to greet customers like she had been weeping all day struck her as comical but *humiliated* fit better as to her mood. The other young female assistant placed the cloth beside Bridget's table. She commented with a casual mirth, "Dublin gets in your nose, doesn't it? You'll get used to it after a bit. I remember when the whole town seemed brown and smelled of sewer!"

"Yes, I've never felt so exhausted from these simple tasks." Bridget wiped her eyes while carefully holding her scissors.

The young woman jotted off her inventory against the active orders. "As much the buffoonery that walks through the door as what the air carries, you can be sure."

Bridget smiled through teary eyes. "My name is Bridget Savage. Very nice to meet you."

The young woman glanced over, taking a moment. "Cassidy Sullivan, same. I have some tea you can try later that should put the hop back in your step." Cassidy pursed a smile and went to gather another load of fabric to carry to the cutting boards.

At the end of the day, Cassidy approached Bridget at the door as she was picking up her hat and belongings. "Off to grab a bite?"

Bridget was fumbling with a pin to hold her hat as she responded, "I thought I might explore my surroundings. It can get so stuffy spending my days inside."

"There is a darling garden near here that helps you nearly forget you're in this cramped city, at St. Stephen's Green. As a bonus, and if you don't mind a brisk pace, we can find a vendor there that has fresh chocolates." Cassidy beamed a welcoming invitation.

Bridget felt humbled by the willing company and nodded. "That would be ever so delightful. Please take me to such a place." She let out a grateful chuckle.

They strolled along Beaux Walk. As Cassidy and Bridget conversed, Bridget saw couples enjoying the weather, hand-in-hand. The birds fluttered and the tranquility was a welcome respite from the industrial streets. As it grew dark, they made their way back to the shop apartments. The lamplighters, sequencing through their assignments, gave some safety to the night.

Cassidy Sullivan became her closest friend there, always subtly pointing out mistakes Bridget was about to make without making it embarrassing for her. Nora was always kind, and among them at times, but her aloof nature was spurred on by her ceaseless responsibilities. After inquiring about Bridget's past, Cassidy asked why Bridget didn't like the balls that Cassidy would be jealous to attend.

Bridget dismissively answered, "Of course, it could be fine. I met a boy though and we were forced apart before the season. I suppose I was foolish but I waited for him."

"He must have put quite the spin on you! Whatever became of him?"

"He was serving aboard a ship and was sending me letters. Then one day, they stopped. I can only assume he changed his mind about us." Bridget was becoming a little visibly restless speaking about it. Cassidy could tell she should disengage.

"I suppose had he remained, then we'd have never met. For that, I'm thankful." Cassidy smiled and refocused on her tasks.

The days blurred and Cassidy's past came up. Bridget learned that Cassidy had previously labored at a brutal flax spinning mill and only gained the opportunity to work at the Clark shop through an apprenticeship, paid for by her father who ran a local bleach field.

Once, after work, all the employees had a social in the shop to celebrate the business anniversary. Beer and appetizers were brought in and everyone mingled. Bridget sat down next to a sharp-looking man named Manus who worked with the head draper.

Politely she broke the ice. "How did you come to work at the Clark shop, Manus?"

He was sipping his beer neatly and welcomed the invitation to share. "I attended a Dublin society school."

Hoping for more to go on, Bridget added, "Is that where you learned about cloth then?"

"No…" He slyly smiled and straightened his collar.

"Oh, well?" Bridget cocked her head and rolled her eyes a bit before chuckling.

"I never considered cloth as an industry where I could prove any value. One summer, after those dreadfully boring school lessons, I would sweep a museum for my father. That's when I saw her. An elegant marble creation. I wanted to sculpt ever since I laid eyes on her. Some Greek creation that seemed impossible to imagine or even yet create."

"So you took classes to pursue that profession. Are you still planning on such a career?"

"I learned that there are very few people willing to pay an apprentice to chisel stone. I decided on a more practical path. One's life always finds the practical path, it seems."

Attempting to be supportive, she offered, "Perhaps fate will place you where you must see your dreams through yet."

He downed the remainder of his drink. "A lot is left to be seen. The Liffey runs deep, does it not?" They both smiled and the rest of the night was popular for all.

Bridget found life in the city to be complementary to adaption from a country upbringing. Food was more preprepared in stalls and cafes across the city which made life easier for those thrifty with their time. Working in a bustling manufacturing jungle made the convenience of comfort items a commodity in itself. She nearly daily ate biscuits with jam and some kebab wrapped in paper when rushed.

Bridget was occasionally frustrated by the step backward she now experienced working in Dublin. The fashions were still friendly to London dress and they took pride in ignoring the progressive styles that Paris embraced. She had to add a petticoat and other heavier clothing to increase her modesty which, dismayingly, added to the weight she bore on hot humid days. She was proud of her figure and didn't understand the need to wrap it multiple times like an overdone construction project. Perhaps she was spoiled but there it was in how she felt rebellion in her senses. When she was at home or with kinder circles, she was elated to wear a bright flouncy dress that hung well. Some associated her style to that of a little girl, but to her, those peacocks had none of the confidence she expressed in her dress.

At night, she peered out her window and marveled at the city's impressive energy. The Grand Canal knew no rest. Packet boats brought scheduled goods without pause. Beef exports and linen yarn filled every dock and warehouse. Dublin Bay had become silted and now, at the Grand Canal, there was always new construction taking place to keep pace with the freight demand. Fewer claiming a farming livelihood drove down labor in the countryside with landowners seeking livestock enterprises for business. Even cattle purchased at Ballinasloe Fair might find themselves coming through Dublin and, later, grazing outside a West Indie port.

She became aware that the most excellent coopers in Ireland made their reputations supplying the ambitious merchants along the quays of the Liffey. Their dry-tight barrels were paramount to successful trade and many skilled laborers were employed. Many of those same men were smugglers before the rebellion, now working respectable jobs. Then there were the districts of the city where some actually made a full purse simply philosophizing over nature and worked to grow closer to it. Francis Street was always active with the upper crust of Dublin society and the shops were in direct competition to attract buyers of their rare imported items. Cassidy would tell her about the notorious drinkers at the secret Hellfire Club meetings but she hadn't encountered the wealthy hooligans. Past the core of the city were the innumerable shacks within which the working class lived. The city could be crowded but she counted herself lucky having comparatively luxurious lodging. She knew the city was unable to accommodate the rapid masses of people that arrived every year.

*****

Bridget walked up South George's Street to meet Cassidy for a drink. Cassidy claimed that to not go to the Long Hall once a week would be certain failure in the fabric business. Bridget had grown a taste for pale beer, and Cassidy wanted her to try a pub that had a section just for women. She walked in and didn't see Cassidy but went to sit at the bar. It was lightly crowded by a cosmopolitan group of ladies and the bartender quickly noticed her.

The barkeep, who had the look of a grown mischievous schoolboy, poured the ale. "I haven't noticed you here before."

"You… I mean, this pub…came highly recommended by a friend from work." Bridget was flustered by her error.

The bartender placed the drink in front of her. A glint in his blue eyes revealed he didn't miss her correction. "Oh, those that ache open our doors."

Bridget chuckled. "Did you say ache?"

"Yes, of course. They want what they can't have so they come here because of the ache. We always have the remedy."

"So I can easily imagine as long as your remedies are poured, not knowing the ailment, then you're only successful if I forget all that came before I set foot through those doors?" Bridget's eyes opened wide, toyingly waiting for confirmation.

"The name is Michael, if you be needing anything more." The bartender smiled coyly then wiped the bar before moving over to another patron.

It wasn't long before Bridget spotted Michael glancing over at her while he chatted with his regulars. The smile was wickedly playful that he shot her way the moment he caught her eye. She noticed how lean he was, stretching his arms across the bar to pass mugs. His white sleeves were rolled and his coal-black hair was swept back to his collar. She could see a metal pendant he wore around his neck flash under the lamps when he leaned forward. She played with the lapel of her jacket and rubbed her palms, thinking about what the pendant was. *Where are you, Cassidy!*

As if a prayer had been answered, in rushed Cassidy who let out a deep breath as if oxygen only existed in this establishment. "So happy you found the place. Have you had to wait long?"

"And where have you been?" She took an angry sip of the draft and looked over to see if Michael was near.

Cassidy slid her tongue through her teeth, smiled, then let an escaped giggle through. "Ahhh, I can tell you noticed the scenery this establishment offers. I knew you'd love the place. I always know the best places to spend the evenings. Now tell me all about this boy you mentioned from Achill." She waved her fingers at Michael and called out, "The usual, darling!"

****

Bridget could see the buildings had makeshift repairs and the streets were littered. The poor of the city scavenged a survival in the filthy properties owned by the manufacturer hungry for willing labor. The agrarian people came to Dublin with little in their pockets and could demand scant luxury in exchange for their sweat. Small children ran across the street like bands of scurrying animals.

In an alley, Bridget saw shillelagh fighting and that instinctively caused her to pull Cassidy along to quicken the pace. Their walk was long since they had to avoid Dame Street, which had many pickpockets, and the brothel along Temple Street was not a place for a respectable lady to pass by. They could easier find typhus than a hackney cab that evening. Perhaps it was the spirits they had consumed as they missed a turn. The Pinking Dandies, known for their lawless attitude, were seen across the street and Bridget became ever more anxious to stay elusive.

A man stumbled out of a shebeen in front of them both. Completely disheveled, he rubbed his one undamaged eye to adjust to the dark street. They could see he had been pitchcapped by his scarred bald head, a marked rebel. As Bridget began to move past him, he tried to stop her.

"Lovely ladies, are you lonely tonight?" He kept raising a hand, even as the women swatted it away, as if his mind was incapable of stopping himself. He kept racing in front and throwing an arm up to them.

"Why do you run? I can pay you. I can pay you!" His breath made Bridget close her eyes a moment. He grabbed onto Cassidy's sleeve and Bridget struggled to shake him off her person. Bridget saw, out of the corner of her eye, no one was willing to help them and some, perhaps, even willing to join in the accostment.

A clamor of boot steps was nearly overwhelmed by the sound of Cassidy shrieking. A wooden club came down on the outstretched man's arm. Then the women watched as a red-uniformed man pushed him down, now unconscious from pain and liquor.

The rescuer breathed heavily then spun his stick back under his armpit. He tipped his shako helmet back and said, "I'm attached to the Irish militia, Twelfth Dublin City. How may I assist you, mesdames?

"You've been a great help. I thought we were in grave danger. Were you on patrol?" asked Bridget.

The sweat trickling down from under his helmet and down his cheeks gave evidence to his exhaustion. "I was having a drink myself, to be honest. I saw you both and thought I could assist. It might be best if you all moved along. This is a poor part of town to be caught unaccompanied at this late hour."

Bridget was loud to say, "I'm sure we'll be quite safe now, sir. Thank you so." Cassidy was too upset to speak at first, trying to hide her shame for what had occurred.

"Thank you, mister…" queried Cassidy.

"Lieutenant Whelan. At your service." She offered her hand and he held it and bowed a moment.

Cassidy fluttered her eyelashes and said, "If you should find yourself along the canal sometime, visit the Clark shop. I would be quite pleased to offer you some tea to repay your gallantry."

Whelan smirked as he seemed reasonably flattered. "I would be so delighted. Until we meet again?"

"Cassidy Sullivan." Her voice was soft and gave away her new affection for Whelan.

The dashing soldier nodded and said, "I have a meeting back at Dublin Castle with some yeomanry so I must depart. I hope tonight finds you safe home, ladies." He left without further pause and the women continued.

Bridget was relieved by the intervening protector. However, she knew what allowed the presence. The police authorities were kept quite busy in Dublin. The British were detaining barges regularly, searching for contraband. Revenue cruisers often caught smugglers on the Liffey and beyond. A substantial presence of law enforcement was as welcome as it was inherently oppressive to the population.

Gorias

Holy chapels were erected by missionaries and prophets at some locations with divine meaning to harness their significance for Christianity. They marked them and then let men forget their origins since it served no purpose for the holy Roman Catholic Church.

The *Mistress* had weighed anchor outside the island of Inis Mór. A soft rain was falling upon the ship as it anchored. Cathal was in his study, partially dressed and holding a steaming drink. He wore only a heavy fur jacket on his lean frame and black belted pants.

A knock brought Cathal's attention. Tymon opened the cabin door and approached wearing a wide leather strap slung over his shoulder, carrying a short sword in an overwrapped scabbard. Cathal looked away from his papers to the broad-shouldered Irishman.

"The hour has been reached, Baron. Let the sailing crew you placed your trust in, for the safety of the voyage, to now also extend that safety ashore."

Cathal smiled and could not help but feel some relief that such spirit still survived.

Tymon continued with an air of declaration, "We know how to capture islands. It has been enough time for us since Puerto Rico. Send us against whatever's ahead and we will not fail you."

The cold waters slapping the hull could be heard outside as Cathal responded, "I'm near my ancestral home. Where the Tuatha de Danann landed in Connacht was once a standing O'Ruairc king."

Cathal rose and walked over to Tymon. He continued, "Whether it may have been demons or Normans that dropped our banner at Dromahair, with you by my side, I shall fear nothing." Cathal took Tymon's forearm and they shook. "Ready your men for a shore party. I know not what will be required so act accordingly."

With nothing more needing to be said, Tymon nodded then left quickly to prepare. Donn was told of the landing party being assembled and said goodbye to Croaghaun over a minute of quiet company.

*****

The men, with lit torches, had crossed over the low hills to a ruined stone building. In the ancient church, the stone arches had demonic heads protruding from the wall. Donn idly queried to Cathal, "What are those creatures?"

"The heralded success of spiritual bounty hunting. A long time ago, chiefdom guardians would put the heads of our enemies on the walls of our home to ward off those that wished our families harm. The earliest monks might vanquish a demon and do the same—brave men that sacrificed a great deal to make our land safe to rest our heads—by putting a few on a wall."

Donn looked at them closer. "So these are a warning. This church has some bragging rights then."

"Yes, it does…"

Cathal chose to say a few words as the crew stood in a pack inside. "How many times I've sat foot in the Lord's house and felt it wasn't to welcome the likes of our people. Our church has been empty for too long and you're the remains of what once stood. English is the language of the oppressors and so is the reformed Bible since not a copy is written for the Irish ear. Both were offered to us at the end of a sword. However, I've been told of a king many centuries ago that sorted out an argument between two men over an interpretation of proper ritual to show God respect. He walked to each man and asked them if they believed God gave them the wisdom to believe it. They each said yes with certainty. So the king said, 'I am not your arbiter nor can your brother be, for God is in each of us and mutual respect shall be shown. Let us worship together as equal brothers and each as a loved son of God that carries a cherished piece of his wisdom.'" Cathal walked over to Donn.

"That couldn't possibly work. Sacrilege would be rampant. People need a shepherd to guide them," said Donn.

"The holy men and their people from the far past had a different perspective than ourselves. They spent every day trying to shorten the distance between them and God through learning and experiencing the world He gifted them. They weren't offended that they were ignorant of much of the divine truth. Like children, they were loved and they loved Him back." Cathal implored Donn, "God loves life and life is about change. To change in order to better serve Him and His glory is a purpose in our lives."

Donn looked solemn. "I see little of such gracious tolerance in neighbors through my memory. It's hard to relate to such a story surrounded by such ugliness."

"We strive for purity in mind despite it being unreachable. Anyway…people get lost, especially when catastrophe greets them at every dawn. It's for us to try for all of them." Cathal paused a moment and then added, "We are resident in two existences. Both of which God gave us but free neither of sacrifice nor responsibility."

Donn saw Judge kneeling with arms open wide, looking up at the stars. His white hair was matted down, free from its fur cover this rare occasion. Donn mentioned with some amazement, "I've never prayed in a stone church. We once held mass in a home but the local magistrates dispersed it."

Judge didn't react to Donn's words, remaining still.

Donn offered, "Are you ready to go?"

The old man slowly responded, "I feel I'm where I need to be. This holy place needs to hear a few words from me." Judge grabbed Donn with a hand and shook him gently. "*Dia duit* and return safely."

The crew gathered at the center of the room. Cathal raised the white rod above his head. "This is the key to travel to other kingdoms. The finger of God presses through the universe. Now we will go to Gorias."

The men looked at each other in both apprehension and antici-pation. Donn's feet felt light against the stone floor as he felt his arms drifting upward. He felt like his mind had been caught up in a vac-uum while the words echoed into the beyond. The night sky moved as if the stars were draining away from whatever center Donn's sight took in. He lost sight of the building as he sensed they were all envel-oped in an orb of moving glints of color, seeming to travel faster than a returning reflection. When they arrived, they collapsed simultane-ously. Donn tried to look out but all he saw were objects cast into prism-like shapes. After a minute, his vision cleared and he felt sense return to his mind. Shipyard checked on each man. All were well. All around them were rolling hills and black trees where before desola-tion had been all around, now completely replaced.

MacIntyre was brushing himself off and having difficulty steady-ing himself. He announced, "I'm going to be sick. I'm going to be si—" He nearly threw up but stopped himself. "Och, this has been a grand vacation. To think there was a time when I never thought I'd set a foot outside Ulster. But this has been enough travelin' for me." He let out a deep breath and continued, "Running from the bits of red at home is looking a damn sight more relaxing now."

Cathal motioned to Tymon to have the men follow him. "We'll pass over these grasslands and head toward the foothills. I wager there will be some establishment placed in such a location."

Sporadic trees were warm to the touch. The excess heat invited strange creatures to populate them. Shipyard reached up to a white-barked tree bearing a fruit that resembled a large red berry. MacIntyre yelled out quickly, "What'cha think you're doing!"

Shipyard, startled, dropped his hand and turned to MacIntyre.

MacIntyre pointed at the fruit and exasperatingly said, "Have you forgotten everything you've learned? We're in a kingdom of the Lord and you want to eat weird fruit off a tree? We'd all be done for."

Shipyard winced in confusion. "I'm hungry, it's food, I don't think Bible lessons include this particular tree."

MacIntyre tipped his hat back, shook his head, and began to move away. "All right, go ahead. Don't let destroying this world get in the way of lunch!" Shipyard hesitated and then moved away from the tree, still hungry and now quite irritated.

The crew passed through grass that was waist-high. They could see cattle, twice the size of those on earth, grazing peacefully. Donn saw Tymon shaking his compass, obviously unable to find a heading.

When some animal would appear, it was often unknown to them. The animals acted as if they couldn't see the Irish or at least devoid of an interest in the visiting men. Twisted-trunk trees shed yellow leaves in the light winds that caressed this country. The fragile leaves, like lost petals, floated in the sky. They felt young as they walked, as if renewed by the calming surroundings. Donn mentioned to Cathal as they walked, "I feel the sun's warmth but I cannot see it." Cathal looked up and couldn't see a sun either. Although a strange land, Donn secretly wished Bridget was there to witness it with him.

Although there was no high ground apparent near them, they made camp on a clearing where the grass had been grazed down. The men used the food carried with them to recuperate beside a small fire of gathered sticks. Donn jotted some words as his head was challenged to stay upright; exhaustion was taking him. He leaned over and set the paper alight in the flames.

Devine, beside him, asked, "Why would you burn your words?"

Donn opened his eyes quickly and responded, "In case we don't return. At least they might find her one day." He then slumped down, too tired to continue.

The crew all slept soundly. Cathal dozed off while still holding his knees. He had a dream of a great tree surrounded by darkness. The heavy branches carried naked warriors slung about them. Their broken corpses were painted as the ancient ones did. He noticed a pair of golden eyes that appeared and disappeared beneath the black leaves. Cathal felt danger lurking. It clawed its way down the trunk, in full view. Its long tail was a lion's and its body was covered in tight long feathers while its feet were a dragon's and its head was a tiger's. The yellow-and-green-streaked creature was twice as long as he was tall and eye to eye in height. The whites of its eyes spun inside its head. He thought he'd be attacked the moment his vision blurred. His dream shifted so that all that appeared was a wooden table with a single candle resting upon it. A feminine voice in the void could be heard, and Cathal walked over and sat at a chair that had appeared. When he looked across, he saw a black-hooded person sitting opposite him.

Cathal casually said, "Can I offer you anything? I'm certain we can imagine some bread and wine to enjoy."

The intruder of Cathal's sleep made no movement but spoke, "The angel Goria once administered here before he was slain in the rebellion. The dominion of this land is unstrapped."

"How can I help?"

""The sword spoke to you, Cathal. You must go confront the beast."

"You mean that adorable-looking cat?"

"Only the blood of a hero can wield the sword. The beast is impatient with those that would disturb him. The beast will kill the unworthy. You have seen those that failed him in the tree of Baal."

Cathal knew the voice he heard. Many dreams, throughout memories past, carried her voice. "What is the beast? How could such a creature take the sword?"

"He is the spirit of freedom. He exists as long as man survives, no matter his unrest."

"All right…" Cathal nodded his head while trying to determine another inquiry. "I know you." He then began to feel himself folding into himself.

Cathal awoke to Donn shaking him. "Yes, good lord, what?"

Donn asked, "Are you well, Baron? You've been motionless for hours after the rest of us have woken."

"I sometimes slip into dreams that are quite an adventure."

"What sort of dreams?"

Cathal rose and dusted himself off. He squinted an eye at Donn. "Did you wake me up?"

Donn cleared his throat. "Yes…yes, I did. I apologize."

Cathal pushed Donn's shoulder with his fingers and began to grab his belongings. "She calls to me in my dreams. Those are the ones I never forget. Let's go."

"How long?"

"Since Montserrat. Come now, no time to waste."

The crew continued the long march into the unknown. MacIntyre watched as a lioness, several yards away, lifted her head with a mouthful of grass. He spoke to anyone listening. "I'm not sure if my fair sense followed me here, perhaps we should have a sit?" Despite the oddities around them, they continued following Cathal who rarely paused his stride.

None could deny the tranquility as they walked together. The weather was a gentle warm day where one could accomplish anything for as long as it took. They all struggled to contain a euphoria that filled them since the feeling of peace drenched their being.

Cathal spoke to Donn as they were realizing the new terrain. "We were on the edge of this place when we landed. Now we'll find what this place has in store for us."

At last, they discovered some dwellings. They could see it was an encampment of very unrefined children that scattered as they saw the Irish approaching. A few of the men attempted to speak to the frightened youngsters but none would leave their pitiful hiding spots. The stick shacks they called home couldn't withstand a kick before collapsing.

Cathal squinted, bemused. He idly queried, "What is going on here?"

Tymon turned the baron by grabbing his shoulder. A stout woman with cropped graying hair was suddenly there at the edge of the camp. She had a sharp focus on the Irish that seemed to warn Donn that she was not to be trifled with.

Her skin carried radiant blue markings that wrapped her body in ribbons that never ended. She went to one knee.

Cathal called out, "Pardon us, we appear to be lost. Whom do we have the pleasure of meeting?"

"Call me Caireen. Why are you here?"

Cathal responded with a direct answer, feeling silly to keep secrets. "To retrieve the sword once claimed by Nuada."

She slapped her knee. "In that case, you're welcome, but if you'll excuse me, I have much work to do." Caireen went to a large cauldron bubbling over a fire and began to stir. The children seemed to relax enough to exit their hiding places and began to stand around the village. The barefoot children hardly had a cloth to cover them-selves, although one could tell that they were well fed.

Caireen stepped upon a platform to a steaming cauldron. She was using a large oar to stir its brothy contents. She seemed in a foul mood when the crew followed her.

MacIntyre wandered close with a disturbed look and asked, "Are you making a terrible potion?"

"I'm making the children lunch."

"How many children have you put in the pot then?"

Caireen looked perturbed and ceased stirring. She looked to Cathal. "Do I need to be worried about him?" Cathal looked up briefly in embarrassment.

With his big paw, Shipyard hooked MacIntyre's neck back into line.

Cathal flatly stated, "We need your help in knowing where to go."

Caireen saw, out of the corner of her eye, Takama washing the dirt off a child's face. "Gather around near the table. I can speak to you as I serve the children."

Donn was looking at a wandering cow moving through the camp. A little girl was examining him from a distance she judged as safe. Her dirty long red hair was bunched up above her head. Donn pointed at the cow and bellowed a moo to see what the girl would do.

The enamored girl mimicked the sound but then burst out laughing before finishing. She then ran back to her friends. Some sailors hoisted some happy children on their shoulders as they gathered to Caireen.

Caireen told a story. "I've been here a long time and I can tell you what I know. Gorias harbors what the great flood—which washed the sin away—delivered unto this place. Lies sit on nature's lips within this land. Time cannot escape the darkest night and redemption is unfound. Where Kaleth sits as ruler, the ash is all that grows in his fields."

Cathal interrupted, "Kaleth? Who is that? Does he have the sword we seek?"

Caireen raised a hand for silence then continued, "It was a desperate prayer I heard one evening. I was beckoned and came to find a crib with a creature not of its parents. I searched for signs. Before long, I came unto the sound of a babe crying down in a valley. I investigated until I saw I was chasing three changelings carrying a child wrapped up in a bundle. I made my furious presence known to them. They went into a burrow and so I followed them into its vast depths. When I arrived here and had killed the kidnappers, I was then introduced to the real villain. Kaleth had made himself ruler of an abandoned realm where he could be free to prey on bloodlines from where His light touches. He is an outlaw who feasts on the blood of God's children. I'll let no harm come to the children as my Creator gave me power to do so, but alas, I cannot stop them from becoming adults."

Cathal shrugged. "How could that be left to happen where the Tuatha de Danann lived? There is no place the Lord does not have dominion."

"The land of Gorias is not on a planet. It's between where the divine may rise and the mortals can thrive. This land exists by a construct of God and only extends as far as one wills it to be. No one is meant to be here as it was merely produced to acclimate the angels to life with your kind."

"We'll leave as soon as we have the sword."

Caireen was serving the kids lining up that had their bowls. "Why do you seek it? The world He gave you needs no such weapon now that the new kingdom has begun."

"I believe without what once brought our people together, we will be kept apart. We are lost without a king to bring back our harmony."

"To find what you seek, you must go over mountains and into the waste of what once surrounded the temporary home of the Tuatha de Danann. Stay clear from the stone structures and you'll find what you seek on the other side."

Cathal showed his lack of entertainment at her guidance. "I'm afraid I missed this geography lesson back in school. Where might we find these mountains?"

Frustrated, Caireen rolled her eyes and grabbed Cathal's shoulder. "You see that hill with the rocky ridge facing us? Go that way." She went to wash clothes in a carved stone basin.

Cathal yelled, "Do you want to come with us? Perhaps together we can free these children."

She spat back, "Perhaps. Or we'd fail and these children would be dragged to Kaleth's keep soon after. Now go on." She waved them off.

Devine whispered to Cathal, "She's a rebel, same as those we chase, Baron. Let us go get what we came for." Cathal gave up his attempt to convince the woman and acknowledged with a nod toward Devine. With a shout, Cathal told the men to gather to leave.

Donn noticed Takama ignoring the Irish regrouping for departure. "Takama, are you joining us?" She simply shook off Donn and left him startled. Cathal approached Takama; Alaster ran up to them.

As Takama was feeding a baby at peace in her arms, she spoke in her native tongue. Alaster translated, "One of these children is Conri's daughter and she'll consider all of them his children now. That's why she stays."

Cathal responded, "They can't return home because their parents would never accept them. Kaleth will eventually slaughter them here anyway. It's pointless."

Takama, dejected, nodded her head and Alaster said, "Perhaps you aren't troubled by the fact he has these children as prisoners."

Cathal sneered. "My blood still runs hot same as yours." He looked up at the sky and let out a chuckle. "Damn life, it gets so complicated." He gripped his hands until they turned white and then sighed. Donn could see Cathal had begun to perspire from the stress of his decisions. "All right. I'll figure something out. Stay safe. Will you be staying with her, Alaster?"

Alaster chirped loudly, "I'm a member of your crew so I go where you go."

Cathal nodded and turned to take the lead with his men.

The trophies of demonic mischief littered the sight of the Christian warriors as they ventured onward. Bits of human bones lay in the patchy grass that was slowly dissolving into desert landscape. Donn did silently dread what he saw as the greatness stripped from the land much the same as Ireland itself.

They made camp and another evening passed. They awoke inside a smoke that crawled along the ground. With some trouble, they gathered their things. Shipyard spoke to Cathal, "This fog isn't dissipating, Baron. I fear we might step off a cliff here."

Tymon peered at where the horizon should be and searched for a marker. With no sun or compass, his options were slim. He saw a golden flicker in the far-off distance. "Follow me. I know where to go," he said. Cathal waved the men to follow Tymon's lead.

They passed by trees that had died from animals aggressively gnawing on their trunks, the bark ripped away. It gave Donn an ominous feeling and he rubbed the cloth wrap on the grip of his sword. They made it through the fog and found the wasteland that met an abandoned city.

The jagged stone hills that surrounded the flat plain between them were artificially hollowed and smoothed out as an encircling bowl. Countless groups of pillars appeared to orderly frame open entries into different establishments within the polished canyon walls. Terraced paths, as wide as a team of six horses abreast, climbed around the shining lime rock to those passages. Upon the flat plain, the crew marveled at the sight. Two piles of boulders were near each other, stacked like pyramids, perilously erected. A low blue stone ring was embedded with a pool of sand. They saw hexagonal pillars of silver mineral standing above the ground at different angles and bunches. Donn thought that each thing they saw was in its own appropriate place, as if for presentation. When he saw a flat-roofed building near some grooved posts, he ventured closer. He could see stalls and the unmistakable scuffs from hooves against the lower wall. The stone posts were snubbing posts. He ran his hand over a stone weapons rack that had slots for spears in it. It was the stable of the Tuatha de Danann.

Cathal was enthralled by the sight. "They trained here. This is quite remarkable. Look at where they lived."

Although everything was abandoned and stripped, it still had a beauty about it.

McIntyre questioned, "Where do you suppose the demon is?"

"They prefer darkness so that's where he'll be." Cathal pointed toward a spire-like building close to the chokepoint of the canyon walls. The crew snuck closer and readied their weapons. They heard shriek-like laughter echo and the banging of people laboring.

A deep and drained stepwell surrounded the tower. That tower opened up like a flower on top, twenty feet above the many narrow wooden bridges that connected to it. Spiraling staircases wrapped the outer wall as well as the tower.

The crew laid eyes on the terrifying residents of the stepwell. The changelings were feasting as blocky barstool-high people with greasy faces. They chortled and ate with a vile gleam in their small bulging eyes. Their chubby hands stuffed their mouths as their naked bodies twitched with the joy of the consumption.

Demons endlessly partied on inexhaustible plenty. Stone statues of Greek godlike figures danced in a fluid ballet, floating in midair before each awning down the stepwell. There was fuel-less matter flamed in bronze bowls all around each level. The shadows of the activity told of legions of enemy below them. Red sprites illuminated the depths of the subterranean structure, and above the men was a wavy dome of blue gases exhausted in spinning currents. Above the gases, the crew could see an open viewing platform where a large demon sat atop the spire that hung over the stepwell.

*****

The Demon King sat on a throne made of the skull of a massive stag. The snout was smashed in for the large pillows that acted as his chair. The skull had been varnished in the red sap of the dragon's blood tree and reeked of death. Small portals flanked the tiled pathways to different rooms in the temple. The fire that the portals emitted reached down and not up as gravity would normally dictate. A floor of ground bone was beside the walkways where another temple may have had a garden. A comparably small red fanged scantily-clad female creature was leaning on his shoulder and noticed a group of human men approach the edge of the stepwell.

The Demon King, Kaleth, leaned forward. His appearance was like the shape of a human but not complete. His skin looked like it was an unfinished carving and his stature was as a goliath. He howled gently and the noise from within the stepwell quieted. A low voice that caused the canyon to tremble called out, "All those that approach shall bow before me."

Cathal responded, more for his men to hear, "We shall not."

The king spoke with disdain, "Carneus once led you children like rays to conquer all that stood before you. Then you betrayed him for that whore Anu and her watermarked followers. Do you see what I've done with the home of your lost cherubim?"

"What I see is a false one breaking God's law."

Kaleth rose forward with such force that the Irish felt the air push into them. Alaster's nose began to bleed from the impact. Kaleth leaned his head forward and clicked his long tongue. "Leave now or never see home again." He then retired back into his tower chamber. The female demon followed him. The changelings began to stir in unison and slip in toward portals spread throughout the walls.

Cathal waved the men on so that they could continue to the mountain passage.

*****

The demon woman crumpled on to the floor as if bracing against a gale. "He comes for me! He'll be my king, my promise of the light you stole from me will be returned by his will."

The Demon King, in an instant, arrived in front of the succubus and, with a strong grip, choked her. Then his voice reverberated in the chamber. "They are nothing, Ninbanda, but game hiding from me." Saliva dripped from his lips. "When they entered my kingdom, they took on a new understanding of existence where they are no longer masters of their world but prey to be hunted." Her tears were shaken from her face and then slapped the floor. Frothing at the mouth, he slammed her against the tile with a second eruption of rage. "How dare you defy me! Your adorers drowned and you were cast off into the desert. You've been blessed as my concubine."

Ninbanda spit blood and trembled with a sort of smile toward Kaleth.

Kaleth snarled. "They had better leave or my full wrath they'll find."

"You're scared of the marked ones! You're terrified!"

Kaleth moved out of the room "I'll deal with you later, little one."

The succubus, writhing around, cried out like she was taunting the sky itself. "You can toss me against a wall hoping I'll break like a glass, but I assure you, I will not!" Her veil of hair caught her gasps of agony as Kaleth disappeared from her.

*****

Donn was walking in the center of the crew. Sweat dripped from his brow as they continued in the heat. The leather of his rifle strap bit into his neck. He was miserable but grateful to not be alone there. He looked up when some commotion caught his attention. Tymon and O'Hogan were walking, right flank of point. They heard a whimper and cough. Tymon gestured to O'Hogan to follow him and they ran over toward the sounds. They found a naked baby boy shaking on the grass. Tymon picked the baby up in bewilderment. He handed the baby to O'Hogan, then began to wave for Cathal's attention. The crew all stopped and took notice. Donn heard a terrified scream and then the brush moving. Tymon could be seen investigating his collapsed shipmate and then quickly drawing his sword. All the crew began to change to a defensive posture as Tymon then ran back to them. Tymon yelled, "We must get out of the grass!"

Cathal was confused but searched with his eyes for the crisis. Then the grass on the horizon shook all across the view in front of them. Things were approaching. Tymon made it to Cathal. "Call the men back, Baron. It was a baby then a snake. There are many!"

Cathal whistled out at the men and then waved to fall back. Cathal shouted, "Show them the steel, boys!" The crew pulled their swords and stepped forward.

The snakes leapt up and flew through the air at the Irish. Then as they got within a few feet of their targets, the etchings on the men's swords began to glow and pulse and the snakes crashed against an invisible barrier. They retreated and the Irish waited a few minutes before Cathal yelled, "Make camp!"

That evening, Cathal remained awake. He smoked a cigar and watched its smoke waft off him into the air above him. He saw a fire flickering off a cave near them. He approached the cave without telling his men. He saw it was an overgrown and eroded fortress entrance. Cathal entered the ancient foyer past a broken gate. Pillars, carved like waterfalls, supported the roof and he could see Kaleth's succubus in front of a freshly lit fireplace.

She was covered completely in recognizable black robes. Her sweet voice defied the horror she earlier portrayed. "This is where your loyal angels rallied to toast the new government." She motioned to an empty corner. "Over there is where Michael sat and plucked the harp your people remember. With each note, the universe itself knelt before it."

Cathal looked about at some smashed furniture and pottery in the room, more like an empty crypt then the hall she described. "It still does. I recognize you. What do you want of me?"

"Ninbanda is my name. It was I whose whisper you heard throughout your life. Long ago, my land was turned into a desert which no mortal could share with me. It was when I discovered you that I wished again to share my existence."

He quickly approached her. "I like to be frank in all things." He grabbed the succubus's elbow. "I can't stand around and let fools waste what little time I have. Let's move on for time's sake. Whose creature are you? I know you serve the beast that destroys this land."

"I'm merely a slave whose service was rendered by a heavier chain the more I resisted. Tell me, was it wrong to beckon you to rescue me from that beast? Do you only save those you find beautiful?"

Her voice lightened Cathal's heart like it was consuming physical joy. "No. It's my sworn duty to protect those that request it. I must confess, I could convince myself I'm speaking to a physical trick of the mind and perhaps…a trap?"

The succubus declared, "Strike me with your indifference like a distant sun that has withdrawn its warmth from its forgotten worshipper. Like the sunlight I cannot see and know its warmth, I see your affection but you spare me none. Turn your gaze upon me and give me a rich soul as certain as the shadow that appears before all. I've sacrificed to bring you closer to me, even knowing I embraced destruction at your flames that have found me by drawing you near."

Cathal said to Ninbanda, "I cannot be sent away. What must pass is here. I know your voice from long ago."

She shook her head and moved a little further away from Cathal. "I've called on my most enviable desire to appear with reckless abandon. I've summoned my love to couple with me in a viper pit."

Cathal gave no ground. "Never doubt us. Cupid's arrow had struck me, and on attempts to draw it out, the pain would drop me to my knees. Let me rescue you."

"If you dare to share my company, then put your sword on that table near you and come join me by the fire."

Cathal didn't move. "Uncover yourself and step forward to me."

That vibrating feminine voice rebuked, "I cannot. I wish not to frighten you, sire. Who I belong to is the shape I take on for his pleasure."

Cathal responded resolutely, "Frighten me then."

She moved toward him until she was under his chin. The creature that pulled its veil off had been suddenly transformed and what was revealed was met with astonishment. The form of the succubus was now made mortal and of such beauty the Greeks would have called it "the woman." Her ivory skin and bloodred lips were overcome by the pair of amethyst stars that saw him. Her eyes took the reflection of a lit candle that wasn't there. He felt an examination taking place.

She spoke cautiously, "You do not turn away. May I serve you? You may have me if you desire."

Cathal responded, "I'm going to shake your cage until I open the gate. You are no longer a slave from this moment forward. Send your heart where you wish."

Ninbanda began to undress them.

"I wish to go slowly," Cathal said quietly. The succubus was taken aback by the request. As he admired each inch he uncovered, perhaps for the first time, she felt vulnerable and self-conscious. He made her feel a wanting that was deeper than lust could dive. He looked at her like a boy who had rediscovered a dream that now existed before him; the gentle touching that followed was an exhibition of the impossible. She could see flames in his eyes and she shuddered, not from fear but out of shame that she was not worthy to be the angel he long sought after. Her wretched manipulation of this man was now pouring guilt into her as a dam, never known before, was suddenly broken, for he returned a soul to her through his recognition.

A kiss became a bite but Cathal moved his head and she lost her grip on his lip. Then she felt something dripping on her chest and noticed that blood was running down his chin.

She pulled a blade from her belt and offered it. "You can cut your name into my chest, if you'd like, so that all who see me know that I belong to you."

"Toss the blade away. I'd have you come to me freely or never at all," responded Cathal. He picked Ninbanda up as she let the blade hit the floor. He placed her on some furs. She pulled at his trousers at the hips and he stroked her.

"Kaleth will never let you near him with the Sword of Nuada. He's too quick for any creature to stand against him," said Ninbanda through heated breath.

"I may yet surprise you."

Ninbanda whispered, "When you slay Kaleth and become the king, will you allow me to stay here with you in Gorias? Would you keep me as your lover?"

Cathal hesitated. "You may stay with me as long you care to. Then a life in Ireland would be your fate as a mortal. This is no kingdom to rule by a just man, even if I was worthy of ever being called a king. Kaleth is in charge of the prison he is captive to and nothing more."

The succubus spat, "Forget pausing before telling a lie, it bores me to read you so easily." She slid out from under him then moved to glass doors and opened them.

Cathal sat up. "The things we do this night will not be washed away by daylight."

Ninbanda pointed out over the balcony. "Misery is their occupation. They await death and that is all. Is it so different in your precious Ireland? I'm used to misery, that unwelcome companion, running itself over my bones through disappointment, like bondage with teeth. Without a master, there can be no order. With no order there can be no peace."

Cathal firmly disagreed. "I would serve my people as a ruler. They were not created to secure my selfish needs. Not one creature was created to unwillingly serve another."

The succubus pulled her hair back behind her shoulders and swung her hips toward him as she closed in on Cathal. She spoke intimately, "Drop the shrouds of a saint you cover yourself with. Never had I a use for one. Within resides both mercy and terror, like plagues that embody you."

She looked at his neck with a scowl on her face. She breathed through her teeth and he thought she might drag them over his skin.

*****

Donn woke to see Cathal standing alone, watching them all. Donn wondered if he had slept at all. Cathal spoke up. "Come with me. Today we finish this journey."

They arrived to where two mountains seemed to be springing away from each other. Beneath the natural archway was an altar made from dolmens that was twice the size of any they'd seen before. The cat-like beast appeared by awakening from behind the altar.

Cathal yelled, "Back!" The crew stumbled back in a line formation behind the baron.

Cathal locked eyes with the guardian then drew his sword. The beast snarled and put weight on his back paws. Cathal then aggressively sliced his hand open and raised up the now-closed fist. Cathal knelt down with care. The nervous crew were waiting, all still to not upset the baron's plans. The streaming blood pooled in the uneven ground. Cathal breathed out heavily and waited. The beast moved to the offering and then lapped it up slowly. Cathal lowered his arm then watched as the beast moved its red-stained face within inches of him. To smell him, he could only guess. The beast then turned away and walked toward the platform. He looked back and growled at him, as if to warn him of his responsibility to him, and then leapt up to the platform. The beast slumped down.

Cathal stood and didn't know what to do next as no sword was visible although convinced, based on his own survival, that he must have satisfied the beast. Then the beast quit breathing. A gleaming wrap of pale-blue energy appeared and enveloped the beast. The eyes of the predator turned white and all his body exploded into sparkling stardust upon the platform. When it settled, Cathal could see a sword not less than two feet in length and grand beyond any measure. Cathal picked up the weapon with his bleeding hand and lifted it into the air. The relieved crew cheered, "O'Ruairc *Aboo*!"

*****

That evening at camp, near the altar, Devine counseled a visibly troubled Cathal. "We can leave. We have the sword. We don't have to face Kaleth. Think of what we have to lose."

"Yes, I know. We are sworn to serve a purpose. I'm not sure if that duty doesn't extend here as well."

Cathal couldn't sleep. He eventually got up with a stoic and determined gait. He pulled his jacket on and declared, "I'm going hunting. I'll return soon." He picked up, loaded, and slung a rifle over his shoulder.

Donn stood up and said, "Baron, do you want me to come with you?"

He shook his head and averted his eyes. "Today I hunt my own prey."

The men alerted themselves to their leader's preparation for departure. With a swipe of his hand, Cathal said, "You all stay here. What I'm going to do is something I have decided for myself. If I'm not back by morning, then go home and finish this." Cathal pulled the rod from inside his jacket and threw it to MacIntyre. The men were silent as Cathal added, "Remember who you are." He pointed around at the men as he turned to leave. "It's not always easy to do that."

As the crew watched him enter the darkness, past the campfire light, there was an uneasiness that stirred them. They looked at each other and then Shipyard picked up a heavy stone mallet.

To a man, they arrived in the darkness to the spire and joined up with Cathal standing before the bridge. On that bridge was an innumerable swarm of changelings acting as irregular sentries, appearing and then disappearing into the shadows. Both parties saw one another and Cathal did not stop to consider more shrewd plans of engagement.

Tymon shook with adrenalin, a true warp spasm that any Irish warrior could be proud of. "Another bridge to take! Say it! Come, Baron, give us the order! We'll bring great slaughter upon them."

Cathal began to walk forward with a serenity in his attitude. "The order is given."

The crew rushed past Cathal, swords drawn, rushing to the end of the bridge and locking in battle with the creatures. The adversaries landed against one another, initially like two waves crashing. Tymon was ahead of the rest, taking on the monsters as a still more vicious monster himself. The changeling tactics evolved to then change in shape quickly; they sometimes appeared like putty rearranging. The enraged creatures leapt and clawed at the Irish but were stymied by the charmed Fiann swords that repelled their efforts. Shipyard swung at them and his mallet would crash against three at a time. The walls were crawling with the enemy; the fight would seemingly take forever. Cathal walked alone through the chaos and through the open entryway.

Donn was taken off guard by seeing Cathal leave them behind. A changeling bit down on Donn's shoulder with its hundred long teeth but couldn't bite through the stag jacket. Donn saw the beast's bewilderment and took advantage of the confusion by slicing its jaw off. Donn could feel a terrible bruise form but felt relieved that his jacket acted as an armor against these wee devils.

Tymon flung the Spear of Lugh through the ranks of changelings and he skewered a trio of them against the door arch. He pulled it back out and was immediately jumped by more changelings with blades. A pack of those predators sprung from the wall above the door and overcame Tymon. He stood up under great strain using the spear to keep them at arm's length, kicking them away as he pressed them back. His sweat and their black blood had drenched his white shirt and he spent energies no man could harbor. Tymon was nearly surrounded, seeing himself cut off from the rest of the crew, so he charged forward, causing five changelings to slip off the bridge to their doom. However, as he attempted to pivot back around, he encountered an overwhelming horde tackling him, cutting all across his body. Instead of losing the spear to the chasm and to whatever fate he was to face, Tymon screamed "O'Ruairc Aboo" and flung the spear toward the Irish center. The force of the pitch caused Tymon to fall back, but before coming off the edge, he grabbed another changeling to continue the fight into eternity. Devine caught the spear in midair and pulled it close to his side.

*****

The ember of Cathal's cigar was all that was visible in the narrow void. The crackle of the burning tobacco was followed by the sound of his exhale echoing off the stone walls.

Cathal could hear ravenous eating as he entered into what appeared to be an immense cathedral. The illumination within the room came from what appeared to be a million stars that emanated from all around him. The reflective floor was made of glass and carried scratches from the struggles of the Demon King's prey, a testament to his enjoyment of the kill. Tightly packed pillars surrounded an altar with a throne atop it. A stone frieze rested above the pillars which then met overlaid pillars above, leading into the unseen reaches of the ceiling. A spinning orb of crystalline light canopied well above the throne which caused the one that sat in the throne to cast a great shadow upon the chamber. The crystal light manifested images of a gate worthy of Zion itself. The throne was placed within a low semicircle barrier.

Cathal saw the giant creature sitting on his throne of human bones while dismembering O'Hogan and feasting on his leg. Blood ran in streams off the dead body and his chin, down the throne and the couple steps up to it. He saw Cathal and stopped his consumption. His head was below an emblazoned saucer, like an eclipsed sun, that hovered above the throne and generated from an unknown source.

The Demon King's low voice reverberated inside his throat. "I welcome you with a story, wanderer. I am the single word that cannot be written. I am the rot of your soul. I've ruled from this throne to ensure the degradation of humanity's descendants for an eon. Time stripped everything but truth away from me. My family beckons me. I do not come. They are fools. I am Kaleth."

"Well put. However, as much as I enjoy a good story, I'm in a hurry to go back home. So…" Cathal pulled his rifle from his shoulder.

Undisturbed, the king's words slowed. "I used to be able to see across the universe but no longer. Understand, I despise you. I know your secrets, the ones never told to you. It was once my charge to oversee you…now I'm free to consume you." Kaleth licked his lips. Amused at himself, he leaned in to catch Cathal's reaction.

Cathal's laughter inserted into the air as if he was the wicked concluder.

Kaleth tilted his head back and spoke as if to a foolish child. "Do you crave life?" Kaleth stood abruptly. "Your destiny is to join the fate that you all will share."

Cathal nodded and checked his rifle. "Destiny, hmmm. Sounds right exhausting. I can't claim that's what this is for myself but whatever works for you, sweetheart."

Kaleth let out a hiss of a cry and flexed his body for battle. Cathal shot from the hip which sent a bullet into the demon's shoulder. He then rolled out of the way from Kaleth who moved with no footsteps to Cathal's last position. Cathal used the butt of his rifle and uppercut Kaleth's jawline. Kaleth was unfazed and caught it. Cathal's rifle was tossed away and Kaleth was now within reaching distance of Cathal. The baron pulled his pistols and fired both into the demon's stomach but to no aid. Cathal was tackled onto the floor without time to flee. Kaleth's fang-filled mouth began to widen as if he would swallow the baron whole. Inside the mouth was a vacuum into nothingness.

The crew had suddenly appeared at the entrance at a fast pace and began to volley shot into the demon. Kaleth looked at the intruders and snapped at them with his fangs, the rounds landing against him not doing any apparent harm.

A blinding light flashed from under Kaleth and then disappeared again as Kaleth winced. He looked back to Cathal who uncomfortably said, "Get off my damn leg, you craggy bastard." Kaleth had been stabbed in the side of the lower torso with the legendary sword known as The Light. Kaleth's face took on the expression of a frown of clown-like proportions. Cathal tore the sword out and a dissolved essence ran down over the guard and upon the floor.

Kaleth spat, "Impossible!" He attempted to bite Cathal but was slammed into by a massive club that sent him tumbling away. Shipyard had tossed all his weight into the swing to free Cathal. The crew all pulled their swords, knowing the rifles were worthless in this battle. Kaleth fell into a heap with his cloak covering him.

Cathal ordered, "Spread out!" The crew moved about the walls around them.

Cathal slowly pulled himself up and slapped Shipyard's shoulder. "Thank you for coming, old friend." Shipyard, breathing heavily, walked over to Kaleth who was hiding his face near the floor. He gripped his mallet tightly and postured for the final blow. Then the ground around Shipyard erupted in movement. Kaleth was gone and Shipyard dropped his mallet, still otherwise. He dropped to his knees and Donn rushed over to assist him. Before Donn could reach him, Shipyard fell to the floor. Blood ran in a pool around his body from a hole where his heart once was. Cathal limped over and they both could spend only a moment mourning. The master gunner looked like a sleeping bear. The shaken crew stealthily searched the throne room for Kaleth. Devine had the spear with him and stood near Cathal. A few changelings began to stumble into the chamber, ready to fight.

Cathal told Donn, "Take the spear. You'll have to finish him for the rest of us."

Donn grabbed the weapon from Devine and ran recklessly into the nearest hallway, looking for Kaleth. He followed blood splatters as he detected them. His heavy breath surely gave his position away so he slowed to a walk. He entered a high-ceilinged pitched chamber that had stone benches lined like a place of worship. The far wall was caved in. There was dim light, entirely of blue flame, coming from a high chandelier. A large censer had been overturned and smoke from incense drifted out of it. Desecrations were painted across the walls as if wild animals had held the brush. Donn saw the back of a suffering Kaleth where a rostrum might have been. Beneath his cloak, he could see Ninbanda whimpering and fighting under his heavy grip. Donn heard a loud pop and cracking as he rushed to attack Kaleth. Donn used a bench to lift up and spring away against which gave the angle of his spear-throw more power. Kaleth tossed Ninbanda's body to the side and looked up to howl. The spear struck through Kaleth and the blow was so great that the destroyed wall blew out. The sun that had, until then, been a stranger poured into the room. Donn squinted and could see Kaleth crushed by the debris. He thought the serene look upon the Demon King's face was terrifying in its own right. Donn then called the spear back and his grip soon met the black blood the spear had extracted. He could hear the shrieks of the changelings below the tower as they burned in sight of God's vision. He searched for Ninbanda and found her twitching on the floor, eyes still open.

*****

Cathal held Ninbanda's hand gently as she lay dying. Ninbanda spoke her words through fragile breaths. "Cathal, my savior, my wait for you is over. I imagined you even before you were born. Don't find me foolish for this. You need to know that I saw our children in my dreams and they were strong. They would have made you so proud."

Cathal's eyes welled up as he focused on her.

Ninbanda weakly remarked, "I prayed here that you would leave here safe. I'm somewhat out of practice but it seems to have worked."

Cathal spoke loudly, "What can I do for you, Ninbanda? How do you wish people to remember you since I promise to carry your memory?"

Ninbanda was slipping away, "I knew the king. At least I shared a moment with him…"

She was gone. Cathal kissed her hand and shed a tear.

*****

Rain clouds had been gathering and the rain finally fell. It washed away the blood and impure elements of Gorias. The stepwell filled quickly and drowned the hiding spots of the changelings.

As the weary crew left the tower, Alaster briefly mourned over Shipyard's corpse through a self-muffling of his agony. Gone was the mirthful child; now a resolute man took his place.

The rainy night abated as the crew assembled to depart. They were at the village of lost children when a rainbow formed in glorious splendor above them. Cathal explained to Caireen what had transpired but she already knew Kaleth was dead. Takama and Alaster volunteered to stay with Caireen to tend the children and build a new kingdom together. The children celebrated their newfound future of safety and hope by playing in the village with an ease foreign to them. Alaster, looking like his innocence had been shed away, felt it was his duty to hand back the colors he wore around his waist. Cathal refused it and said, "You are a valuable part of my crew and I cannot spare your service. You will stay here but in service to us. Make us proud as you have before."

Alaster nodded and stood straight like his sadness had been replaced with duty. The crew said their goodbyes and gathered around Cathal. Caireen picked up two smiling toddlers in her arms and they waved.

Cathal raised the white rod.

*****

I bet you were never more beautiful than before this moment. However, I am foolishly not there. I'm twenty-one tomorrow. If I live to be 109, I'll still wish to have again your hand in mine and your lips to press. To hear your musings and take on life together may never be but I still long for it. For now, I'll be foolish. For now, I'll dream. Dream with me sometimes when you care to. I'll find you there.

The Decision

Bridget and Cassidy had become followers of the rising stars in the Anacreontic Society of Musicians. At times, they'd strike up conversations with the performers after events. An evening after seeing a dramatic play at the Crow Street Theater, they were invited back behind the scene room for refreshment with the cast. An actor from the performance, who fancied himself quite the attraction, introduced himself as Patrick Kerley. He sat down with the ladies and spoke with a teasing nonchalance. "Brave souls have come to see how we thespians behave when the audience is absent! Go on. Take it in. I promise to try and resist posing." He paused and raised his chin up above his shoulder. He peeked an eye out to the ladies before bursting out a laugh.

Cassidy enjoyed the silly banter. "You are a strange one, aren't you! You've granted us a peek into the madness behind the curtain so I must thank you, yes."

He spoke with flamboyance and pointed a finger at one who passed by. "He believes he walks on water since he played in the Hanover Square Rooms. Know now though, his single greatest achievement was shaking Samuel Wesley's hand." Patrick chuckled and slapped that man's leg. "I suppose your oboe will be heard tonight at a gambling hall on Smock Alley." The embarrassed musician slowly retreated with a strained smile. As Patrick looked past the table, he asked, "Have you tried a banana? Like candy turned to cream. One of the more enjoyable benefits of working in theater is the gifts from admirers. Fruit and flowers seem to always be in fashion!"

Bridget and Cassidy were flattered by the attention but Bridget asked, "Your performance of *Macbeth* was amazing. Why are not all the seats filled?"

Patrick breathed long as if someone ruined his fun. "Without the Crow's matron, the late Mrs. Barry, or her hallowed husband, Spranger, this theater is spiraling down. The competition to find competent tragedians for Irish stages is nearly impossible with the demand. However, so many started here and later became the toast of Drury Lane that our dreams are permissible… I think, quite right."

The party began to dissipate as the fur-covered shoulders of the actresses evacuated. As it grew quieter, with only the lights still lit to glory the green room, Patrick became more serious as if he was remorseful.

Bridget said, "What moves you to suffer on this circuit of performances across the nation?"

Patrick shot a glance about the room then lifted his glass to the ladies. "A kitchen never without saffron. To eat with silvery cutlery, but above all, an adoring crowd."

It wasn't long after Patrick started slurring his impromptu renditions of great performances. Bridget and Cassidy were tired by the late hour but they bid Patrick a gracious farewell.

*****

Bridget would volunteer to teach orphan children as a way to fill her heart or at least distract it. Although the ground rents at St. Stephens Green contributed to the education of Irish children, the need was great. Each time Bridget made a child smile or learn a lesson, she felt like she had made her day worthwhile. More than that, she felt consequential in a world that seemed to pass over her. Bridget considered how the older she became, the more layers to her there were. Her innocence was misshapen through disappointment and her hesitation grew with each day passed. Bridget knew herself to be someone quite different than who she portrayed but she couldn't recall who that was.

Bridget and Cassidy ventured out to Smock Alley. Bridget was inebriated before long. She beamed, red-faced, at Cassidy. "I've come to love music over these past months in Dublin. They perform at the halls in such an improvised fashion that it seems to celebrate living. Before it was all so formal to the ear that I never felt a part of it, just an intruder to a song played in Eden."

As the night waned, Cassidy could see her friend beleaguered by an unseen burden. Bridget rubbed her temple and closed her eyes. Her thumb and index finger, on the hand next to her drink, pressed against each other. "I'm cursed, Cassidy. I fell in love and gave myself to a man. I pledged myself to him and he left. Every man I've met since has been driven off."

Cassidy weighed her response. "Do you still love him?"

Bridget looked at Cassidy and timidly said, "Of course. And what matter that?"

Cassidy placed her hand on Bridget's, resting on the table. "I know very few certainties, Bridget, but I know it in my heart that your man will return for you. Chin up, darling. Chin up, please."

Bridget returned in a less-than-dignified composure to her apartment. Fresh correspondence was on her table left by Nora. She expected to see letters from her family but she spotted one from Deirdre. She tossed her shoes aside and hopped up onto a soft chair. The moonlight had cascaded through the window into the sitting room.

She briefly regained her senses. She reflected on why she was deteriorating instead of thriving in Dublin. Inside her guise of innocence resided a struggle. Promises given were unkept and a conclusion that was denied was pressed far beneath her psyche. She waited and didn't let every moment without him tear her mind apart. She had long ago decided, Donn was hers and she was his and that was that. Now it had been four years and she awoke in the morning to find another sun rising without him and had to convince herself he ever existed and she wasn't mad to be so devoted. On her nightstand still rested Donn's timepiece. Her hand placed itself upon it, her eyes taking in the sight of a quiet Liffey beyond her. She thought she would wear off its varnish as tightly as she had held it over such a long period. Like pages in an old diary, she ran through every memory until those memories were faded and edited down to simply feelings and shadows of the moments that made her fall in love. Memories became tattered pages in a book written for her.

She opened the letter and read. She put down the message and nearly cried out as she pressed her fingers against her mouth. Deirdre would be wed that September in Bohemia, swept away by a merchant. Deirdre had written in detail about how she came to meet the suitor.

*****

Deirdre had met a man that designed chandeliers for the famed Harrach family. His name was Johan Pohl and held residence in the Harrach Estate, east of Dresden. The Harrach's trademark propeller marked many fine crafts and was known throughout Europe.

Deirdre arrived early the day of a dance. She was inside a room just updated in the latest decorative fashion that Johan was working in. At an estate befitting a noble, under the lights of many half-crystal chandeliers, she spotted him instructing laborers to hoist another. She admired his wondrous creations and bravely interrupted him with a compliment. He did a double take, one-half distraught and the final half then entertained.

After a few questions, careful not to get in the way of his arms as he directed where the laborers should guide the ropes, she saw that Johan was becoming more interested. Deirdre had asked why he had to travel to market the sales instead of devoting himself to his art. He responded, "The expensive glass isn't in demand because of the conflicts across Europe so I've been sent to solicit the business myself."

Later at the dance, Johan was never far from her company. "You are…" Deirdre watched the words leave his lips. "Enchanting. I would ask for your hand but I feel I might have to warn you that I may find it very difficult to let it go again."

"I won't ask you to. Can you waltz, though, Mr. Pohl? Since we seem tied together otherwise."

It wasn't long after they began that Deirdre began missing steps. Her lack of experience dancing with a man was beginning to show through so she guided Johan away before making a spectacle of herself. "I apologize, Lord. Perhaps the music overwhelmed my senses."

"Was it the violins or brass horns that infected you? I would be inclined to learn to play them." Her cheeks flushed and she flinched to the side before giving an involuntary open-mouth smile. No, she thought, why she blushed wasn't at his jest but at his eyes that, although warm, were upon her like a hawk finding prey.

Johan stood quietly after the waltz. When the music stopped, they stood near the wall under a painting of some Babylonian scene where a lion was calmed by intruding angels. The Czech never took his eyes off Deirdre before he spoke, "Would you mind if I courted you?"

Deirdre blushed and shook her face in a sort of swoon and then said, "You'll have to be a gentleman and let go of my hands first because if you wait for me, then I fear it may never happen." She smiled up at him and she could see a warmth behind his eyes that was all for her. She loved that he had an obsessive look when he dealt with her. His interest was authentic and hungry for more of her company.

"You're not going to get any help here," he replied resolutely. She began to reconsider if it was a hardwood floor she stood on and not a bog since she suddenly needed to hold a rope to remain standing.

She heard hushed words to her she didn't recognize; it sounded like *pol lip pamyah*, then he moved forward and once pressed his lips forcefully against hers. As the blood ran back into her lips, her eyes opened again to see him. There was a ruthlessness in how he took the kiss but she found she wanted a man to want her kiss enough to take it unapologetically.

Suddenly tonight had become more than just another outing with her family. Now she was pursued by whom she believed to be the most dashing man in Ireland. How her whole world could change so rapidly in one evening was as much unsettling as enchanting to her. She intensely studied him as if she was encountering her entire future suddenly thrust upon her. His silly chin thrust out like something that might be imperially struck on a coin—his mustache tailored to hang over that mouth that could speak ever so sweetly to her and the blackest hair that shook over his forehead in a fashion that teased against his serious manner. *Oh*, she thought, *could this be the man meant for me?* She considered that he was much too charming and attractive to be enamored by her after so little time had passed. She decided instantly that if doom was what he offered her in the end, then she'd see herself through this glorious interlude to its conclusion. She found truth in the conviction of his tone, so free from uncertainty or doubt. She would be a fool to disbelieve him and she would be a fool *for* him if that is what he required. Throughout the carriage ride home and into the late night before slumber at last found her, she imagined that she danced with him to every melody she could remember.

*****

In the letter, Deirdre implored Bridget to be at her side at the wedding. She would be accompanying Deirdre's family at Brussels onward.

Bridget considered the request to venture so far. Perhaps it was the need to escape the dark cloud that seemed to rest over her lately but she would book passage on a ship to see her old friend.

As slumber found her that evening, her thoughts carried her back to the hills of Achill. It had become like a land of enchantment left behind, ever calling her back.

The Wedding

After a passenger sloop, two broken carriage wheels, and some of the most stomach-upsetting cuisine in Europe, Bridget had finally made it.

Bridget arrived near Harrachsdorf where Johan had his residence in a beautiful country house owned by the Harrach Estate. An oasis of noble pride was in the valley, surrounded by towering trees twice as tall as the building. Over a small stone bridge that crossed a seasonal creek, the carriage dropped her in front of her destination. She was in one of many valleys in the area of the village. It seemed like the Harrach holdings stretched as far as one could imagine. The large house Bridget arrived at was charming with its apricot-orange stone brick edging and white-plastered walls. A company caretaker took care of the grounds. Johan even had a two-story round tower guest house in the rear of the house.

She walked in but didn't see Deirdre. Nay, not a sound was heard. She decided to sit at the waiting bench to be polite.

*****

"I'm tiring and must retire I'm afraid… Will I expect you darling?" Her eyelashes fluttered quickly, offering the question with alluring charm.

Johan gazed at her and then curled his lips in a knowing smile. "I must spend time drawing designs unto a late hour. Sweetest dreams, my darling."

The next day Deirdre was frustrated again.

"Why will you not join me today? I have nothing I wish to do if not with you."

"I have some errands and drawings to create. Certainly there are some details of the wedding you must tend to." His eyes fell to his papers again.

"I'm not a child, Johan. I'm your betrothed and I expect to stay with you wherever you go. Have you grown bored with me?"

Johan, shocked, stammered first in his native tongue and then slowed before responding, "Deirdre, darling..." He grabbed her hand. "Politically the Harrach's have to play a careful game. *Holznot* is the word meant to extort money from successful glassmaking. The idea that we're using too much of the forest is preposterous, especially when you ask them if we should stop sending them these marvelous creations. I'm always instructed to make some design or another to send to the nobles at a reduced charge, of course. It's not because I don't wish to be with you, only that I work to keep our future secure."

"I know *you* understand why you must treat me as such, Johan, but I do not." She turned and left his presence.

Deirdre sulked around the house. She would pass family members and only gave obligatory nods or single-word responses. She enjoyed her tea and to be left to her quiet thoughts. However, her temper was causing her muscles to ache so she decided to retire early.

The backdoor of the house opened and a head carefully popped out. "Hello?"

Deirdre was flummoxed but recognized the voice. "Bridget!"

Bridget and Deirdre saw each other and ran past garden beds flanking the rock paths and nearly lost their balance. They hugged as their eyes welled with happiness.

Bridget sobbed. "It's been so long, my dear!"

"That it has. Oh, tell me everything! Tell me of home."

"Take me to where we can hide my spectacle and I will do just that." She wiped beneath her eyes.

They laughed together uncontrollably and walked back into the house.

*****

"The wedding is off! I couldn't possibly marry that man."

Bridget felt as if the ceiling fell down upon her. "What are you talking about? What changed so quickly?"

"Since I've arrived here, I'm now ignored. He puts me off for other affairs he feels are more important. I'm to be wed to this man who thinks his investment in me has been enough to fulfill an obligation. Can one put on a disguise for a time to trap me and be forgiven?"

"Is he unkind, Deirdre?"

"Worse than that, he is brief. He is dismissive. If I knew anything about glass, then he'd pay more attention to me! I need to be his destination. I wish to be where he longs to go."

"You know that's not how it is. You have hope. So much more than even myself. You drove something within him that is inarguable."

"I feel like I've been fooled, Bridget. I won't be put on a shelf to collect dust. I cannot overcome it. I must be valued each day or be left without him."

"I'm certain he does value you. Have you spoken with him about how you feel?"

Deirdre spat her words as if she was cursing. "I don't care for excuses, only actions speak to me." She shook her head and then composed herself. "I'll never be that woman I grew up knowing. The one who has to lie to herself each day to justify the loneliness, the contempt she must endure."

"Calm yourself and consider that you are in love with him, and since you are, then he must not truly be what you condemn him to be. He wouldn't have gotten this far with you. Deirdre, you've found a joy that awakened your soul and I fear you've decided to turn away from it."

Deirdre impatiently waved her hand and then shut her eyes. "You don't understand, Bridget…"

"Make me understand, my dear friend. You've invited me here because I pray you know I won't guide you toward ruin. You're seeing things that may not be there at all, and I beg you to challenge him openly to abate your fears."

Deirdre placed a hand on a circular stool to steady herself and widened her eyes. Bridget noticed Deirdre was seemingly paralyzed before saying, "I'm not sure I know how."

Bridget stood up and grabbed Deirdre's hands gently. "You'll find a way. Just be yourself, proud and forward. I hope you know you deserve him and you'll let that man know that he very well deserves you."

They hugged, and through teary eyes, Deirdre began to laugh. "Had he been any closer the last I saw him, I would have killed the poor man." Deirdre moved away and took a deep breath. "However, there is more… I've been led to believe, through rumor, that he was matched with another before coming to Ireland. He then bribed Mr. Browne to put himself on my dance card, threatening others to stay clear of me."

Bridget opened her eyes wide. "Oh my."

Deirdre, exasperated, began pacing in front of her old friend. "Can the prattlers calm their tongues and grant ladies, frequently admonished, reprieve to trust that long faith toward their matches and just allow due acclaim?"

"Dearest Deirdre." Bridget tensed her face and averted her eyes. "I hear your bereavement and cannot add sympathy. You've been met by a sweet fate and blessed to share your love with a man who will not vanish!" Her eyes nearly gave a tear away.

Deirdre spoke softly to prevent a tremor in her voice. "He will neither confirm nor deny the rumors. I can't say I'm not hurt by the manipulation, if truth lay behind it."

Bridget firmly stated, "You have a man that would tempt scandal to have your hand. He wouldn't jeopardize a union by leaving it in the hands of the fates. Dear friend, if you love him, then I pray you will see in time the triviality of your concern or even the passion he must have for you in pursuit."

Deirdre sighed quietly but then remarked, "Perhaps. You know, his kisses could make me forget all he's done." Both girls exchanged a laugh and then the door opened. With her renewed strength, Deirdre saw Johan and walked over to him with a smile.

"Deirdre, *jak se máš*?" Johan turned her hand over, kissed the palm, and then closed it.

Deirdre smiled at his impromptu language lesson. "Oh, *božský*, my love."

She introduced Bridget to Johan and they went about the day in pleasant conversation. Bridget remained concerned that Johan was unaware of Deirdre's fragile state.

That evening, in their bedroom, Johan was flipping through his paper and idly remarking on the death of the eminent writer, Friedrich Schiller. "Perhaps Schiller was returned to his garden of wonder by Calypso herself. Trust that the magic that surrounds us seduces the angels still, my dear."

She kept her eyes on him. He looked so regal in just his robe. Johan noticed she was staring at him from bed.

"Twirl for me, Deirdre."

She stood up and spun for him and then looked again at him.

"Twirl again."

She twirled again.

"And again."

She twirled again, with her arms out and her eyes shut, and when she was done, Johan was directly in front of her. Her breath was stolen by his suddenness. They made love until they both fell asleep in each other's arms.

*****

The smiling young couple exchanged good mornings and then Johan sat at a desk, still in his nightshirt, and began to read some newly arrived correspondence.

Deirdre was gathering herself, still on the bed, when she lovingly asked, "How should I wear my hair? I was considering pinning it up with a brooch."

Johan didn't look over to her and remained transfixed on the letters. "Any way you prefer, my darling."

Deirdre became frustrated by his dismissiveness. *Does he not care for me?* She feared. She spoke up a little. "Perhaps we might go to the shops together and explore what my new home offers to a lady?"

Johan responded, "Yes, I believe Sophie would enjoy that. You should go with her and we can meet later at dinner."

Now Deirdre was steaming hot and she'd seek revenge for his detachment. Without wasting another word, she quickly dressed in a heavy riding dress and tied her hair back. She wore a smart light-brown dress with twin rows of brass buttons beneath a rust-colored lapel with buttoned sleeves. She tied a matching rust-colored scarf tightly above the ruffles of her white blouse. She fumed that he brought her to this foreign place and, now secured, chose to ignore her. She'd never allow him to dare such a belief. She'd never be his ornament. She determined to remain as radiant a presence in his life as she felt when they first met. She marched right past Bridget who was having tea in the sitting room. Bridget attempted a good morning but swallowed her words when met by Deirdre's determined look.

Deirdre had a horse saddled and she rode the grounds for hours. It was an overcast day and the fog snuck around the area. She wanted to be unavailable to him long enough for him to take notice. She was near a thicket across the long green meadow before the great house. Across that manicured lawn, she spotted Johan pacing outside, obviously trying to locate her. She noticed something red he was carrying. He waved at her so she trotted slowly back to him, projecting an indignant pride.

He acted coy in his approach. "Deirdre, my dear, I had the gardener pick these for you. Did you not wish to go shopping with Sophie?"

Annoyed, she took the stems in her gloved hand. Deirdre then tossed his roses into a mud puddle and held her gaze upon Johan. The delight on her face must have seemed cruel but her challenge had been declared.

Johan grumbled, "Look here, the way you toss away bouquets without mercy, I'd consider you as ruthless as Oliver Cromwell himself. Well…say I were to call on you soon for dinner in the village, would you turn me away?" She turned on her heels, away from his shocked expression.

She mounted her horse and galloped away from Johan, pretending to wish to escape him. If he would not pursue her, then she had made the wrong match so the risk was irrelevant to her. She arrived at a tower atrium with old stone arches capped with a modern lookout. She dismounted and scampered, nearly on all fours, up the wooden stairs wrapping the tower. She made it to the far railing and turned to wait for her pursuer. She could hear his steed kicking up clods below and her name being called out.

She could hear his boots pound the stairs as he ran up. He confronted her by slowly walking up and breathing with some rage beneath it. She reached forward and violently ripped his white shirt open, beneath his wet black leather button jacket. He pressed her hands to her hips, effectively pinning them. He spun her around and squeezed her neck. He dropped his belt and scabbard to the wooden floor with a thud that caused Deirdre's pulse to race. They tasted each other's collected raindrops across their skin as the rain curtained over open windows from the domed roof. The hanging vines that choked the structure were in reddest bloom around the found lovers. Johan swept a spurred boot under her dress and, with a jerk, sent her skirt to land in a pile behind him. Her stance was nearly lost to collapse if it weren't for his arms about her. Her wool bodice was all that delayed his further capture.

"Deirdre, my darling, you fell from your horse and tore your dress."

"It is a dangerous path in the twilight to travel. Would you tend to my person, sir?"

They made love and it fulfilled her demand. She needed the promise renewed that his eyes made to her on their first evening together.

As his hands inspected his prey, her mind wandered. She sensed the wickedness within him that could be lured out by his desire for her. She also held the chains of true love in her grip that harnessed his will. She knew that the slightest gesture would be the equal to giving him more leash to be closer to what he craved. She thought, *What woman baited and drew in such a rival to Adonis?* He delivered her passions like flowers slapped across her cheek and she would not be satisfied with less.

Johan gallantly rode her back home, in his arms, with her horse in tow. She spoke with some reservation as they went. "I've been ignored before, by a man I love, and I won't let that happen again. My father acted as a ghost as I grew up in his home. Be the man I need, can you?"

Johan answered resolutely, "Yes. Always."

*****

Bridget accompanied Deirdre as she went with Johan to a concert being held in Neuwelt. Johan was quite delighted that the *konzertmeister* of Prince Esterházy graced their area with his talent. They were seated in the open. A troupe of musicians lit the black forests around them with their sounds beneath a ceiling of stars. The genius Hummel orchestrated, and then near the close of the evening, he played the piano. His intimacy with the keys swept up emotion as he was in complete control of his audience. Johan explained after the concert that the area had been blessed by refugee composers as a recompense for the burdens of war against the French. Bridget thought about how nice it was to spend an evening with two that were so in love. She mentioned how nice it was to dress up for such an occasion but stopped short in fear of appearing plain to such well-to-do company.

The couple was to be wed on a Wednesday and the entire household was busy with preparations. Bridget was the patient laboring pillar to lean on that Deirdre needed. The wedding dress had been altered numerous times, at least half being legitimately needed.

They arrived at the church in Neuwelt on a pleasant day. The vaulted ceilings of the church were as high as a prayer and radiated colors down on those in attendance by way of towering stained glass biblical depictions. The church was overspilling, full of friends, family, and colleagues of the groom. An event such as this was enhanced by the endorsement and patriarchal jollity of the resident Harrachs who were also present.

Bridget had just helped Deirdre put on her veil as she took her place at a pew to the sound of organ music. Johan was beside the pastor, standing like a statue depicting Czech manhood. The flower girls tossed up pinkish-white flower petals with an infectious glee as they moved down the center aisle. Deirdre appeared in a white gown with a silver tone that sparkled in the candlelight. Her dress had a train that draped back so far that four bridesmaids had to carry it behind her. Bridget shed a few tears as the couple kissed in matrimony, but her resolve of resisting the full elation collapsed when she saw the custom of the couple sharing a loaf of bread.

When they went to the reception in the village hall, the true celebration began. Twirling skirts were tossed in the air by booted men in the presence of the clapping attendees. Deirdre and Johan were not spared from the rapturous activity as many dance partners stole them away to complement their routines. Those whose work was to blow glass or clean shop were pouring the wine into anyone's empty glass, and everyone mingled like family.

A shriek was heard out in the crowd and Bridget swallowed her breath. The musicians stopped their melody abruptly as the struggling noises continued. Bridget realized Deirdre was thrown over the shoulder of some party guests she didn't recognize and was hurried out of the hall. Bridget was further confused by some laughter that followed. It was explained, through some broken English, to her by a stranger that she had been kidnapped and Johan must prove himself to win her back. The helpful stranger's laughter left her dumbfounded but at least her heartbeat slowed.

The guests rushed out of the hall in a disorderly fashion with Johan leading the way. In the courtyard, Karl Harrach was gleefully standing upon a fountain and waving a sword around.

"Johan! You don't deserve this prize." Karl pointed his sword toward the captive Deirdre and added, "For a lady so fine, you shall have to drink from a swiveling cup. I know just the one." His seething smile was wicked as he proposed. "Retrieve my family marriage cup where we hunted as boys together so you two may drink as one. Until then, you're not married and you cannot have her."

The crowd quieted for Johan's reaction. Johan's fists were on his hips as he seemed less than amused. He knew the place Karl spoke of as the old Harrach Estate in the Giant Mountains, miles from where they stood. It was only used for hunting in certain times of the year and otherwise boarded up.

Johan shouted, "Bring my horse."

The crowd around him cheered and applauded. He was soon upon his wiry mount, its muscles twitching for an impending race that it sensed from the energy in the air. Karl threw him the house keys with a laugh, and Johan made haste as the retiring sun was flooding the distant purple fields of alpine flowers with a fiery glow. The clacking of his shod horse announced to the village his epic departure. He galloped his horse past the Harrach glassworks and then through the blue flax fields. After a couple of hours, he made it to the estate and entered. He had to throw many sheets off the covered furniture before he found the cup. The heirloom was a standing silver woman in a full petticoat dress holding a little bowl above her head. He left and started on his way back.

The lumbering ashy clouds had been crawling across the mountain range during his journey. The light had vanished, and Johan had trouble keeping track of the path from the thick forest. Above him exploded thunder as if the mountains were caving in from a battle with the sky. A downpour of rain began and his horse became weary of its steps on the sloppy ground. A lightning strike cracked a tree near him and his mount reared, falling to the side. He was planted onto the muddy slope as his spooked horse disappeared into the distance. Johan was frustrated as he pulled himself up, filthy but uninjured. He walked carefully down the slippery mountain, wishing to save time not taking the winding path. The occasional luminescence the storm granted helped him somewhat keep his direction true. He relished the thought of punching his dear friend Karl in the nose as soon as he saw him again.

As Johan rested a moment against a boulder, he heard a whimper. He squinted and looked about, considering it a figment of his tired mind. Then he saw a bundle against a tree. A fragile woman, huddled on the grass, was soaked with the rain. Johan approached her in dismay. "What are you doing here? Where did you come from?" The old woman, with her gray hair matted against her gaunt face, couldn't respond to Johan. The storm raged above them as he touched her shoulder. He tried to shake her awake. She acted despondent and weak. *Perhaps she was injured*, he wondered. He took off his black riding jacket and draped it over the woman. With little thought as to alternatives, he picked up the woman and cradled her in his arms as he stomped down the mountain once again. He could feel his feet cut in his boots from the added weight of the woman and the uneven terrain. He had to press her against himself with a tighter grip since she might slip from his arms. Every step was out of faith since he couldn't wipe his wet brow to clear his vision.

After many hours, he made it to the edge of Harrachsdorf Village. Then he felt her head lift. Her eyes opened and she said with no labor, "You may put me down now, kind sir." With an agony rippling up his back, he set her on her feet. The rain ceased at that moment and the winds abated. She took off his jacket and handed it back to him. "You are welcome in my mountains. I have a gift for you as my new friend." Her hands closed together, and then as they parted, a translucent red goblet appeared upright upon her open palms. He took the cup and was dazzled by its ornate design. Horses could be seen dancing around in a regal scene.

She smiled and asked, "Do you like it?"

He shook from the trial he'd been through as he looked at the elderly woman who looked peculiar since she never blinked over her hazel eyes. "It's beautiful. I've never seen such glass in all my years working. You have no need to give me a gift. Are you all right?"

She nodded, completely at ease, with a soft gaze at him. "Since you like it, its secret I'll share with you." She moved toward him and whispered in his ear then walked past him. Johan was exhausted and he took a moment to examine the goblet, but when he turned to thank her again, she was gone.

"Hello?" He was too tired to figure out how she could vanish so he turned away. He did wonder what she meant to tell him when she whispered.

He tossed his jacket over his shoulder, his white dress shirt completely filthy from the storm. He didn't bother adjusting his clothing since most of the buttons had snapped and he looked like he had wrestled a startled bear. He began to wonder how this cranberry-colored glass could be created when an epiphany occurred to him. "Of course. I know I can." He felt alert, despite the late hour, and he picked up his pace back to the reception.

His heavy wet clothes slapped upon his frame when he returned to the hushed guests. Deirdre was speechless, having a glass of wine in hand from the celebration. The lone sound echoing in the courtyard was a center showpiece fountain.

Karl Harrach sprung up and walked up with apologies ready to deliver from his lips but Johan quickly said, "It's fine. Here." He collapsed to the ground in exhaustion. He lifted the cranberry colored glass, much to everyone's astonishment. Deirdre took it and kissed him while pleading with him to stand. She hugged him. Johan's bay horse appeared from the dark road behind him and Johan pointed at him.

"My bride's price is with him. She'll drink from my cup. I'm taking her with me now and forever."

The Return

Damn these terrors. His once reality was so forgotten that the grim fantastic had become his old neighbor. He was enduring his self-torture with another night of brooding when a familiar face appeared.

"What news do you have for me, Jana?"

Jana wasted no time with pleasantries, although she averted her eyes. "She thinks you're dead. She was sent to Dublin by her parents."

How did this happen? Why didn't you stop it!"

"I wasn't with her. I couldn't."

"Where were you?"

"I was imprisoned in a mound by my old brethren since I was never supposed to return."

"You were a prisoner again. That's just fine. Perhaps I was wrong to ask you to do such a task, aye?"

"I'm sorry that I failed you. She is not with anyone. She merely works in Dublin. You can still be with her if you hurry."

Donn calmed himself and steadied his hands back upon his hips. "How did you escape?"

"I had to make a poor deal. It will require my return to the mound soon, but my obligation to you gave me some grace to be here now. What was Gorias like?"

"I didn't much care for it."

The clurichaun told Donn where to find Bridget. Without much pause, he moved past Jana and went to the baron to make his demand.

*****

Donn pleaded, "I can't seem to remember her face. She's becoming so distant from me. Do you understand that I can't wander any farther from her? Without her, all this doesn't matter to me."

"There is still the need to unite our people. Don't give up when you served so long and now we're so close," Cathal implored.

Donn hesitated and then offered a question, "What do you expect might happen should we survive to reach Tara?"

"There the guardian tree should appear if I have earned the right to lead our people. I've seen it, in my dreams. The rod in my hand will be my crown and our lands will be liberated."

Donn said, "My father told me that all the guardian trees were cut down by rival tribes."

"No, one is for the Danaan, the rest were once seeds gifted to the powerful families that protected the kingdom. The tree at Tara is as much spiritual as physical so it cannot be cut."

Donn paused and then stated plainly, "My place is with Bridget. Just as it was the morning I found her walking. I knew I belonged to her from that day on. You follow your heart, Cathal. So must I."

Cathal said, resignedly, "It's well understood since man walked barefoot in Eden that he'd give up everything for a woman. That particular one of yours fits that fate."

"I'm going home to Bridget. You'll know where to find me if you have need of me."

"Am I not invited to the wedding?"

Donn looked at Cathal, slightly thrown off. "Yes."

"Then let's all go. If you change your mind at the altar, then I'll have a fast horse for you."

The crew were informed that they were to gather all their belongings for the last time. The *Mistress* was then unceremoniously scuttled, partly because the growing navies of France and the coalition forces were making moving undetected impossible but mostly by the promise from Cathal that they were home for good.

*****

When I sleep, wicked visions upset me. I call for you and you cannot hear me. I approach you and you cannot see me. I grab you and you cannot feel me. My mind works a poison within me and I become what I fear such as the dead that might haunt the living. I pray you drop away from the drift of time and tend to your heart. Beware of that which may stray you from my love. I cannot chance the thought that I didn't offer enough of that love I have for you. In your life I'm a truth you can embrace. Tell me, darling girl, that I'm your man as we walk.

Angels Rejoice

Dublin Port, December 24, 1805

Bridget was one of many tired passengers in the flotilla of currisks that reached the little stone landings to moor upon. She stepped up off the small boat that brought her up the Grand Canal from the main dock a few miles east. The streetlights and lanterns, carried by the baggage handlers and tied to the coaches, showed a lively scene before the Liffey River. The seasonal damp chill was overcome by the excitement in the air as families reunited. The joyous carollers were singing, holding candles and welcoming the disembarking passengers. The cobblestone canal street was like the many rooftops, covered in the whitest snow, with her every footprint short-lived as the snow fell like sugar through a sift. The travelers' hats and jackets collected a film of the white powder that glistened under the lamplight. There were hugs, laughs, and kisses surrounding Bridget. She received her bag beside her. A tear found her cheek before she reached down to pick up the luggage and then turned to locate a hackney for hire to return her home.

She was being passed by a vendor selling warm gingerbread when she heard a newsboy shouting out headlines that included a possible British invasion through Holland to face the French. It had only been a couple of weeks since Napoleon had broken the coalition at Austerlitz. Perhaps that national drama made the holidays all the more important. She wiped her tears and silently chided herself not to be sad surrounded by such joy.

The fog that wafted off the waters was illuminated by all the streetlights. As it rolled off the canal, into the houses, she saw a standing shadow out on the overpass bridge. The fog only allowed her glimpses but she was transfixed since the shadow appeared to be moving toward her since she first saw it. She wiped the frost from her eyelashes and focused where she thought it was coming from. In those clouds, the cut of a man she knew all too well began to appear.

That man walked up to her and she recognized those eyes immediately—Donn. He pulled his black gloves off and took her hands. The leather jacket she recognized, under black cape, looked worn upon him but now smaller on his muscular frame. The busy commotion of the city went past her, unnoticed now, as she thought she might be dreaming.

"Bridget, I'm here now."

She placed a hand to his tired face as if to check if he was a ghost.

"My rock? Oh…" She trembled.

He placed his hand over hers, pressing it against his cheek. "Do not leave me, although I deserve you not for my failures toward you."

She shook her head and asked, "How did you find me?"

"I had a little help." His words ebbed off as he moved slowly closer. He squeezed her hand, looked upon it, and said, "I half-expected a ring to be there. I used to terrify myself through sleepless nights from the prospect." He let out a careful chuckle with a smile.

"I never expected to see you again. Do you really still care about me, really, Donn?" Bridget blushed and looked away. "I don't know if I'm the same girl you knew on Achill."

"I'm sure I've changed too, Bridget, but when it comes to you, I never moved on from the last moment I saw you. I wonder, can the hand remember how to touch you after being used for so much violence? I feel that need now. It was never misplaced but it was somehow kept from overtaking my senses years ago—my love for being with you. I tremble at the thought of losing it again. I love you, Bridget."

Bridget felt her heart skip as she said, "Well, where are you heading tonight, stranger? Perhaps you don't have Christmas plans, as before I remember, you enjoyed my company."

Donn put a hand beneath her chin and moved forward. The lovers kissed and held each other tightly. It wasn't just a kiss because a kiss couldn't make the world turn a little faster like theirs did. When her eyes opened again, she thought a miracle had arrived and life could never be so grand as that moment. Donn took her bag and held her hand. They shared a second look with each other to cherish this that they had so long sought. They strolled and carried on with stories to share as they wasted no time in this perfect courtship.

He had the scent of a man who had been traveling—of horse, sweat, and forest. That smell was wickedly drawing to her and each pause in her conversation could be linked to her awareness of it, his scent the bait and his eyes the hook.

As they strolled back to Bridget's apartment, Donn spoke of his return. "I rode from the west, as quickly as I could, to be with you again. Before that, I was delayed at sea by the winter storms. However, it was the same weather that allowed my return since only the maddest seaman attempted to voyage despite it. We kept far from the Bay of Biscay on our way back to Ireland for fear of the tides. The winds swept away the British blockade long enough for both Bonaparte's navy and the *Mistress* to cross over the Celtic Sea."

They arrived at her home and ran through the shop. They kissed by the door before they poured into the entrance. She led him up the stairs and to her bedroom, tugging at his wool sweater. Her body was a spring meadow and his like her own Irish legend reborn. They found themselves again after these lost years and recognized the bodies they so yearned for. She marveled at the little changes. His beard was unkempt and looked like black flames erupting downward off his jawline, burning her face when he kissed her with that over-powering nature. She experienced a hunger that she readily surrendered toward.

He pulled her dress up and away like matadors flourish a bull near impact. The kisses made landings upon her quivering lips, flushed cheeks, chilled neck, and beating chest as, all the while, he was loosening each corset loop behind her back. Then he pulled at them sternly, releasing her body from the garment's grip. The sudden relaxation of her body, combined with her senses in disarray from his targeted mouth, boiled her skin in ecstasy. He loosened her chemise and dropped it from her naked form. She had been unwrapped by him like a conquest won, and now, his spoils she had become. Then her feet left the ground, as weightless he proved her, and she was carried to her bed. There was no question or suggestion in his action. She was at the whims of his will and she was enraptured. She leaned in and rested her left hand against his chest. He pulled a ring from his jacket, took her hand, and slipped it on her left ring finger. She looked briefly at the gold ring, with its two hands holding a heart under a crown, as he spoke to her. "The jeweler said if it didn't fit, we could get it adjusted. The effect I'm told is to capture the heart for the one that placed it there. Is it working?"

She eagerly grabbed his face and kissed him repeatedly as she stammered out, "Yes."

"Good." He chuckled. "Then I'd like us to be married with all haste."

She excitedly nodded and said, "Yes!" through joyous tears.

They drew a bath and Donn pulled from his bag that unusual gift from Derne. She noticed the white soap and some red splotches upon it. "Is that blood, Donn?"

"Well… I imagine I have much to wash off to make myself ready to be your husband."

She smiled and they stepped into the tub. They washed each other and kissed all the while. Her hair dripped on his bronzed body when she rose above him. She couldn't keep her notice a secret as her eyes kept darting.

The absence of her words and tensing muscles alerted Donn to the new atmosphere that had invaded their evening. Donn calmly remarked, "They don't hurt. It's nothing, really."

She kissed his scars, and the soap dissolved as the suds sparkled like diamonds across the candlelit pool of water. They loved each other without restraint. Bridget gently moved her fingertips to the raised scars left from a past hasty field stitching. "I pray you understand me. How many ways was our fate together nearly amiss. You know, not everyone that falls in love gets to be together, Donn." She shook her head and her eyes became as submerged as their bodies.

They stepped out of the tub so she could make them drinks and he could stoke the fire. He then walked over to her and placed a hand into her dripping hair. She looked back then into his eyes. When he saw her red lips, his grip tightened. He pressed her back into a chair and she sat upon it, trapped in a corner. He placed his leg in between her thighs as she straddled him. Her breath quickened as he dropped his towel and her hand was brought to his ready manhood.

He took full advantage of her vulnerability in that naked state, whereas it was clear he was his most magnificent unclothed. He dropped her neck back and punished it with his burning lips pressing against her. She could feel him grunt softly as she caressed him. She found herself sliding her hips as his thigh muscle tensed. She began to sweat again; whether ruining or realizing the effect of the bath oils, she was unsure. Her eyes shut and the cinnamon scent that wafted off the lit Christmas candles made her relax. Her mind was at ease as he feasted on her.

She broke off suddenly and took up her glass. She took a sip then swiped its wet rim across her cheek. Her hand flung the glass and she heard it shatter against the wall. She grabbed the hair on the back of Donn's head and threw herself at him like a famished animal.

After hours of lovemaking, they refreshed themselves by opening the windows and pouring more drinks. Bridget then told him she would be right back and left him in the disheveled bed. When she returned, she strolled through the light white curtains that billowed about the room. Her fingertips glided across them as she made her way to him. He sipped honey wine and saw her body reappear many times like musical notes that had just been composed. Her neck was weighted down with the jewelry that was now hers. Her hair was pinned up with the Spanish brooch that Donn had brought her. The moonlight that shot past the windows lit up her lips, necklace, and eyes. She looked on him with a gaze of delight, with her body standing in front of a window of falling snow. His relaxed attitude was a ruse because he truly was marking every second with sharp focus.

The fireplace light washed over the bed with all its gold and green, contrasting against the gray of the room.

Donn spoke whimsically. "In the chambers of Aphrodite, there should stand a statue of you for her to gaze upon." She nodded at his compliment and returned to his arms.

The lovers had been reunited on this Christmas Eve, and the moon shone so bright that it seemed to have taken the light of day as a prisoner.

She felt the sunlight warm her eyelids. Softly awakening to a golden flood from her bay window was her day's morning greeting. She made herself snuggle into Donn's side and slept more to enjoy this great peace. She could feel the ring on her finger and it filled her with bliss.

She was content at last. *I've become the sea. You're my shore. My rock. Calm me, sweet boy.*

Donn awakened to a curtain whipping. A brilliant light fell upon the bed. Her body peeked out of the sheets. She lay on her side and her long leg and milky-white rear projected out to the side. Her arm was above her with the hand in frozen greeting, at rest in her long hair. He felt as a motionless guardian overlooking her radiance like a precious gift. He mused that she might sprout wings soon and fly up to heaven.

She opened her eyes and looked at him and spoke slowly. "How dare you for frightening me, darling one. So many days I missed you and you never ever would come back to me. It's as if you came back from the dead, but now, I realize you brought me back from a type of oblivion." She pressed her fingers upon his lips as if to see if he was real. "Now you're going to stay still. Let's get you cleaned up. I don't want this hair hiding your face from me." She grinned and shaved his face while playfully biting her tongue as she took care not to cut him. She left his wild sideburns, declared herself finished, then wiped the soap from his face. When she was done admiring her work by kissing it all again, they had breakfast and enjoyed every simple act together.

Bridget was flummoxed by the charm of his presence, the same as when she first met him. His eyes held such warmth for her that the depth of his love revealed its power over her. She found herself accommodating Donn with a gusto that could be accused of being silly because her subconscious was soaked in fear that Donn might disappear.

She wrapped herself in his cape, flipped her long hair over, and then twirled for him. The wet black cape pressed the ground but she admired her man's gallant attire. Her levity beamed from her as she smiled at him. She watched him stare at her with a deep craving in his eyes, his amiable nature vanished. Her neck looked small and delicate. Her body appeared tiny in his large cloak, her lips flushed at his aggressive presence, moving ever closer.

His closed jaw tensed, then he tore the neck of her thin gown below her bosom. His chest was so close, her elbows bent her hands back near her face, but instinctively, from fright, she slapped him as best she could. He caught her fingers before they escaped and pressed them hard against that same cheek for a moment. He didn't hesitate and she knew there was no controlling him. He flipped her dress up against her torso and moved into her, sending her off balance. He cupped his iron hand over her open mouth as he forcibly positioned her left leg around his hip. Her panting wet the inside of his palm and she soon found a finger fall within her lips. Her heartbeat rumbled as his erect manhood brushed her inner thighs. He cascaded her neck with his tongue and kissed like a predator softening his meat. Whimpers crept up from her, smothered by the finger she held her teeth upon. He held her breast firmly. Sweat formed and ran against her eyebrows while her eyelashes soaked up tears. She felt a slickness that his manhood rubbed and he trailed it up to its origin.

He dropped the hand off her mouth and hooked it under her arm and placed his fingers in her mane. As the fresh cold air entered her lungs, he moved inside her. She let out a shocked noise one might let escape after a surprise punch to the stomach. He moved his hand from her breast, ripened with blood flow, back to her leg where his fingers embedded themselves into her soft flesh so hard it felt like his grip would bruise her. He gently lowered her to the floor and began his driving thrusts into her.

She slid against the cape, the cords pulled tight enough to make her lightheaded. Her hair draped the floor above her; and to Donn, she appeared like a long-held dream captured. He took her wrists with one hand and placed them on top of her head and used the other hand to press her lower back against him as he pounded gunpowder into the fire within her.

His member was so hard she imagined it mimicked the aroused phallus from a herculean Greek statue she saw once in a museum. Donn's grunting became lower and fiercer as if he was overcoming a wild animal. She could feel his heavy breath against her face as her body was filled with currents of paralyzing euphoria so she bit her lip as well as rubbed her feet against the cape to break up the surge of energy within her. She thought of him on Croaghaun riding around her, scaring her and making her feel safe all at the same time. She thought of his rough hands. Her breath stalled.

She then felt nothing but the center of her and the motion he moved her in. A pronounced movement bloomed within her, finally reaching a pinnacle moment where she felt as if she had merged souls with him and that intense joy flowed out of her, her nails dug into his hand, then the following was the feeling of being thrown onto a shore of absolute contentment.

She lifted her head up against his sweaty chest and attempted kisses but could merely graze trembling lips against him as a result of the faintness she felt. His final thrust came soon after and she never felt more wholly possessed by another. He released his grip on her wrists and she wrapped herself around Donn and remained still in tranquility's sanctuary. He laid his head down upon her breasts and she placed a hand on the back of his head to comfort his departing beast.

A horn sounded like a distant cry. One may have thought it was a foghorn but Donn knew immediately what it was. He looked over at her and smiled. "Do you have a white dress, Bridget, to wear today?"

She turned to him with surprise. "And what might I need such a dress for?"

Moments later, she spotted the dress she thought of in her trunk. She carefully lifted the white garment by the sleeves and held it up to the light. It was adorned with a thin linen belt, high-waisted, pinched together with a pearl brooch in front. The low-cut dress shimmered and rustled as she examined it. It was so light yet so luxurious she was excited to feel it against her skin and then appear before Donn. She dropped it over her head and it draped beautifully. The small careful stitching was proof of its worth. She loved the look of the intricate lace design that floated gently around her ankles as she walked.

They walked out of the building together, hand in hand, where the crew of the *Mistress* were filling the street with lively banter. The well-groomed crew stood and a select few, including MacIntyre, sitting on chairs, began playing instruments. The horses had been washed and brushed and lined the street. Each man had a flower to give the pretty bride and politely handed her them as she passed slowly with Donn.

Judge, round-faced with a bursting joy, married Donn and Bridget with a blue cloth to tie their hands together. Blessed be the Peacemakers was the prayer he announced to the young couple as the people were quieted by the honor to be present at such a ceremony.

Judge's voice boomed off the building walls and down the narrow street. The people who had gathered rejoiced at the kiss of the young couple and festivities were commenced, even by those who had no inkling of who the couple were. The celebration began in the street and those that caught the spirit took turns showing off steps.

Finally Bridget was pushed into the center where she gave the crowd her best kicks. She was twirled by the chuckling crew and she was caught, finally, by Donn who rested her back into his shoulder as the others continued.

Bridget was beaming with happiness, but then suddenly, Cathal shouted out, "Crew of the *Mistress*, mount your horses!"

Bridget's constitution was shaken as all the men began preparing to leave.

Donn said with haste, "I'll return quickly, then we can set off for Achill. Can you manage to settle your business until I return?"

Bridget had a look on her face as if someone slapped her rear end. "You'll do no such thing! Where do you think you'll be off too? You have no right!"

"I'll only be a few days, darling. I have one more duty left to perform. I must be present for the coronation of Baron O'Ruairc."

Donn mounted Croaghaun. He looked magnificent to Bridget but the act appeared like a cruel joke to deprive her of her husband so soon. Bridget shouted up to him, "You hope you've escaped me, boy, but you best return to me soon, safe and sound, or I'll be after you myself. You would hope a monster might have torn you to bits if I should have to come find you…" She paused then, more concerned, adding, "You will be safe this journey, will you not be?"

"Ohc! Toil not of all the false fates but spend this sweet night absent of unrest. I know of our promised tomorrow when I will find your hair crowned in jasmine blossoms where skylarks do fly in a peaceful strath."

Cathal shouted out, "We go to Lia Fail, lads!"

Dr. Cassart didn't mount a horse. He whispered some words to Cathal, and Donn watched as Cathal nodded. The two shook hands and parted. Donn figured that the doctor must have ended his journey with the crew. As the horses passed, a few hands reached down to shake the gentleman's hand that had protected them through so much hardship.

The group of riders soon vanished down the road and swept Bridget's new husband away like a visiting fog. She stood there, holding her flowers, and wandered back inside the shop, dizzy from the event. She arranged the flowers in a vase and placed it on her small round table. She thought about how each flower, diverse in selection, represented a different man who had gone with Donn to change Ireland forever.

She found herself unable to let go of her smile. Suddenly a married woman, she twirled about the room and saw the world anew. Silent prayers crossed her thoughts that her dreams may be playing tricks on her and she'd wake up from this most happy day. It didn't matter though since she felt again what she had given up for the fantasies of a young girl. When she finally sat, she decided that she'd write her family, starting with her parents, on this change of fortune. So many plans she needed to make, it caused difficulty in choosing the words to commit to paper.

Shortly after she began her writing, her hand almost shaking with excitement, a darkness fell over the room. It was strange that she couldn't see the paper so she looked over at the window to see why. Then she heard a paralyzing scream howl through the room. The pen dropped to the rug below the table.

The Battle for Ireland

The last of the crew of free Irish moved through the countryside like a current of hope. They wore their sashes and carried high a long blue banner, their sabres at their sides and pistols strapped to their chests. They passed poor beggars on the dirt roads to Tara. They would stand still to watch in disbelief at the cavalry passing them on that winter day. An impossible sight was before them, watching an Irish noble lead his gallant knights with glorious purpose in their eyes. The poor people they passed, victims of a failed harvest, looked broken with tattered clothes and empty bellies. They carried the look that they may be hallucinating from hunger upon seeing the horsemen pass through The Pale. Donn was distressed by the countryside through which they passed but he instinctively felt the need to only project confidence. Although none of the crew needed to scavenge for food, the game was never to be seen.

Since the borabu horn had blown, quite the number of priests had stumbled through the branches and undergrowth over boot-robbing bogs to retrieve weapons. Most were stored in sunken barrels to keep for as long as need be—and the day was near. By lamplight, the carefully pulled barrels from the bogs were cracked open and out spilled ancient weapons. What had been lost in countless shipwrecks, across the Irish shore, would now be put to use. Markings were placed for wandering knights and fire signals were lit on holy hills to gather these weapons to protect their would-be ardri, the high king.

The cold was bitter but their blood was hot with grand expectation. As the crew rode down the dirt paths in a narrow column, their numbers grew. Loaded wagons would also find them waiting to join the march. Kite Collins and the whole of the Fianna arrived to attend and do battle if necessary.

Judge spoke up over his trotting horse to Donn. "I do believe that after all the tragic calamities that have befallen us Irish, it may well be time enough for our Israelite release." He raised his eyebrows and chuckled. Dark humor was the only humor available if one wished to laugh at all.

Cathal, that day, wore a saffron tunic over his clothes as was the custom among the old chiefs of Ireland. Cathal spoke resolutely. "We know whose design this coming famine is. We will sort it out."

Later, on the path to Tara, Cathal was riding alongside Donn. Cathal amused himself with debating old customs. "Some say these horses transfer their souls instead of ever really dying. A gift from the goddess Etain. You realize that would mean Croaghaun carries a longer memory than us. Can you imagine the secrets whispered in his ear by warriors past?"

"I wonder. I cannot tell by his pace if he disapproves of our wishes." Donn furrowed his brow over the incredible claim. "Have you had a conversation with your horse today about our path?"

"I haven't the foggiest, really, how to go about that. However, I'm sure a guarantee of some oats would be worked in." Cathal had a wry look after that statement. In a more serious tone, Cathal asked, "What will you do when you return to Achill? How will you treat your people if we are successful? You'll then be a part of a renewed nobility, you know."

"I know my home. Everyone that also calls that island home feels responsible for it. When you're from Achill, you always feel like Ireland is largely a place you speak of, separate from what we have there. We exist with all the rights to be there like the birds that fly over these lands. We should be at peace like a stag that stands on the edge of his forest. That's the Achill I hope to give back to its children."

Cathal nodded. "Chains and charity compose the politics of the Irish lords these days so we'll give our people new ones."

As Judge rode alongside the band, he sought out those in the party that may be wounded in a way where no blood escaped. He saw MacIntyre, or rather a man who reminded him of that jolly soul, disguised by wet cheeks that revealed his demeanor. All Judge did was ride up a horse length beside and wait for confession. It was made with a question.

"Holy father, what mind have you of our coronation upon Tara? Earnest voice of my ethos disturbs my mettle and I blink to consider our right."

MacIntyre, so troubled, took off his hat and placed it over his riding hand. "What if death is what we seek for it alone?"

"Shall lowly hero be withheld entry upon Mag Mell's plains if his kind Eudaemon testify to Dagda of that eternal claim?"

"I had not expected such preaching from you, Father, as a Christian."

"I do not blind my eyes to keep faith nor do I fall short of Irish nor Christian stead. Ease yourself now. Were not fishermen drawn out by our Lord Jesus Christ to trumpet His coronation? We follow, and if our cause is true, fear not our fates as they are but instruments of His grace on earth."

The army arrived at the Lia Fail where Cathal's coronation was to be made. They continued deploying on the low hill of Tara which was above an old Fomorian prison that the Tuatha de Danann had filled with great number. Cathal pointed at a covered stone well in disrepair. "That is the entrance to the prison of the Lord's enemies which none can escape. He orders that the iron lid on the well be removed…so that it's ready for new guests." A few pushed the dome lid off and it hit the sod with a thud. They peered into the blackness and shuddered at the thought of what was kept within it.

Cathal shouted out among the men scattered about, "Prepare for the coronation and the defense of this hill. We will not take this day without a struggle. Our enemy is gathering from the mounds and dark places whence they hid."

*****

Sir O'Donel was an affable rake but no one that knew him thought him a fool. When he was woken from his slumber to a lit oil lamp, held by a shrunken woman, caution overtook him.

Jana secured Donn's property through an ensuing intense negotiation. A downturned hat covered the face of the little negotiator. Clouds of smoke from her long pipe smashed against the legal documents and radiated up to the ceiling. Long pulls she took off her pipe in rigid mental concentration. "All future pending annuities of aforementioned land do transfer to the new title holder. All benefits, not excluding benefits derived from future royal grants, shall pass on to Donn Feeney and his named successors."

Sir O'Donel was quite impressed by this episode he was experiencing but an Irish raising taught him enough about these moments not to act disrespectful. The contract and deed were signed. The bag of treasure was in the corner of the room no matter how many times he blinked to see if it would disappear.

*****

It wasn't many years before that the United Irish fell at the Battle of Tara. Some of the knights had family that died there. Their responsibility was not to fight the British that day, however, gossip was rife among the soldiers. A bitter old man, who one might guess lost a son at that battle, brandished a curse. "Tell those that wish peace that they'll find it standing in a puddle of English blood."

Cathal consoled the long-held grievances by stating, "The Act of 1719 proved our right to govern our own people was counterfeit. Long repealed but well-remembered. We will have a complete separation from England after this day."

The old soldier spit to his side. "The landowner I've known my days is as much guilty as an Englishman. Corrupt is he and his plate plentiful since our land's wealth becomes his banquet. He dines on sin, the vespers prayers are unmet, and his manor's hearth fire warms only himself."

Cathal nodded. He knew much would need to be reformed and much more time was needed to heal.

*****

Donn saw the many that gathered and the diverse groups gave a legitimate claim that the whole of Ireland was represented. The scuffs and tears to the leather belts that held their weapons lent tale of past violent strife. They carried the weight of their armaments with labored steps as if all these years, their burden was finally felt. Those men were prisoners of the swords and firearms they carried as they wandered through life. The Fiann, the inheritors of the Red Branch, the United Irish, and many others were there to see the baron become the high king.

That evening, the winds picked up and the tents rattled. The hill was covered with campfires, and at the center was Cathal, toasting the Fianna with all splendor afforded. The horsemen raced about the coronation stone with celebration as their kinsmen saluted them sword in hand. A relief gripped them like living a dream that had become reality.

Donn woke to see Croaghaun nudging him awake. The sun had begun to appear and a slow-motion rise of men was taking place, slapping their jackets free from dust. That day, they shook hands with glorious peace, or death, and they were eager for the introduction. Donn soon found Cathal, kneeling at the coronation stone. Judge beckoned Cathal to step upon the holy stone. The stone let out a tone after Cathal stood up above it. That sound came from all directions and committed any heart yet reserved. Across the breadth of Ireland, all would hear although be ignorant of the meaning. A raspy voice cried out, "Behold the ardri!" Cathal lifted the white rod high.

The crowd shouted, "Hail!" Again and again until he stepped down to the reaching hands of those who might remember when they shook the hand of their new king.

Others heard the sound as well, those who were threatened by the event.

A snow had begun to fall. The Irish had set up firing lines in three lines of defense facing the Girley Bog in the distance. Cathal sent Kennedy to the old double trenches which were made secure with soldiers and supply. The bulk of the infantry waited on the side of the hill which comprised the majority of the Fianna. With MacIntyre in charge of the artillery, cannons at the crest of the hill were draped to hide their presence. A semicircle picket line was placed in front of the cannon as a final line of fallback. Much of the cavalry dispersed to position for possible flanking maneuvers led by Devine and Kennedy. The mounted knights appeared wearing polished breastplates. Their armor was French, of the cuirassiers, and came to be in possession by the Fianna by way of the monks salvaging a wreck from Wolfe Tone's failed invasion. The distinctive blue sashes draped down from their waists on to the horses. They had long lances in hand, over nine feet in length, and kept their sword and firearms equipped. Donn wondered if ever a prouder assembly of horses had been fielded on Irish soil and he watched them twitch, unsettled as if on a race day. He guessed that no fewer than three hundred cavalry and nine hundred infantry had been rallied. He would act as a courier for the baron and an unattached officer during the defense.

On that rolling hill, the men spread out. On the marshy ground, they stepped forward. Their focus was because of Cathal's commitment but they honestly had no idea when they would give up looking for a tree when there was none. Trenches were dug with white stones filling them. Sun-capturing stones for old magic were popular with the ancients. The trenches formed a straight line with one dash to the right.

Meanwhile creatures climbed from the mounds and bogs west of Tara. The thick mud of the peat had long covered the slumbering Fomorians. With a plop and splat, they pulled themselves from their tombs. The Fomorian leader made her presence known to her ranks through a war cry like a predator bird. She stood in a chariot pulled by a team of rattling skeleton horses where her chains, tied to their bits, snapped loudly enough to echo across the valley. She cackled at the task before her and welcomed her gathering officers.

The massive Fomorians, the shortest not less than eight feet tall, marched in line formation twenty ranks thick. They carried large battle axes or bronze spears. A thick moving ether, with a tint of blackness rolling upon its outer dissipation, wafted off the skin of the Sidhe that had given battle. As they walked, some of that mud smeared off their skin and caused that area to burn.

As the creatures pushed through another bog, their pace became slowed. As they began to emerge on the other side, they were joined by even more of their brethren. The enemy were so many that it was as if the horizon was smudged with their numbers. The Irish could hear what sounded like leaves being crushed underfoot as the enemy approached. When the terrifying foe waded across the near bend of the River Boyne, not a man hiding in the forest had spit left in his mouth, beholding the sight of the hostile leader jumping her chariot across the river's breadth with ease.

Many men had surrounded their ardri on the muddy ground. The weather was ripping at the tents, and the flames of the campfires were nearly smothered by the winds. Cathal ordered pipes and drums be played, knowing it would drown out the fear from his soldiers' minds and also bother the enemy by its indignant nature.

Judge was consoling some of the troops needing spiritual bracing near the bell. They were kneeling in meditation as they listened to his words. The old priest exclaimed, "We'll ring the bell so they know the Lord is here! It being baptized Patrick's Praise, we'll humble our enemies low."

Cathal shouted out above the shoulders of his nearby men. "Soldiers of Ireland! Those Fomorians across the field arrive to meet their fate. They who hide in the shadow dare give battle against the guardians of His earthly kingdom. I hold in my hand our common birthright, a promise only we can keep. Today we trade our blood for freedom." He raised the white rod above his hand and the men cheered. The snow had ceased to fall and the sun beamed through the clouds upon them all.

With the mound dwellers now in sight, Cathal raised his hand and the Irish officers were set in motion. The Fianna atop the hill saluted their baron. Those horsemen then disappeared behind the hill to the rear. Cathal remained mounted with other officers behind the lines of infantry, blue banners fluttering overhead. The trained muskets were waiting in the fog. Donn saw that the wintery sunlight that they ventured through was causing the burning of the enemy in corresponding intensity.

The cannons were uncovered and a firing commenced. The iron balls that skipped across the turf tore through ranks of Fomorians. The shrapnel from the ground that erupted from impacts cut into the enemy. Donn saw the arm of an ax-wielding Fomorian come off at the impact of a ball and then its bones flew over to kill another. Despite the carnage, the Fomorians marched on without fear, empathy, or hesitation.

Kite raised his sword near his men in the forward trench and proclaimed, "A king's banner is above us. Let us serve him honorably."

The infantry, tightly packed around him, yelled, "O'Ruairc Aboo!"

Judge stood beside a large bell that had been hung between two stone pillars atop the hill. He was busy blessing the kegs of gunpowder when he heard the men murmuring loudly. Out in the far distance, he could see the Fomorian leader and recognized her as Cethlenn, the wife of Balor. Her missing eyes and floating white hair were a terror to behold. Judge prayed for the men and got a bit misty because he knew so many would sacrifice for this valiant defense. "My Lord, for thee again we drop our knee. Our trust is in your pocket. Our place is where you need. Our courage is at your will. In your name, we pray. Amen."

As the Fomorians arrived below the hill, they were in musket-firing range. The evil legion raged across the valley, now in sight of the Irish. Cathal drew his sword and yelled out, "You may commence your fire, MacIntyre!"

The brave men who filled the trenches took turns standing and firing in successive volleys which allowed a constant fire while others reloaded. Although one bullet would not stop an enemy this dangerous, the intense fire did prove fatal to many.

Cethlenn had great arrogance in her challenge that day. She had no Dagda and no harp to send the Fomorians away, just these sheep to face. Cethlenn brandished her silver sceptre and whispered a chant. She caused the lifting of the snow off the ground in a freezing fog that made the Irish volley of shot inaccurate.

An armored Fomorian officer in the rear blew his horn. The Fomorians gave an unbalanced charge like an army wakened from a night of drinking. The old armor they wore, decorations of ancient glory, clung to tunics worn to rags. Their skin was no longer smoldering since the sun was no longer able to touch them. The ground shook as if cavalry was charging.

The first line of troops began to engage the forward skirmishers of the enemy meant to break up the concentrated fire. The men knew to hang low and move at angles. To stop moving even a moment meant certain death. They stabbed at an enemy and quickly moved to the next target further into the monstrous ranks, however perilous. As the weapons of the Lord's army struck the creatures, many were vanquished. They were turned to light that escaped their physical being and swept away toward the dungeon to its eternal fate.

Cathal pointed his sword on the hill to direct the cavalry to engage. The flanking maneuver was to begin. The cannons ceased firing.

The Irish cavalry was a fine sight to behold—blue undercoats made with wool with grayish-blue jackets topped with a red collar with white piping. Many of the soldiers added a long gray overcoat to brace against the cold, but others wore whatever cloak they had. They didn't wear helmets but instead wore dark-blue caubeens. Their high black boots were worn with white linen trousers. A woolen saddle blanket topped each horse. Their filled scabbards hung down beside the horses' flanks and rifles were slung behind the soldiers' backs. The steel breastplates were strapped over the shoulder by leather straps and the hearts of courage within were the most powerful weapon at their disposal. Devine lamented a moment with Donn. "I'm as much a cavalryman as you're a baker." He looked at Donn as he petted the long neck of his charger, muscles twitching in anticipation. "Thank you for being here."

Donn was pensive as he responded, "The honor is mine. We'll follow wherever your mount decides to take us." Devine chuckled at that remark.

Judge approached quickly and then stood before the cavalry, hands high open to them, and spoke with a booming voice. "Life… requires a nearby star so then God, through an act of joy, filled the universe with His candles. Each star in the sky is a statement of His love for us. Those that inhabited His kingdom existed by bathing in His glorious warmth. Those that rebelled could no longer share in the treasure that fed us and had to exist in flight or suffer His judgement. Now that judgement will be fulfilled by us. Ride out and meet them with the courage through knowing His love. Ride! Ride! Ride and raise your flag, your weapon, high so He may know your joy!"

Devine lowered his spear and shouted, "Gentleman! To the hunt!" His horse leapt and began its gallop. The rest of the mounted Irish let loose their horses upon the frozen field before them. Donn bade his mount with the slightest pull on the reins and that unleashed a rush of violent energy through the horse's speed toward the enemy. As if Croaghaun had been waiting an eon for this one battle, they hurried along as the grass ripped away below them. Every few steps, he snorted and accelerated more as if the closer the recognized enemy, the greater the animal's fury. A sudden stop would be deadly to both him and Croaghaun so Donn gave him rein to react as needed. He was being carried into perilous battle *with* Croaghaun as opposed to leading his mount into it.

Judge had ridden up to the top of the hill to be with the baron. Cathal nodded at Judge. Judge dismounted and threw his robe off. He walked over to the bell and spit into his hand. Then Judge hammered on the bell with full swings. The bell was rung, causing the Fomorians to stumble over their own feet as they kept moving. Cethlenn shrieked in distaste. As some of them were shot, they acted as obstacles for those in the rear. Some of the Fomorians threw their spears with tremendous thrust which found their targets in bloody impalements. Judge maniacally chuckled as he hit the bell.

Snorting warhorses bunched shoulder to shoulder while at full gallop in a display of spears as packed as a porcupine. The Fomorians could see a light through the snowy haze, resembling sunlight on running river water. The Irish banners whipped in the violent charge as the valiant Irish threw up a battle cry to please their ancestors.

The sound of the battle cry and hooves echoed an erupting volcano through the countryside. The lancers wrapped the rear of the Fomorian ranks and shed many of the bewildered enemy. Individual beasts found themselves with no escape from the spears that would impale them. The fierce attack faltered the advance of the Fomorians who now were in a confused melee in all directions. The newly formed Irish lancers were all trained horseman but experience with a lance they did not have. Nor did they possess a place at their stirrup to hold the weight of the pole. Therefore, when the Irish charged, they attacked only one adversary before dropping the lance. Once the lance was dropped, they would shoulder their carbines. A scattering of opportune targets was shot from close quarters to keep the pace of the horsemen. The first rank of lancers was followed by Irish cavalry armed with sabres to vanquish the remaining standing enemy as they swept by.

Those horses that did venture too close were grabbed by the giants and mangled into the ground with blunt blows and tosses. Unlucky riders were plucked off and their limbs torn off, especially was the case when the giants would close the gap between lance and rider. Donn saw one halted horseman failing to swing his lance to abate the enemy, pulling his sabre too late to prevent his demise. The cavalry raced through the stumbling ranks of the enemy. The horses were pushing over some Fomorians while the spears and swords sliced down others. They had successfully turned the marchers. The cavalry kept passing through since they were vulnerable at a pace any less than a lope. When they found themselves finally on the plain past the Fomorians, they kept riding in a final J-shape back to the high hill. While some comrades fell back into a hellish fate in the frozen shroud, the charge was successful. The cavalry quickly began to regroup on the opposite rear flank of the enemy.

Cethlenn screamed in anger and dropped the fog back down. She began to wave her staff above her which caused the birds above to mimic her waving.

Meanwhile Cathal, seeing that the cavalry had cleared the field, ordered the cannon to fire grapeshot. The cannons initiated a fire in sequence. The discharged explosives massacred waves of the enemy that were approaching the first line of muskets.

The ground shook again like thunder. Cethlenn's right flank was turned by the oncoming attack. As the Fomorians again saw the cavalry, their panic was completed by the sun breaking through the fog against the shining steel chest plates the riders wore. The eyes of the enemy were blinded and the sound of approaching Fianna crippled their resolve. After they pierced the enemy ranks and fired their carbines into the Fomorians, they drew other weaponry while keeping pace. The fire from their pistols discharging, and gleaming swords, added to the impending disaster the enemy felt in the ensuing chaos. A wall of armor crashed against the Fomorians. The clamor of hundreds of weapons crashing against iron and bone did drown the screams and shouts to the ear. Donn felt the blood, from sources unknown, splatter him throughout the cruel affair. The valiant were extinguished in vicious moments where horror and glory coexisted. With every second still blessedly granted, they survived by divine pleasure as much as skill to dispatch souls. The swords of the Irish carried the white light of the sun and tore beams into the enemy bodies. The fallen Fomorians smoked on the field, and the spirits within them withdrew from the corpses and flew into the dungeon.

Cathal could see Cethlenn, employing her powers as a sorceress, spinning the sceptre in the air. She controlled the flocks of birds that circled that field. They began to dive down and peck the eyes of the Irish horses and their riders. Cethlenn cracked her reins and her chariot moved her into the thick of the fighting. Her sceptre grew long as a spear when she lowered it for striking. The sceptre's end glowed and became so hot it could melt steel upon contact. The Irish who were struck by her blows were immediately deprived of their lives. As she swung the sceptre, it grew longer to reach those that would vainly attempt to dodge its bloody reach. The Irish, suffering a collapse of cohesion, began to fall back to the next trench, making the second line far more reinforced to brace against the rapid assault against them.

MacIntyre, next to Cathal, blurted out, "We need the harp to send Cethlenn back to hell! We can't stop her, Baron!"

Cathal ordered, "Continue the cannon barrage and have the men fall back to our final line!"

Donn was in the midst of the confused riders as they were being slaughtered. He saw Devine, bravely trying to rally the center of the cavalry formation, fall to a swarm of axes. Donn saw the birds ravaging the men which also caused them to be easy prey for Fomorian attacks. Horses collapsed, and just as quickly, their riders were brutally killed. Donn yelled in fury, "Leave and fly from here!" The birds began to lift away from the soldiers and disappeared into the smoke-filled sky. He regrouped the few remaining cavalry, barely escaping an enraged Cethlenn, and swung them back to the top of the hill.

Meanwhile the battlefield was filled with war cries as the dirt flew from the impact of crashing bodies. A particularly vicious ax-wielding Fomorian made it to the second line of defenses. The pickets were pushed aside as waist-long hair shot around his head as he sprang in shuffled steps to heave the weight of the terrible weapon. The Irish that collided with it were severed into pieces. Through his advance, other Fomorians were able to follow and threaten to collapse the last Irish line of defense. Cathal then signaled to his staff to attack the breach; he led the assault himself. Donn saw Kite instinctively dashing in to grab onto the shaft of the long-handled ax. He was immediately thrown back, unable to maintain a grip to stop its harvest. Kite pulled his face off the ground and gasped to recover. Donn saw him nod his head and mumble something before attempting another attack. As the Irish began to deal with trying to contain the breach, Kite drew his sword. He again closed the distance quickly so the ax was too long to strike him. Kite got between the monster's arms and used his momentum to ram the full bearing of his shoulder into its stomach. He turned away from the Fomorian and brought up his sword and swung from overhead with both hands down, slicing the weapon in half. The Fomorian had the end of the ax in one hand and used his other to grab Kite by the neck and pick him up. Kite began to twitch, unable to even lift his sword arm.

As the mounted Fianna closed in on the surging enemy through the broken line, Donn knew where he would aim. Donn and Croaghaun, together, turned their heads toward the beast holding

Kite. Croaghaun threw his head down to contest the adversary and Donn gripped the reins as his charger lit out in a blast. At full gallop, Donn stood up in his saddle and leapt in the air. He had his sword gripped in both hands above his head as he landed it into the top of the Fomorian's head that had Kite in his grip. Kite dropped safely to the ground and the Fomorian fell dead. Donn landed on his boots and pulled his sword out as the Irish finally moved past to plug the breach. Kite then heard the trumpet recall and ordered the men to fall back.

In a haphazard dash up the hill, the Irish grazed death with every move. They tossed themselves over their comrades and into the trench. As the cannons rang out for close combat fire, the creatures were shredded in a gross comedy of patterns that littered around the combatants. The artillery crews moved on instinct as the smoke blinded their eyes and the noise shook their balance. The last line of defense was filled with the exhausted and wounded Irish. Cathal and his officers rushed in to bolster the defense. Cethlenn was in full charge up the hill, even mowing over some of her soldiers to keep pace. Cathal made a valiant effort, leaving his pistol shot in the enemies followed by his devastating sword that could not be blocked. However, the number of Fomorians climbing the blackened hill was like a flooding river that must ultimately rupture even the strongest dam.

MacIntyre was trying to keep some fire effect from the few cannons that hadn't been overrun with hand-to-hand combat. The Irish line was being driven away from the cannon emplacements. He found himself the lone survivor of the cannon crews and then below the terror of Cethlenn's horses. He attempted to light his cannon but was immediately stabbed by her sceptre and had an arm nearly severed completely off. MacIntyre withered in pain on the field. He clenched his teeth and tossed the lighting stick into the gunpowder kegs that had spilled contents everywhere. The barrels blew and it caused Cethlenn to be ripped up onto the flames and fury of the explosion. Her body incinerated and the skeleton horses fell into a pile of bones.

MacIntyre was picked up off the ground and flung back up the hill, nearly in a backflip. He landed and said idly, "Resurrect from that, you bitch." He lay with his hat some feet down the hill and stared at the clouds.

The ferocious Fomorians, with the strength of bulls, pushed the Irish around like children throwing toys about. Donn himself was slammed by a club and tossed through the air into the shoulder of MacIntyre. At first sitting, Donn slumped down like a heap of rocks upon the grass. MacIntyre's delirious look carried an amused smile. He had his wits and his anger at full disposal but took a breath as the intoxicating chaos happened around them. MacIntyre spoke, "I wish Conri was here. He'd make a real mess of them."

Donn looked over and saw MacIntyre with a vacant look and he knew death had found his friend.

Cathal was sliced in a leg by a battle-ax which felled his mount. He was stabbed in the shoulder by a spear before the Irish could redouble their efforts to protect their baron. The line was crumbling. Donn found Judge and aided in making a last stand before the innumerable enemy still approaching.

Cathal pushed away from his horse that had pinned him down. He had to cut away at the enemy who approached him. Then a flash of lightning wrapped the highest clouds above them and a fire brewed behind them. The sun was setting on the horizon but the flames above illuminated the hill below. A star was seen hovering above the hill of Tara.

Cathal crawled back up the hill to meet it. The last of the Irish, scattered about the hill, threw themselves into a final defense against those that would capture their leader. Donn crushed the eye socket of one that grabbed Cathal's injured leg. The scamper of clawed feet, heard by Cathal, rushed up the hill and many was soon met by grace-filled blade. Drawing upon what their will still had left to offer, Cathal's desperate bodyguard tumbled down the hill in exhausted rage with their targets. Mutual death met the adversaries but Cathal could still move on. Cathal could hear the chaos behind him as he pulled the mud past him. That trail of blood that seeped from Cathal's leg lengthened with each second as the reckless enemy sprang to extinguish its source. All actions in the bloody affair boiled down to that struggle from the living to see their king secure their kingdom. Cathal's hot spitted breath shot against the cold mud as he grunted forward. A rhythm of guardianship followed Cathal up the hill with every mortal survivor slaying his next pursuer. All the men were covered in the earth before they met that bloody conclusion that gripped them as a permanent blanket. The hill was crawling with the countless enemy which was a closing abyss. The sun was setting and its rays draped the backs of all creatures with a crimson-red glow.

Cathal came to eye level with the descending star and Donn watched, from afar, the baron speak to it.

*****

An angel appeared to Cathal. "Hear my words. We've always been with you on your journey. I remember watching you as a boy, learning to serve Him. You carried His cross for the congregation to follow. It was there you had the idea to do the same for your people." Cathal thought back to his time as an altar boy, walking down the beach for many processions. The cross always gleamed a blinding light under the sun. "Your life spent in his service is known throughout His kingdom. He sent me to escort you to Him after those vile are imprisoned."

"What of my crew?"

The angel gently placed a hand on Cathal's shoulder. "Each one of them has a chair."

*****

The charioteers held the reins of their horses, swimming in fire, and cracked them to begin the descent from the clouds. The chariots came down from the sky and landed upon the turf at full speed. Their wheels tore the ground up like sea waves. Mere proximity to the heavenly rescuers was enough to incinerate the Fomorian horde. The charioteers shot arrows at those that attempted escape to the underground.

And so, rain fell upon the hillside.

The ashes of the wretched were washed away from the battle-field for all eternity.

*****

Donn arrived by Cathal's side, having slogged up the hill in his mud-covered boots. The baron was lying with a knee up, barely moving. He fell to one arm next to the baron and saw the faraway look in his face.

Quietly Cathal asked, "Did you see him?" He looked at Donn with a pleading look in his eyes. Donn put his sword away and looked all about but saw nothing. The baron grabbed Donn by the jacket and continued, "He was pleased with us. He said he heard his horn. I asked him if he had brought the harp. He told me it would be brought to free us all when the Lord returns."

"Rest easy, Baron. I can get you some help." Donn looked about the field below and he saw no one moving that wasn't already gravely injured themselves. He put his hand on his brow as the sound of dying horses and burning trees could be heard. He saw Judge barely conscious next to his bell which had broken off its support onto the turf.

"She died because of me." A pause passed as Cathal's eyes wet and he delivered a confession. Donn placed his hand on Cathal's shoulder to share his presence with his great leader during moments he knew would be their last together. "All my life, searching for a way to restore the throne of Ireland. I was really looking for her."

Donn gripped Cathal's hand. He remembered when Luke died and would give Cathal his final peace. "Redemption is not a sin, Cathal. The harp was never to be for anyone, if not for you… The Lord must think us strong enough to stand without it."

Cathal's glassy eyes were losing their focus and his words began to fade. "I'll be sure when I visit with him… She was so very lovely." He gazed out above and lost his grip. "There now…"

Cathal went still; his soul departed. Donn placed his baron's arms across his chest, with the white rod resting upon him, then stood. He walked over to Judge who was trying to prove he wasn't injured by poor attempts of mirth.

"Look at this! You survived! Well done, young man!"

Donn asked with care, "What will you do?"

Judge winced as he sat himself up against the bell. "Maybe I'll visit Caher Island. Both times we went to Achill, I think I only saw Clare Island. I had an old friend that went on pilgrimage there. I'm told it feels like when man first walked the earth." Judge was trying to hide his grave wound, beneath trembling hands, from Donn.

Judge chuckled and pushed himself up. "I'm going to bury our friends. You should go get your girl then so I might smile about it later on."

A tower of disconnecting light was spiraling along the country-side; Judge and Donn spotted it in the dim light. The banshee threw herself through the night. Her spinning form, which emitted a bath of light, sped over the hills.

Donn recognized Bridget within its long whipping cloaks as the banshee neared. Donn yelled out, "Stop!" but to no avail as the banshee vanished with a loud *pop*.

Judge spoke quickly to Donn. "It's taken her to the dungeon of the Tuatha de Danann. We send our demons to that hell. Nothing is retrievable from there."

Cathal's broken body was at peace beside the coronation stone. A cackling crow landed upon the stone edge beside the baron. Donn picked up the white rod from the fallen king's hand. Donn ran over to the coronation stone. Judge, in his blood-soaked robe, saw him step up upon the stone and cried out, "No, man, it cannot be undone! Nothing can bring her back."

Donn responded, "They have nowhere left to run, you mean. I'll bring her back."

He straightened his jacket then rested his hand on his sword pommel.

"My name is Donn Feeney, knight of the Fianna." He raised the rod. "Take me into the dungeon of Tara!" Donn was transported in what felt like reality around him, blinked, and when his eyelids opened, he had arrived.

*****

Bridget was trapped in a whirlwind that pinned her arms and legs back and tumbling was all she could accomplish. Falling without control of her bearings made her feel faint. She could try and scream out for help but the task would be fruitless while the banshee screech masked all sounds. And then she was tossed upon the ground like a sack of flour.

Bridget saw a weeping woman at a stream, her recognizable black shawls covering her completely. The woman was busily cleaning blood from children's clothing in the running water. She knew it to be the torturing hell of her captor. Bridget reached out to touch her shoulder to give sympathy. As her fingers met the shawl, the pale woman turned and screamed toward Bridget, embodying a horrific distorted expression. Bridget stepped back and saw the woman rushing toward her with her long bird-like claws reaching to cut at her stomach. She felt the swipes slice through her dress as she cried out in pain.

The banshee climbed up onto Bridget, now collapsed upon the turf. She felt the banshee's tears burn her skin as they landed against her. The banshee lifted Bridget and slammed her down again and again. Finally Bridget no longer sensed the banshee's presence above her. She was alone, suddenly standing with a long blade in her hand. She began to hear the wailing and it pierced her soul. She could feel its pain as if it was her own. The invading agony dropped her to her knees. She couldn't stop from hearing the screaming, the blade trapped in her hand. She held it up and decided that she must plunge it into herself. Then she heard, "Away, banshee!"

Donn had drawn his sword and, with it, drove back the malignant creature away from Bridget a few steps at a time. Donn picked Bridget up in one arm and held the sword toward the banshee. The banshee slipped away into the corners of that false reality.

The distress of the banshee had infected Bridget's soul. Her tears flowed down her cheeks. She couldn't look at her rescuer as she was dazed in and out of consciousness. She was overcome with anguish. Donn could not make Bridget acknowledge his presence.

Bridget shook her head in disapproval. With closed eyes, she sadly said, "Love is as destructive as anything in the world. Love leads to loss, to loneliness!"

Donn gripped her tightly. "To not know love is to not feel it missing. We have what all desire—our precious love—that which all the good in our lives will spring from."

With solemn pause, Bridget averted her gaze and a hand toiled with the hem of Donn's sleeve cuff. "Although my tears land in the dust and I am spent like cinder, past injuries are sadly remembered. Has ambition's thirst been quenched so the satisfaction of family be enough for you now?"

Donn kissed her gently and said, "Without love, here most clearly, lost one remains. I'm taking you home with me. Where we'll never part again."

Bridget looked into Donn's eyes, uncertainty painting her face.

"Come with me, wife. Your rock is here with you." Donn put his sword away and raised the white rod. A blinding light tattered the false reality.

*****

I can find you through the void as I'm drawn to your light for doesn't the shining stars pierce the night sky?

Fadó and Ever After

Donn and Bridget returned to Achill as husband and bride. He carried the title for his own land in a leather case as they made their way to Slievemore.

As they traveled by hackney, Donn asked, "When you were a girl, you faced east and never west. Now that we're tied, you're further led away from garden picnics on noble estates. Does it not trouble you?"

Bridget looked down at her gloved hands and seemed to check for dirt. "You may still see me as the girl you knew years ago." She mock shifted her eyes about the cab while brushing some loose hair back behind her ear. "You certainly thwarted my plans to rule high society. Anyway I'm quite content. You'd never get along without me watching over you. I really have no choice but to stay here with you." She tucked her chin and smiled.

Donn quickly slapped his knee. "I do appreciate your burden. Might you please forgive my elation for your sacrifice and consider this permanent stay happily met?"

Bridget leaned closer, shut her eyes, and kissed Donn's upper lip. "Forgiven, sir. Home every day to me and never drag in mud on my floor." She caressed his bristled cheek and sat back.

They dropped in on every old friend should they yet inhabit Achill. Smiles, laughter, and handshakes filled up the entire day, and behind him, Donn closed the journey that began long ago.

Arriving at his childhood home, Donn kicked over a dusty wooden bucket inside the door, testament to the abandonment his old home faced this many years. He saw the hand-hewn rocking horse his father had given him. A sadness rushed through him and he picked it up. He ran his hands over the weathered wood grain and decided he would repaint it and give it to his first child. He saw the crib standing in the corner, covered up by blankets. He only glanced since that's where his father had told him he found his mother when she passed.

Bridget noticed Donn's distress and gave him a hug. Donn took a breath and then said, "When I was young, I never thought anything would change. I think a lot about the farm and my parents. What I didn't realize, as I do now, was everything was constantly changing. Life was changing always, even when it seemed so permanent."

*****

Donn saw to it that an estate house be built on the west hill of Slievemore. Donn and Bridget started a family and their days were idyllic, away from strife that might fill the rest of the world. Donn employed many ex-soldiers that returned home with little prospect but made excellent herdsman for him. Donn's herd flourished, and he saw that wicked Mr. Hanlon be run off from the Ballinasloe Fair. Bridget had a son. And then she had a daughter. Then she was pregnant a third time as Donn couldn't keep his hands away from his beautiful wife. Daley and Ella enjoyed their grandchildren and were happy to live their days close to them, and even on the rare tide, Deirdre would return with her family. Ashling, who had only begun attending socials, was an enthusiastic aunt and visited at every opportunity.

One day, Donn walked over into his stable with joyous news. He saw his old mount and greeted him. Donn rubbed Croaghaun's snout just beneath his eyes, which always calmed the horse, and said, "My boy, Cathal is three years old today. You were there to see him born. Who knew that you'd be there for all the change in my life, old friend. It feels like yesterday we were on the mountain together, getting to know each other."

The horse tilted his head, hoping Donn would give him a good scratch behind his ear. Donn rubbed his neck quickly and patted him. "Cathal liked the rocking horse. Perhaps one day, he'll take you for a ride on the mountain where we first met."

The horse was alert and ready to be saddled.

"You should rest. Who knows what tomorrow may bring to this island." Donn winked at him then moved away.

Croaghaun watched him leave and gave a disappointed snort. There was no great challenge to face and nothing fateful asked of him. Such was the maddening curse of having found tranquility in life.

Donn walked into their home and saw Bridget tending their second child next to the hearth. He dropped his head and gazed directly at her. He made an offer like a cat to a canary. "Come to bed and I'll tell you a story." He pulled off his suspenders as he walked away to the bedroom.

She gave a knee-jerk smile. "I'm sure you would!"

Donn climbed into their bed and pulled the heavy blanket over him. Bridget snuggled in close to him.

"My feet are cold!" She pressed her feet against his legs.

His eyes opened sharply from the sensation. "I saw some socks by the bed."

She playfully punched his chest. "That's not what I want." She mused, "I never knew how much better a bed would feel with a rock in it."

*****

Like Mongolia, post the great Khans, empty of its untamable warriors and once-great treasures, Achill is now as it had begun. It is a pastureland for the herdsman, still producing glorious sparks of the rugged bloodlines that survived her wild environment these centuries.

If Donn was quiet and gazed out past the shore of Achill, he could still see the ships that had reached their shores once again. He could see the brave crew standing before him. He easily imagined what one of them might say to situations he encountered, like welcome ghosts that shared his days. The world was a finer place where dreams were pursued while they moved among us.

*****

A gathering of branches was burning upon stone ground. Another branch was tossed into it. The *seanchaí* stood above it, watching the smoke rise. He let out a long breath which swirled the gray air. His aged hand gripped his walking stick like an old friend, holding him upright.

"If your hearth still burns this late hour, I would offer you a story. You can share it again to those who may warm themselves in your home in the years to come. Do spare your questions, for I am a storyteller. I will not judge you for doubt that may fill you as you listen, for I'm a simple guide of my people's time and you are favored to hear this tale."

ABOUT THE AUTHOR

Jim farms the northern plains, continuing the tradition of his Irish forebearers in America who arrived in the 18th century. He is a graduate of Lake Forest College. Jim is the proud father of four children. Living with him as well is a drool-face St. Bernard named Cassius and 2 quarter horses, Johnny and Scotch. Walker, his red roan that was never outpaced, went to the last pasture before this book was completed. Jim continues with the threat of a sequel.

Lightning Source UK Ltd.
Milton Keynes UK
UKHW010310080223
416649UK00009B/175/J